BRAVERY'S SIN

MASTERS' ADMIRALTY, BOOK 5

MARI CARR
LILA DUBOIS

This story is dedicated to Lila's mom and her ankle. Her surgery and hospital stay while we were writing the book inspired the character, Patty--that poor, poor woman. - Mari

Patty was the name of my mom's drug-seeking, TV hoarding, oversharing, hospital roommate. She deserved it. - Lila

The hospital stay is also to blame for two-thirds of the violent acts in the book. Lila doesn't do well in hospitals. - Mari

The therapist said I should get a healthy outlet for my feelings. Imagining ways to kill people is healthy, isn't it? - Lila

If I ever go missing, tell the police it was her. - Mari

PROLOGUE

"What's happened?" Nyx asked, in lieu of a greeting. On her laptop screen, the image clarified, revealing a picture of Josephine with her bright red hair, freckled face, and ever-present grin.

"How are you feeling, Nyx? Oh, wow. You look loads better."

Nyx considered the other woman, who hadn't answered her initial question. As was her habit, Nyx remained silent. She found that silence made other people nervous; however, she enjoyed it. It made it easier to think and wonder.

Josephine fidgeted. Though Nyx could only see her from the waist up, she was sure the other woman was bouncing her heels against the floor. Josephine was never still, a trait that occasionally made Nyx want to tape the other woman to her chair.

"Why does something have to have happened? Can't a woman call her girlfriend to check up on her?"

They were friends? Nyx blinked several times, still silent.

"I've been worried about you, Nyx."

"Thank you for your concern." Nyx frowned. She hadn't been trying to sound rude, but more than one person had told her she could come off that way if she wasn't careful. She cleared her throat and tried again. "I am much better. And I do appreciate you thinking of me."

"Is the infection cleared up?"

Nyx pressed a hand against her lower abdomen, over the spot where a knife had sunk in deep. When people looked at her, they could see the first wound she'd suffered that terrible day in Bucharest—a long scar bisected her cheek from eye to jaw. It had healed, and in a testament to the skill of the surgeons who'd helped her, the scar itself was a thin, pink line that would fade to white in time, but the slice had cut through muscle. Damage to the underlying tissue had resulted in a slight furrow. She could cover up the scar itself with makeup, but no makeup could hide the crease in her face or the unevenness of her smile.

"Yes, thank you." Nyx lifted her hand off her abdomen. Josephine had been referring to the other wound, the less visible one. She'd also been stabbed, and it had perforated her bowel. She'd developed sepsis and been ill for months. "And the wound has closed."

"You could have come to Dublin. Colum and I could have taken care of you."

Nyx blinked again. "You would have taken care of me?"

"Of course!"

"I... Thank you." Nyx smiled, before she remembered she shouldn't do that anymore. It didn't look right. "I would have enjoyed meeting the archivist."

"Oh yeah. Well. I should warn you now. Colum doesn't have my people skills."

Nyx was amused. Josephine did have a way of endearing herself to others.

"He prefers books to people."

"Something he and I have in common," Nyx mused.

Josephine's eyes widened. "What? You're great with people."

Nyx had no idea what she'd done to give Josephine that impression, but this conversation had already taken too many odd twists. "So your brother is shy?"

Josephine shook his head. "No. Just socially awkward. And he's smart enough to know that's a shortcoming, so he basically stays away from people."

"All people?"

"He's okay with me and Eric, but that's different, isn't it? He's uncomfortable meeting new people, and don't get me started on crowds."

"What happens in crowds?" Nyx had been curious about the Archivist prior to this conversation, merely because the academic in her wanted access to the historical documents surrounding the Masters' Admiralty. Now her interest had been piqued by the man.

"Colum prefers one-on-one conversations, in private. When there are three or more people in a room, he simply shuts down, unable to concentrate on anything. He's always been that way. Eric and I get it. It's one reason why Colum could never be placed in a trinity marriage. He'd probably implode."

Josephine grinned at her own joke.

"Thank you for explaining that to me. I shall keep that in mind should I ever have the opportunity to meet your brother," Nyx said. "But I would still like access to the archive." And Colum was the only one who could provide it. Nyx loved information. She loved the way information influenced belief, and in turn, influenced behavior.

"Brilliant. When you're better, we can make a day of it,

sure we will. We could go to tea at this little inn near Trinity that does lovely scones. There are a few shops around there as well. Then we could hit the archive." The Irishwoman was grinning, her fingers drumming rhythmically.

What Josephine was describing sounded like something out of a movie. Nyx had always assumed no adult women actually did anything like that. Though she had come close once, during the day she'd spent with Leila Virtanen in Bucharest. They'd walked and shopped. She'd even bought the Finnish woman a gift because she'd seen something that she'd thought Leila would like.

Of course, they'd been bait, trying to lure out Ciril, one of the mastermind's many puppets. No part of that excursion had been about friendship.

And the day ended with her in the hands of a killer. She would have died if Leila hadn't shot the man between the eyes, even as he'd held Nyx in front of him as a shield, his knife buried deep in her abdomen. Lucky for her, her pretend girlfriend, Leila, was a sniper.

Josephine's fingers hadn't stopped tapping, and Nyx twitched with the urge to reach through the computer and put her hand on Josephine's to make her be still.

"Anyway, we can do all that when you feel better. And when things are calmer."

When things are calmer. What a lovely euphemism. Leave it to someone from Ireland, a nation that called their civil war "the troubles."

She and Josephine were both members of the Masters' Admiralty, an old and powerful secret society. They'd been secretly ruling the world—well, Europe—since the Black Plague. Membership was selective and based on merit, even for people like her, whose parents were members. As a legacy, she'd still had to prove herself worthy of joining.

Though in her case, there had never been any doubt she'd be accepted, not when...

She pushed that thought away, focusing on the present.

She was a religious scholar, which was far less practical than being a politician or barrister, but the Masters' Admiralty valued not only the traditionally powerful, but scholars and artists. She'd originally planned to study law, but after her eighteenth birthday, things had happened that made her choose a different path.

In the recent past, the society had been terrorized by a killer they'd dubbed the mastermind, a ruthless villain determined to bring the Masters' Admiralty to its knees. In order to catch the mastermind, she and Josephine, along with several others, had been recruited into a think tank, a group they called the librarians. The more dangerous and deadly members of the Masters' Admiralty were tirelessly hunting the mastermind, following the clues left behind by the various and many crimes. She and her fellow librarians weren't meant to face down danger. They were instead studying the case, analyzing and hypothesizing.

They weren't supposed to be "in the field" as crime dramas would term it, but each of them, besides Josephine, had ended up in harm's way.

Every time they thought they'd gotten close to discovering who was pulling the strings, more unraveled. The mastermind had acquired an entire network of apprentices and "pets," who helped him carry out his crimes. One of whom was the serial killer Ciril, who had first kidnapped and tortured Leila and Karl—another librarian—before taking his knife to Nyx.

"How is Karl?" Nyx asked. A second after she asked the question, she realized to Josephine it would have sounded like she was changing the subject, since Josephine was not privy to Nyx's thought process.

Josephine's restless tapping stopped for a moment. "He's holding it together. Things are tense for him and his new trinity. No honeymoon for them."

The founding principle of the Masters' Admiralty was an arranged ménage marriage. When the society first started, powerful couples were matched with a third, who at that time were priests. The concept was created in an attempt to counter the influence of the church. Over time, it had evolved into the merging of powerful trinities, unions meant to strengthen society through politics, economics, the arts.

"Unfortunate," Nyx said. She made sure no expression marred her face. She didn't like to think about the trinity marriages.

Josephine wrapped her knuckles twice on the table, like she was knocking on a door. "I know what I wanted to say. Did you read that article in *Stern* about mobile phone usage?"

Nyx leaned forward, as if by peering at the screen she could make sense of Josephine. It was, as much as her question about Karl had been, an abrupt change in subject. Was Josephine trying to alter the course of their conversation, or was this the genuine reason for her call?

"*Stern?*" Nyx asked.

"I assume you read it."

"I do." Nyx read the German newsmagazine on a semi-regular basis, though it was more for entertainment, as she preferred other sources for actual news. It was a rather odd thing for Josephine to assume she read, though the librarians had once had a side conversation about their favorite light reading. Maybe she'd mentioned it then.

What had Josephine's original question been? Something about an article about mobile phone usage. She thought for a moment before remembering. The article had been about the history of communication, a sort of pro-con argument about whether the ease of communication was good for human behavior.

And it had started with an amusing anecdote about the telegraph.

"I thought it was just fascinating," Josephine continued, her fingers tapping on her desk once more.

The article hadn't made any new observations or contributed any original research. Nyx found it highly unlikely that Josephine, who was a brilliant scholar, found it "fascinating."

"I did read it," Nyx said slowly.

Josephine said something else, but Nyx ignored it. She was listening to the sound of the tapping.

Morse code.

Nyx was chagrined that she hadn't realized earlier. Josephine must have been incredibly frustrated by how dense Nyx was being. In her own defense, Josephine was always in motion, so the tapping hadn't seemed out of place.

Suddenly, this phone call made sense.

Josephine smiled even wider as she stopped tapping for a moment. Then she began again. Probably from the beginning.

Nyx reached for a pad of paper and a pen, keeping both of them out of sight of the camera. If Josephine was going to all the trouble of using Morse code, hiding the real communication inside an otherwise unremarkable video call, it meant she thought their communications were being monitored. The Masters' Admiralty had encrypted email systems, secure phone lines, and courier services.

Apparently, Josephine didn't think any of those could be trusted.

Nyx listened, writing down each letter as she heard it.

"Ah well, listen to me," Josephine said after she stopped tapping, her voice lilting. "I'll leave you to it then."

"Yes." Nyx forced herself not to look at the paper and begin deciphering the message. "Thank you for calling, Josephine."

Perhaps it was foolish, but the other woman's smile seemed genuine as she said, "I really do hope we can get together in Dublin, Nyx. For tea and shopping and the archive."

"I...would like that," Nyx said, and it was the truth.

They ended the call, and Nyx turned off her laptop, just to be safe, before pulling the paper toward her. She had a long list of letters written at a drunken angle across the page. Picking up her pen, she tried to simply divide it into words. That yielded nothing useful, so she treated it like an anagram, but again, she couldn't make it work.

Code. It was in code.

Ten minutes later she'd figured it out. The message was in Welsh with a Caesar substitution cipher applied.

Nyx sat back, propping her feet on the balcony railing. From here, she had a beautiful view of the Mediterranean Sea. This chair, this spot, had brought her peace during her long recovery. And her host had made her feel safe.

There was a knock at the door. Nyx knew who it was, knew the cadence of that knock, but still, she turned around to look as she called out, "Come in."

She couldn't stand to have someone behind her.

Grigoris Violaris opened the door, leaning in and smiling at her. His Greek heritage was obvious in his appearance. In a word, he was beautiful. With olive skin, straight nose, large dark eyes, and brown hair, streaked with gold, he was a prepossessing vision.

As always when she saw him, her feelings were a tangled mix of longing, relief, happiness, regret, and desire.

She wanted him, wanted him more than she'd ever wanted any man. He hadn't hidden the fact that he felt the same. The moment she'd met him there'd been a spark of connection. When she'd been well enough to leave the hospital in Bucharest—and she'd been frantic to leave—he'd swooped in and brought her here, to his home on Cyprus.

He was a patient man. It was what made him such a good and dangerous predator. She knew he was waiting for her. Waiting for her to tell him, either by words or action, that she was ready to acknowledge the attraction between them and act on it. Ready to slide herself into his arms and raise her lips for a kiss. He thought she was still hurting, emotionally if no longer physically, and that was why she kept him at arm's length.

But it wasn't.

If she wasn't lying to him every single day by omission, she would have gone to him right now. Kissed him and then pulled him to the bed. She wanted the man's hands on her the way a woman in the desert wanted water.

"How are you today, *o ángelós mou?*"

He'd started calling her his angel in Bucharest. The term of endearment always touched her heart, made her feel warm and cherished.

Nyx held up the pad. "We need to go to Dublin."

He frowned and stepped into the room. "What do you mean?"

She quickly explained about the call, and the Morse code message, which in turn needed a cipher.

Grigoris took the pad from her hand, reading the translated message aloud. "Dublin Friday at close. War council.

Bring the Greek." His face took on a grim expression. "How sure are you about this message?"

"Very. Josephine is friends with the fleet admiral."

"Friends? With the fleet admiral? Is that a thing?" Grigoris raised a brow.

Nyx smiled, remembered, and quickly dropped the expression.

Grigoris caught the movement. "Don't hide your smile. It's beautiful, and you are too."

Nyx looked away, her heart aching. She had to tell him the truth about who she was.

But not now. Not today. She wanted—needed—more time.

"I am sure," she said again. "I think you were just invited to a meeting of the librarians."

CHAPTER ONE

G rigoris stayed at Nyx's side. He would have preferred to fall back, to protect her from anything coming up behind her. Tactically, that would make sense, since she was the one who knew where they were going. But Nyx couldn't bear to have anyone at her back, and that, plus the physical scars she bore, were his fault. He'd been in charge of the operation in Bucharest that resulted in her nearly dying.

"A moment," Nyx murmured, placing her fingers on his arm.

Besotted fool that he was, he felt that touch through his whole body.

A fool he may have been, but he was a security officer, and he immediately stopped walking, scanning the area in front of them for any threat. They'd entered Trinity College through the College Green main gate and headed for the Old Library where the famous Long Room was. On the flight here, Nyx told him a bit about the librarians—a think tank group working on the "why" of their current situation, rather than the who, when, where, and how the fuck to stop it.

Her explanation made sense of some of the things he'd been wondering since the first day he'd met her. She'd arrived in the midst of his investigation of Ciril with the now-admiral of Rome, Antonio Starabba, and two other members of the Masters' Admiralty, Leila and Karl. He'd wondered why and how Nyx had come to be involved with the odd trinity. Now, it was suddenly clear.

It was 4:30 in the afternoon, early enough in the day that it should have been light outside, but a low-hanging blanket of clouds covered Dublin, making it feel more like evening. The air was heavy and cold, and Grigoris wondered why people chose to live like this when his beloved Mediterranean was no more than a day's travel away.

Nyx indicated a freestanding silver sign with a nod of her head. It was positioned in the middle of the large cobblestone square, which, according to the map he'd grabbed both for information and to ensure no one would look twice at the "tourists," was called Parliament Square.

The sign board was one of several that were clustered together, some of which were clearly aimed at students, announcing events and important dates. There was one bearing an image from the Book of Kells with an arrow pointing toward the Old Library building. According to the sign, the library was closing in half an hour, so Nyx's message had instructed them to arrive at close.

Nyx walked closer to the little clump of signage and tapped one. It was a simple A4 piece of paper, taped to, and partially obscuring, the menu for a campus cafe.

The Viking Traitors Workshop.

1937 Reading Room.

"It seems we've changed from our normal location," Nyx murmured.

Grigoris pulled the map from his pocket, checked it, then

pointed to a small detached building not far from where they stood, which, according to the map, was the 1937 Reading Room. He approved of the architecture. It was classically Greek with Doric columns.

"I want you to wait while I check it out."

Nyx nodded and followed him to the freestanding campanile in the center of the wide-open area in the middle of Trinity. She put her back against the brown stone, and anyone who looked at her would think she was merely leaning there. Grigoris knew better. Knew *her* better. Tension was in the set of her mouth and the way she held unnaturally still.

He also knew how to blend in. It was one of the things that made him dangerous, and he'd come prepared. He ducked into the campanile and shed his long jacket. He pulled a thin sweater from the pocket, shook it out, and put it on over his dress shirt. A pair of lens-less dark-framed glasses, rumpled hair, and he was ready. Draping his jacket over his arm, he hunched his shoulders and hustled out of the dubious cover of the campanile, striding quickly toward the reading room, projecting "frazzled academic."

He glanced at the front of the reading room as he walked past, then circled around the back, pausing a moment before returning to Nyx.

As he walked away from the reading room, three people mounted the steps. Grigoris recognized Mateo Bernard, who, prior to the assassination of the previous fleet admiral, had been Head of the Spartan Guard, an elite squad of military men and women whose sole job was to protect the leader of the Masters' Admiralty. Since stepping down from his role, Bernard had been placed in his trinity. Given the protective way Bernard and the dark-skinned man with him flanked the attractive woman walking between them, it was apparent these were his spouses.

The trio hesitated when they read the "closed for private event" sign before Bernard opened the door, and the other two preceded him inside.

Grigoris walked back the way he came, past Nyx, and once he was in shadow, slipped on his coat and took off the glasses before circling around to join her. "It says it's closed for a private event, and I just saw Mateo Bernard walk inside."

"That's Cecilia St. John and her trinity," Nyx corrected. "Though, yes, Mateo is one of her husbands, as is Dimitri."

"And she's one of the librarians."

It hadn't been a question, but she answered as if it had. "Yes."

Grigoris held out his arm to her. Nyx looked at him for a moment before grabbing his forearm. Though she showed no outward signs of distress, she was trembling. He'd never met someone who could hide their thoughts and feelings the way Nyx could. It both fascinated and enraged him because he was certain that something, or someone, had taught her to be that way, long before Ciril carved her up with his knife.

Grigoris walked with purpose, projecting a surety that he found usually stopped people from asking him what he was doing, even when he was in places where he shouldn't be. Without hesitation, he and Nyx mounted the steps to the reading room. He opened the door and ushered her inside. Given that a former Spartan Guard was the last person he'd seen enter, he was taking a calculated risk that if this was an ambush, the attacker would be trying to take down Mateo, leaving Grigoris to protect Nyx's back.

There was no attack waiting, and instead they found themselves in a beautiful octagonal room. The ceiling of the central room was two stories high, while the floor was occupied by large library tables, each with four chairs waiting for scholars to pull them out and have a seat. Off each vertex of the octagon, short hallways filled with books beckoned anyone with the desire to learn to retrieve one of the dusty volumes and bring it back to the central hub. The second-floor hallways ended in railings that allowed someone in the stacks to look down on the scholars in the center.

He took in the architecture and layout in a single glance before focusing on the people who were already in the room. Nyx had assumed this was a meeting of the librarians, but it was clear that was not the case. Given the bewildered looks he saw on more than a few people's faces, it was obvious none of them knew why they'd been summoned here, either.

Grigoris continued to look around, then nodded his head briefly at Antonio Starabba, who stood with one of his spouses, Karl Klimek. The two of them were chatting with Antonio's sister, Sophia—the *principessa*—who was married to James Rathmann and the admiral of England, Arthur. Karl and James were both librarians as well.

Mateo and his trinity remained apart from the others. Grigoris appreciated the way Mateo had positioned himself and his spouses near the exit. Like him, the man was on guard, concerned—as Grigoris was—that this could be an ambush.

They were, after all, at war with a faceless villain determined to bring down their society.

He let his gaze travel around the room until he spotted James and Arthur with another man he didn't recognize.

"Who is the admiral of England speaking to?" he asked Nyx.

Nyx followed the direction of his gaze. "That's Hugo Marchand. He's also a—"

"Librarian. Are all of you here?"

Nyx looked around the room, then shook her head. "I don't see Josephine yet. But the rest of us are here."

"I know everyone Antonio is speaking to, but I'm not familiar with the woman standing next to Hugo."

Nyx studied the woman. "My guess is that is Hugo's new wife. The two of them were married a few weeks ago. Their third is Lancelot, one of England's knights. Sylvia, the woman, is American, a fact that fascinates Josephine to no end. She called me shortly after Hugo's binding ceremony to tell me that Eric had stolen Sylvia from the Trinity Masters."

The Trinity Masters was the American counterpart to the Masters' Admiralty. The American secret society was in its infancy when compared against the long history the Admiralty claimed. Despite the similarities in the two organizations, the relationship between them was contentious to say the least.

Grigoris could only assume the fact Eric "stole" one of their members wouldn't help to improve that state.

A side door opened, revealing a man with a bag over his head being forcefully pushed into the room by two other people. Grigoris tensed, and around the room, people drew to attention, hands dropping to sword hilts or sliding into jackets to touch whatever weapons they had.

Grigoris recognized one of the escorts as Leila Virtanan, but not the man with her. Given the sword hanging from the man's belt, he assumed this was Lancelot. He narrowed his eyes. Actually, the man looked familiar upon closer inspection.

The territories, while allies, didn't openly share information. However, he'd heard that Lancelot hadn't always been a knight, that he was in fact one of the English security officers who'd switched to being a knight. As was tradition in the

English territory, he'd taken on the name of one of the knights of the roundtable. Grigoris was fairly sure the man now known as Lancelot had been Charlie Allerton, a security officer with plenty of blood on his hands.

Lancelot and Leila each had a firm grip on the man's arms, which were chained together at his back. Despite the fact he was clearly captured, the man continued to put up a fight as they shoved him toward a chair and pushed him down onto it.

The man tried to rise, but Lancelot pressed a hand on his shoulder and murmured a quiet warning. Grigoris wasn't sure what the knight said, but the man in the chair stilled.

Josephine was the last to enter, grinning widely as if they were all attending a party and there wasn't the slightest thing odd about the captured man in the center of the room.

A massive blond man appeared at the second-floor railing and cleared his throat. Grigoris watched as half the audience tensed further, while the other half seemed to relax at the appearance of the fleet admiral.

Eric Ericsson was massive, both in height and in the width of his shoulders. He was heavily muscled, which was —purposefully, Grigoris thought—on display, thanks to the thin black T-shirt and dark pants he wore. He'd been nick-named the Viking, both for obvious reasons, and because, if rumors were to be believed, he was prone to berserker rages.

Eric looked over the crowd, making sure his gaze landed for a split second on each person, before looking at where the rumpled man with a cloth bag over his head had been forced into a chair.

"Let him loose," Eric ordered.

Lancelot pulled the bag off the man's head.

"Who's that?" Grigoris asked Nyx.

Josephine ducked, smiling tentatively at the prisoner, while Lancelot kept a hand firmly on his shoulder.

"Hi, brother," she said. "Please don't be cross at me."

The man shook his too-long hair out of his eyes. His glasses were on crooked. "You're a great gobshite! Always getting me into trouble."

"Don't be rude," Josephine scolded.

"You kidnapped me, and I'm the rude one? I'm going to tell the rector."

Josephine laughed. "You haven't been to church in years."

"Why didn't you just ask me to...wait..." The man looked around. "Are we at Trinity College?"

Josephine nodded, but the man didn't notice her. His gaze was raised to where Eric stood.

"Would you still have come if you knew I was the one asking?" Eric called down.

"Ah, ye great Scandinavian fucker, I wouldn't have been—"

The man's accent was suddenly so thick Grigoris could barely understand him. Nyx hissed, and he whirled to her, heart in his throat. "Nyx? What's wrong? Are you hurt?"

"The Archivist," she murmured. "He's the Archivist." Nyx started forward.

Grigoris reached out and placed two fingers on her upper arm. He didn't grab her or try to hold her—both those things triggered bad memories.

"Who is the Archivist?" he asked. It was more to distract her than because he needed the answer.

"The Masters' Admiralty has an archive. A record of everything, that also serves as a vault. Like the Vatican Archives. I hadn't ever heard about them. None of us, except Josephine, had. And she only knows because the

Archivist is her brother. And I want access to those archives."

"You're a member," Grigoris soothed, "so after this you can—"

"The archive, the Archivist, and the city of Dublin all exist outside the structure of the Masters' Admiralty."

Now that was interesting information. "Dublin is neutral territory?"

"They didn't like that the territory was called England. Refused to obey an admiral based in England. Apparently the society had been storing information and documents in Dublin for years. They leveraged that into declaring themselves neutral territory. I need to see what's in there."

As a Greek Cypriot, who was under authority of the Ottoman territory, he was a bit irritated that Dublin had managed to declare themselves neutral territory.

"You're doing that terrifying scholar thing again," Grigoris murmured to her.

That stopped her, and Nyx turned, lips curling up into a smile. He'd first used that term when she'd been peer-reviewing an article for a journal. It had been just after she'd been well enough to sit up and work on her computer, the sepsis finally under control. He'd walked in to check on her to find her staring at her computer with a sort of terrifying intensity, like a cat stalking a mouse.

He'd dubbed the predatory look "terrifying scholar" and every time he used the term, it made her smile.

Grigoris lived to make her smile. To make her feel safe.

"I suppose demanding he give me access isn't a priority right now."

"No, I don't think it is," Grigoris agreed solemnly. "Why was he black-bagged?"

"I don't know."

They returned their attention to the front of the room. Lancelot was looking back and forth between Josephine and Colum, who were now arguing with each other in a different language. Colum would occasionally look up and yell something at Eric.

"Knock their heads together," Eric called down to the knight. "Trust me. It works."

Josephine backpedaled, Colum started cursing, and Lancelot just sighed, before unlocking the cuffs on the Irishman's wrists.

"Would you two shut up?" Eric demanded.

"Don't talk to my sister like that, you great Danish fuck."

"Lancelot," Eric barked.

Lancelot put a hand on Colum's shoulder, forcing him back into the chair before he said, "Shut the fook up, mate."

Everyone in the room had been watching this odd little byplay, but now their attention switched to Eric.

The fleet admiral braced his hands on the railing. "You all know why you're here."

"No, we don't," Dimitri, Mateo's husband, called out.

"Make an educated guess," Eric grumped. "Or get your wife to explain it to you. God knows she's the brains of your trinity."

Cecilia St. John's lips twitched, but she managed not to smile.

Sophia Starabba whispered something to her husband James, and they walked out of the room, leaving Arthur behind.

"I don't like the game we've been playing," Eric continued. "So I'm changing the rules."

"Game?" Karl said. He didn't shout, but rather raised his voice to carry. "What has been happening is not a game." The trinity from Rome was toward the center of the room, Leila sitting on the table, Antonio standing beside her, and Karl sitting in a chair.

Antonio put a hand on his husband's shoulder and pulled his wife against his other side.

Sophia and James appeared behind Eric. When Sophia touched the fleet admiral's shoulder, the Viking didn't jump. He'd known they were there. There was a quick, whispered conversation, and then Eric stepped back, gesturing for the other two to come forward.

Sophia stepped up, hands resting delicately on the railing. She looked calm and composed. Grigoris knew that her father, the admiral of Rome—though due to injuries sustained in the bombing of his villa, it was a title in name only—had intended Sophia be the next admiral. Instead, she was married to the new admiral of England, and if rumors were to be believed, she was the power behind the throne.

"Thank you, to each of you, for coming here." Her voice carried well, and her tone and posture were calm. "If you are here, then it means you know, or are known to, the small group called the librarians. The threat to our society is many faceted. Many of you in the room now are knights or security officers for your territories. In those roles, you've been fighting our enemies. To support that effort, those we call the librarians have been working on the less-direct threats, analyzing and dissecting the information we have."

"By enemy, you mean the mastermind," Dimitri called out.

Sophia nodded. "*Esattamente.* For the sake of clarity, I have suggested to our esteemed fleet admiral that we review what has happened."

James stepped up beside his wife. "We're going to try to do this fast. If you have questions, you can ask your librarian afterward."

"Are you my librarian?" Grigoris asked quietly. He'd meant it as a joke, but it came out heavy and hopeful.

Nyx stiffened, then sighed. "I belong to no one, but yes, I think in this case, I'm yours."

Skatá. He wished she would talk to him, but he wasn't going to push her. Nyx had been to hell and back these past few months, recovering from one of the most brutal attacks he'd ever seen.

And while he knew what she needed was time, it was getting harder and harder to put his feelings for her on the back burner.

James recapped what had happened. "Chronologically, it began with the poisoning of former Fleet Admiral Kacper Kujakski. Starting several years ago, a member of the Spartan Guard, Derrick, and Kacper's wife, Manon, began switching out his prescription medication with poisoned tablets."

"There are some things that happened before that," Eric called out from the shadows behind James. "But they're not mission-relevant at this point."

Grigoris made a mental note to ask his librarian about that, but given the way she was frowning, it seemed like she wasn't sure what Eric was talking about.

"The death of the trinity in Rome, at the hands of serial killer Ciril Nowak, is what began the current series of connected events," Sophia continued. "Clues were left with their bodies, clues that pointed to a threat on the fleet admiral's life by the Domino."

James picked up again. "As many of you know, the Domino is an old enemy of the Masters' Admiralty. Traditionally there was the Domino and a single apprentice. When we—Sophia, myself, and Arthur—took the evidence we'd found to the fleet admiral, Kacper was attacked. A man who we assumed to be the Domino's apprentice used a dart gun mounted to a drone to shoot the fleet admiral. The chemicals in the dart gun interacted with the poison already in Kacper's system, killing him.

"That resulted in calling a conclave to choose a new fleet admiral. The conclave, held in a secure location owned by the Admiralty of England, was booby-trapped," James said. "A state-of-the-art heat sensor had been installed in the meeting room. A sniper, using a high-powered rifle, was able to use that information to shoot into the room from a nearby building. The admirals of England and Castile died that day, as did the English knight Gawain, and Tristan—now Arthur —lost his arm.

"It was later discovered that a similar heat sensor had been installed in one of the buildings owned by the Admiralty of Rome—a place that was as likely to be the location for the conclave meeting as the site in England."

"So the mastermind knew where the conclave might meet," Josephine added.

"Hurry it up," Colum said nervously, looking around. "I didn't realize there were so many people in here."

"A second conclave was held at an inaccessible location," Eric said. "Leaving me stuck with this job, since I was the only one qualified. Santiago became admiral of Castile and Tristan had to change names and became Arthur, admiral of England."

"In the investigation that followed, we found the sniper— a young American named Griffin Rutherford, who was also involved in an affair with Kacper's wife, Manon." Sophia looked around the room, taking in the reactions. It seemed there were a few people who hadn't known about that.

"Turns out the Spartan Guard hadn't bothered to do anything about the fact that one of Kacper's wives had left him," Eric grumbled, looking at Mateo.

Mateo obviously felt the insult and stiffened, but Cecilia put a hand on him to calm him.

Sophia resumed her calm, concise narration. "Manon and Griffin both died when we cornered them in a hotel. They were aided by Derrick, the traitor in the Spartan Guard, though we were unaware of it at the time. It was during Mateo's investigation into how Kacper was poisoned that it was revealed both who the traitor was and that Derrick had also been having an affair with Manon and a third woman, Alicia Rutherford, Griffin's wife."

"For those of you playing along at home," James said. "You'll notice this is way more than two people, and if it was the Domino, there should have only been two. The drone operator, the sniper, Manon, Derrick and Alicia, whom we eventually caught in America, all referred to themselves as the apprentice."

"The person who did not use this language was Ciril, the serial killer who murdered the trinity in Rome, kidnapped and tortured Karl and Leila, and wounded Nyx."

Grigoris reached down and took Nyx's hand as people turned to look at her. Her face remained expressionless, but her fingers squeezed his with a desperation that made his heart ache.

"Ciril kept referring to his 'friend' who both helped him evade capture and provided him with targets," Sophia continued. "Ciril himself had a tenuous connection to us, but no knowledge of the organization. That was provided to him by his 'friend'."

"And then there's the bombings," James added. "The safehouse in Bucharest and several vehicles were blown up, killing German Ritter, Hungarian Harcosok, and security officers. Good people died that day, and Bucharest ended up under martial law as we had to declare everything a terrorist attack."

Grigoris felt ill. He'd been in charge of the operation in Bucharest. The blood of those who'd died that day was on his hands.

The silence hung for a moment before Sophia started speaking, perhaps with a bit more emotion than before. "We dubbed our enemy the mastermind. He is not the Domino, or at least not just the Domino. He used that idea, and the term, to recruit apprentices. He also befriended and became the benefactor for at least one serial killer. He also restarted and supported a second old enemy of the Masters' Admiralty, the Bellator Dei—a Catholic extremist group who opposes our way of life. Their preferred form of attack is bombing, and they often use innocent people to carry out the attacks, as was the case in Rome."

James and Sophia exchanged a glance, then both looked at Eric.

Grigoris stiffened, and Nyx placed her hand on his shoulder as if to warn him to brace himself.

"We've been dealing with the mastermind's minions, his puppets," James said. "But we haven't been able to get closer to the mastermind himself, until Hugo and Lancelot followed Alicia Rutherford to America. Thanks to their work, and the help of our new member—hi and welcome, Sylvia—we got a name. Alicia called the mastermind Varangian."

"And no," Eric said. "It's not a *Star Trek* term. Hugo, the big geek, checked."

"Hey," Hugo protested as a small laugh ran through the room.

Eric's face hardened. "Varangian was—sorry, Josephine, I'm not going to give the long academic explanation—a Greek and Rus term for Vikings."

There was a beat of silence and Grigoris stiffened. Around the room he saw others do the same, rising to their feet as if preparing for battle.

"The mastermind is calling himself Viking," James said.

"He's trying to frame the fleet admiral," Sophia spoke calmly, ignoring the murmurs of conversation that followed. "Those of you in this room are those we—the librarians, and Eric himself—trust."

"The fact that he's using that name, that he's setting it up to throw suspicion on me, means we can't wait," Eric said. "We're taking the fight to him. We're going to find the mastermind, kill him, and then dismantle the rest of his operation."

"The mastermind is one of us," Sophia said. "And not just one of our own, but someone in a position of power."

"Josephine, Sophia, James, and I have compiled a list of suspects," Eric said. "A fucking long list. That's why each of you is here. You're getting homework."

"Why not take this to the security officers for each territory?" Dimitri called out.

"Because everyone not in this room is a suspect," James said softly. "Including all the admirals, vice admirals, and security ministers."

"Your job is simple," Eric cut in. "And not simple. Investigate the people on this list. Narrow it down to something we can fucking work with. I want this bastard before any more of our people's blood is shed."

"You say the admirals are suspects," Arthur called out, "but the admirals were all in the room at the first conclave. Any one of them could have been killed."

Eric grunted and crossed his arms. "We've been over this, so I know you're just asking for their benefit. Fine. Yes, for almost everyone on this list, there is a reason why they aren't the mastermind. Everyone in our society has lost something since this shit started, even if it's just a sense of security. You find that reason and rip it apart. We're going to assume guilt and prove innocence. Not the other way around." Eric looked down. "And if you need information, especially historical records, you go to Colum, the Archivist. By the way, we have a secret archive, and an archivist who is the only fucker in the whole society who doesn't have to listen to me."

"I have to talk to all these people?" Colum yelped.

"You can do it one at a time," his sister soothed. "I'll help you."

"Josephine, can you pass out the lists?" Eric rubbed his hands together. "Homework time."

Josephine grabbed a small stack of papers and walked around the room as Eric called out assignments from above. "Cecilia, you and your trinity are going to investigate the leadership from the territories of Castile."

"Okay," Cecilia said.

Mateo frowned but nodded.

"You have a problem with that?" Eric asked.

Mateo didn't answer immediately. "I'm close to the new admiral. Santiago is like an uncle to me. But no, Fleet Admiral. I don't have a problem. I want the mastermind caught as much as you do."

"No one wants it that much. Also, try not to fuck this up." Eric turned his attention to Hugo. "You, Lancelot, and Sylvia are going to investigate France."

"Eric," Lancelot interjected. "We just got married and—"

"Trust me, that won't matter to him," Antonio murmured.

"So take her to the south of France and buy some wine while you're there." Eric shrugged. "Moving on. Arthur, you keep an eye on England, though suspect-wise, England and Rome are at the bottom of the list."

Arthur grinned. "You want me to investigate Lorelei? No one gets too close to Lorelei. It's dangerous."

Eric pointed to him. "There. See? That. And I don't want you to investigate. Just stay alert. I need you and Antonio to run your territories, protect your people.

"Karl. You and Leila are going to investigate Germany and Kalmar. James, I want you in Bohemia."

"What do you want me to do?" Josephine asked eagerly.

"You'll work with Colum," Eric said.

Josephine turned her nose up, but her brother seemed to like the idea a lot. "That works," Colum barked out. "You can deal with the people."

Eric rolled his eyes. "And, Nyx, you're in charge of Hungary."

Nyx stiffened but didn't say anything.

"Fleet Admiral," Grigoris broke in. "I don't think—"

Eric shook his head. "This isn't a discussion. Nyx is going. You're going with her, as her backup. You got a problem with that, Violaris?"

Grigoris ground his teeth. "Sir. Nyx is still recovering. I will go and investigate—"

"I need her in Hungary." Eric stared at Nyx. "For obvious reasons."

"What reason could be good enough to risk her health?" Grigoris asked.

"She can get close to Petro. She's the only one who can because Petro is a paranoid fuck."

"I will find a way to get close to him," Grigoris said.

"No. Nyx is going." Eric looked at her and something passed between them. "After all, Nyx is Petro's wife."

CHAPTER TWO

"I'm giving you one more minute to quietly freak out," Eric declared.

Grigoris whipped his head up, looking around the small gathering. They were in a back office of the reading room. Eric had called him in for a second, smaller meeting, only moments after dropping the bombshell about Nyx's marriage.

Marriage.

Married.

She was married.

"You can be an ass," Arthur said in a casual tone to Eric.

"He is an ass," Antonio corrected.

"I'm your boss," Eric pointed out to the admirals.

"Changes nothing." Antonio folded his arms and leaned back against an untidy desk that took up most of the space in the small room.

Grigoris forced himself to stop thinking about Nyx. About the fact that she was married. She'd be on her way back to the hotel by now, safe with Dimitri, who he'd stopped to talk to on his way to answer Eric's summons.

"There were kinder ways to tell him." Arthur was looking at his prosthetic right hand, though he spoke to Eric. The fingers of the lifelike appendage were flexing, each one touching the tip of the thumb before relaxing. Grigoris vaguely wondered how Arthur was able to control it.

"Kind." Antonio snorted.

Grigoris looked around, really seeing the other men for the first time. His shoulder muscles tightened. It wasn't like him to be so unaware of his surroundings. Then the implications of what they'd just said sank in. "You know how I...how I feel about Nyx?"

"Yep," Eric said.

"I was in Bucharest. I saw the way you cared for her," Antonio added.

"James told me she's been with you since then." Arthur was the only one who looked at all sympathetic. "I'm sorry, Grigoris. I assume you didn't know about her marriage."

"No. I didn't." And that hurt. Yet there had to be an explanation. "What do you need, Fleet Admiral?"

"Ignore your feelings and focus on the job. I like it." Eric had been slumped against a filing cabinet, but now he straightened. Grigoris had been in the fleet admiral's presence several times, yet when the Viking straightened, Grigoris was once again struck by just how big the other man was —tall, broad, and muscled. Grigoris himself was tall, but he knew how to move his body to minimize his height when needed, and he didn't have the bulk of the other man.

There had been rumors about what Eric had done in the years between his wives' deaths and him being forced into the role of fleet admiral, and looking at the man, it was easy to believe each and every story.

"You two are here," Eric pointed at the admirals,

"because I want updates. And I want Grigoris to hear the updates. Right now, he's my best piece."

Grigoris raised a brow, but didn't object to being referred to as if he were a game piece. As not only a janissary, or knight, of the Ottoman territory, but the chorbaji of the janissaries, he had both the skills and authority to act on behalf of the Masters' Admiralty. His admiral, Hande Demiratar, had temporarily relieved him of his specific duties to the territory so he could head a joint task force in Bucharest. That operation had gone bad. People had died, Nyx had been wounded, but in the chaos, Leila, Antonio's wife, had managed to kill Ciril.

He'd brought Nyx back to Cyprus but continued working on the investigation from there. One of the bombs had been a suicide bomb, and he'd spent a month running every possible lead to see if the bomber had any connection to the Masters' Admiralty. They hadn't, but they had been a member of a very conservative orthodox church in Romania. He'd been working on tracing the finances of that church to see if he could find any connection to someone in the Masters' Admiralty.

"I need you two to keep your territories running. Which brings me to the first update—Antonio. How is your father?"

"Awake and talking." Antonio suddenly looked tired. "The weeks in the coma did damage to his body. The recovery will take some time, given his age."

"Is he going to step down?" Eric asked bluntly.

Antonio winced. "I hope not." He glanced at Arthur. "If I could have my sister back so I don't have to be admiral..."

"No." Arthur's tone was polite, but his eyes were hard.

"The faster you start accepting that you're not getting out of it, the better." Eric clapped Antonio on the shoulder. "You know how I feel about it, and I hate to force you."

"But you will."

"I will," Eric confirmed grimly. "Any news on your bombing, Antonio? Grigoris is like a dog with a bone on the Bucharest ones, but the fact we had to use terrorism to cover it up is making everything hard."

"We have a new lead," Antonio said. "The security officers found and detained the brother of the man who constructed the bomb. There was residue from explosives in his home. We're tracing his connection to the society back and continuing to question him."

"An actual lead?" Eric put a hand to his chest. "I might faint."

Antonio snorted.

"And don't kill him," Eric added.

"We have no intention of killing him." There was an unspoken "yet." "We have him in protective custody. I'm more concerned with making sure the mastermind doesn't get to him."

"Good." Eric's expression didn't change, but his stance relaxed a little. Though no one said anything, an air of hope filled the room. Grigoris looked at Antonio and he prayed, though he wasn't a religious man, that the Italian was on track to bring an end to all this.

"Arthur?" Eric asked. "What have you learned?"

"Nothing as promising. But since I was looking into a decades' old crime, I suppose it's to be expected."

Grigoris frowned but didn't interrupt.

"I think you were right to look into those older murders. Dr. Bernard's records are missing. All of them." Arthur looked at Grigoris. "Eric asked me to look into the murder of Mateo's parents. He's a legacy and was being raised by two members of the trinity. He didn't know about the Masters' Admiralty until after they were killed."

"What made you want to look into it?" Grigoris asked Eric.

"The way they died. Grisly murder scene, message in blood. Too close to what they found in the cave in Rome."

"If they were killed decades ago, Ciril would have been far too young," Grigoris pointed out.

"I know, but how many serial killers can we have running around killing our people? Not that fucking many. I looked it up." Eric focused on Arthur once more. "Which Dr. Bernard are we talking about?"

"Both of them were doctors," Arthur explained to Grigoris, then to Eric said, "His mother. The neurosurgeon."

"Any idea of when the records went missing?"

"That's what makes it interesting. A few days before she was murdered."

"Shit." Eric crossed his arms. "She knew something."

"That's a leap," Arthur cautioned.

"Leap? This is a goddamn logic freefall, but I'm going with it. Dr. Bernard knew something that someone didn't want her to, and it was in her records. They stole the records, then murdered her. Who would care about some missing files when they're distracted by a grisly murder?"

Grigoris nodded in agreement. "Whoever murdered them has the same homicidal tendencies as our latest killer, Ciril."

"Which means that Ciril's 'friend' is probably the same person who killed Mateo's parents."

"Another pet serial killer," Antonio added.

"Exactly. But maybe the mastermind was sloppy when younger. Maybe clues were left, or that killer was told more than he or she told Ciril."

"That also means the mastermind is older. At least forty, but most likely fifty," Antonio pointed out.

"Which is why the younger admirals aren't on my list for first-round investigations." Eric looked at Grigoris. "Which reminds me of why I wanted to talk to you. Petro *is* on my list, which is why I'm sending you and Nyx."

"If they're estranged..." Part of his mind had been puzzling over the issue of Nyx's marriage, and that was the only thing that made sense.

"They probably are. Hell, I didn't even realize they were married until I started making my suspect list and checked the records." Eric shrugged. "And while she's the logical one to get close, I won't send her in alone."

Grigoris wouldn't have let her go alone, no matter what Eric said.

"But there's something else. I'm worried about Lazar Markovic, the vice admiral."

"You think he's the mastermind?"

"Maybe. He hasn't been seen outside his territory. Last thing I found in Kacper's notes was that he was sick."

"In the head?" Antonio asked.

"No. In the hospital. Not expected to make it, but a month later he was released, apparently healthy enough to go home." Eric pointed at Grigoris. "Investigate Petro, find Lazar." Eric's expression softened, and something that looked like regret appeared in his eyes. "And protect Nyx."

Grigoris nodded. He would protect Nyx because he loved her. It was as simple—and as complicated—as that.

But first he was going to find out why she'd hidden the fact that she was married.

Why she'd let him believe that maybe, someday...

Grigoris ran his hand through his hair, fighting to dismiss the thought. They were members of two different territories. This wasn't some goddamn fairy tale. He was never going to get the girl, ride into the sunset, live happily ever after.

But that didn't mean he hadn't longed for it, realistic or not.

"That's all I have," Eric said.

When the fleet admiral dismissed him, Grigoris turned on his heel and strode out of the room. It was time to talk to Nyx.

NYX STOOD at the window of the hotel, looking down at the streetlights below. Grigoris had booked them two suites at the Westin in College Green so that they could walk to Trinity. The historic stone building had been modernized into a luxury hotel and was situated close to many wonderful attractions in Dublin, including the River Liffey and Abbey Theatre. Under normal circumstances, Nyx would have enjoyed a visit here, as she had the many other times she'd explored Dublin pre- and post-librarians' meetings. Normally she opted for more utilitarian lodgings, but this room was warm, inviting, comfortable.

Not that Nyx was comfortable at the moment.

After Eric casually revealed her darkest secret in front of not only a room containing people she considered colleagues, but the one man she'd resisted revealing the secret to, the fleet admiral had then pulled Grigoris away to talk to him. Dimitri, Cecilia's husband, had escorted her back to the hotel.

In the moments after the announcement, Nyx had tried to study Grigoris' face. One of the reasons she was so drawn to Grigoris was that, unlike her, he was open with his emotions, prone to smiling and joking. That was, she'd come to realize, part of what made him so dangerous—he'd cultivated a nonthreatening manner that allowed him to both blend in to most situations and put other people at ease.

Yet once he'd learned who she was, what she was, his expression had been perfectly blank. He hadn't even looked at her, though he'd stopped to ask Dimitri to escort her.

Dimitri had walked her all the way to her suite. She wished Grigoris had been with her. She'd come to rely on him as a safeguard. And while it pained her to admit it, she needed him. Needed to have him nearby.

She'd been off-kilter since Ciril's attack. The strong, independent woman who was used to—even more comfortable— being alone was gone. She'd retreated, leaving this person who was frightened, uncertain. The only time she felt steady these days was when Grigoris was with her. She'd allowed him to prop her up, keep her moving.

She couldn't keep doing that, but she couldn't figure out a way to stop.

Nyx caught sight of her reflection in the window. Reaching up, she ran her finger along the pinkish scar, sliding it beside her eye, down her cheek, touching the side of her mouth.

There was no pain. Yet, there was the memory of pain. A white-hot burning sensation that often woke her, left her crying out in the middle of the night. It was those times she longed for Grigoris the most. Because he would come to her. He would sit beside her, hold her hand, and stroke her hair. He would assure her she was safe, alive, brave, and that everything would be fine. His soft voice would lull her back to sleep and for a few moments, she'd allow herself to pretend everything he said was true.

Nyx's eyes returned to her reflection. Had she been a vain woman, she might have mourned the loss of beauty, but she did not. Part of her actually welcomed the scar. In her experience, her appearance had been a disadvantage, a distraction, to many men. Men ruled by lust, by sexual desires. Men who did not hold women in esteem, but rather viewed them as pretty objects they could possess—existing only for their pleasure.

Men like Petro.

Her husband.

Her mouth twisted in a sneer as she thought the word, but the flash of angry disgust was short-lived.

Nyx should have told Grigoris about her sham of a marriage before this. She had considered it countless times, but she simply couldn't say the words. Not to him. Not even to herself.

She'd pushed that truth away for so many years there were times she almost believed it was simply another bad dream, something else Grigoris could chase away with his gentle voice and caring eyes.

She glanced at the clock. It was late. She wondered if Grigoris had returned yet. Part of her had expected him to come see her, to fill her in on his meeting with the fleet admiral. The fact he hadn't shown concerned her.

Now that her secret had been revealed, she knew it was time for her and Grigoris to put words to all the things she'd forced them, with her silence, to ignore.

Nyx considered going to his room but discounted it. Perhaps the coming conversation would be easier in the morning. She walked to her suitcase and pulled out her silk nightgown. Shedding her clothes, she lightly touched the uglier scar on her abdomen. The cut had gone deep and she'd lost consciousness, her body's only way to combat the intense pain.

The dark stillness of her room felt too intimate, too...inviting. It was best to save this conversation with Grigoris until tomorrow.

She pulled the nightgown on. It was the color of water, cool, soft. Then she drew the matching silk robe on as well, loosely tying it around her waist. The sleepwear set had been a gift from Grigoris, shortly after he'd checked her out of the hospital and taken her to his home in Cyprus to recuperate. He had told her the color reminded him of her eyes, pale blue, crystalline, mesmerizing.

Nyx pulled back the sheets, about to climb in, when there was a soft knock at the door.

He'd come.

Walking to the door, Nyx's heart began to pound harder. Since the attack, Grigoris had become...important to her. She couldn't bear the thought of losing him.

Peering through the peephole, she saw him standing outside her door in profile. Ever the vigilant bodyguard, he was studying their surroundings, making certain nothing was amiss.

She twisted the dead bolt and opened the door.

Grigoris turned to face her, and the mask he'd worn back at Trinity College was gone, his emotions laid bare. He looked shocked. Shattered.

Nyx stepped to the side. "Come in."

Grigoris walked into her room, closing the door behind him, throwing the dead bolt once more.

Nerves made her stomach tight. She couldn't look at his face, and as the silence stretched between them, she couldn't bear it. "What did the fleet admiral say?"

She should care, but she didn't. She just couldn't stand the tense silence. When she'd been recovering, unable to speak without risk of opening the stitches on her face, Grigoris had sat with her and talked—told stories of his childhood, read to her, made her laugh, though she'd had to press one hand to her face to make sure amusement didn't cause damage.

"Why didn't you tell me?" Grigoris asked softly, running his hand through his hair. It was already mussed, sticking out all over the place. Her first thought was that it was windy outside, but now she could see he'd done the damage himself. He'd done a similar trick earlier, before they'd walked into the meeting.

She was always amazed at how much he could alter his looks with just a few subtle changes.

Nyx crossed her arms, well aware it was a defensive—or perhaps protective—posture. "I should have."

"That's it? That's all you're going to say? You 'should have'. You're married."

Nyx drifted across the room to the wingback chair, dropping down exhaustedly. "There are reasons. I'm not like you."

"Dammit. Don't do that." Grigoris followed her across the room, claiming a spot on the couch. He sat there for approximately four seconds before bouncing back up again to pace the length of the room.

He came to her chair, kneeling in front of it. "Why didn't you tell me?" he asked again, gentler. Curious rather than accusatory.

"Because I don't accept it."

Puzzled, Grigoris shook his head. "As members of the Masters' Admiralty, we gave up the right to choose who we marry. We can't disregard our admiral's choice for us just because we don't agree."

"I joined the society because it was all I knew growing up. I'm a legacy. My parents are members. Their lifestyle is what feels normal to me. But more than that, I believe in the mission of Masters' Admiralty."

"Then you have to accept an arranged marriage." He looked away. "You're married to an admiral. Petro is powerful, wealthy."

Nyx tugged her silk robe closed more tightly, then leaned forward. "And admirals are the only ones who choose their own spouses." Grigoris stiffened, and his eyes narrowed as he considered exactly what she'd just said. "Petro is my admiral. He has been the admiral a long time."

"You don't like that the admirals get to choose when no one else does?"

If he hadn't been kneeling at her feet, Nyx would have gotten up to pace. "No. That's not why I object. Why I refused." She didn't want to say this next part, didn't want to talk about something that made her feel dirty. "Petro didn't choose me because of my intellect or my accomplishments. He selected me because I was young and pretty. A legacy. Good lineage." She met Grigoris' eyes. "I was placed in a trinity—he chose me for himself—when I was only fourteen."

Grigoris' features shifted in horror, then disbelief. "No. How? You weren't old enough to even be a member."

"No, I wasn't. He called it a betrothal." She looked away, hating how small and weak talking about this made her feel. "The legal age of consent in Hungary is fourteen, but he couldn't form the trinity until I was eighteen and a full-fledged member, rather than a legacy." And at fourteen, she'd been torn between horror at how old her husband was and pride that she'd been picked. Her parents had been so happy, it had been hard for her to voice her disquiet.

Grigoris reached for her but stopped, his hand hovering in the air. "Did he...?"

"No. He didn't touch me then, and shortly after, I went

away to boarding school. Once I was away from him, from my parents, I began to understand what exactly was going on. I saw my story, my circumstances, reflected in the annals of history. To Petro, I was not a person, but a prize he'd earned."

"That's abhorrent," Grigoris said. "I can't believe it. That goes against everything our society stands for. One of the reasons our society was founded was because people didn't agree with the way the church treated and abused women."

She nodded, feeling somewhat numb. She'd lived this nightmare over half her life, but it didn't make it any easier to face. "While I was at school, he chose another pretty young woman to be his second wife. Hanna was fifteen when the three of us were betrothed." Nyx was aware that technically, she should consider Hanna her wife as well, but she'd never felt any connection to the woman.

"You said you don't accept the marriage. I can see why, if you were only fourteen." Grigoris looked disgusted, and his clear revulsion of the idea helped her finish the story.

"I am not blameless."

"You absolutely are," Grigoris said vehemently.

"No, I'm not. Because I still joined the Masters' Admiralty the day after I turned eighteen. I flew to the Isle of Man to formally join the society. I stood in front of the fleet admiral and didn't say anything about the betrothal or my objections. Two days later, I returned to my home territory for the first time since I was fourteen."

Grigoris paused, considering. "You're a legacy, so I understand why you still joined."

She snorted. "Do you? I thought I could affect change. I had plans. The kinds of plans that only revolutionaries and juveniles think are viable. I was so sure in my own hubris. I walked into *Isten Palotája* prepared to transform the world."

"*Isten Palotája.* God's Palace," Grigoris translated the Hungarian.

"Petro's home in Lake Balaton, Hungary."

Finally, he touched her, his hand laying lightly over hers. "I'm sorry, Nyx."

She smiled, but it was fleeting. She wasn't used to smiling, wasn't good at it. She was trying, when she was with Grigoris, to let him see how he made her happy. Even though she'd lied to him. "Petro let me talk, explain, argue. Then he ignored me, called Hanna in, and married us."

"That *malakas.*"

His outrage on her behalf made her feel good. She wanted to reach out and touch him but didn't.

Grigoris scowled. "This can't be true. There's no way the fleet admiral would approve the marriage, not if he knew you'd been picked at fourteen. And if you'd only just joined, he might have told Petro to wait."

"He didn't approve it." Nyx smiled, and this time it was a cold expression she was much more comfortable with.

Grigoris rose, claiming the side of the couch near her chair. Instinctively, he reached for her hand. He'd held it so often these past few months, it felt unnatural for her hand not to be in his. "What do you mean?"

"The fleet admiral has to confirm every trinity on the Isle of Man."

"Right."

"I simply refused to go. My marriage was never formally recognized." She turned to look at him. "I refused to get on the plane, and then I left. I went to England, to Oxford."

Nyx's escape came through higher education. She'd heard that Hanna attended the University of Budapest, graduating with a degree in chemistry while remaining at home, warming Petro's bed each night.

Part of her felt guilty for leaving Hanna behind.

"While I was at the university, Petro could brag about his brilliant, beautiful wife. However, after I received my doctorate, I remained away. I was twenty-six and living in fear. Fear that he would use his power to force me back to Hungary. That my visa would be revoked or, as I applied for professorships, that he would ensure I never got a job."

"And you've stayed away all this time?"

"Yes. I believe Petro's pride wouldn't let him force me to go to Man. I think some part of him is...amused...by me."

That rankled, in no small part because she feared that even now, after everything she'd done to protect herself, Petro could get to her if he wanted to. "I think he considers himself an indulgent and patient man."

Grigoris fell silent for several minutes. Nyx could see something was weighing heavily on his mind, but he seemed to be debating whether or not to talk about it.

"What is it?" she prodded. She'd spent far too long harboring this secret, hiding in shadows. Finally talking about this to someone, after all these years, felt freeing.

"Did Petro ever...did he force you to..." Grigoris swallowed heavily.

"No," she replied quickly. "Never. I thought I could stop the marriage. I was wrong. I ran out of the house right after the ceremony. Hid at the home of—" Nyx stopped herself short. "Of a family friend. He allowed me to stay there until I was able to discreetly arrange to leave Hungary, to make my way to Oxford. Without his help, I..."

Grigoris closed his eyes and released a short, relieved breath. "I am glad. We should go to Eric, tell him about this. This marriage goes against everything the Masters'—"

"No." Nyx shook her head. "I've had a very long time to think about this, *motănel*."

A ghost of a grin appeared. Grigoris liked it when she called him "my dear".

"Though you and I can feel repulsion over Petro's actions, he technically didn't do anything wrong by the standards of our society. He is allowed to choose his own partners and he waited until we were of age to perform the wedding. Besides, what happens if Eric refuses to confirm the marriage? I still belong to the Hungary territory and Petro is still my admiral. I don't want to consider what he might do to punish me for refusing him. Perhaps it is better this way."

"Better? No. It's not."

Nyx squeezed his hand. "He thinks I am still his. Believe me, I am safer as long as that is so."

"I will always protect you, Nyx."

She smiled, not bothering to hide the brokenness behind her hand. "I know you will, *motănel*. I know."

They sat there for a long time, neither speaking.

Now that the truth was out, it seemed as if the wall she'd erected between them had fallen.

However, another higher wall had taken its place. Now Grigoris fully understood why this attraction between them could never be acknowledged, never be allowed to blossom. To give in to it would only lead to disappointment and unspeakable pain. The two of them were destined to long for something they could never have.

She mistakenly thought Grigoris was feeling that same pain, but then she realized there was something more he wanted to say.

"Grigoris?"

"I know Eric asked you to investigate Petro. Given what I know now, I want you to let me handle that."

Nyx instinctively started to shake her head. She had been given an order by the fleet admiral. There was enough of the woman she'd been before the accident left that the idea of shirking her responsibilities didn't sit well with her.

After all, this wouldn't be the first time she'd come face-to-face with her husband during the course of this hunt for the mastermind. Somehow he had discovered she was in Bucharest, which was partially in his territory. The bulk of the country of Romania belonged to the Masters' Admiralty territory of Hungary, and he'd sought her out. As always, he'd asked her to come home. She had refused.

However, this time, she would be seeking him out, returning to a place she'd sworn to never step foot in again.

Her fear halted her outright rejection of Grigoris' offer. Regardless of Grigoris' promise to protect her, only a fool would fail to acknowledge Petro's power. What if he found a way to force her to remain, to stay, to accept her position as his wife?

"I…"

"I can report back whatever I find to you. Go back to my home in Cyprus. I have people there who can keep you safe. I'll dig up all that I can on Petro, try to discover what happened to Lazar Markovic, and then—"

"Lazar?"

Something in her tone slowed Grigoris down. "Yes. You know him?"

"Of course. He's the vice admiral. What happened to him?"

"Apparently, no one has spoken to him in years."

Nyx thought back to the night she'd fled Petro's house after the wedding. Lazar had found her, and she'd expected him to return her to Petro, that she would have to go through with the honeymoon. Instead, he'd risked everything to hide her from their admiral. It was Lazar who'd arranged safe transportation out of Hungary and who had helped set her up at Oxford. Nyx didn't know why he'd assisted her. She'd never asked.

Now he was missing.

She couldn't step aside. He'd helped her when she had needed it most.

"I'm going with you."

Grigoris frowned, releasing her hand as he stood. "Nyx. Please. Let me handle this."

"No." She stood as well, certain of what she must do. "The fleet admiral was right. I am in the best position to get close to Petro."

A low sound emanated from deep in Grigoris' throat. "I don't want you close to him. I have a plan. I can investigate him on my own. You've been through enough, Nyx. You're still recuperating."

She appreciated his concern, even though they both knew she was well enough to return to her normal life. "I'm going to Lake Balaton...with or without you."

Grigoris stalked away from her, standing before the window. His back to her, she could only see his face through the reflection in the glass. He wasn't happy.

Nyx could almost imagine him cataloging all the arguments, compiling a list of ways to convince her. After spending so much time in close contact with him, she sometimes felt as if she could peer inside that incredible brain of his.

She wouldn't be swayed. She couldn't. She owed too much to Lazar. "Let's don't argue about this anymore, *motǎnel.*"

His shoulders drooped as he released a long sigh, then he turned to face her. He was upset with her decision, but he wasn't going to fight her. "We leave tomorrow afternoon."

She nodded once, and then watched as he crossed the room to the door. He faced her as he opened it.

"Lock the dead bolt behind me."

Ever the guardian.

She followed him to the door. "*Szia.*"

He left without another word.

CHAPTER THREE

N yx twisted from her stomach to her back, grimly contemplating the ceiling of the hotel room. She'd tossed and turned ever since crawling into bed after Grigoris' departure.

She was going back. Back to Lake Balaton.

Glancing to the nightstand, she sighed. It was three a.m. Only twenty-four minutes had passed since the last time she'd looked at the clock. She considered rolling over and trying again, then gave up.

Rising, she pulled her robe over her shoulders and drifted to the chair by the window. Looking out over the Dublin skyline, she thought back to another night when sleep had escaped her...

Nyx stared out over the horizon. Sleep had deserted her tonight, so she'd left the comfort of her bed and crept quietly down the hall. There was a doorway at the end that led to a lovely balcony with the perfect view of the Mediterranean Sea. She'd traveled extensively and spent more than one night alone, far from the lights of any city or town, and yet she was uncertain when she'd ever seen a sky so full of stars.

Grigoris had whisked her away to his home in Southern Cyprus a week earlier. The doctors had insisted she needed more time to recuperate, but she couldn't stand to spend one more night in the hospital, or Bucharest. Grigoris had promised her the sea air would heal her more quickly than anything else.

She'd agreed to go with him, despite her normal preference for being both on her own and dependent on no one. Grigoris had invited her to his home, though there'd been a hint of command in his words, and she'd accepted without argument because...well...she was terrified. The only time she felt safe was when Grigoris was with her. He'd been by her side since the attack, there each time she woke up. He'd gone so far as to set up a mini-office in her hospital room, continuing his work tracking down the mastermind from her bedside.

Nyx wasn't sure when their relationship had shifted from adversarial attraction to...this. Whatever this was.

Upon first meeting, they'd gone head to head, trading verbal barbs, attempting to outwit the other. She was certain the male occupants of the room at the time—Antonio and Karl—had mistaken their banter as animosity. However, Leila had picked up on the sexual undertones almost instantly. Nyx hadn't denied her attraction to Grigoris, and to her surprise at the time, he'd also indicated a sexual interest in her. Yet that hadn't changed the way he treated her, which was atypical.

Nyx had, in addition to finding him attractive, appreciated Grigoris instantly, though he'd engaged in all the typical male posturing and rituals that were both part of cultural norms in most societies, and very tiresome. There was no denying he was clever or witty. He was also one of the most attractive men she'd ever met. He was tall, but he didn't use that height to tower over the people around him. His hair was rich brown like freshly turned soil, streaked with gold, and touched by a bit of curl. Seeing his home, she had no doubt that the bright Mediterranean sun had lightened his hair, as well as aided in giving him the warm brown complexion so typical of his Greek ancestors. His nose was long and straight, his eyebrows two dark slashes. When his personality didn't animate his face, it was an intimidating countenance. But unlike her, he wasn't hiding inside his own skin.

Something soft rubbed against her ankle and Nyx smiled. Grigoris had introduced her to "the love of his life"—his cat— the day they'd arrived.

Fengári was a beautiful, petite tortoiseshell cat. According to Grigoris, one night Fengári had come down from the mountains surrounding his estate when she was just a kitten. He'd just finished a night swim in the small lap pool and was drying off, preparing to go inside for the evening, when the kitten had stepped out of the shadows and into a bright beam of moonlight. If she hadn't done that, he never would have seen her. The kitten had been saved by moonlight and according to Grigoris, he'd been saved by her.

"Come here, lovely *pisoi*," she whispered in Romanian, speaking out of one side of her mouth. Fengári hopped onto her lap, curling up within seconds and purring as Nyx stroked her soft fur.

Since coming to Cyprus, she and Grigoris had spoken only in Greek. His Romanian was nonexistent, his

Hungarian halting at best, while she was fluent in his native language.

Nyx idly ran her hand over the tiny cat's back as she looked out over the horizon. Grigoris hadn't lied. She wasn't sure if it was the sea air or simply the sheer beauty of his home, but she had found both peace and succor in Cyprus, a combination she hadn't experienced in two decades—since she was a teenager.

A door opened behind her. Nyx knew Grigoris, a master of going unseen, could enter and travel the entire length of a room without ever making a sound, yet with her, he was careful to never take her by surprise.

She shifted in her chair, trying not to disrupt the dozing cat, while also not wanting Grigoris, or anyone, at her back.

"Nyx."

He came to stand in front of her. She hadn't yet specifically spoken of her newfound phobia of having anyone behind her. In the hospital it hadn't been an issue, since due to the bed and the equipment, no one could physically manage it. With Grigoris, it appeared she didn't have to say anything. Somehow, he just knew.

"Are you in pain?" he asked.

She started to reply, touched by his concern, but the healing skin beside her mouth grew tight. The stitches, both the internal and external ones, had finally dissolved, leaving behind a different kind of pain as she tried to make those muscles work once more. She lifted her hand to her cheek, her expression falling. "I am fine."

Grigoris took a moment to study her face in the moonlight, and then his gaze drifted to the cat on her lap. "You have company."

Nyx stroked the cat once more. "I do, but there is room for more." She gestured to the chair next to her.

Grigoris sat down and for several quiet moments, the two of them simply soaked in the beauty of their surroundings.

"You were correct," she said.

Grigoris gave her a cocky smile. "I am right about most things."

She narrowed her eyes. "I find that doubtful, but I see you don't lack the self-assurance to be expected from a man of your age, appearance, race, and status."

"Appearance? You like how I look?" he asked with a wicked grin.

"You know I do." There was no reason to deny it. "You are very attractive." She turned her head, glancing him up and down in a deliberate manner. "It's your arrogance that is both frustratingly alluring and infuriating at times, though I acknowledge your expertise."

He settled back in his chair. "What am I right about this time?"

She looked out at the water and sky, the moonlight that touched both, before painting the gold and green landscape of Cyprus a dozen shades of silvery blue.

"This place is healing," she admitted softly.

Grigoris reached out to her, his palm up. He didn't seek to grasp her hand. Instead, he gave her the choice.

She placed her hand in his, fighting back the brief flash of panic that he could use that grip to hold her helpless.

"Stay as long as you need."

It was on the tip of her tongue to ask if the offer was literal or a quirk of language and expression. Was he offering to shelter her here for the rest of her life? Was forever too long? After so many years of constant motion, dodging her past, the idea of retreating from the world, burrowing into the shelter provided both by his presence and his home, blunted the sharp edges of her ever-present fear.

More than that, a lifetime on this beautiful island in the middle of a sea sounded like bliss.

Ordinarily, Grigoris filled the silence with sound, sharing stories, telling little jokes to provoke the smile she couldn't give him—at least not fully.

Tonight, he was quiet.

"Are you well?" she asked.

He gave her a short nod.

Nyx wished she knew how to create easy conversation the way he did. It wasn't normally something she cared about, but with him, she wanted to be different than she was. She wanted to be not only who she'd been before, before the fear took up residence, but the woman she might have been had her life been different—charismatic and magnetic, able to put others at ease. She wasn't that person, so she asked the only thing she could think of. "What is happening with the investigation? Are there any additional leads?"

Grigoris frowned briefly, and then shook his head. "Some, but so far no ties to the Masters' Admiralty. I fear more people will die before we can figure out who the mastermind is."

After weeks spent in his company, she'd come to know him, to understand what drove him, what made him so uniquely Grigoris. As such, she knew he blamed himself for the deaths of every single janissary and ritter killed in the bombing in Bucharest and, by extension, the bombing in Rome, which could theoretically have been prevented had the mastermind been caught. Before Ciril, Nyx had been confident that intellectual work would identify the mastermind. She'd been convinced the librarians would find a way to uncover the villain's identity and bring him or her to justice.

She'd been so confident, she'd risked a visit back to

Bucharest. Romania was her home, yet she'd never willingly returned since her marriage to Petro. That was, until the investigation demanded her presence.

Bucharest ceased to be her home the day of her trinity marriage, and now, she viewed it as a place to avoid, to fear.

"You will capture the mastermind," Nyx said. While her confidence in herself was shaky, she had the utmost faith in Grigoris.

He squeezed her hand and gave her a sad, tired smile.

She waited for him to say more, but it appeared the weight of his burdens were too much for him tonight. So it would fall to her.

Her gaze drifted back to the sky, words springing to mind. Switching to English, she recited the old poem. "'The stars are mansions built by Nature's hand, and, haply, there the spirits of the blest dwell, clothed in radiance.'"

She glanced over and realized Grigoris had shifted in his chair to face her. "Wordsworth?"

Nyx nodded, impressed. "I attended Oxford. Developing an appreciation for the English language, which is otherwise imprecise, but was a benefit of walking halls trod by the Romantic poets."

"I must admit, Nyx, I've always been curious. Why did you choose to study religion?"

"It isn't religion that I study, but people."

"I thought that was anthropology?"

"Anthropology is the study of people as they are. The understanding and documentation of daily existence. It seeks to understand how people exist, where they live. It is a look out, and sometimes down, at humanity." She gestured with one hand at the expansive view.

"Ah," Grigoris said. "I see where you're going with this.

You want to know not who, how, and where. You want to understand why."

Satisfaction made the corners of her eyes crinkle, and she attempted a small smile. "Yes. Religion is why. Or it has been the why. Will it continue to be? That is one aspect of my research."

"Do you teach classes?" Grigoris tipped his head, as if considering her. "You'd be a good teacher."

"No. My position is purely research-based." She realized how short that sounded and tried again. "But thank you for saying that. To teach is a skill I don't possess, and a calling I won't answer."

He nodded, but she could tell from the sly smile growing, he was getting ready to tease her. He'd be upset to know he had tells, little giveaways that told her what was coming next.

"What a shame. All those young, impressionable men will never have the chance to indulge their crush on the hot teacher."

She shook her head and, once again, tried to find a way to smile. Every time she made the attempt, the pain returned.

The two of them faced the night horizon once more, sitting in companionable silence for a long time.

"It's late," Nyx said at last. She was more comfortable hearing his stories than telling her own. As long as the stitches had been there, she'd had an excuse to remain quiet, but now...in this serene, lovely place, with the sound of the sea in the distance and the moon casting a soft, yellow light over them...the intimacy that had been impossible to find in the hustle of the hospital blossomed.

Grigoris stood. His movement woke the sleeping cat, who jumped down from Nyx's lap. He used his grip on her hand to help her rise. "I will walk you back to your room."

It wasn't necessary. She felt safe here. Something she

hadn't experienced in the hospital in Bucharest. There were too many doctors and nurses coming and going. And always, in the back of her mind, she wondered if any of them were working for the mastermind.

In Grigoris' home, it was just them, hidden away from the rest of the world.

Regardless, she didn't reject his offer to walk with her. The foolish, selfish part of her wanted to steal every moment with him she could.

This time was fleeting. Forever wasn't a possibility.

They stopped outside the door to her bedroom. His was just across the hall. He'd left his door ajar when he'd come to find her, and she could make out the rumpled sheets on his bed. Had he been restless like her, or had she woken him up when she'd left her room?

She turned, lifting her face to look at him. Grigoris was standing close.

It would take very little for her to lift up on her toes and press her lips to his. As if he could read her thoughts, Grigoris' eyes drifted to her mouth.

He wanted to kiss her as well, and he had for a long time. She wasn't blind.

They remained there, eyes locked, her heart racing, until...too much time had passed.

Nyx moved a half step away. "Good night," she whispered.

Grigoris looked for a moment as if he might pull her back, pull her into his arms. She wanted that as much as she feared it.

His eyes gentled. "Good night, *o ángelós mou.*"

Nyx returned to her room, then ran her fingers over her lips, longing for that kiss. Now, she was afraid she would never know the feeling of his lips on hers.

She had no right to kiss him. She had to be alone. But maybe, for a little while longer, she could stay here with him, safe and at peace.

Nyx shook herself from the memory and rose from the chair. Turning her back to the window made her feel too exposed, so she walked to the corner, placing her back to the wall there, and considered the bed. It represented both the possibility of rest and respite, and the impossibility of achieving either when she felt this way. They were flying to Hungary, specifically to Budapest, tomorrow. She needed her rest, needed to be sharp, to have her wits about her.

The last time she'd been in Budapest had been when she was eighteen. The last time she'd been in the territory of Hungary, in the Romanian capital of Bucharest, just weeks ago, she'd come face-to-face with Petro, but the ordeal of seeing him again had paled in comparison to what had happened when Ciril caught her.

Ciril was dead, and while that thought brought her some ease, she was under no illusions as to how dangerous returning to Hungary would be.

But she had no choice.

Shrugging off the robe, she climbed back into the bed and closed her eyes.

Grigoris didn't see Nyx again until they met the next morning at the airport, thanks to a dawn call from Eric informing him that he'd thought of more things he wanted to tell him. When the fleet admiral mentioned that Grigoris would need to go straight to the airport after their meeting,

Grigoris had balked. He wouldn't leave Nyx—despite the uneasy mix of emotions he'd woken up feeling—to make her way to the airport alone. Before he could continue his protests, there'd been a quiet knock at his door. Dimitri had been standing in the hall, looking alert and deadly, despite the hour.

The meeting with Eric had provided more details, in particular about the Rome bomber's home life and the name of the hospital where Dr. Bernard had been in residence. Grigoris has listened impatiently, waiting for the opportunity to tell Eric about Nyx's marriage. The fleet admiral had to do something about it—what Petro had done was abhorrent.

Time had run out before Grigoris could say anything, and he'd realized that was a blessing, as, despite his anger at her situation, he didn't have the right to say something to Eric without discussing it with Nyx first.

He'd arrived at Dublin International only an hour and a half before their flight, but thanks to first-class tickets, he'd been able to slide through check-in and security quickly. Someone had been fast and efficient in making travel arrangements for everyone after last night's meeting. He and Nyx were traveling directly to Budapest from Dublin.

He found her in the first-class lounge, holding a cup of coffee, an untouched plate of fruit on the table in front of her. Nyx was sitting in a corner, her back to the wall, the floor-to-ceiling windows that provided a view of runways to her left. He claimed the seat across from her, setting down his small overnight bag. They'd packed light, and he could see her bag tucked in beside her chair. It meant they wouldn't be waiting for luggage when they landed, which was a good thing.

Grigoris had had some questions of his own for Eric, most of which the fleet admiral hadn't been able to answer. Questions like—did Petro have travel alerts set up? Would he know they were coming?

The element of surprise would be beneficial. It would give the admiral of Hungary less time to prepare or hide evidence.

Grigoris—still not having spoken to Nyx—rose from his seat and went to get a cup of coffee. He took a sip and grimaced. Ireland wasn't exactly known for its coffee, and this stuff was as far from a good cup of *sketos* as two beverages technically made from the same base ingredient could be. He changed to a cup of tea, adding milk until it was the color of the soil in Cyprus, before returning to his plush chair.

There were only a handful of other travelers, and no one was near them. It would be safe enough to talk about what he'd learned this morning, and more importantly to discuss their plan for when they reached Budapest. He was going into a complex situation with limited intel. Anything she could tell him about the admiral's residence, which was technically in Lake Balaton, would be helpful.

Privately he had something else to grapple with—the fact that right now, he wasn't objective. Not at all. He wanted Petro to be the mastermind. Wanted him to be the villain of the piece, simply because Grigoris hated the man after everything Nyx had told him last night.

He opened his mouth, ready to begin his inquiry into what she knew about where they were going, but what he asked was the one question he still didn't think she'd truly answered the night before. "Why didn't you tell me?"

Nyx looked away from the window, toward him. Given the dark circles, he assumed she hadn't slept any better than him the previous night. The silver-tinged light of a Dublin morning painted the line of her scar, making it seem to glow white against her tanned skin.

"I don't consider myself married."

Grigoris felt his shoulder muscles bunch, and he rolled them to work out the tension. "Then you could have told me you'd been placed in a trinity when you were a child. Could have told me you were running from him. From what he did to you."

Nyx's spine straightened, her whole body stiff and tense. "I am not running."

Grigoris looked at her, and then planted his elbows on his knees, leaning forward. "You're smarter than that, Nyx."

"Is that what you think of me?" The question was softer, not so stiff and formal.

"I think you should have told me."

Her head tipped to the side, the vulnerability leaching away from her expression. She studied him the way he imagined scientists studied lab animals. When he'd first met her, she'd seemed distant and arrogant. She'd been beautiful, infuriating, but the arrogance, the way she seemed to think she was smarter than everyone else in the room, had irked him. Then he'd gotten to know her and realized she usually *was* the smartest person in the room. Once he figured that out, he saw past the facade she kept up as a barrier, saw that she sometimes struggled to relate and interact, and that for all she could seem cool and distant, she felt things deeply.

He'd seen what lay behind her layers of defenses. Ciril had stripped those away, and Grigoris had stepped in front of her, helping to protect her from the world because he'd known how much she would hate for others to see her weak and scared.

He'd thought he knew her, yet she'd kept this from him.

"What happened, how your marriage took place, is unacceptable." He'd been thinking about this a lot. "And I think now, with Eric, maybe you could do something about it."

She turned to look out the window, but he saw her swallow.

Grigoris wanted to reach out and take her hand, the way he had a hundred times while he'd sheltered her in his home on Cyprus. His hand curled into a fist. He wouldn't. Not only because now that he knew she was technically married it seemed wrong, but because he was hurt. He'd sensed the bond between them was growing tighter with each day that passed. Now, he felt like an *anóitos*, a fool, certain he'd felt more for her than she did for him.

"You know how I feel about you." Grigoris' voice was low and rough with repressed emotion. "You knew, and you let me make an idiot of myself."

Nyx jerked as if she'd touched a live wire, but she didn't look away from the window. "I never meant to hurt you."

"Just lie to me?"

"I never lied to you. I am not married. If I had done what I wanted..." Her throat worked, and something inside Grigoris broke. "If I had kissed you, if I had gone to your bed, touched you and let you touch me, it would not have been wrong."

He wanted to agree, but he loved and respected the Masters' Admiralty. He was a janissary, a knight, and their rules, their laws, meant something to him. "There's no question what Petro did was wrong, and your trinity marriage shouldn't be valid." He reached out and touched her knee. When he did, she looked at him. "But if, in your mind, you're not married, why didn't you kiss me...let me kiss you?" He hated having to say this, but it needed to be said. "I think, in your own mind, you *are* married, and that's why you stopped this," he gestured between them, "from happening."

Nyx shifted in her seat, deliberately sliding her leg out

from under his hand. "You'll see, Grigoris. When we reach Petro's house, you will understand."

"Understand what?"

"That it wasn't shame or some moral objection to betraying vows I never gave that stopped me." Nyx looked at him, and there was something haunted, hunted in her gaze.

The speaker above them chimed, and the first-class lounge attendant called their names, informing them their flight was boarding. Nyx rose, picking up her bag. She looked down at him. "I didn't tell you because being Petro's means I'm tainted, and I was trying to protect you from that."

Grigoris sat, horrified and stunned at her words, as Nyx walked away. He forced himself to pull it together, racing to meet her at the lounge entrance. In silence, they walked out, side by side but miles apart.

CHAPTER FOUR

G rigoris glanced out the window of the plane, though there was precious little to see. While the sky was bright and blue, they were riding high above the clouds, obscuring all view of the world below.

Nyx had reclined her aisle seat and closed her eyes several minutes earlier, but he didn't think she was asleep.

He put his head back and shut his own eyes. Forcing thoughts of Petro—including all the ways he'd like to hurt the man—and the MIA vice admiral from his mind, he let his thoughts wander, countless memories briefly flashing. Some of the recollections were terrifying, like the image of Nyx crumpled on the ground, Ciril's dead body beside her. He would never forget the horror he'd felt, riding in the ambulance with her to the hospital. There had been so much blood. So much.

Then he pictured Nyx sitting on the terrace of his house, her hair pale, her skin slick from sweat, gilded by the Mediterranean sun. In truth, when he looked back on these last few weeks, he thought they were some of the best of his life. It felt odd to describe them that way. After all, Nyx had been healing from very serious injuries, not only to her body, but to her mental state as well, while he had been painstakingly slogging through the same clues, seeking out new leads, remaining in constant contact with the security officers in all nine territories, making sure no new threats had arisen, no members had gone missing.

He knew he'd seen a side of her few people were privy to, and that it was because she'd been hurt. He'd been concerned she wouldn't find a way back to being the powerful, confident woman he'd first met. Knowing that action would help her find that confidence again, he'd been considering how, or what, he could do to help her, when she'd come to him with the perfect solution.

GRIGORIS STRIPPED off his shirt and wiped the sweat from his face with it as he entered the back gate of his house. He was just a few moments away from diving into the chilly, clear water of his pool. It was the perfect way to cool off after a run.

He pulled up short when he realized Nyx was sitting on the edge of the pool. She was wearing a soft cotton skirt and a T-shirt, the outfit feeling out of place on the elegant woman. The clothing she'd had with her in Bucharest had been limited, all of it elegant, tailored but simple pieces, none of it right for spending days and nights sitting beside his pool.

She'd tried to make do with the clothing in her luggage, and he'd done his best to help by buying a few things he thought she'd need. A week after their arrival in Cyprus, she'd requested that he take her to the store. It had been a brief trip, and she'd been tense and wary the whole time they were out. She'd grabbed rather than selected clothes, but the casual attire, including a few rather garish tourists T-shirts, were better suited to her current activities than what she'd brought with her.

Watching her, Grigoris had realized that Nyx didn't think much about what she wore and didn't seem to care about her appearance. If he had to bet, he'd say that her normal elegant wardrobe probably had more to do with purchasing high-quality, timeless pieces that would last, rather than fashion.

He'd taken her to Polis to shop for new clothing. He'd been rather looking forward to spending the better part of an afternoon feeling like the hapless husband in some romantic comedy, following her from store to store, lugging her count-less shopping bags. Instead, they'd been in and out in less than an hour, and he'd spent the entire time focused on making sure she felt safe.

Her current outfit was the result of that shopping trip. He grinned. "I'm not certain I've ever seen you looking so...comfortable."

Nyx tipped her head to the side, though there was no anger in the expression. "Physically or spiritually?" she asked.

That was too big a question for his brain to tackle right now. "I was just about to take a swim," he said.

Nyx hadn't ventured into the water yet. The wound to her abdomen had healed, but it would take time for her core strength to return, thanks to the damage to her abdominal muscles, and she was still skittish about doing anything that might set her back in her recovery.

She waved her hands in a "be my guest" gesture.

The devil in him couldn't resist teasing her as he tossed his sweaty shirt onto the patio table, before dipping his thumbs into the waistband of his running shorts. "Typically, I swim in the nude."

Nyx gave him that small flash of a half smile. "Sounds refreshing."

Grigoris stepped closer to her. "You're welcome to join me."

He regretted his invitation the moment he issued it. Nyx's shoulders stiffened. He silently cursed himself for being a fool, for reminding her of her injury.

"I don't think that would be the wisest course of action..."

"Of course not. I understand, Nyx." He headed for the deep end of the small lap pool, preparing to dive in. He was definitely keeping his running shorts on. Her next words stopped him.

"I came here to wait for you. I need to impose on you once more." She looked away then, face unreadable.

"What do you need?"

"I need to not panic whenever someone is standing behind me."

Grigoris' heart clenched. It was the first time she'd said anything about her phobia of having someone at her back. It made sense. Ciril had snuck up on her, grabbed her from behind, and inflicted unspeakable pain. He knew that and understood it. As such, he was always careful to place himself beside or in front of her.

"I refuse to spend the rest of my life standing against a wall. Ciril already took things from me." Her hand drifted to the stab wound in her stomach, which he knew bothered her far more than the scar on her face. "'We can easily forgive a child who is afraid of the dark; the real tragedy of life is when men are afraid of the light.'"

"Plato." Grigoris walked over to her, offering a hand to help her rise.

"I don't want..." She paused, looked up at the sky. "I will not be afraid of the light."

"Good for you. Tell me how I can help."

"Teach me to defend myself."

Self-defense was a great idea—proactive, and it would give her a sense of control, but it wasn't going to be simple. Running his hand through his damp hair, he tried to decide how best to do that. She was skittish as a newborn kitten. He'd spent every moment since her attack protecting her, taking care not to add to her fears by making any threatening or untoward moves.

He'd earned her trust...and he wanted to keep it.

"Very well. The most important thing when it comes to defending yourself is to trust your instincts. If you sense something is wrong, something bad is going to happen, believe it. Don't discount it."

She nodded intently.

"If possible, you need to remove yourself as a target. If you see someone walking toward you who looks dangerous, cross the street, enter a shop, take yourself out of the line of fire."

"I understand, but if that's not possible, what do I do if someone grabs me from behind?"

Grigoris raised his hands. "Keep your technique simple. Aim for the sensitive spots. Play as unfairly as you can. Best places to hit are the eyes, throat, and groin."

He reached for her hand. "An open palm is the best way to ensure that you don't hurt your own hand when fighting back. Consider an eye strike. That's simply driving your fingers toward the assailant's eyes." He cupped her hand and slowly pulled it toward his eyes. "You could do some serious damage with those nails of yours."

She lifted her hand from his and sighed. "I'm badly in need of a manicure. Continue."

Grigoris wanted to take her hand back in his, simply because it was the only way he could touch her without scaring her. He'd tried to hug her...just once...shortly after they'd arrived in Cyprus. Nyx had gone rigid for a split second, then backed away quickly, excusing herself to her room.

"The knee strike is another effective move, but you need to move fast and use the element of surprise."

She didn't nod again, instead she looked impatient. "All of that assumes I see the attacker coming, from the front. What I need to know..." Nyx swallowed heavily, and then the beautiful, brave woman turned around, leaving her back to him. It was the ultimate show of trust, and Grigoris was so moved by it, it took all he had not to twist her back around and kiss her.

Nyx shivered slightly as she glanced over her shoulder. Her breathing was labored, as if she was the one who'd just done a five-mile jog along the shoreline.

As she watched, he shifted closer, slowly. "I'm going to wrap my arms around you, Nyx. Just loosely. If it's too much, step away and I'll release you."

"I know you will." Despite the physical cues telling him that she was fighting against a very powerful fear, her voice was steady, strong.

He moved directly behind her and slid his arms around her waist. Holding her in his arms felt every bit as good as he'd imagined it would.

"Now what?" she whispered.

"Your elbows are your power in this position. Bend slightly forward at the waist."

Nyx complied, doing as he instructed. She moved carefully, and he knew she was being careful of her healing stomach.

"Then twist to one side, driving your elbow up toward my face. Then counterattack with the other elbow. Fast motions, quick thrusts. And keep doing it until you can break free of my grip. Try the motions a few times to get a feel for it."

Nyx twisted and threw an elbow that, if she'd put any speed or force behind it, would have hurt. She moved quickly, throwing the left elbow, then the right, then the left again. She was a quick study. He should have realized.

Grigoris had to force himself to release her, to step away. He'd spent weeks longing to hold her. "Once you've broken free, you can spin around and try that knee or eye strike. You remember those moves and then—"

"Attack me."

"Excuse me?"

"Theory is excellent. However, lessons are learned through practical application. Theoretical knowledge in this instance is not enough."

"You want me to attack you?"

She nodded. "Yes. Unless you're afraid I will hurt you."

Grigoris was no stranger to fights and he'd lost count of how many fists to the face he'd taken in his lifetime. His concern wasn't that she would hurt him. It was that he'd trigger some sort of PTSD and Nyx would fall apart. "That's not what I'm afraid of."

"You're afraid you'll hurt me."

He didn't hesitate to respond. "Absolutely."

"Please."

There was very little he would deny her, though he thought this request might be one of the no's. Until that word.

"Nyx."

Before he could finish, she turned her back to him once more.

"Stubborn fool," he muttered, low and quiet.

She'd heard him. "'The greatest lesson in life is to learn that even fools are right sometimes.'"

"Churchill," he grumbled, not bothering to hide his growing grin. "I can play this game all day."

His heart skipped a few extra beats when she gave him a genuine smile before turning back around, instructing him to "proceed."

Grigoris took several deep breaths, trying to convince himself he wasn't making the biggest mistake of his life. Nyx had asked for his help as she sought to heal the broken parts deep inside.

He wouldn't let her down.

Before he could talk himself out of it, he moved toward her, grabbing her from behind, his arms wrapped around her waist like before. This time, he didn't warn her, didn't assure her he wouldn't hurt her. He simply moved like a genuine attacker.

She didn't hesitate, didn't consider that he was a friend. Grigoris wasn't entirely sure if she remembered that at this point.

He grabbed her and she reacted, exactly as he'd shown her. Her right elbow connected with his cheekbone painfully and, before he had a chance to even acknowledge how fucking bad that blow hurt, she delivered a second to the other side. And then the right side again.

His hands loosened, and she used that to her advantage, twisting out of his grip. He tried to reach for her again, but his eyes were watering like crazy and he wasn't completely able to focus on where she was. She used that temporary blindness to her advantage, grabbing his upper arm to pull him forward while kicking out his leg.

One second she was in his arms, the next he was sprawled out on the concrete next to his pool, eyes clenched shut, while fighting to take a deep breath.

Grigoris was a trained fighter. He knew how to ward off blows, but Nyx had done exactly as he'd shown her, and on the first try. She'd taken him by surprise. He'd expected her fears to weaken her response.

A rookie mistake.

It was her terror of the situation that lent unexpected speed and strength to her movements.

He hated that he'd scared her, even if it had been done at her request.

He remained on his hands and knees for a few moments, not entirely sure Nyx wouldn't continue the fight. When he'd gathered his wits—and felt somewhat certain she was finished —he pushed himself upright, kneeling on the ground.

He looked up to find her staring down at him. He expected to see her standing there, wild-eyed, crazy. That was certainly what her attack had felt like.

Instead, he saw Nyx, cool, calm, almost regal. It was the way she'd looked when they'd first met. If her breathing was a bit heavy, and there was a lingering trace of fading panic in the depths of her gaze, both of those were overshadowed by the satisfaction and relief he could sense.

Grigoris smiled, even as he reached up to touch his puffy cheeks. Jesus. He was probably going to have two black eyes. "I let you win," he joked.

She laughed, reaching up to hold her cheek, to shield her smile, as she did. Regardless of that, it was an honest-to-God laugh. "Liar."

CHAPTER FIVE

N yx grew still and silent as Petro's estate came into view. The admiral of Hungary's helicopter had been waiting for them when their plane landed in Budapest. There would be no surprise arrival. Grigoris had cursed when they'd been greeted by two of Petro's security officers at the airport exit and led to the helipad.

Her stomach twisted into knots, though she knew there would be no outward sign of her turmoil. She'd learned to draw everything deep inside—her feelings and reactions— leaving a cold but poised exterior. The last time she'd made the trip to Lake Balaton this way, she'd just finished boarding school, just turned eighteen. That flight had been different. She'd been full of youthful arrogance, certain in her ability to control her own destiny.

She'd been wrong.

Perhaps she would feel differently about this return if it had occurred prior to Ciril's attack. Or perhaps not.

It had become her habit these last couple of months to attribute her fears and her waning self-confidence to the attack. But hadn't she spent her entire adult life running and hiding from this man? She'd been offended when Grigoris said she was running, but was he right? Was it now adult adjuration that had her making excuses for her cowardice and for the fact that she couldn't make her hands stop shaking?

Grigoris reached over and patted her hand covertly, then pulled it away. He couldn't hold her hand as he had in Cyprus, not with the two security officers in the front of the helicopter. If they witnessed any act of affection between her and Grigoris, it could be reported back to the admiral. Did these two know she was technically married to Petro? Surely there were questions about who, and where, his third was.

Nyx didn't want to consider what Petro would do to Grigoris if he thought she was having an affair with the janissary.

Grigoris didn't look at her face. His gaze was glued to the scenery outside. She forced herself to look as well. If she were able to view the estate with an objective eye, she would admit it was probably one of the most beautiful places she'd ever seen.

Petro was one of the wealthiest men in Hungary, perhaps all of Europe. And it was important to him that everyone he came into contact with knew it.

His estate, *Isten Palotája*, was indicative of that. A huge French-style chateau, it was situated in the middle of a large vineyard. Petro loved to tell people that he made his own wine, though Nyx knew for a fact, he'd never so much as picked a grape.

Limestone terraces decorated with countless water features and fountains led to a large outdoor pool, surrounded by plush loungers. The terraces also led to an indoor pool and sauna. The three-story house had nine bedrooms, each with their own en suite bathroom, and a custom-designed master suite—a massive bedroom with an equally large bed. Off the central bedroom was Petro's walk-in closet, a palatial bathroom with three sinks, and two "dressing rooms"—enlarged closets that also contained narrow daybeds and well-lit vanities. Those rooms, accessible only from the main bedroom, were for his wives. One of the rooms was hers. She'd seen it once, and only once.

She'd wondered, in her masochistic moments, if Petro had planned to force her to sleep on the daybed, only calling her into the main bedroom when he wanted to fuck her, or if he'd make her sleep beside him, sending her to sleep in the dressing room if she displeased him. She drew the rancid fear the memory caused deep into her core, rolling it up with all the other emotions and burying it deep.

The estate's opulence was stifling. Not at all like Grigoris' home, which Nyx loved. Petro's home was meant to impress, rather than provide comfort.

As the helicopter landed, she turned to Grigoris. Neither of them had spoken during the trip from Budapest to Lake Balaton, unable to have a private conversation through the headphone connection shared by the security officers.

He gave her a quick wink that she knew was meant to be reassuring. Instead, it only drove home how much she wanted to be anywhere else. The last time she'd stepped foot in this house, she'd had the rug pulled out from under her. It had taught her never to underestimate the admiral of Hungary.

Once on the ground, one of the security officers helped her out as Grigoris and the other man retrieved their bags. She and Grigoris walked side by side, following the security officers after a brief, silent denouement at the landing pad. The officers had waited for her and Grigoris to precede them, but she shook her head, gesturing for them to lead. They were confused by her actions, but Grigoris stood steadfastly beside her, making it clear they weren't moving until the officers did.

She simply couldn't bear the thought of those men walking behind her.

A butler opened the grand front door as they reached the entrance, bowing to them in a solemn, respectful way. "Madam, welcome home."

Home. The word made her feel sick.

"If you will both follow me to the living room, the admiral will join you in a moment," the butler continued.

Nyx took a long, deep breath, holding the air in her lungs, fighting to keep the ball of fear deep inside, as they crossed the long, elegant foyer to the grand living room. She wondered if Petro, who typically received visitors in his office, had chosen the living room on purpose. It was the room where he'd listened to her arguments against the marriage, then claimed her and Hanna as his brides anyway.

If he expected that memory to rattle her, he was mistaken. One thing Petro would never have the satisfaction of seeing from her was fear. Her fingers twitched with the need to keep from reaching for Grigoris' hand. She let a little tendril of anger escape the banked fire of her rage. It rose to the forefront of her emotions, a weapon she could grab if needed.

Grigoris, in the meantime, walked behind the butler as if he didn't have a care in the world. She'd come to recognize that persona, realized that it was simply a mask meant to set people at ease. She also knew that if she quizzed him upon entering the living room, he would be able to tell her exactly how many doors and windows they'd passed, what portraits were hanging on the walls and where the defensive weaknesses in the foyer were. He'd probably catalogued every decoration, every lamp, every chair in his mind in terms of best potential weapon to least.

"If you will wait here, I will tell the admiral you have arrived." With that, the butler left them alone in the living room, closing the double doors behind him.

Nyx watched Grigoris as he quickly scouted the perimeter of the room. She wasn't sure what he was looking for or if he was merely familiarizing himself with the area in case of an emergency, but she let him do so in silence.

Small talk was beyond her realm of ability at the moment. She needed to concentrate on remaining calm and in control. Every meeting with Petro—though she'd done everything she could to make them few and far between—was a fencing match, as the two of them lunged and parried, opening small wounds. Death by a thousand cuts.

A door at the back of the living room opened and Petro stepped in. Nyx held her breath, waiting to see if her control held, or if she'd be overcome with some combination of rage and fear. Her emotions stayed safely balled up, except that small thread of anger, and she was able to objectively study the man who was, by the laws of their society, her husband.

Petro was of average height, but seemed shorter due to his stocky build. He was wearing most of a tuxedo—the custom-made inky black pants, crisp white shirt with onyx shirt studs and matching cuff links. His bowtie was draped around his neck and the top button of his shirt was undone. It was late afternoon, and it looked like he was getting ready to go out somewhere—that thought made Nyx want to sag with relief. If he was attending the opera in Budapest, he'd have to leave soon.

The relief was short-lived. Petro had known they were coming. He wouldn't leave her and Grigoris alone, though she was sure the house was full of servants. Which meant the evening dress had something to do with them. Petro was a master strategist when needed, and a bulldozer when he wanted to be.

Petro started walking toward her, hands outstretched. He stopped midway across the room, his expression twisting into one of revulsion. "Your beautiful face!"

Nyx didn't bother to hide the small smile his reaction elicited. She'd never been vain, and the stab wound in her stomach that had nearly killed her was of far more concern than her scarred face. "Hello, Petro."

"I will fix your face. The best doctors in the world." His lips were twisted in an expression best described as regret—the way someone regretted knocking over and cracking a pretty vase.

"There is nothing to fix. And speak English or French. Chorbaji Violaris doesn't speak Hungarian." For now, they would keep the fact that Grigoris understood some Hungarian a secret.

Petro sniffed, glanced at Grigoris, but then back to her, dismissing the janissary as unimportant.

A mistake. Good.

"I will take you to Korea in a few days. The best face surgeons are there."

"I will not be going to Korea with you, Petro."

His expression hardened for a moment. "Do not forget where you are, *hitves*."

"Of course not, *admirális*." She inclined her head in a shallow bow.

Nyx knew it would be easier for Petro if she were outwardly defiant, the way she had been when she was eighteen. Then he could play the patriarchal husband/master role. Instead, she remained civil if not polite.

"Admiral Sirko," Grigoris said in English. "Thank you for providing transportation from the airport to your home."

"It was my pleasure. I pride myself on knowing who is in, and taking care of those who enter my territory. Both people who are mine and those who are guests."

The message was clear—*I knew you were coming, this is my territory, tread lightly.*

Grigoris' easy smile didn't change. "And I thank you for that."

"Now that she is home," Petro said smoothly, "one of the harcos will see to my Nyx's safety."

"I would appreciate any additional security they can provide, but I have given my word to personally guard Dr. Kata while she travels."

"Ah, I understand. A penance for your failure in Bucharest?" Petro clucked like a disappointed father.

Nyx's heart clenched for Grigoris. He hadn't failed in Bucharest; the mission had been doomed because they'd set out to catch a serial killer. There'd been no way to know the mastermind had also recruited bombers.

Grigoris' jaw clenched, but he said, "Of course."

"I am surprised Hande let you take on this duty. Perhaps she doesn't know?" Petro asked. "Or perhaps she isn't aware of how vulnerable she's made herself by allowing the leader of her knights to abandon his duties."

This time Grigoris visibly stiffened. "I have not abandoned my duties."

"Oh, of course not." Petro shook his head in mock sadness. "My English isn't always good." Petro was fluent. He knew exactly what he'd said.

"My admiral knows where I am and allowed it, since I'm here at the request of the fleet admiral."

Petro's eyes narrowed, and for a moment he looked...satisfied? Dread coated the inside of Nyx's mouth, but then the expression was gone.

It was in that moment she realized something—she wanted Petro to be the mastermind. She wanted him to be the villain because he was the antagonist of her personal story. She'd been sent here to investigate Petro, but she hated this man in a bone-deep way that meant she'd never be impartial.

She glanced at Grigoris, wishing she could talk to him. Grigoris was staring at the admiral, an amiable smile on his face. She wondered if Petro could see through that to the deadly predator beneath.

The door Petro had entered through opened once again, and Hanna stepped into the room. Hanna was gorgeous, and a near-perfect contrast to Nyx's coloring. Her hair a brown so dark it was almost black, it fell in waves around her face and shoulders. She wore it loose and long, with a single jeweled clip holding it back from the side of her face, exposing one ear and the massive pear-cut diamond earring. Her skin was pale and flawless, her body sweetly curved, her impressive breasts on display, but not lewdly so, in the red off-the-shoulder mermaid-style gown she was wearing.

Petro was most definitely planning something. They'd flown commercial, so it was possible, probable even, that he had access to flight information, and had known the moment they—or more accurately, she—booked a ticket. Still, in less than twenty-four hours he'd orchestrated something.

"Nyx," Hanna said softly. "It's good to see you."

Nyx met the other woman's gaze and guilt made her stomach roll. She'd run, but Hanna had stayed. Hanna had obeyed their laws, accepted the marriage.

"You look well," Nyx said quietly.

Hanna glided up to Petro, taking his hand and leaning

into him. Petro raised their linked hands and kissed her fingers. There was real affection there. Nyx was shocked by the longing she felt, not to have Petro kiss her, but by the closeness she saw between them. It was the closeness and affection of spouses.

That could have been you. You could be safe and happy. Have a family. Not be alone.

"I am well." Hanna's English was stilted and hesitant. "It is good you are home."

"I am not home," Nyx said quietly in Hungarian. She wanted to make sure Hanna understood. "I am just here to check on you."

"Check on us," Petro replied in the same language. "What do you mean?"

Grigoris cleared his throat, and Nyx switched back to English. "Other admirals have been attacked. Someone is trying to hurt the Masters' Admiralty." She quickly repeated what she'd just said in Hungarian for Hanna's benefit.

Hanna gasped and turned to Petro, her mouth rounding into an O of worry.

Petro was frowning in concern, some of his arrogance gone, revealing the intelligent man beneath. "You're here because the fleet admiral doesn't trust other methods of communication."

Nyx nodded, happy Petro was drawing his own conclusions as to their presence.

"Then we will talk, but privately, and later. First, we will have dinner. I'm having a small party." Petro's arrogance was back in place, and he gestured to his and Hanna's attire. "A formal dinner, with people you'll want to meet, Nyx."

Nyx inclined her head. "Thank you for the gracious invitation, but Grigoris and I would prefer to wait and talk to you afterward."

"Oh, but you have to come," Hanna said in Hungarian, apparently able to follow along with the conversation enough to respond. "I have dresses for you, in your room. Whenever I go shopping and see something that would look good on you, I buy it, in case you come home to us."

Guilt bit at Nyx, so sharp and deep that it stole her breath and her anger, nearly breaking her control.

"If you would prefer to wait," Petro said to Grigoris. "I will have my staff show you to a room."

"Come with me," Hanna said, walking to Nyx, hands outstretched. "I know just the dress."

"No," Nyx said. "I'd like a guest room."

Hanna stopped short, as if the words were a physical blow. Petro looked disappointed but not surprised.

"Come, Hanna," Petro barked, his tone sharper than it had been. The way Hanna jumped to obey made Nyx sick to her stomach, and some of her guilt metamorphosed back to anger. "I trust you know your way to the dining room?"

"Yes," Nyx said. "What time is dinner?"

"In one hour." Petro patted Hanna's hand, then led her back the way they'd come. Before the door had closed, the butler who'd let them in opened the door behind them. Nyx jerked, spinning around, her heart thudding.

I can defend myself. It's okay if someone is behind me.

That thought calmed her enough that she was able to follow the butler out of the room. Grigoris fell in step with her. He cast her a few quick glances, but they didn't say anything to one another. The butler showed her to one of the guest rooms then started to lead Grigoris away, but with a smile, her beloved janissary walked into the room beside her.

The butler, a bit taken aback, couldn't see a way to get him out and into whatever room Petro had wanted him in.

Nyx took a seat in her room, angling the chair so her back

was to the wall, and waited until a different servant brought her bag, setting it just inside the door. She murmured one quick request, and he left to get what she'd asked for, returning a moment later. On that man's heels came a woman bearing a garment bag. Hanna had sent her a dress.

She laid everything over a chair. Only then did she close the door, leaning back against it. Her control held for a moment longer, then Nyx started to shake, sliding to the floor as silent sobs of terror wracked her.

CHAPTER SIX

Grigoris stepped out into the hallway the moment he heard the door to Nyx's bedroom open. She gave him that slight half smile when she saw him in his slacks and button-down. He raised his hands. "This was the best I could do. A formal dinner wasn't on the itinerary when we packed for Dublin."

She walked over to him, holding up her hand to show him the necktie. "I asked the butler for this," she confessed as she slid it around his neck, after glancing around to make sure no one was coming. Grigoris allowed her to tie it on him, taking advantage of the momentary closeness. She smelled like jasmine and looked amazing.

He wolf-whistled playfully. "Nyx. You look stunning."

She wore a gold V-neck gown with cap sleeves accentuated by sequins and crystals. It was elegant and understated. With her pale hair and sun-kissed skin, darker than it had been when he'd first met her, thanks to all those days spent lounging on the terraces at his house, she looked like a gilded goddess. Given her simple makeup and hairstyle, he was sure

Nyx was trying very hard not to draw too much attention to herself.

He didn't have the heart to tell her she'd failed. Every head was going to turn when she walked into that dining room, and not because of her dress, but because of her mere presence. She was the type of woman who could command attention simply through the way she held herself, the way she spoke, the intelligence in her translucent eyes. In a word, she was mesmerizing.

Grigoris studied her dress once more. "Hanna has wonderful taste."

Nyx ran her hands over the sides of the garment. "Actually, I fear her taste is driven by Petro. I suspect the gowns Hanna purchases were clearly chosen to please Petro. His taste is exactly as you might imagine, chauvinistic in its revealing nature and ostentatious, so that he can show off all the pretty things he owns."

"He doesn't own you, Nyx." Grigoris' eyes had been opened earlier in the living room, just as Nyx said they would be. Seeing Petro and Nyx together proved she'd been lucky to escape this house. He'd already imagined the worst of the admiral of Hungary, but it went far beyond anything Grigoris could have conjured—because Petro wasn't overtly authoritarian. It was more subtle and insidious.

Nyx didn't respond to his assertion. "The gown is impeccably made," she said instead.

"It's lovely. You're lovely."

Under different circumstances, perhaps Nyx might have smiled at his compliment, but her impassive expression told him she was nervous about the coming dinner. Nyx had warned him several times not to assume things were the way they seemed with Petro. While he gave the outward appearance of a kind man, Nyx assured him the admiral was a snake in the grass, always poised and ready to strike. Usually when his victim least expected it.

Grigoris had realized while he was getting dressed that if Nyx hadn't told him about the marriage, he would have thought of Petro as arrogant but not hateful.

They had a job to do, and Grigoris needed to be very careful that he used logic, rather than his emotions, to assess the admiral of Hungary.

Grigoris offered his arm and they slowly traversed the hallway, talking quietly. "I asked the butler who would be in attendance, and I did some recon on the guest list. Petro has some very impressive, powerful friends."

"He does. Who is attending?"

"Apparently, the Hungarian prime minister, a politician named Nikolett Varda, as well as the entire Masters' Admiralty leadership in Hungary. The security minister, all three finance ministers, and the vice admiral."

"I thought no one had seen Lazar in years?" she asked.

"I'm wondering if the fleet admiral got bad intel."

Nyx gave him a dubious look that said she doubted that was the case.

"I'm most anxious to see Lazar. You trust him?" Grigoris asked.

Nyx nodded. "Yes. I do. With my life."

"It's been a long time since you've seen him."

"I know. But people don't change that much. Lazar helped me the night I fled Petro. He made sure my passport wasn't suspended. He ensured my visas stayed valid. Petro could have made it impossible for me to leave Hungary, could have forced me back by manipulating the government, which I'm sure you now understand would be an easy task for him."

Grigoris stopped, turning to face her. "The vice admiral is the one who helped you escape right after your marriage?"

"Yes."

"Do you think you could pull Lazar aside at some point tonight? Somewhere private where you could ask him where he's been the last few years? Why apparently no one has seen or spoken to him?"

"I had already planned to speak to him about that," Nyx said.

"Good. Don't tell him anything about our true reasons for being here."

Nyx narrowed her eyes slightly, telling him she knew perfectly well how to be circumspect.

He squeezed her hand. "Sorry. I'm used to giving orders. It's a habit I don't try to break, though I realize there are times when my guidance isn't necessary. What about the other guests attending? What do you know of them?"

"I've never met the current prime minister in person, nor have I met the other politician attending tonight. Though I have heard very good things about her."

"Yes, yes," Grigoris said. "Nikolett Varda. I've heard she's making waves in the National Assembly, taking a strong stance in the opposition party."

"I've been very impressed with several of her speeches in parliament, as well as in interviews. She's intelligent and unafraid to speak her mind."

Grigoris pressed the hand she rested on his arm against his body in a flirtatious way. "Sounds like someone else I know."

Nyx acknowledged the compliment with a nod before continuing, "I only have a passing acquaintance with the three finance ministers. And my last experience with the security minister, Hans Molnar, involved him sending one of his security officers to attempt to kidnap me from my apartment in Oxford during grad school to force me to return here.

He was unsuccessful, thanks to the big dog my roommate owned, and mace."

"I'm hoping for the opportunity to speak to the admiral's wi— To Hanna, without the admiral present." He knew Nyx didn't consider herself married, and he didn't want to upset her by referring to Hanna as the admiral's wife. Tonight was going to be stressful enough. Nyx was shockingly, worryingly calm, which he now knew, after spending months with her, was not a good thing. Her very stillness had triggered a healthy dose of paranoia in him. He'd tucked a knife in a strap around his ankle, and there was a naked razor blade taped to the inside of his belt near his right hip.

"Hanna?" Nyx glanced at him. "You think Hanna can tell you something?"

"I don't know. The two of them looked very much in love earlier, but perhaps Hanna is no happier with her fate than you are."

Nyx seemed to consider that. "If that's true..."

Neither of them finished that thought aloud. Nyx had run, escaped with Lazar's help. What if Hanna had been as anxious to get away from Petro as Nyx had been, but was either unable or unsuccessful?

They descended the stairs, the sound of voices growing louder as they neared the parlor. Apparently drinks and hors d'oeuvres would be served there prior to dinner.

He and Nyx entered together. Scanning the room, it appeared most of the guests had already arrived. Petro and Hanna weren't here yet, but Grigoris suspected the admiral made it a point to always plan a grand entrance. His own admiral, Hande, often did the same, and it was impactful, despite being a rather obvious tactic.

Grigoris led Nyx to a quiet corner, where she would be able to engage in conversation without the concern of someone approaching her from behind. A waiter appeared with a tray of champagne, and Grigoris took two glasses, handing one to Nyx. They tapped glasses in a silent toast to camaraderie and took a sip.

"Hello, Nyx. Welcome home."

Nyx stiffened slightly as Hungary's security minister, Hans Molnar, approached them. The man was built like a two-ton truck, his neck so thick and muscular it was practically as wide as his head. He looked uncomfortable in his tuxedo as he ran his fingers under the collar of his shirt as if to loosen it and his bowtie at the same time.

Nyx lifted her hand to Hans' outstretched one, shaking it. "Hello, Hans. Please allow me to introduce Chorbaji Violaris from the Ottoman territory."

"Please, call me Grigoris," he said in a friendly manner, shaking the man's hand as well.

"I am familiar with you and your work, Grigoris. I was sorry our paths did not cross the last time you were in our territory, but I had business here in Budapest that prevented me from traveling to Bucharest. If I had been there, perhaps there would have been less bloodshed."

Grigoris stiffened at the slight. "I would be interested to hear what you would have done differently."

"Perhaps at another time I will teach you some things," Hans said, glancing at Nyx, his chest puffed out. The man was far too full of himself. "We wouldn't want to offend female sensibilities."

Hans nodded farewell before drifting off to talk to one of the finance ministers and her husband.

"Do you have a weapon with you?" Nyx asked coolly.

"Always," Grigoris said.

"Good. Kill him with it."

Her coldhearted demand soothed his wounded pride,

and he chuckled. Before he could answer however, the room quieted as everyone's attention turned to the parlor door.

Petro and Hanna had arrived, arm in arm, smiling and greeting their guests. Petro's gaze traveled around the room until he spotted Nyx. The admiral's expression tightened, and Grigoris thought he saw a flash of rage in the other man's eyes when he saw how close Grigoris was standing to Nyx.

Grigoris considered putting an arm around Nyx or taking her hand. He loved her, and he wanted her to know she was cherished, was adored, for who she was. He wanted to stake his claim to this woman in front of the man who'd preyed upon her by claiming her when she was far too young.

But Grigoris was also a knight. It was his job to uphold and protect the laws of the Masters' Admiralty, and though their marriage hadn't been confirmed by the fleet admiral, Nyx was, technically, Petro's wife. The idea made him sick, and he'd lain awake thinking about ways of getting Nyx out of the marriage. Until that happened, and he doubted Eric was going to do anything else until the mastermind was caught, Nyx was married.

Making sure his internal war didn't show on his face, Grigoris inclined his head to Petro, lifting his glass slightly. Petro's attention shifted from him to Nyx, and then to the other people in the room. Grigoris was studying Hanna, so he saw the moment a strange expression flashed across her face —some combination of anger and cold calculation at odds with her pretty, soft appearance.

Was that emotion directed at Nyx?

And if it was, could he blame her?

An attractive woman in a shimmery royal blue dress approached them, speaking English. "Nothing like a grand entrance," she said sarcastically. "Petro is nothing if not annoyingly bourgeoisie."

Grigoris and Nyx turned their attention to the newcomer. Grigoris recognized the woman from the research he'd done in his bedroom. Nikolett was a slim young woman, of average height with long dark hair she'd pinned up, allowing several strands to fall loose and curl over her shoulders. Her black eyes were intelligent and piercing. When neither of them replied immediately, the woman continued speaking.

"I'm Nikolett Varda," she said, her hand outstretched to Nyx.

"It's lovely to meet you. I'm Dr. Nyx Kata, and please allow me to introduce you to Chorbaji Grigoris Violaris, from the Ottoman territory."

Grigoris and Nikolett exchanged handshakes.

Nyx was focused on Nikolett, and it appeared that the other woman's appearance served to distract her, something Grigoris was grateful for.

"I've followed your career with interest," Nyx said. "You are the youngest female to serve on Hungary's parliament. I've been impressed by the legislation you've introduced. You have a wonderful grasp of what needs to change if Hungary hopes to thrive in the future."

Nikolett grinned. "The old boys network is frantically trying to figure out how to shut me up."

Nyx covered her cheek as she smiled.

"It turns out I know who you are, as well," Nikolett said. "I read your paper on the role of religion in promoting ideas of sexual ownership and exclusivity for women."

"Dare I ask what you thought?"

Nikolett laughed. "I thought it was wonderful. However, I cannot say the same about *your* work," she said, turning to Grigoris.

"Excuse me?"

Nikolett gave him a smile that instantly put him on alert, especially when paired with her friendly voice. Because the expression and tone didn't match the words. "The last time you were in our territory, half of Bucharest was blown to pieces."

Nyx's champagne glass was halfway to her lips, but she lowered it. "It was hardly half."

Nikolett ignored Nyx, her gaze locked on Grigoris. "Why are you here?"

"Nyx wanted to visit old friends. I accompanied her."

Nikolett shook her head. "I expected you to be a better liar, Chorbaji Violaris."

"Grigoris, please," he said. He'd always found using first names put people more at ease, however, Nikolett's expression hadn't changed. She still looked friendly, which left him struggling to find the best way to respond.

He recalled Nyx's description of the woman—intelligent, forthright. It was evident when she wanted to know something, she kept inquiring until she got the answers she sought. But more than that, she donned masks the same way he did, using her soft smile and kind voice as the weapon.

If they weren't here investigating the mastermind, investigating someone who had managed to outwit some of the best minds in the world, he might have respected that. But instead, he found himself questioning her motives.

"Does the fleet admiral know you're here?" she asked sweetly.

Grigoris lifted one shoulder casually. "I'm sure the fleet admiral can find out where members are at any given time if he's curious."

Nikolett didn't back down. "Did he send you?"

Nyx had dropped out of the conversation, allowing him to answer the questions. He was glad. She had a keen mind, and he could tell she was not only listening to Nikolett but watching as well. Later, he would ask Nyx about the other woman's body language, her intonation and facial expressions, to get her take on whether the politician should be added to their list of suspects.

"Nikolett," Grigoris replied. "Surely you must understand that if the fleet admiral did send me, I wouldn't be able to tell you."

"I'm going to call that an answer. Why did he send you? What is he looking for in Budapest? How many people have to die this time?"

Grigoris catalogued her questions, tried to analyze the words. It was her last question that bothered him the most. Was she asking out of concern for the people, or was she making a veiled threat?

Petro stepped next to Nikolett. Grigoris had been so shaken by Nikolett's questioning, he hadn't noticed the admiral approaching. He couldn't make mistakes like that, not with Nyx to protect.

Nikolett, however, didn't appear to have missed a thing. "Petro," she said. While her tone when questioning Grigoris had been sugar and honey, all pretense of that dropped in the presence of her admiral. There was no mistaking her outright disdain for the man. With Petro, she didn't bother shielding her opinion of him.

Interesting.

"Nikolett, how nice of you to join us this evening. I was afraid your busy schedule would prevent your attendance again." Though his words were nothing but kind and welcoming, there were tight lines around Petro's mouth that betrayed his true feelings, especially in the way he said "again". He obviously didn't like that she'd rejected past invitations. He was a man who liked to pull the strings, and Nikolett didn't strike Grigoris as the type of puppet who would dance.

Grigoris chalked that up to Nikolett's earlier comment. No doubt Petro was president of the old boys' network that would resent an intelligent, powerful woman trying to break into their ranks. He had noticed the same attitude from the admiral earlier in the living room, when he'd subtly insulted Grigoris' admiral, Hande, another strong female leader.

"I see you've met my lovely wife, Nyx, and Chorbaji Violaris."

"Your wife? The missing wife?" Nikolett asked, her gaze drifting to Nyx with a curiosity that didn't linger. Nikolett was very quick to put the pieces together. "I see. I consider myself fortunate to be here tonight. I am fascinated by Dr. Kata's work. She is truly a leading voice in understanding and exploring the role of religion in maintaining and sustaining the patriarchy." She stressed Nyx's title and surname, after taking obvious objection to Petro's condescending intro-duction.

Petro's jaw clenched, widening the smile into more of a baring of teeth.

Nikolett certainly knew how to push the admiral's buttons, how to insult him without ever saying anything negative.

"Charming as ever, Nikolett," Petro said.

"Sir," the butler said in Hungarian, bowing to Petro. "Please pardon the interruption, but the chef wanted me to inform you that dinner is prepared."

"Very good," Petro said, dismissing the butler. "Well, my dear guests. Should we move our conversations to the dinner table?"

Slowly, people started to move. Grigoris made sure to pretend he hadn't understood, and made a point of looking

around curiously, as if he were trying to figure out what had
been said by context clues. He, Nyx, and Nikolett stayed
back, waiting for the others to leave.

It was obvious from Nikolett's hesitance to move that she
was unhappy about not getting her answers. Grigoris was
debating whether it would be wiser to fabricate lies for the
politician so that he could ask some of his own questions, or if
he should avoid her for the rest of the evening until he could
investigate her more fully.

"You don't typically attend the admiral's parties?" Grigoris asked Nikolett once Petro had moved away from them.

Nikolett shook her head. "No. I'm only here tonight in
hopes of pulling the prime minister aside for a few minutes.
I'm introducing legislation, and I would like five minutes to
present my case for it."

When everyone else was gone, the three of them followed
the admiral to the dining room. Hanna had already led the
rest of their guests to the table. The place cards revealed that
he and Nyx were seated at opposite ends of the long table.
She was seated to Petro's left, while Hanna occupied the spot
across from her at the admiral's right. Petro claimed the head
of the table as if he were lord and master, his concubines at
his sides. Grigoris gritted his teeth at the patronizing way
Petro smiled at Nyx.

Seated midway between them was a hunched man who
hadn't been in the parlor. From the way Nyx was looking at
him, Grigoris was sure it was the vice admiral. The man
didn't look well.

Grigoris was forced to look away when a male voice said,
"It looks like we'll be dining next to each other this evening."

He smiled genuinely as the prime minister claimed the
spot next to him. Nikolett was positioned in the center of the

table next to one of the finance minister's spouses. She was obviously displeased with the seating arrangement as well.

Glancing around at those seated next to him, Grigoris realized he had the opportunity to speak with three of the suspects on Eric's list.

Let the interrogation commence.

CHAPTER SEVEN

"If you'll excuse me," Nyx murmured to Antal Noth, one of Hungary's finance ministers. Petro was leaning away from her, speaking to Hanna, and he barely spared her a glance as she spoke. They were on the first of three dessert courses, and all the food and wine had mellowed the previously formal atmosphere.

Antal nodded amiably, turning his attention to Hans, who was on his other side. Grigoris looked up sharply as she rose from her seat. She glanced quickly at Lazar, who was being helped from the table by a servant. His hunched shoulders and uneven gait were painful to watch.

Nyx slipped out the door closest to the bathroom, hoping people would assume that was why she'd gotten up from the table. Once outside the dining room, she ducked down a hall, praying she remembered the layout of the house. As a legacy, she'd attended several Masters' Admiralty parties and events at this estate—and Petro's many other properties—with her parents. She and other legacy children would, in the ways typical of youth, race through the halls, making a game of exploring the building.

She got turned around once and was worried she'd missed her opportunity to talk to the vice admiral privately. When she rounded a corner and spotted him, she realized there was no danger of missing him, not at the pace he moved.

Another servant held the handles of a wheelchair, and Lazar dropped heavily into it. Nyx strode up, flicking her fingers in her most imperious manner. It worked, and the duo of servants melted away. Nyx grasped the handles of the wheelchair.

"Hello, Lazar," she said softly.

"Nyx," he wheezed in reply. "Take me to his office. I have some of my medicine there."

Nyx guided the chair to Petro's office, aware that she didn't have long before she'd be missed. Lazar directed her to Petro's desk, where he reached into a drawer, pulling out a small machine. She helped him plug it in and opened the small capsule of medicine, pouring it into a circular reservoir. Lazar turned it on, and the machine started to hum.

"A breathing treatment," Lazar explained, holding up the mouthpiece. "Helps me breathe." He put it in his mouth and took a deep breath.

This was going to severely limit their ability to converse. "I wanted to talk to you, to thank you."

Lazar briefly took the tube from his mouth. "Nothing to thank me for. You needed to be free."

"But Hanna..."

Lazar inhaled more medicine before replying. "She didn't."

Nyx stiffened. "You agree with what he did to her, and to me?"

Lazar looked tired, and so frail, she felt like a bully for her aggressive question. "It wasn't a matter of what I agree with. Petro is my admiral, and I obey my admiral."

The two of them shared a look that said they both acknowledged the one time he did not obey.

"He's also your friend," she said.

"He was. But being the admiral changed him."

Nyx frowned. "Was he angry at you for helping me?"

Lazar didn't reply. He inhaled and exhaled, the machine humming.

"Lazar, what's wrong with you?"

"I'm dying, my dear. I've been dying for a long time."

"I mean what disease?"

Lazar's eyes were opaque, unreadable. "My own foolishness."

Nyx couldn't help the shiver that worked its way down her spine. Her thoughts were whirling, and she didn't try to examine and dissect each possibility or conclusion. Other people had accused her of making the occasional leap of logic, but she always connected the pieces, always knew the path between basis and conclusion.

"Lazar, did Petro do this to you?"

"Petro didn't do anything I didn't deserve."

It was time to make one of those leaps. "Lazar, how did Petro punish you for helping me?" Her words were hurried and tense.

Lazar laughed, but the laughter quickly turned to coughing. The coughs were deep and wet, and a moment later, a different servant opened the door, rushing in. She cast an accusatory glance at Nyx, who backed up, getting out of her way. Nyx felt helpless, and worse, confused.

"You should not pester him," the woman accused.

"Patty, this is Nyx." Lazar had caught his breath, but it

was clear the coughing spell had taken something from him. "Patty is my helper," he explained in a reedy voice. "She was supposed to have the evening off."

Patty began to fuss over Lazar, and it was clear their conversation was over.

Some part of Nyx was sure, beyond a shadow of a doubt, that Petro was responsible for Lazar's deteriorated health. Lazar hadn't denied it. Hadn't been shocked by such an outrageous implication. Instead, he implied that if Petro had been responsible, that it was because Lazar deserved his current suffering. The Lazar she'd known was a forthright, moral man, so it was possible he felt he deserved to be punished for helping her, if he considered his actions immoral. On the other hand, it wasn't like Lazar to prevaricate.

And there was the possibility that Lazar's mind had been affected by whatever illness was ravaging his body.

If she stepped back and put aside her hatred for Petro, the situation could be viewed from an entirely different angle. Petro had helped Lazar hide his failing health, ensuring he could retain his position as vice admiral, which Lazar had taken great pride in. Petro kept necessary medical equipment in his private study, and the servants all knew how to take care of Lazar. From that perspective, Petro was caring for Lazar, both physically in the most literal sense, and emotionally by helping him keep his position, long after it was clear he should have stepped down due to his health.

Nyx retreated, casting one glance back at Lazar. It wasn't until she saw him looking so small and sick that she realized how much of her own sense of security had hinged on him being strong and powerful, able to protect her from Petro.

Lazar wasn't protecting anyone. Did that mean Petro

wasn't bothering to come after her? Had he given up and let her go?

No, he'd told her he was going to take her to Korea to "fix" her face. That was the action of a man looking after a prized possession.

Nyx raced back to the dining room, pausing to compose herself before she reentered the chamber. This would all be so much easier if Petro were the villain, if he were evil in the most absolute terms. But he wasn't. He was a monster, her monster, but he might also be the hero in other stories.

Grigoris waited for her to sit before casting her a quick glance. She shook her head once. She'd talked to Lazar, but it had left her with more questions than answers.

She listened as the small talk around the table continued, then released a sigh of relief when Petro stood, his silent, powerful way of saying the meal was over. Her relief was short-lived when he invited everyone to his den for after-dinner drinks.

She caught Grigoris' eye, then glanced around, trying to find some way of pulling him away from the others so they could talk.

It was clear he hoped for the same as he made a beeline for her. He was about to place a hand on her arm to hold her back, when he remembered that there were people in the room who knew Nyx was Petro's wife, and it would be inappropriate for him to touch her.

Instead, he angled his body, directing Nyx to a portrait that hung prominently on the wall as the others continued into the den.

"What a lovely portrait," he said, loud enough to be overheard by two of the finance ministers walking just ahead of them.

Nikolett glanced at them, one brow raised, before she followed the crowd out of the dining room.

GRIGORIS WAITED for the others to leave, pretending to study the portrait. "What did Lazar say?" he asked quietly.

"He wasn't...wasn't as I remembered him." Nyx's lack of expression told him how much that disturbed her.

Grigoris frowned. Lazar's health was certainly an explanation as to why no one had seen him. Deteriorating health, plus the passage of years, could also explain why he seemed different to Nyx. "Did he say anything about Petro?"

"I asked him if Petro was the one who made him sick."

Grigoris blinked at her. "You're not great at subtle questioning."

Nyx shrugged. "Time was finite."

"What did he say?"

"He said that if Petro had been the one to make him sick, he deserved it. Then he said that I needed to be free...but Hanna didn't. I thought he'd helped me because he objected, but what if I've been wrong? What if he holds no moral objection to Petro's actions?"

"We'll try to question him again later. Perhaps when he's feeling better, and maybe more lucid."

Nyx gave him a dubious look that told him exactly how ill Lazar was. "Did you learn anything revealing?"

"Nothing relevant to the mastermind." He kept his voice low. "The people I was seated with were more interested in figuring out if I knew you were Petro's wife."

She flinched, and Grigoris wished he could take the words back.

"Gazsi Balogh and Nikita Ursu know," he added. Gazsi was the prime minister and Nikita a finance minister.

"They would. They've been in power a long time. He would have told them."

"What was your impression of Nikolett?" he asked, aware they would have to enter the den soon or risk raising suspicion.

"You think she's the mastermind?"

Grigoris thought everyone in this house—with the exception of himself and Nyx—could be at the very least pawns of the mastermind. Nikolett was someone they needed to keep an eye on. If he were a less suspicious man, he would dismiss her as being too forthright to be a possibility, but that forthright manner might be a very effective shield hiding the truth. "I'm curious to know your thoughts."

Nyx considered the question. "She is intelligent and driven, unwilling to accept the status quo, which makes her either a mad anarchist or a principled rebel, depending on your point of view."

"Smart and driven—that describes the mastermind."

Nyx tipped her head to the side. "And she's progressive, in that she not only wants, but is demanding sexual equality, social justice, and religious freedom."

"The Masters' Admiralty has protected and fought for those things too. Without the Masters' Admiralty, the church would have far more power today than it has had, and most of Europe would still be ruled by monarchies, so that eliminates her."

"Does it?" Nyx asked quietly.

"The mastermind is trying to take down the Masters' Admiralty. Without the society, and its influence and access, her job would be far more difficult."

"Or," Nyx said quietly, "she dismantles the society as it

exists now and remakes it. Our foundation may be one of intellectual excellence and social equality, but the Masters' Admiralty isn't revolutionary. Not any longer."

Grigoris hissed as he realized Nyx was on to something. "She's angry about all the things the Masters' Admiralty hasn't done."

"Exactly."

"We might have a new prime suspect for the mastermind."

Nyx's shoulders slumped. "I want it to be Petro."

The need to touch her made his palms tingle, but he couldn't risk someone walking in the moment he did. "Even if he's not the mastermind, it doesn't mean he's not a villain."

"He's a good admiral. Strong, smart, determined. He's held the territory together for a long time."

Grigoris wasn't sure how to respond. These were the first words of kindness he'd ever heard her say with regards to Petro. "Nyx, do you...I mean...he is your husband."

"No," she spat the word. "He's not. He never will be. But I know the world isn't black and white. No person is wholly and singularly good or evil, but a combination of both. For me...Petro is evil. What he wanted from me, and how he sees me, is an anathema." She hugged herself, which was for her a profound sign of distress. "Because of that, I cannot be impartial. I cannot be trusted to see what is, rather than what I perceive." She shook her head once, then dropped her arms, straightening. "The fleet admiral ordered me to come here to investigate him, but the burden falls to you."

"I understand. We'll keep looking, keep talking to people. The mastermind has been so active this past year that people around him—or her—would have noticed something. Maybe we'll figure out a way to get invited to Nikolett's house."

"It hope it's not her. I like her."

"I do too."

Nyx looked up and sighed. "I would prefer the man who wanted to marry a child be the villain, rather than the intelligent woman."

"Don't forget, it might be neither of them."

Nyx nodded. "True."

Grigoris stepped back, giving her space to fall in beside him as they left the dining room. By the time they reached the den a few people had left, and others remained, including, to Grigoris' surprise, Nikolett. They had apparently missed Petro's invitation to everyone to stay the night.

He toyed with but didn't drink a glass of sweet port, and when Nyx rose to excuse herself, he offered to escort her. He'd made it clear to his dinner companions that he was here in the capacity as her bodyguard, but even so, he thought he saw a few people glance in Petro's direction as he followed her out.

Servants were trotting through the halls, preparing yet more guest rooms for those who planned to stay overnight, so after doing a quick sweep of Nyx's bedroom and bathroom, Grigoris bade her goodnight, not daring to do anything more.

Once in his room, he sat down on his bed, propped up by a mountain of pillows, staring at the wall between his room and Nyx's. He imagined what she might be doing over there and briefly wondered if he'd be able to hear her cry out if her nightmares returned. In Cyprus, he'd kept his bedroom door ajar so he could go to her if she needed him.

For months, he'd offered her everything he thought she needed—a friend, a protector, a counselor. Tonight, those roles fell away as he longed for something that would only bring turmoil and chaos to both of their lives.

Because he was in love with Nyx Kata, the wife of the

admiral of Hungary, and he wanted her...in his bed, his home, his life.

Nyx struggled out of the dress—the beading made it hard to undo the hidden side zipper. She had the zipper undone, but the dress still on, when the wall opened.

She was standing at the foot of the bed, unconsciously facing Grigoris' room. If it hadn't been for the decorative mirror over the bureau, she wouldn't have seen the secret door opening, wouldn't have seen the intruder enter. The door swung inward in silence, and Petro's footsteps were silent on the thick carpet.

Shock was quickly replaced by a panic that ripped through her. Nyx whirled around, taking two quick steps back so she could put her shoulders against the wall.

Petro smiled. "Good. You know when to be afraid."

Nyx was still caught by panic, her brain dragging the memory of Ciril's attack to the forefront. *Calm, calm. He isn't Ciril. You know how to handle him.*

The thought helped her beat back the panic, and she took a deep breath, raising her chin. "A secret door? Really, Petro. It's beyond cliched."

Petro kept walking, his gait too casual to be predatory, but there was a sense of arrogance about the way he moved, as if he had her right where he wanted her.

And that thought ate away at some of her self-control.

"Did you think you'd surprise me, showing up the way you did?" He was now less than a meter from her. "You are intelligent, which makes you both more desirable and irritatingly hard to control."

"You can't control me."

"Oh, but I can. I'm almost done letting you play at having your freedom."

"I am neither your wife nor your slave, though I suspect you see the terms as interchangeable."

Petro's smirking arrogance was gone in an instant. His face contorted in rage and he lunged for her.

One hand grabbed her throat, and the force had her head bumping against the wall. His other hand grabbed her left wrist, pinning it beside her head. She tried to bring her other arm up to deflect him at the same time she raised her knee, but he twisted his hips and dodged the blow she aimed at his eyes.

He squeezed her neck, and Nyx raked her nails over the back of his hand, then grabbed his wrist, trying to force him away so she could breathe.

Petro leaned into her, his heavier body pinning her in place. "You're mine." The words were fetid in her ear. "You were born to be mine and will die being mine. I'll fix your face, but until then, I guess I can fuck you from behind. Like a pet."

He chuckled as if amused by that idea. Nyx was able to just barely drag in air through her restricted windpipe.

"Behave yourself, or I'll treat you like a disobedient pet. One who always runs away and needs to be taught to heel when her master calls."

He released her left wrist, and she tried to gouge his eyes the way Grigoris had taught her—why hadn't she paid more attention to what to do when an attack came from the front? She was light-headed from lack of air and her aim was off. Petro easily dodged.

One hand still on her throat, he grabbed the neckline of the dress, yanking it roughly. With her arms raised, he couldn't pull it completely down. "This dress, this body. They are mine."

Nyx felt tears of terror prickle her eyes, followed quickly by rage. Rage she could use. She would fight him. Kill him with her bare hands if she could.

Petro released her and stepped back. He tugged the cuffs of his tux, adjusting them with a practiced motion.

Nyx crumbled to the floor, gasping for air. She tried to stand up so she could attack him, but her shaking, oxygen-starved muscles wouldn't obey. Her will, the fire of her anger, couldn't counteract the survival instinct that prevented her from doing anything but breathing. She coughed, sucking in air, only to cough again.

"Remember who you belong to, little girl." Petro squatted, making a tsking noise as he looked at her. "I think we will get that face fixed first. Rest now, and in the morning, you'll tell me exactly why you are here, why the Greek is with you, and we'll discuss your return." He straightened, brushing at his slacks. "Welcome home, Nyx."

Petro turned and walked out of the room, pulling the hidden door closed behind him. It blended seamlessly with the paneled walls and vertical-striped wallpaper.

It took a long time for Nyx to stop shaking, but once she did, she knew what—who—she needed.

CHAPTER EIGHT

G rigoris picked up his knife, the blade along his forearm. The hold allowed him to either conceal the weapon if that knock at the door meant there was no threat, or to strike out and surprise the attacker as his blade slid across their flesh.

His hair was still wet from the shower, and rather than pajamas, he'd put on well-worn black tactical pants that were comfortable enough to sleep in. He also planned to sleep in his socks and boots. Though Petro was not the villain he'd hoped, there was an air of tension and suspicion in the building that was making the back of his neck itch. Some of that was their fault—Nyx's unannounced arrival had no doubt stirred up questions and suspicions among those who knew who she was.

Grigoris had a feeling this would not be a restful night, so the knock, when it came, was not a surprise.

Keeping his body behind the door, he opened it. It was dark in his room, but there were lights on in the hallway outside and a narrow wedge of light spilled in. The person on the other side would be looking in at a sliver of seemingly empty bedroom.

"Grigoris?" Nyx asked hesitantly.

Surprise sent a little electrical shock through him, and he stepped out of the way, opening the door fully. She was still wearing the gold dress she'd had on at dinner, but it was loose, and her right hand pressed against the bodice, as if holding it up.

"Nyx, are you all right?" he asked, speaking Greek. If anyone was listening, they might not understand what he said.

In reply, Nyx stepped into the room. She placed her fingers over his where they held the edge of the door. With a gentle tug, she broke his grip, then closed the door behind her.

The door was heavy, solid wood, and when it closed, the only light in the room was a faint shimmer of moonlight that leaked in from around the curtains he'd drawn.

"Nyx, what are you doing here?" There was no place he'd rather have her, but it wasn't safe. "You shouldn't be here. There are too many people staying in the estate tonight. Someone might have seen you."

Nyx cocked her head to the side in that way that was achingly familiar. "I don't care." There was something odd about her voice.

"Nyx, what's wrong?"

Silence stretched between them. Her breathing was a little louder than it should have been. As if she'd been running...or as if she was nervous. Nervous because she was afraid?

Or nervous because she was excited? Nervous with anticipation?

Grigoris forced himself to take a step back because he

didn't trust himself so close to her. The urge to take her in his arms was nearly overwhelming.

Her next words were so soft, he almost didn't hear them.

"I need you to touch me."

He didn't move. He didn't dare. Every emotion, every desire he felt for this woman came rushing to the surface.

His vision had adjusted, and he could just barely see her face in the moonlight. She looked both fragile and strong, her chin raised not in defiance, but regally. She was beautiful, a beauty that had nothing to do with her features, and everything to do with how she carried herself.

"I need you to touch me, even though we can never have more than a short-term affair."

Grigoris prided himself on being a logical person, but that fell away with her. His heart refused to believe they couldn't be together even though he knew she was right. He still planned to talk to the fleet admiral about getting her out of this marriage, even though that didn't mean the two of them could be together. But now wasn't the time to discuss it.

"You are a moral man, Grigoris Violaris. I am asking you to do something immoral—to touch another man's wife."

"You're not his wife," Grigoris ground out. The statement wasn't true, in the most legal sense—at least by the laws of their society—but it was, he knew, true for her.

And he wanted it to be true because he wanted to touch her. He'd never wanted anything more.

"I'm not his." She dropped her arms, releasing the fabric she'd been holding up. The dress slid down her body, the weight of the beading helping gravity to guide it over the soft curves of her hips.

She stepped out of the dress, wearing nothing more than a pair of small black bikini underwear. Her breasts were pale in the moonlight, and by far the most lovely breasts he'd ever seen.

"I need you to touch me."

It was the third time she'd said it. Nyx wasn't the sort of person to admit she needed anything from anyone. He knew, though they'd never spoken of it, that it had cost her something to let him take care of her. That her pride and her need to be self-reliant had changed during her time with him.

He held out his hand.

Nyx made an odd little noise—somewhere between a whimper of need and a groan of pleasure. She placed her hand in his, and he drew her into his arms.

Her naked breasts met his bare chest. Her nipples were tight—it was cool in the room—and when she rose on tiptoe, bringing her lips to his, her sweet nipples dragged across the plane of his chest.

Grigoris started to cup her face with his left hand, his right snaking around the small of her back. Then he realized he'd be touching her scar. He stopped, hand a mere inch from her head.

"I'm not afraid. Not of you." She leaned her cheek into his palm.

Grigoris had never received a more precious gift as he accepted the weight of her head.

"I may be a coward," she whispered. "But not with you. You make me feel strong."

"You are not a coward. You could never be a coward." He tipped her face up, lowering his mouth until he was whispering his next words against her lips. "You are brave and smart. I have never met a more courageous person, man or woman. You came to Bucharest when we needed your help, even though it meant entering Petro's territory. I didn't know then how brave you were, but I knew you were brilliant. Fierce. And I wanted you the moment I saw you."

Nyx rose the fraction of an inch needed to bridge the gap between their mouths. The kiss was soft and still, as if they were posing for a romantic portrait—her raised up on tiptoe and leaning into his body, her arms around his middle, one of his around her waist, the other cupping her face.

Nyx pulled back when the kiss ended, and in the faint light he could see surprise in her eyes. "Oh, that's lovely."

"I've been dreaming about kissing you."

"I'd like to do that again."

"Wrap your arms around my neck."

Without question, she did, twining her hands over his shoulders, tentative fingers brushing his hair.

Grigoris grabbed her hips, hiking her up and grabbing her sweet ass. "Wrap your legs around me, *o ángelós mou.*" She was an angel, his angel, sent to save him.

She sucked in air as he pulled her close, the insides of her thighs tight to his hips. He swore he could feel the heat from her pussy, and it made him lightheaded with desire.

Grigoris took three big steps back, then sank down, sitting on the side of the bed. He wanted to make sure Nyx felt safe and in control. That need to provide her with a sense of security didn't stop him from giving her ass a squeeze before he slid his hands up her back, settling them on her shoulder blades.

Nyx propped her elbows on his shoulders. Sitting on his lap, her head was only slightly higher than his. "Sometimes I forget how big you are."

"If I were a lesser man, there's a crude joke I could make."

"Is your penis proportional to the size of your body?" She looked genuinely curious.

Grigoris choked, then coughed, finally chuckling. He

wrapped his arm snuggly around her, then lay his forehead in the crook of her neck.

She slid her fingers into his hair and tugged his head back. She dipped her lips to his, repeating the slow, still kiss from before. Grigoris tried to be patient, not wanting to make her feel physically threatened, though having her straddling his lap meant his cock was rock-hard and aching in his pants.

Nyx pulled back, a little line between her brows. Before he could ask what was wrong, she grabbed the back of his head and sealed her lips against his. This time it wasn't still and sweet, it was raw and needy. She nipped his lower lip then licked the seam of his mouth. Grigoris let out a groan and loosened his own tightly held control.

What he wanted to do was roll her onto her back on the bed and devour her—leave no millimeter of skin untouched, unloved, unkissed. What he did was slide one hand up into her hair, cupping the back of her head and holding her still so he could take control.

He coaxed her mouth open with soft passes of his tongue, then, when she yielded, he invaded. She tasted sweet and hot. When he ran the tip of his tongue along the inside of her lower lip, she whimpered, pressing herself hard against his chest. Grigoris slid the hand not in her hair around her ribs. He thumbed the side of her breast, unable to do more while they clung so tightly together.

He tugged her away, wanting to change the angle of the kiss—and wanting to access her breasts, to let his fingers toy with the nipples that were so clearly ready to be pinched and fondled and...

"I suppose now is when I should tell you that I haven't done this before."

Grigoris froze, one hand hovering over her bare breast. She couldn't possibly mean... "Haven't done what?"

"Had sex."

"You're a virgin?" He might have yelped the word.

She raised one brow. "The term virgin has been fetishized by men, via societal structures, particularly religion, for tens of thousands of years, possibly since the advent of—"

He gently laid a hand over her mouth. "We won't use the V word. You haven't had sex before?"

She shook her head, her lips sliding against his palm.

"Then we'll take this slow." He moved his hand to cup her face, thumb sweeping over her cheek. He would be her first. God, he would be even happier if he could be her only.

"I don't want it slow." Nyx put her hands on his shoulders, trailing the tips of her fingers down his arms. The touch was so featherlight that he had goose bumps. She grasped his wrists and drew his hands up to her breasts.

She gasped when he pressed his palms to them, her head falling back, the line of her throat begging for his lips, tongue, and teeth.

Grigoris squeezed her breasts, then leaned in, drawing his tongue up the line of her neck, then nipped her chin. "I want to savor you."

Nyx looked at him, her pupils wide in the dark bedroom. "And I want you to fuck me. I want to forget about anything, anyone, but you."

Grigoris stiffened because her words were setting off alarm bells, but before he could ask her about it, she was sliding off his lap. She looked at him for a moment, then hooked her hands in her panties.

Grigoris reached out, stopping her. "Wait."

Nyx stiffened. "You don't want to do this?"

"Oh, I very much want to fuck you," he purred. Grigoris rose and slipped around the foot of the bed. Grabbing a small armchair, he tugged it over to the window. Rather than open the curtains, which might allow someone to look in, he draped the fabric of the curtain over the chair, pulling it away from the glass. Bright moonlight spilled over the floor, brightening the room.

Grigoris turned to her. "You said you needed me to touch you. That's what I'm going to do. I'm going to touch you. Every part of you. And when you're so hot that you're about to scream, if you beg..." He winked. "Then I'll fuck you."

Nyx lifted her chin, but she was shifting her weight from foot to foot, a restless gesture that he knew meant she was already aroused.

"Get up on the bed, *omorfia*, beauty."

With an alacrity that made him want to roar with satisfaction, she leapt onto the mattress, sitting back on her heels.

"No, I want you standing, hands on the ceiling."

She blinked in surprise. Her pale hair—painted silver by the light—swished softly around her cheeks as she hopped to her feet. He crooked his finger and she walked gingerly to the foot of the bed, standing near the edge of the mattress, her hands raised and palms flat on the ceiling.

Nyx looked quizzically down at him. "I've watched a considerable amount of ethically produced pornography and I've never—"

Grigoris reached out, grabbed her panties, and yanked them down to her ankles in one quick movement.

Nyx gasped and wobbled but found her balance.

"Step out of them."

Gingerly, she did, and Grigoris rubbed the damp fabric between his finger and thumb. "You're already wet."

Nyx's shoulders hunched with embarrassment and she turned her face into her arm.

"No," he said. "Look at me. I want to see your face when I touch you."

Nyx looked down at him, and he wished he could see her better because he was certain there was a blush on her cheeks. He'd never seen her blush. Later...

There was no later for them. Not really. She'd said short-term affair, so clearly Nyx wasn't imagining this as a one-night stand, but for them, "later" was a brief and fleeting thing.

Grigoris tucked her panties into his pocket, then set his hands on her ankles and started his exploration. He stroked her calves and the back of her knees, placed hot, open-mouthed kisses on her thighs that left damp patches of skin. He blew on one and watched her shiver.

When he went north, toward her sex, Nyx held her breath. He cupped her ass, kneading the cheeks before separating them slightly. She made a little yipping noise of surprise.

"Shhh," he reminded her, "you have to be quiet."

"Are you going to touch me?"

"You mean am I going to slide my fingers deep into your pussy? Am I going to spread you open and lick your clit?" He made sure his mouth was close enough that she'd feel the puff of air as he spoke.

"Yes...that."

"Say it, Nyx. I want to hear the words."

"I'm not...I've..."

"And I've never seen you at a loss for words." Grigoris blew gently over her pussy, which was neatly trimmed, then bypassed it, kissing the skin just below her belly button.

"You are a diabolical man."

"And you are a delectable woman." He kissed his way up her torso, as high as he could reach. "Drop your arms."

Nyx tentatively lowered her hands from the ceiling, her palms nervously tapping her thighs.

"Remember, stay quiet," he warned.

"What are you going—"

Grigoris hooked his hands behind her knees and yanked. She toppled back, arms windmilling for a moment before she bounced down onto the plush mattress, the downy duvet cradling her body. Grigoris planted one knee between her legs, inching them open, then leaned forward.

She looked up at him, wide-eyed, and smiling with an almost innocent delight.

"Enjoy that?" he asked.

"Unexpected," she answered.

"I'll take that as a yes, and I think you'll enjoy this even more." He lowered his mouth to her chest and took her right nipple into his mouth.

Nyx gasped and her fingers slid into his hair, tightening until his scalp tingled. He smiled against her and swirled his tongue around her nipple before flicking the tip a few times.

Nyx's hips rose, bumping into his abdomen. He transferred his attention to her other breast. Bracing his weight on one elbow, he used the other hand to toy with her now-wet nipple.

He started gently, stroking and circling, listening to her breathing and the small noises of pleasure she made, keeping his tongue's attention to her other nipple consistent. After toying with her long enough that her skin had dried, and her hips were rising and falling of their own accord, he intensified the contact. Pinching her nipple gently, he gave it a little twist. Nyx sucked in air and held it. He twisted her nipple between finger and thumb, as if rotating a dial. Nyx shrieked in pleasure.

He raised his mouth from her breast, releasing her with a pop. "Shh..." he whispered.

"I need..."

"What do you need?"

"I need you to touch me."

"Ah, ah, ah." He kissed her sternum, her chin. "You'll have to be more specific. Which part of me do you want touching you and where?"

"I want...I think I want you to either..." She paused to clear her throat, and though he couldn't see it, he could hear the blush in her voice. "I would like you to manually stimulate my vulva and clitoris."

Grigoris ducked his head so she wouldn't see his smile. She was so intelligent and so well-spoken that her current discomfiture was, for lack of a better word, cute.

He switched arms so he could play with the nipple that had, until now, only been touched by his lips. He didn't wait as long this time to transition from soft touches to more forceful twisting and plucking.

"Try again, *omorfia*. What do you want?"

"I told you." The words were breathy.

"You gave me clinical terms. I like to talk dirty, and I want to hear *you* talk dirty."

"You are infuriating," Nyx whispered.

"Maybe I am. And maybe I'm going to give you everything you want. Maybe, if you talk dirty, and beg, I'll slide my cock so deep inside you that you'll forget your own name."

"Doubtful," she gasped, but as she said it, she was arching up into his hand, only to fall back and raise her hips.

Grigoris was hit with a wave of love, and it softened both his amusement and his desire to hear her explicitly say what she wanted. He tugged her panties from his pocket, laying them on the bed, then rose.

Nyx looked up, her face registering shocked dismay for a moment before her expression shuttered. She started to roll away, but he grabbed her legs, yanking her down the bed far enough that he could spread, and then step between, her knees.

"Look at me, Nyx."

She glanced at him, her body relaxing back into the bed as it became clear he hadn't been leaving her. He dropped his hands to his waistband, unfastening his pants.

Slowly—since he had no desire to get any part of his cock stuck in the zipper—he finished unfastening his pants. His cock was hard, but trapped in his boxer briefs. From the wide-eyed look she gave his crotch, she was either nervous or impressed. Given that this was her first time, he was guessing nervous.

Slowly, Grigoris lowered both his underwear and pants, stepping out of them when they fell to the floor.

Nyx inhaled deeply then blew out a breath. "I'm well aware of the mechanics of the act of copulation—"

"You know how sex works."

"—but I admit the physical reality of an erect phallus—"

"My cock, which is rock-hard because of how much I want you."

"—is somewhat disconcerting."

Grigoris grabbed her hand. "Nyx. It's me. Look at me." She raised her gaze to his, and he smiled softly. "I won't hurt you."

The tension around her mouth and between her eyebrows smoothed out. "I know. And I trust you."

He guided her hand to his cock, wrapping it around the shaft. She was tentative for a moment before she started to explore him with her hand. Featherlight touches traced the shaft and head. She tentatively curled her fingers around his balls, then went back to his cock. She wrapped her hand firmly around him and stroked up and down.

Grigoris grabbed her wrist, his breathing labored. "Stop."

"Did I hurt you?"

"No, but if you don't stop, I'm going to come on your stomach." That thought reminded him that he didn't have a condom. "Hold on, I need to check for protection."

"I'm on birth control," she said softly. "I won't mind if you...if you ejaculate inside of me."

He lifted her hand, kissing her knuckles. He held his lips there, eyes closed, fighting down the knot of impatience churning inside. Holding back, taking the care he needed, was going to be almost impossible. It wasn't helped by the voice in the back of his head that warned this could be it. Tonight could be all they ever got.

He sucked in a long, deep breath. And then another.

Finally sure he was back under control, Grigoris lowered her hand back to his cock. "You touch me while I touch you."

With his hips between her outstretched knees, Grigoris finally slid his hand to her pussy. She jumped, shocked when he cupped her, letting her simply feel the weight of his hand. Her fingers tightened around his cock, and he had to bite the edge of his tongue to make sure her gentle, tentative touch didn't send him over the edge.

Carefully, he parted her pussy lips, exposing her soft, slick core.

Nyx's breathing was uneven, and her free hand went to her breast, pinching and plucking the nipple. Grigoris slid two fingers up and down the valley of her pussy as he watched her play with herself.

She wrapped her legs around him, hooking her ankles together at the small of his back, which spread her knees open even wider. In reward, he brought his fingers to her clit and started to circle it, a soft, steady rhythm.

"Your clit is so soft. Next time, I'm going to spread you open and study you, then taste you." Around and around he stroked the smooth, wet bud, her breathing speeding up with each rotation.

"Once you come, we'll scoot up on the bed so I can fuck you," he said softly, his own breathing a tad choppy. Nyx's fingers were still on his cock, squeezing and relaxing rhythmically. "I don't want you to feel trapped, so you're going to be on top and—"

"I want you on top," Nyx burst out. "I want you on top of me while you slide your cock into my pussy. I want you to fuck me hard and I want to feel you heavy on top of me. I want you to...no. I'm begging you. Touch me. Fuck me. L—"

Her delicious stream of dirty talk cut off as her eyes shot open wide and her mouth opened to scream in pleasure.

He'd thought she was close, could feel the rising tension in her legs. Grabbing her panties, he stuffed them in her mouth, even as his fingers kept circling her clit. She arched up off the bed like a drawn bow, and her thigh muscles quaking, one hand fisted around his cock, the other digging into her breast until the flesh plumped up between her fingers.

As her orgasm started to recede and she collapsed back onto the bed, he pressed his thumb to her clit and slid his long middle finger deep inside her. She arched up once again, screaming into her panties.

"You like it when I finger-fuck you while playing with your clit, don't you?"

She nodded frantically.

"Want me to fuck you?"

More nodding, and now she pulled on his cock, drawing it toward her pussy. Grigoris slid one arm under her, lifted her enough so that as he climbed onto the mattress, he was able to slide her to the middle of the bed.

"Spread your legs. Good girl. Now put your heels on the bed. Yeah, like that." He guided her into position, and then plucked the panties from her mouth. She'd come, but he was still half-mad with need. "Could you taste yourself? Next time I'm going to taste you."

"I want that," she whispered. "I want you to lick my pussy."

That was it. His control was at the breaking point. "I'm going to fuck you now. You tell me if it hurts."

"And if I want it to hurt?" She frowned briefly. "In a sexually masochistic way, not a self-flagellation way."

Grigoris briefly dropped his head to her breasts, huffing out a breath. "We'll explore all that later—rough sex, some kink. But right now it's just about us."

"Us," she breathed.

Grigoris shifted his hips, planting his elbows alongside her torso. "Wrap your arms around me."

Nyx slid her fingers into his hair, lifting herself enough to kiss him softly. "I'm glad you're my first," she whispered.

Grigoris didn't have the words, not anymore. He flexed his hips, the head of his cock finding the warm, wet valley of her pussy. He slid down to her entrance, her breathy gasps the most beautiful sound he'd ever heard.

"Nyx, look at me," Grigoris said.

Nyx met his gaze, and there was something so innocent and trusting in the way she was looking at him. He doubted someone who didn't know her, didn't understand her the way he did, would be able to see it.

Grigoris slid the head of his cock into her body. Her eyes rounded, and he held still, though he was shaking with the need to thrust in deep, to claim her in the most primal way.

"Am I hurting you?"

"No. No. It feels...right."

Grigoris maintained eye contact as he slowly, centimeter by centimeter, slid all the way in. When he was fully seated inside her, he had to close his eyes. The combination of the physical stimulation of her body tight around his cock and the emotional stimulation of looking at her were too much.

She sighed against his neck and wrapped her arms around his shoulders. "Make me yours," she whispered.

"You *are* mine," he growled. "Mine." He withdrew halfway then slid in again.

Nyx sucked in air, and he sealed his lips over hers, muffling the sound of her shrieks of pleasure as he started to fuck her in truth. He wanted it to last forever, but he was too ready, and she felt too good in his arms. He felt her tense once more, either another orgasm or a residual one from before, and then go limp under him. That evidence of complete satisfaction was all he needed to finally allow himself to find his own release. He thrust in once, twice, a third time, and then he was muffling his own sounds of pleasure against her shoulder.

He collapsed down on her, breathing hard, for only a moment before holding her tight and rolling so she was on top of him, his still-hard cock inside her. Nyx sighed heavily and nestled her head in the hollow of his neck. He stretched out his arms, gathering the sides of the duvet and flipping the soft comforter over the top of them.

Even as he closed his eyes, Grigoris acknowledged he'd just experienced the most important event in his life.

And for the first time, he questioned whether he'd have the strength to do the right thing. If he'd be able to walk away from her when the time came.

CHAPTER NINE

He was moving before the sound fully registered. At some point in the night, Nyx had slid off him and was curled up with her back against his side, her butt nestled against his hip. One moment Grigoris was asleep and content. The next he was in motion, instincts developed from years of maintaining the safety of Ottoman members in a territory rife with political upheaval triggered a response before his brain had fully registered exactly what the sound was.

Gunshots.

Two echoing cracks, muffled by walls and distance, but clear and recognizable.

"Grigoris?" Nyx asked sleepily, rising on one elbow.

"Those were gunshots. Grab some of my clothes, get dressed. Be ready to run if I come back for you."

"Gunshots?" She sat up, crossing her arms, holding the blanket to her torso.

Grigoris hiked his pants into place and fastened them, quickly and efficiently sliding knives into pockets and hidden sheaths with the ease of practice. He grabbed a long-sleeved T-shirt, shrugging it on. "Stay here. Be ready to run."

"Don't go out there." Nyx rose to her knees on the bed, eyes wide in the darkness. Her hair was silvery pale in the moonlight. "Stay with me."

Leaving her would always be difficult, but if there was a threat outside this room, he wanted to deal with it head-on and on his own. She would be safer here. Protecting her... loving her...they were the same thing, held the same level of importance for him. A world without Nyx wasn't something he ever wanted to consider. "I want to, *o ángelós mou*, but I need you to trust me to do my job."

Less than two minutes had passed since he'd heard the shots, and now there were other sounds—shouts, the faint pounding of footsteps. Nyx's gaze slid to the door and there was fear in her eyes.

"Nyx." He said her name like a command, and her attention jerked to him. Her breath was a little uneven, and he could only pray that she wasn't going to have a flashback-induced panic attack. In Bucharest, Ciril had used the panic and confusion caused by bombs going off to grab Nyx. He held her gaze, and then winked, smiling as if he didn't have a care in the world.

Nyx blinked in surprise, her body relaxing a bit. "Grigoris, you shouldn't go out there."

"I'll be right back. Be ready for me." He winked again, and he thought he saw her blush.

Before she could say anything else, he slid out the door. The moment he was in the corridor, the smile slid from his face. He glanced up and down the hall. A few of the other doors were open, and sleepy-looking dinner guests were peering into the hall. He motioned silently for each of them to go back into their rooms. Nikolett Varda looked like she was going to argue. He frowned and started in her direction, when a scream pierced the air.

Grigoris took off running.

He took the stairs two at a time and paused for only a moment, listening, before turning on the ball of his foot and racing toward the room Nyx had pointed out as Petro's office.

A harcos jumped from the shadows, raising a Hungarian saber. Grigoris skidded to a halt, managing not to decapitate himself. At the same time, he slid his long knife from the sheath hidden under his sleeve, raising it in a wicked under-handed slice.

The harcos' eyes widened as he and Grigoris stared at one another, frozen in place, a saber inches from Grigoris' throat, the tip of his knife against the other man's belly.

"What happened?" Grigoris asked in English. Now would be a good time to use what little Hungarian he knew, but with his adrenaline up, he needed to speak one of the languages he was fluent in.

The man—who Grigoris was fairly sure was named Ivan —responded in kind. "The admiral was shot."

"Shooter?"

The door to Petro's office burst open and a blood-covered, wide-eyed Hanna stood there. She said something in a language Grigoris didn't know—Ukrainian, possibly?—then started to sob.

Grigoris and Ivan sheathed their weapons, but it seemed like Hanna hadn't really seen them.

Ivan responded to her, then quickly ushered her back into the study. Grigoris went with them, pulling the door closed.

The inside of the office was brightly lit, and cold, thanks to the wind that blew in through the shattered window, beyond which was the vineyard they'd seen as they'd flown in. A second knight was kneeling by Petro, who was flat on his back on the floor.

For a moment, Grigoris thought the admiral was dead.

The relief and joy that surged through him was quickly followed by shame. He was a janissary. It was his job to uphold the laws of their society. Wishing harm—nay, death—on an admiral merely proved how deeply in love he was.

And how utterly fucked.

Petro let out a groan of pain. The knight with him adjusted the pressure on the bandage he was holding to Petro's right upper chest.

"What happened?" Grigoris snapped.

Ivan, who'd led Hanna to a chair, glanced at him, face stony. His expression was pure I-don't-have-to-tell-you-shit.

"What can I do to help?" Grigoris asked, changing tactics.

"Get my wife out of here," Petro wheezed in English.

"No, my love, I won't leave you." Hanna slid out of her chair, ignoring Ivan, and dropping to her knees beside Petro.

Ivan turned his head slightly to the side, gaze unfocused. Grigoris knew that look. He was listening to something. Probably an earpiece. Ivan grimaced, then glanced at Grigoris. The man made his way over to him, and then he started speaking quietly.

"At approximately two-forty a.m., two shots were fired through that window." He pointed to the broken front window. "The first shot hit the admiral in the torso. He was able to drop and cover before the second shot."

"Sniper?"

"Unknown, but the wound seems smaller caliber. Probably a rifle with a .223 caliber bullet."

From the way he said it, Grigoris thought Ivan might have experience with those types of wounds, which undoubtedly meant he'd been in the military—most armed forces used rifles with .223 caliber bullets. "Did you get him?"

Ivan's eyes went flinty. "All available security personnel are searching the grounds. The perimeter gates and walls have been locked down and electrified."

"Perimeter fences? I didn't see anything when we came in."

"Hidden in the tree line, forty meters from the house."

"How soon were they after him?"

Ivan's face tightened. "Very soon. We have two knights here, myself and Fedir." He motioned to the man kneeling with Hanna and Petro. "But we're here because of the dinner. Normal security for the admiral's residence is provided by security personnel from one of our companies."

Grigoris nodded, understanding. Most of the territories owned and ran security firms that not only employed, and often trained, the territory security officers, but also additional security professionals, who provided security services to member businesses and institutions. "There were territory security officers here yesterday, not just security personnel."

Each territory had six knights, though their titles varied. Like him, they all served as both law and order for the territory, ensuring laws were obeyed and violations were punished. In counterpoint, there were six security officers, who were more like mercenaries or spies than law enforcement. They had independent authority within their territories.

Ivan's eyes slid to Grigoris, then away. "Yes. The admiral wanted security officers to help escort Dr. Kata."

Given what he knew, Grigoris was fairly certain Petro had wanted to intimidate Nyx.

He glanced at the admiral, who grimaced in pain, Hanna bent over him, her dark hair falling around her face. She wore a long silk nightgown with a matching robe, while Petro still had on his tux from earlier.

"Once they heard the shots, two of the guards entered the office to assist the admiral, and two more started sweeping the grounds until we arrived to take over caring for the admiral."

"How many are searching the grounds for the shooter?" Grigoris asked.

"Six—the two security officers, and the four regular night guards."

"Has anyone called the fleet admiral?" Grigoris asked.

It was Petro who answered. "No. But I need to. A phone. I need—" He broke off, gasping in pain. His breathing sounded funny, and Grigoris wondered if his lung had collapsed.

"If the gates are closed, how are paramedics getting in?"

"We're going to fly him out, once we have the shooter. We can't risk moving him before then." Ivan glanced at his admiral.

"He's right. We need to call the fleet admiral. Get word to the other territories. This might be another attack like in..."

Like in Rome.

Grigoris grabbed Ivan's arm. "We need to search the house for a bomb."

Ivan's eyes widened. "What?"

"A bomb. In Rome, it was a car bomb. If the attacker got close enough to shoot the admiral through the window without being seen, he could have planted a bomb."

Ivan raised his cuff to his mouth and started barking out short, hard commands.

"Bomb?" A female voice asked.

Grigoris whirled around to see Nikolett standing in the doorway. She looked at Petro, eyes widening. In the next moment, she darted into the room, racing to Petro. Hanna was—rather uselessly, in Grigoris' opinion, though that was hardly fair since not everyone reacted well in a crisis—sobbing and clinging to Petro, while the harcos kept pressure on the wound.

Nikolett placed her hands on top of the harcos'. "Press harder. And you," she said to Hanna. "Stop crying and get something we can use as a dressing. A towel, a shirt, something. It will help clot and seal the wound. Hurry now. We have no time to waste."

"You have experience with this?" Fedir asked.

"I was nearby during a terrorist attack in Budapest a few years ago. I attempted to help the injured, but I didn't know enough. After that, I took courses in first aid. Press harder," she said.

The harcos applied more pressure until Hanna returned with a sweater.

Grigoris wasn't sure, but he could have sworn Nikolett muttered, "Fucking cashmere."

The harcos lifted his hands and Nikolett pressed the soft sweater to Petro's skin. She gestured with one quick nod for the harcos to resume applying pressure.

"We need to get him out of here," Nikolett snapped at Ivan.

"Not until they've cleared the grounds."

"If there's a bomb in the house, don't you think we should leave?" Nikolett asked coolly.

"Bomb?" Another female voice entered the room, one he knew.

Grigoris whirled, raising a hand to stop Nyx from walking any farther into the room. "The admiral was shot. They're looking for the shooter, you'd be safer..." Grigoris trailed off.

Nyx raised one eyebrow. "Safer in my room? Hardly. Not if, as Nikolett put it, there's a bomb in the house."

"I'm pulling two people in to help sweep the house," Ivan said.

"No, keep them on the shooter. I'll sweep the house," Grigoris commanded.

"That would be highly dangerous, since it seems most likely the shooter is one of the guests," Nyx said.

The whole room stilled. Grigoris resisted the urge to grab Nyx and shake her. He'd been starting to think something along those lines. Nyx thought fast, finding connections then declaratively stating her conclusions. It had made him crazy when they first met.

"Nyx, be quiet," he said softly in Greek.

She glanced at him, and then stiffened before stepping around him into the room.

As she did, he got his first good look at her since before they'd gone to bed. She must have slipped back into her room because she was wearing dark pants and an ice-blue sweater that made her golden skin seem to glow, while highlighting the pale shades of blond in her hair.

And a line of blotchy red bruising circled her throat.

Grigoris' blood went cold. Had he done that? No. He hadn't touched her neck, had he? For one insane moment, he wasn't sure.

She'd left the door slightly open when she entered, and out of the corner of his eye, he saw two men slam in the front door then race up the stairs, presumably to rouse the other guests.

"You want to help?" Ivan asked him. "Help us get the guests out. We'll evacuate the house just in case."

"And make us all easy targets for whoever shot the admiral?" Nikolett said from the floor, looking at Ivan like he was stupid.

Grigoris was only half listening. He was looking at Nyx.

And Nyx was looking at Petro.

Whatever Nikolett was doing had stabilized the admiral. He turned his head, meeting Nyx's stare. She looked down at him, icy cold, but the rage was there, in the set of her shoulders and the very stillness of her face.

Petro smiled at her, and it was a cruel expression. His gaze slipped to her throat and his smile widened.

Grigoris' whole body flashed white hot with rage.

Petro. Petro had hurt her. How? When? He'd made sure she'd locked her bedroom door from the inside, and he knew she wouldn't have opened it for anyone but him.

But Petro had gotten to her. He'd hurt her—tried to kill her? Or just strangled her enough to scare her?

That's why she came to you. Not because she wanted you, but because she was terrified.

That idea shook him to the core as his eyes traveled to her neck once more. There was no denying what he was seeing. The bruises were the shape of fingers.

Nyx hadn't come to his room because of desire. Instead, it had been a knee-jerk response to an attack. As hurt as he was, he wouldn't leave her with Petro. He stepped in front of Nyx, ostensibly to talk to Ivan. "Nyx and I will help clear the house. You have transportation?"

"There's a garage with a fleet of vehicles behind the house."

"We'll take the guests there. You get the admiral to the helicopter and a hospital." Grigoris turned, stepping into Nyx's personal space to force her back a step.

She didn't move. She was frowning. "How do you know there's a bomb?"

"We don't, but given what happened in Rome, I'm not planning to take chances. Someone got close enough to shoot him, and—"

"Most likely one of the guests."

"That's the second time you've said that. Are you accusing me of something?" Nikolett asked.

"Though I suppose it's possible the attacker brought not only a gun, but a small incendiary device with them," Nyx continued. "But if that's the case, I don't think the hypothetical bomb is in the house." Nyx looked up at him and raised an eyebrow.

Grigoris cursed. "The helicopter or the cars. Shoot the admiral, then wait for him to get into a vehicle to be taken to a hospital, then blow up the vehicle. Take out the admiral and probably a couple other people too."

"Precisely," Nyx said.

Grigoris looked at Ivan. "I'll take the helicopter. You take the garage."

Ivan raced out, Grigoris right behind him. As he passed her, Nyx's fingers brushed over the back of his hand, a small, secret touch, a fleeting moment of contact that made him pause, his emotions at war.

He felt like a silly young girl with a daisy.

Does she love me? Does she not?

CHAPTER TEN

Nyx wanted to turn and watch Grigoris leave. More than that, she wanted to call back her words and hold him to her. She'd been so focused on unraveling the puzzle, assessing the situation, running each possible outcome that she hadn't thought about what would happen if she voiced her conclusion.

Normally, it didn't matter. Normally, there were no emotional consequences to one of her statements. But this time her statement had sent the man she'd just made love with running away from her and into danger.

She was a scholar, and, as far as it pertained to the current crisis with the Masters' Admiralty, she was a librarian. She discussed and analyzed with like-minded scholars, and the one time she'd gone out to help, she'd ended up nearly dying. Now she found herself in the middle of another crisis, and rather than feeling fear or the need to flee, she'd focused on assessing. Clearly, she was better suited to working behind the scenes.

They were searching the house for the bomb, but given

the current series of events, the house was not the most likely target.

It was a testament to how safe Grigoris made her feel that she hadn't shut down the moment she realized there had been an attack. Or maybe her vicious satisfaction at seeing Petro hurt and bleeding was overriding her fear.

Fedir glanced at Nikolett, indicating he needed her to take over as he stood.

"First aid kit," Nikolett snapped at Hanna. "Where?"

"I...I don't know."

"You don't have one, or you don't know where it is? This is just a sweater, and we need proper bandages, especially if our only ways out are about to be blown up."

Hanna pressed her hand over her mouth, dark eyes rounding with horror.

Nyx suppressed the uncharitable urge to sneer.

Nikolett closed her eyes, and Nyx could practically hear the prayer for patience the woman was silently praying. "Fine. I'll go find it. Here, I folded the sweater into a better compress, but you need to apply pressure."

Fedir had his hand to his ear. He paced to the broken window, drawing a sword from his belt and peering out into the night.

"It hurts him," Hanna whispered in horror. "You're pressing down too hard."

"Right. You're useless. You." Nikolett looked at Nyx. "You hold this while I find the first aid kid."

Nyx's blood went cold, followed by a hot flash of rage. She made sure none of that showed. She crossed her arms and raised a single brow.

Nikolett stared at Nyx, her expression shifting from determined to genuinely shocked. "Um, he's your admiral. You have to help."

Petro laughed, a gasping noise that was, for all its weakness, cruel. When he spoke, it was in Bulgarian. "I'm more than your admiral, aren't I? I'm your husband."

From the confused looks on Hanna and Nikolett's face, neither of them spoke Bulgarian. This was a private conversation then.

"You are not my husband," Nyx said. "And I will never be your wife. You can force me. Drag me to the Isle of Man, hold a gun to my head so I say the words, but I will *never* be your real wife, a partner in your trinity."

"You will do all that and more. And in the end, you'll beg me."

The words echoed what Grigoris has said to her hours before in his bed. The words were the same, but the meaning was entirely different. She smiled coldly at Petro, but inside she was shaking. She couldn't forget the feel of his hands around her neck.

Nyx looked at Nikolett, switching to Hungarian. "I'll hold the bandage down, so you can go find whatever first aid supplies you need."

Petro bared his teeth at her, but spoke to Hanna. "The pantry in our private kitchen. There's an emergency kit."

Hanna stood and raced toward the door. Nyx stepped out of her way, but the other woman paused for a moment, hand on the door. It was, Nyx realized, the first time in their entire life the two of them had ever been in a position to speak without Petro hovering nearby.

"I'll see you burn in hell," Hanna whispered.

Then she was gone.

Nyx stared after her in shock that she didn't have time to indulge. There were sounds coming from the rest of the house, as those who hadn't been roused by the initial commotion were woken by the guards searching the house.

She was tempted to leave, but if she did, Petro would be alone with Nikolett and the harcos who was on the other side of the room, his back to the room as he scanned the night beyond the broken window.

She hated Petro with a passion. He'd destroyed her life, and only hours ago assaulted her.

Nyx looked at Nikolett, and there was no denying the razor-sharp intelligence in the other woman's eyes.

As much as she hated Petro, her personal feelings were not of greater import than taking down the mastermind, and if she walked out of this room, she just might be leaving an admiral—a wounded, vulnerable admiral—alone with a distracted knight and a woman who, Nyx was starting to think, could be the mastermind.

She was still staring at Nikolett, trying to decide what questions she should ask, and if she should alert the harcos to the potential threat, when the bomb went off.

Outside the window, the night was, for a moment, bright as day. From where she stood, she could see pieces of the helicopter hurtling into the sky.

Cold horror poured over Nyx. "Grigoris!"

"You have feelings...for the Greek?" Petro's laugh was cruel. This time he hadn't bothered to switch languages, and Nikolett looked from him to Nyx and back again.

Nyx's insides had turned to liquid, and she wanted to run, to run toward the now-burning mess that had once been the helicopter. To find whatever was left of him and weep over his body.

The door behind her opened. "You were right. A bomb was on the helicopter."

Grigoris. That was Grigoris' voice.

Nyx pressed a hand to her mouth and whirled, throwing her arms around him. "You're alive!"

Grigoris hugged her tight, and then she felt him go stiff. He eased her away from his body. She looked up then followed the line of his gaze. Grigoris was looking at Petro, who was watching them with a hard, cruel expression.

"He's not yours," she said quickly in Bulgarian. "You can't touch him. He's a knight. He's the chorbaji."

Grigoris looked sharply at her, recognizing his title in her statement.

"You are mine," Petro said, but this time he didn't bother to speak Bulgarian. "You belong to me, wife."

"Admiral." Ivan raced in, Hanna just behind him, holding a large red duffel bag. "We located the bomb, and for safety, detonated it remotely rather than attempt to remove it."

Petro's enraged expression shifted as he looked away from her. Nyx stared at the far wall, aware of Nikolett's attention on her and Grigoris' tense presence at her side.

"Good," Petro said. "Was anyone hurt?"

"No, Admiral. And another helicopter is ten minutes out. We're going to take you on a stretcher to a point just outside the walls. We still haven't caught the shooter, and we don't want the helicopter landing and you transferring where you might be vulnerable."

Two more men entered, forcing Nyx and Grigoris to step deeper into the room. They laid a narrow yellow stretcher out beside Petro. Nikolett opened the duffel bag with one hand, then started barking orders at the guard closest to her as to what she needed.

Ivan walked over to Grigoris. "Nice shooting, Janissary."

"Who is going with him?" Grigoris asked.

Ivan pointed to himself. "Hanna, myself. That's all there's room for."

"Just you," Grigoris said. He raised his voice loud enough

for everyone in the room to hear. "No one except the admiral and one guard is allowed to leave."

Hanna look incensed. "I will go with my husband!" Her gaze darted to Nyx as she said 'husband'. Now that she knew the other woman would "see her burn," she no longer had to waste time feeling guilty about not convincing Hanna to join her when she'd run.

"You have no authority to give orders," Nikolett said, not looking up from whatever she was doing to Petro. The admiral was grimacing in obvious pain, which was undoubtedly the only reason he wasn't asserting his authority.

"The Admiralty, and territory of Hungary, were just attacked." Grigoris' words rang out. The door to the office was open slightly, and Nyx could see the worried faces of some of the other guests where they stood in the foyer, doubtless corralled there as the guards finished sweeping the house. "I am leader of the task force assigned to address these attacks." Grigoris looked around the room, and he seemed taller and broader than he had moments before. He was always tall, but he decided to stop hiding it while he took control of the situation. "Which means I am in charge. And *no one* leaves here without my permission."

Nikolett sat back, cleaning her bloody hands with a small wipe. "If there was one bomb, there might be another in the house. I have no intention of staying here."

"You will stay here. We will sweep the house a second time. Additional security is on its way with equipment."

Two men loaded Petro onto a stretcher and lifted him. He grimaced as he was jostled. He had a mask over his mouth, and Hanna stayed by his side, peering worriedly at him, one of her hands on his shoulder as they carried him out.

"You can't keep me here," someone else said, though Nyx couldn't see who'd spoken.

Hanna shot Nyx a venomous look before she disappeared, leaving the door open wide enough that Nyx could see more of the crowd in the foyer.

Hanna was going to go with Petro. Nyx was sure of that.

Grigoris stepped forward, raising his voice to quiet the murmurs that had followed as people got a good look at Petro.

"As of right now, you are all suspects in the attack on the admiral. No one leaves."

Grigoris walked through the crowd. He had a small conference with the men who'd searched the house. Then they started herding everyone into the dining room and den. Nyx tried to catch his attention, to warn him that Hanna had left, but he was occupied, and it was already too late.

Nyx went with the crowd until a strong hand halted her.

"Come with me."

Nyx hadn't panicked at the touch because she knew it was Grigoris. She nodded her assent and followed him away from the crowd.

"Are you alright?" Grigoris asked, pulling Nyx into a small alcove.

Nyx nodded numbly. Exhaustion and adrenaline were warring for dominance at the moment. Too much had happened in too short a time frame. She hadn't had time to process any of it.

She'd moved from the terror of Petro's attack in her bedroom, to Grigoris' bed, to Petro being shot, to the bomb and her brief certainty that she'd lost Grigoris.

She needed time to herself to sit quietly and process, but given the intense look in Grigoris' eyes, it was apparent she wasn't going to get that until he got answers she didn't want to give.

Grigoris wasn't appeased by her nod. Tipping her head up with a knuckle under her chin, his fingers drifted to her neck. She couldn't see the bruises forming, but she could tell from his touch, they were there.

"What didn't you tell me?" His anger was almost palpable, though Nyx knew it wasn't directed at her.

Nyx wrapped her hand around his wrist. "I didn't think it would be wise to tell you."

"Did Petro do that to you?" he asked hotly. "Did he put his hands on you? Strangle you?"

Even now, cold fear snaked its way along her spine as she recalled struggling for air. Terror gripped her as she considered Petro's hand tightening around her throat and her very genuine belief—though brief—that he was going to kill her.

"He came to my room after dinner. There was a secret passage...I didn't realize."

"What did he do? What did he say?"

Nyx closed her eyes, unwilling to repeat the vile words, Petro's threat to fuck—rape—her from behind, to treat her as his pet. Telling Grigoris about that would only add to the stress he was under, that they were both under.

"He made threats and then he left."

Grigoris shook his head, his fingers gentle when they touched her neck once more. "It was more than that."

Nyx was too tired, too frustrated. It made it difficult for her to shield her words, to consider their impact. "I thought he was going to rape me...kill me."

Grigoris went white with rage, but his coloring was the only thing that betrayed the intensity of his emotions. His hands were steady, his voice unnaturally calm when he spoke again. "You don't have to worry about either of those things happening. I will kill Petro before he ever lays a finger on you again."

"He is an admiral. You cannot—"

"I don't give a fuck."

"We have too much to do, too many knots to unravel. We need to work, to think rationally. Our emotions cannot blind us to the task at hand."

Grigoris took a step away from her, and Nyx instantly missed the warmth of him standing close to her. Without him, she felt so cold, so alone.

"Why did you come to my room?"

Nyx stilled, confused by the question. Surely he knew, surely he understood why. Her tired mind whirled, searching for an answer. Not to his question, but to what had driven him to ask such a thing.

"I came," she said, haltingly, "because I only feel safe with you."

"You came to feel safe?" Pain dripped from his words, and suddenly it all became clear.

She shook her head quickly. "I came to you because I wanted you, desperately. I've spent a lifetime alone and cold. I'm so tired of being numb. With you...with you, there is warmth; with you, I come alive. And I feel. Not pain, not fear, but hope."

Grigoris studied her face and she steeled her expression, desperate that he see the truth in her words, in her heart.

"Nyx," he whispered her name, like a prayer.

She reached for him, gripping her fingers into his shirt to pull him back. "Please, Grigoris. I need...you near me."

Grigoris pulled her into his arms without a moment's hesitation. The embrace was too brief. Though they were tucked into the alcove, they would be visible should anyone walk by.

"I will always be with you, near you."

"That is a promise you cannot make. Better to leave out the 'always' and add 'for now'."

The scowl on Grigoris' face told her he didn't like hearing

the truth any more than she enjoyed saying it. "You can't go back to that bedroom. You'll stay with me, where I can protect you."

"Petro is gone." She motioned to the door. "He won't be using that secret entrance again soon. Besides, it isn't possible for me to share a room with you, not here, in his house."

While Nyx didn't consider herself married to Petro, nearly everyone else in this house—with the exception of Grigoris—did. To flaunt her affair so brazenly would be the height of foolishness, not to mention dangerous.

Grigoris blew out a long, slow breath. "We can't leave. We have to unravel what happened here tonight. For the first time, the mastermind failed, and that means we might have a chance of figuring out who he is, based on *how* he failed."

While she felt like death warmed over, he appeared energized, ready to take on the world.

"All right." She needed coffee.

"But first, you need to rest. Unfortunately, until we've swept the house with a dog and equipment, I don't want you in a bedroom. You'll stay with the others."

"If you think there could be a bomb, perhaps remaining in the house isn't a prudent idea." It wasn't lost on Nyx that Nikolett had said something similar only moments ago.

Grigoris' lips quirked in a little smile. "Don't want to get blown up?"

"Not particularly." She didn't tell him how terrified she'd felt when the helicopter blew up and she thought he was dead.

His expression turned serious once more. "If the shooter is still out there, it would be too easy to pick off people while we moved you."

"I also do not particularly want to be shot," Nyx said.

Grigoris chuckled. "Come on. I need to help them search.

You can rest, and maybe listen to what the others are saying, but the priority is to get some rest."

"What about you? You haven't slept much either."

"I'm fine. Once it's safe, and everyone can go back to bed, I'll come with you. Set up my laptop in your room. Work there while you sleep."

"Like you did in the hospital," she murmured.

"Exactly."

"But the situations are not repetitive. I'm not going to sleep while you alone reason out the identity of the mastermind's latest pawn." Nyx paused, considering what she'd just said, considering the people who'd been at the party tonight—all powerful and intelligent. She looked at Grigoris and lowered her voice. "Or perhaps this attack was carried out by the mastermind himself."

Grigoris nodded once, stepping out of the alcove. "I know you're tired, but keep your ears open."

"I will." She was also going to keep her back to the wall.

CHAPTER ELEVEN

By 6 a.m., the house had been declared bomb-free. Grigoris appeared at the door to the den. Nyx knew he was there even before she saw him walk in with Fedir—she could feel his presence, like a warm breeze that helped her breathe deeply, gave her an instant sense of calm.

She let her body relax, and she sank deeper into the padded bench where she'd been sitting for the past few hours. There were far more comfortable places to sit, but here she had her back to the wall and had been able to keep an eye on everyone. Particularly Nikolett.

"The house is safe," Fedir said in Hungarian. "You may return to your rooms."

"When can we leave?" Hans asked, straightening from the chair where he'd been slumped, eyes half closed. He'd spent some time right after they'd been herded in here railing against Grigoris for treating him like cattle, rather than respecting his title of security minister.

Nyx had mostly ignored him, watching Lazar, who'd been brought in by Patty. Despite the crowd in the room, Lazar had been given a whole couch. Patty had stayed with him, seated on the floor. Both of them had fallen asleep, which meant Nyx didn't have a chance to have a follow-up conversation with Lazar. She needed to know what he'd meant when he said anything Petro might have done to him would be something he deserved.

"The house? Not until I've spoken with each of you individually." Grigoris had shed his easygoing, inconspicuous cloak and looked tall and menacing. The stubble along his cheeks and dark circles under his eyes added to the effect.

"You think one of us shot the admiral," Nikolett said. "Why? And you think the bomb detonated here is similar to the attack on the admiral of Rome?"

"Yes, this was an attack, just like the one in Rome."

"Who is behind these attacks?" Nikolett's gaze slid to Nyx, who didn't move. They'd had a very interesting conversation several hours ago, when nearly everyone else in the room had been asleep. Nikolett had invited herself to take a seat beside Nyx and not bothered with pleasantries before she'd begun asking hard questions.

"WHY ARE YOU HERE?" Nikolett asked quietly.

"I needed to speak with Petro," Nyx replied. She kept her eyes half closed, her body language relaxed, as if she was half asleep though she was fully awake. The adrenaline from earlier had faded, leaving her shaky and tired, but she wouldn't fall asleep. She needed to watch and listen. If Grigoris was right, the mastermind, or a close associate of the mastermind, was in the room right now.

"Uh-huh," Nikolett said. "You show up, and suddenly the admiral is shot and his helicopter blown up."

Nyx forced herself to remain calm. "I think it's possible Petro was shot because someone didn't want me to talk to him."

Nikolett didn't mince words. "Or you shot him because you hate him."

"I didn't shoot him."

"You have an alibi?"

She did. A good one. One no one could know about.

"You said this is the first time you attended one of these dinners. Interesting that the first time you are here, Petro is shot and his helicopter is blown up," Nyx replied, throwing Nikolett's words back at her.

Nikolett's brows rose. "Ah, it's like that then, is it? The gloves are off? I have no wish to go to war with you, Nyx, but I will if I have to."

"It's like nothing," Nyx said softly. She considered leveling a veiled threat at Nikolett, to gauge her reaction, but something stilled her tongue.

"I don't know who you are, or why you're here," Nikolett said quietly. "I didn't do this, though if you ask around, I'm sure there will be plenty of people who tell you I have a problem with Petro. I don't support the way he's created silos within the territory. He's secretive, as if Romania and Hungary, all of Eastern Europe, were still communist. He doesn't see the future. He doesn't see how we need to change."

Nyx's heart beat faster, but externally all she did was make a small humming noise, before saying, "I hate Petro." Nyx felt it as Nikolett's attention dropped to her neck. She didn't give Nikolett a chance to ask about the marks. "Nothing will change my feelings toward him. But I do not deny he has provided stability for the territory."

"Stability is just another way of saying maintaining the patriarchy."

"Very true."

Nikolett tapped her palms on her knees before she stood. "I don't know why you're here, but if you're a danger to the people I represent, the people I want to protect, don't think I won't do everything in my power to stop you."

With that, the other woman walked away, leaving Nyx feigning exhaustion, while internally her heart was pounding.

"WHO DID THIS?" Nikolett repeated, determined to get an answer out of Grigoris.

"That's what I'm going to find out. As I said, I think someone here is responsible for the attack on Petro."

"You're sure it's connected to what happened in Rome?"

"There are too many similarities."

Nikolett frowned. "You mean the bomb?"

Everyone, even Lazar, was sitting up and watching the back-and-forth between Grigoris and Nikolett.

Nyx needed to talk to Grigoris. They needed to have a council of war between themselves before anything else was said in front of the group. Before Grigoris could respond, Nyx got to her feet, walking not up to him, but to Fedir.

"Excuse me. I need to sleep."

"Of course." Fedir stepped out of her way, and that broke the tension that held the room.

As she passed Grigoris, she let her fingertips brush the back of his hand, needing that small moment of contact. She felt his hand twitch under hers, but then she was gone, headed through the foyer toward the stairs. At the top she paused, looking around. No one was in sight, so she slid into Grigoris' room.

It was a risk, but she wasn't going back to her room, not with that secret entrance, even if Petro was away from the estate. It left her vulnerable to too many other threats. Still, she leaned against the wall in the corner, where she couldn't be seen by someone coming in the door.

Half an hour later, the door opened.

"Don't stab me," Nyx said quietly. She'd known it was him by the sense of calm and warmth that spread through her.

Grigoris closed the door and locked it. He looked over at her, winked, but did a quick search of the room. He walked casually, as if he were just checking out the amenities, but the knife he held in a backwards grip, the blade along his forearm, offset the nonchalance.

When he was done, he turned to her, sliding the knife into a sheath hidden by his sleeve.

"Hey, beautiful *ángelos*."

"We need a council of war."

Grigoris smiled. "An avenging angel, I see. Perhaps I should call you Michael. Have you come to help me banish Satan's dragons?"

Nyx personally related more to the archangel Ariel. However, there was no time for a discussion of the Book of Revelations, though she made a mental note to bring the topic up again later. She and Grigoris had engaged in quite a few religious debates during her time on Cyprus. He'd known the best way to counteract her fears was to shut down the hypothalamus and left side of her brain by stimulating the right frontal cortex through lively discussions about theology, spirituality, and morality.

"There were no dragons slain tonight." Nyx walked

across the room and sat on the side of the bed. A vivid memory of what they'd done on that bed flashed through her head and she jumped up, striding over to the window instead. She started to open the drape, pulling it away from the chair he'd draped it over to give them more light.

More light to see one another as they'd had sex.

Made love?

What they'd done had felt like making love.

His fingers closed over hers, stopping her from opening the drapes. He was at her back, and despite how much she trusted him, she tensed for a moment. His lips brushed her hair, and he murmured something in Greek. She was too rattled to translate, but when he touched her chin, tipping her head to the side, she sighed and let him do it. He pressed open-mouthed kisses to the spot below her ear, then moved down, kissing the marks on her neck.

His hands were gentle on her hips, but she didn't want gentle. If he was going to touch her, she wanted to feel it. She grabbed his wrists, pulling his hands around and up to her breasts. His palms closed over them, and there was something both arousing and comforting about having his hands on her.

Grigoris slid his lips to her shoulder, nuzzling aside her collar. He licked her, then added a little nip.

Heat rushed through her, and she wanted to turn around and devour him. To lose herself in his touch.

"Based on the criteria of intelligence and vision, there are two viable suspects from among the people here tonight," Nyx said.

Grigoris stilled, then thunked his forehead against her shoulder. "Nyx, my sexy brainiac, you sometimes confuse me."

She patted his hands, which still cupped her breasts. "I want very much to have sex with you again, which is precisely why we need to have this discussion now, before we get distracted."

Grigoris stepped back. He adjusted the drape, leaving it over the window but no longer covering the chair. He held the chair for her, and Nyx took a seat. Grigoris sat on the end of the bed, facing her.

"Who do you suspect?"

"Nikolett and Petro."

"Nikolett is on my list too," Grigoris said. "But, as much as I plan to kill Petro for daring to lay his hands on you, his injury was not self-inflicted. It's impossible that he shot himself."

"Shot himself, no. But he could have orchestrated it. Gotten one of the security officers or harcosok to shoot him."

"What's his motive?" Grigoris asked.

"To shift suspicion off of himself."

"Because he's the mastermind?"

"In this hypothetical, yes."

"And if he's the mastermind, what's his motive?"

"I don't know," Nyx said slowly. It was something that had plagued her and the fellow librarians—what did their foe hope to accomplish? "Maybe he wanted to be made fleet admiral. He killed Kacper, assuming he would get the job."

Grigoris shook his head. "There wasn't time to talk about it when we were in Dublin, but I'm not sure Eric is right about all the old admirals—I mean the ones who held their positions before all this started—being suspects."

"Why?"

"Because they were all in that room in London. They could have been shot as easily as Winston or the admiral of Castile, Ricardo Garcia."

"You were there?" Nyx asked.

"I was one of the knights in the room," he confirmed. "I

was there to guard Hande. It was chaos."

"But the tech the sniper used was state of the art, wasn't it?" Nyx persisted. "Perhaps the sniper knew who he wasn't allowed to shoot."

"It showed heat signatures only," Grigoris said quietly.

Nyx stiffened. "I think you underestimate Petro. If he is the mastermind, tonight is merely another example of him putting himself in the line of danger in order to throw suspicion off himself."

"Or it's a second good reason why he shouldn't be a suspect," Grigoris said. "The mastermind has in the past used an expert sniper. This would have been an easy shot for even a moderately accomplished marksman—the lights were on in the office. It would have been easy to take a head shot."

NYX NODDED. "THAT'S TRUE."

"I know you want it to be him, but—"

"I don't want it to be him," Nyx said sharply, though it was a lie. She'd already admitted she wanted it to be him. "I just know how manipulative he can be. I know that he is the sort of man who will go to great lengths to get what he wants, or what he thinks he deserves." She kept coming back to what Lazar had said. What had Petro done to his vice admiral in retaliation for the way Lazar had helped her?

Grigoris frowned. "That's also true. But if what he wanted was to be fleet admiral, why isn't he? Why was Eric named?"

"We need to talk to one of the admirals who was at the second conclave. The one they held in secret."

"And we need to talk about your second suspect," Grigoris said. "Nikolett."

"We had an interesting conversation." Nyx briefly

recapped their exchange.

Grigoris' frown deepened. "That might put her at the top of the list."

"She's a strong candidate for the mastermind. She's too straightforward to be manipulative, but I believe she could recruit people to her cause, the same way a cult leader recruits, through philosophical devotion and belief."

"But we know the mastermind used sexual manipulation, at least for Manon and the Rutherfords."

"Nikolett is beautiful," Nyx pointed out. "And her forthright manner is most likely not the same approach she uses when it comes to sexual relationships."

Grigoris stared into space.

After a moment, she asked, "Grigoris?"

"I was thinking about the timeline."

Nyx blinked, realizing instantly what he was talking about. "Nikolett might be too young."

"Kacper was being poisoned for years. Would she have had time to recruit people in order to put all these things into place?"

"And if she were the mastermind, why wouldn't her attacks have started here, in her own territory?"

"Don't shit where you eat," Grigoris pointed out.

"This brings up another interesting point. Where the first attacks took place might be of more significance than we've allocated." Nyx rose to pace. She always thought better when she was moving.

"You mean maybe Winston, and England, were targeted first for a reason?" Grigoris asked.

"But they weren't the first victims."

"The murdered trinity in Rome." Grigoris sat back, frowning.

"Following our previous chain of logic, Giovanni

Starabba would be on the shortlist for the mastermind; however, he was injured, and nearly killed, in the attack on his home."

Grigoris held up his hands. "You said maybe Petro shot himself in order to throw off suspicion."

"And I am steadfast in that conclusion. The degree of magnitude cannot be discounted."

Grigoris nodded. "There's a world of difference between a bullet wound to the shoulder and having a building fall on you."

"And Antonio Starabba was in the building when the bomb went off. Giovanni's dedication to his children is legendary. I doubt he would have risked his son's life."

"He made his son a security officer. That is not a low-risk occupation."

"No, but again, it is not the same as being near the epicenter of an explosion."

Grigoris stood, and as she passed, he reached out and grabbed her shoulders, forcing her to stop her pacing. "We're talking in circles. And we shouldn't narrow our suspects. There were a lot of people at dinner last night."

"And you're sure it was one of them?" Nyx asked.

"No. I'm not sure of anything. But it's the most likely scenario. There are no cameras in or around the house, but there are cameras on the perimeter wall of the estate. There's also an electric fence embedded in the top that is turned on whenever a lockdown is initiated. The instant the harcosok saw Petro had been shot, they flipped that switch, meaning anyone going over the wall would have gotten an electric shock strong enough to drop them. Nobody, and none of the cameras, were disabled."

"If the shooter isn't one of the people who was in the house, they could be hiding on the grounds."

"The extra security we brought to check the house is doing a full sweep. And Fedir is testing the hands of all the staff for gunshot residue."

"If it was one of them, they were manipulated by Petro," Nyx said instantly.

"Most likely, since none of them are members, but they have to know at least something about the society."

"True," Nyx agreed.

"Tomorrow..." Grigoris looked at the morning sun that peeked around the curtain. "I mean this afternoon, I'm going to talk to a few people." He touched her cheek. "Lazar is on that list."

"He couldn't have held a gun long enough to fire it."

"Are you sure?"

Nyx frowned. "The same emotional bias that leads me to suspect Petro could blind me to Lazar's involvement."

"Exactly."

Nyx wanted to keep talking, sure that if they just studied the patterns of behavior and potential motives long enough, they'd find a solution. There were so many things they hadn't yet dissected—Rome was the first target, so who among the suspects, either those in the house or among the other admirals, would want to hurt or cripple Rome? What about the pathology of Ciril? Would he have accepted an order—or "help"—from a woman? It seemed likely that he was a misogynist, though she'd want to discuss that with Leila, who'd been kidnapped and tortured by the man. If that was the case, it might rule out Nikolett. At least rule her out as the mastermind. Maybe she was yet another of the mastermind's pets.

Nyx was about to say all this, but when she opened her mouth, she yawned.

"Sleep," Grigoris said. "We both need it. I emailed Eric

about what happened today."

"Emailed?"

"I'm too tired to deal with a pissed-off Viking. Besides, Lazar, or Security Minister Hans Molnar should be the ones to report this to the fleet admiral, but I doubt either of them did."

"I'm staying with you," Nyx said. "My previous statements about sharing a room are rescinded. With that secret entrance to my room, I don't feel safe. Even with Petro away from the estate."

Grigoris went pale, and then his arms came around her, hugging her so tight her ribs creaked. It felt good.

"I checked your room and didn't find it. I'm so sorry," he whispered in her hair.

"I don't blame you, and you shouldn't blame yourself." She raised her hand, touching his cheek. As she looked up into his eyes, she realized that she'd declared she would stay with him, rather than ask. A little trickle of uncertainty slid through her. "Can I...can I sleep in here with you? If you'd rather, I can—"

He scooped her up into his arms and carried her to the bed. "Don't be stupid."

He lay her down on the bed, then circled the room, running his fingertip over every wall, checking for a secret door. Nyx let him do it, not bothering to tell him she'd checked after he'd left earlier, scared that Grigoris had been lured out of the room so Petro could attack her a second time. Staying on the bed, she stripped down to the sports bra and panties she'd put on before heading downstairs. She tossed her clothes over the nightstand where they'd be in easy reach.

When he was satisfied, he came to bed, stripping off his shirt. He kept the knife strapped to his arm, and seeing him shirtless and deliciously dangerous, thanks to the straps of the sheath wrapping around the sexy muscles of his forearms, made her body heat in a way that was newly familiar.

Grigoris lay on his side, facing her. He traced a single finger down the midline of her body, starting at her nose. She nipped his finger as it slid over her lips, moaned as it teased her cleavage, and held her breath as his finger slid down her belly, lower, lower...

...only to stop at the waistband of her panties.

Nyx's eyes popped open.

Grigoris was grinning down at her. "Get some sleep, *ángelos.*"

"You are quite evil."

Grigoris chuckled as he lay back, gathering her against his chest. She thumped her fist against his stomach, but he'd seen it coming and tightened his stomach muscles, so it probably hurt her more than him.

"Do not doubt how much I want you," he whispered against her hair. "But we aren't safe, and the next time I make love to you, I want to take my time. I want to look at you. I want the room lit by a thousand candles so I can see every inch of your skin, watch your expression as I pleasure you."

Her irritation dissolved under a wave of arousal so strong that her nipples tightened inside the confines of her tight sports bra.

"I want you too." The words were so pale and simple, not at all representative of how she felt.

Grigoris kissed her hair and pulled the blanket over them. Despite her arousal, her awareness of the way his bare skin felt under her cheek, Nyx's eyes closed and she drifted off.

Her last thought before she finally fell asleep was that he'd called it making love.

Love.

At last.

CHAPTER TWELVE

W hen Nyx awoke, she suffered a brief flash of panic as she tried to recall where she was. Grigoris' room in the harsh, bright light of day looked very different from the soft, warm dimness of night.

The guest room was certainly reflective of the admiral's home. The elegant furnishings, including this oak four-poster bed, had been chosen with the utmost care, so visitors were constantly reminded of their host's immense wealth.

She blinked her eyes several times, fighting to focus. When she did, she realized Grigoris was no longer in the bed.

Nyx sat up quickly, startled, a soft cry of distress escaping.

Her sudden movement drew the attention of Grigoris, who'd been sitting—shirtless—at an antique raised panel roll-top desk in the corner. He had been tapping away furiously on his laptop, but seeing her awake, he crossed the room to her in a half dozen long strides.

While she felt rested and refreshed, it appeared Grigoris hadn't managed to shut his mind off enough to sleep.

The dark circles she'd seen last night as he'd investigated the shooting were even darker, and his face was creased with deep worry lines. He sank down on the mattress beside her.

"Are you well?" he asked.

She ignored his question. "You didn't sleep," she said, her words almost an accusation.

"I managed to rest for a couple hours."

"That's not enough." She reached for him, cupping his cheek in her hand. "You should lie down."

He shook his head. "I've been building a case against Nikolett, researching her career, cataloging her travel, her connections, but there are too many gaps, too many parts that don't match up to the mastermind."

"Put it away for now, *iroa mou*." She used his native language for her term of endearment. In Greek, she was his angel. And he was her hero.

Her savior.

Grigoris ran his fingers through her hair, the soft expression in his eyes telling her how much her words meant to him. "There's still too much to do, Nyx."

She understood his frustration, felt it. Grigoris had spent months caring for her. Now she had the opportunity to take care of him.

"And there is time to do it. But not now."

Grigoris looked like he would continue to argue, until she reached out and ran her fingers down his chest, toying with his brown nipples as she did so.

The fires had been banked last night—actually, this morning—as their exhaustion had overwhelmed their desires. Nyx wouldn't, couldn't, be denied again. She'd spent a lifetime in theoretical study when it came to sex. There was a time for books, but that time had passed.

"Will you join me in bed?" she asked. "I know how to help you relax."

Grigoris' lips tipped up in a sexy grin. "Oh, I know you do."

Nyx resisted the urge to smile. It was unusual for someone to tease her, to joke with her. She had accepted long ago that her serious nature intimidated others, seemed to discourage easy laughter and playfulness.

Lately, Josephine had started to breach some parts of those walls, but Grigoris had scaled them all, right from the beginning.

"Take off your pants," she directed him.

Part of her expected Grigoris to continue to resist, to insist on continuing the investigation. So she was surprised when he rose from the side of the bed, unfastened his pants, and shoved them off.

He stood before her gloriously nude, but he made no move to join her on the bed. When his gaze slid lower, she understood why.

Nyx slipped off her sports bra, enjoying Grigoris' soft intake of breath as she revealed her breasts to him. Then she slid her fingers into her panties, lifted her ass, and pulled the lacy underwear off.

Grigoris placed a knee on the mattress, intent on taking control, but she shook her head.

"No," she said quickly. "I am helping you relax. Remember?"

Grigoris was unlike any man she'd ever known. Petro and her father were men of action, old-fashioned, chauvinistic. Neither of them would dream of taking orders from a woman.

Her beautiful janissary respected and trusted her, and he showed it in countless ways. However, now, when he lifted his hands out, palms up in surrender, her heart nearly burst with happiness...and love.

"Sit on the bed, in the middle," she commanded. "And cross your legs."

Grigoris moved with purpose, assuming the position she'd suggested.

Once his legs were crossed, she positioned herself in front of him, mirroring his body.

"Have you ever practiced tantra?" she asked.

"No," Grigoris said.

"The word tantric is from ancient Sanskrit. It literally means to weave energy."

Grigoris gave her a tired smile. "Energy sounds good."

Nyx placed her palms on her knees and Grigoris followed suit. She spoke slowly, softly, as she explained. "Tantra is a way to enlightenment. It's a way to transcend the spiritual and the sexual through meditation. It's about physical and spiritual awareness. I have practiced it alone for many years." She hesitated before adding, "I would like to experience it with you."

"Show me," he whispered.

Nyx intended to start as they were, facing each other on the bed. Though they were so close their knees nearly touched, the distance felt too great.

So instead, she shifted forward, until she was sitting on his thighs, her ankles crossed behind his back. "This is called the lotus." In this position, she could feel his heat. His cock was thick and hard against the valley of her pussy, the head nudging her stomach slightly.

She held his gaze. "Match your breathing to mine. And don't look away."

Nyx drew in a deep breath, holding it for several seconds before releasing it. Grigoris was with her on the next intake, the two of them breathing in unison, his kind eyes focused on hers.

She could get lost in his eyes.

They remained there for several minutes, neither of them speaking. Words weren't necessary. The tension she'd recognized in the set of Grigoris' shoulders relaxed. She felt his body begin to loosen, the same tranquility she felt reflected in him.

Nyx moved first, lifting her hands to his shoulders, drawing them over the thick muscles, letting herself feel the texture of his skin, the coarseness of the hair covering his arms. She leaned closer on the next intake of breath, drawing in the smell of him, the faint scent of his soap, the piquant aroma of his body. Over and over, she slid her hands over his arms, leaving no part of them untouched.

Through it all, Grigoris remained still, his eyes locked with hers, his chest rising and falling in time with hers.

When her hands returned to her knees, Grigoris took his turn, though he didn't start with her arms. Instead, he reached out to cup her breasts, feeling the weight of them in his palms before he started to knead them. His thumbs circled her tight nipples until it was nearly impossible for Nyx to keep her eyes on him. She wanted to close them, wanted to purr, wanted to arch her back to stretch closer to his touch.

Like her, he took his time, touched every part of her breasts. A soft sigh escaped her lips.

She caught the slight upturn of Grigoris' lips a split second before his gentle ministrations turned wicked. He pinched her nipples. Hard.

Her easy breathing became labored in an instant.

Grigoris released her nipples, palming her breasts in his large, calloused hands. "Breathe," he murmured, drawing her back to him, to them. It took several attempts until she managed to match her breathing to his once more.

Once she had, his hands returned to his knees.

It was her turn.

Though Grigoris claimed he'd never had tantric sex, he mastered it quickly. For the next hour, the two of them simply explored, leaving no part of the other untouched, neither of them forgetting it would take very little effort for him to lift her onto his rock-hard erection, to give in to the desires that had her body pulsing and throbbing almost painfully.

When Grigoris finally kissed her, Nyx thought she would explode, the pressure of his lips on hers, the taste of him so vivid, so inviting. Neither of them sought to break the kiss, both taking the time to learn each other's mouths. She ran her tongue along the roof of his mouth, stroked his teeth, nipped at his lips, and Grigoris did the same.

When they parted, Grigoris placed a strong hand on her shoulder, pressing her until she lay on her back, her legs stretched wide as he knelt between them.

He held her gaze briefly as he parted her labia, then he looked down. Nyx fought to control her breathing once more as Grigoris studied her.

"*Omorfi theá,*" he whispered in Greek.

Beautiful goddess.

With him, she felt beautiful, celestial, holy.

Grigoris pressed two fingers deep inside her, curling them until he found the spot he was seeking.

Nyx arched, her eyes closing in bliss. One more stroke and she'd be there.

One more stroke and...

"Don't give in to it," Grigoris demanded. "Push your orgasm away."

Her eyes flew open. She began to tell him that wasn't possible, but she knew it was necessary. She'd been the one to initiate tantric sex. Orgasm control was part of that.

It had been easy for her to control her orgasms when she was masturbating alone. However, now, with Grigoris, she realized she'd never truly been tested.

He stroked her G-spot again. Nyx fought to clamp it down, every muscle in her body going stiff with the effort. She clenched her eyes closed, gritted her teeth, held her breath until she was able to stave off the orgasm.

She started to open her eyes, to smile victoriously, but Grigoris wasn't finished. He grazed her G-spot once more before bending lower to suck her clitoris into his mouth.

She cried out loudly, her hips rising from the bed. Her body was forsaking her. Nyx trembled as she clenched her hands into the bed sheets.

"Please," she begged breathlessly.

Grigoris pressed a third finger inside her, stretching her, but he was careful not to touch her G-spot again. Not that it helped.

Nyx had spent the last hour attempting to show Grigoris how to relax. He'd destroyed all that hard work in seconds. Every part of her was tense, fighting against something she wanted more than her next breath.

"Please," she whispered again, weakly.

Grigoris loosened the suction on her clit, then slowly extracted his fingers from her body.

It took several moments before Nyx could find the strength to open her eyes, to look at him. When she did, she expected to see some semblance of satisfaction.

What she saw was naked desire tinged with the same overwhelming, intense, painful need she was suffering.

Nyx bolted upright, taking Grigoris by surprise. They weren't finished here. Not by a long shot.

She twisted them until their positions were reversed. He was on his back, she was kneeling between his legs.

"Nyx." Her name sounded like a plea...and a prayer.

She bent over him, running her tongue along the underside of his cock. It was the one part of him left to explore. She'd saved the best for last.

Nyx cupped his balls in her hand, playing with them as she continued to lick his cock. Grigoris attempted to lie still throughout her ministrations, but the way his fists were clenched by his sides, the tautness of his body, betrayed him, told her she was doing everything right.

"Don't give in to it," she said, repeating his demand, mere seconds before she took the head of his cock into her mouth.

He groaned.

Nyx took him deeper, smiling when he muttered, "*irgalmazz*" in Hungarian. She didn't have a clue how he knew to beg for mercy in her native language, but it only made her want to drive him crazier.

She took him to the back of her throat, one hand wrapped around the base of his dick as the other cupped his balls.

She continued to move her lips along his shaft, increasing the suction until Grigoris gripped the side of her face, holding her still.

Nyx's eyes lifted to his.

"I'm only human," he said, his rueful grin touching her heart.

Nyx released him, pushing herself up in a sitting kneel. "I was hoping to massage your prostate as well. I have read that men find great pleasu—"

Before she could finish, Grigoris had flipped her to her

back on the bed once more, his cock nudging at the entrance to her body, pressing forward, deeper.

Both of them released their held breath in unison when he was fully seated inside her.

Grigoris cupped her cheeks in his hands and kissed her passionately, hungrily.

Nyx lifted her legs, locking her ankles around his hips. When the kiss ended, she sensed Grigoris holding back.

"Tell me what you want," she whispered.

"This isn't about what I want."

"I don't understand."

Grigoris' voice was hoarse, as if he was in pain. "I want to be gentle. I want to protect you. But, Nyx, right now..."

Enlightenment dawned, and she smiled, ignoring the way her scarred face protested the expression. "Take me the way you want, *íroa mou*. I want the same. With you, I'm no longer so numb from the cold that I can't feel anything but fear and loneliness. You make me ache and burn, but you do not hurt me."

Grigoris kissed her once more, hard, possessive. Then he released the reins and gave in to his baser instincts. He withdrew from her body, returning with a hard, deep thrust that sent waves of electricity throughout her body.

Nyx didn't even try to hold back her orgasm this time. Instead, she gave in to it, let it crash over her, drowning in the pleasure. Then she let him drag her to shore, only to shove her back into the rolling swells again. And again.

The third time she fell, he was there with her, her name on his lips, his come filling her.

It was rough and brutal.

And all she'd ever wanted.

Nyx opened her eyes, staring up at the ceiling. Glancing at the clock, she realized she'd only slept an hour.

Grigoris lay next to her on his side, his hand resting on her breast. She smiled at the slight twinge between her thighs. She was sore, but she would never complain about it. In fact, if she didn't realize how badly Grigoris needed the sleep, she would twist the man to his back, straddle his hips, and take him inside again.

Slowly extracting herself from the bed, she gathered her clothing and dressed. The house was quiet. She could only assume that the rest of the guests at the estate were dozing as well, after their sleepless night.

With Petro and Hanna at the hospital—Grigoris had decided forcing Hanna to leave Petro's side was unwise, given the potential massive political fallout and potential perception issues—Nyx felt the need to do some investigating of her own. Walking to the bedroom door, she glanced back toward the bed. Grigoris was sound asleep and, given his state of exhaustion, she suspected he'd remain that way for at least an hour or two more.

Which gave her time.

Opening the door, she slipped into the hallway, returning to her room. Nyx wiped her damp palms on her pants as she leaned against the door. Her heart was racing, and while she tried, she failed to master the deep-breathing techniques she knew would help calm her.

Her eyes traveled around the room, stopping on the entrance to the secret passageway Petro had used last night, when he'd strangled her.

Nyx knew what she needed to do.

Shoving her panic aside, she ran her fingers along the

edge until she found the latch. It opened silently, and she slipped inside the narrow, concealed hallway. She almost lost her nerve as she tried to look down the narrow corridor, lit only by the light from her bedroom. She wasn't sure how long it was; there wasn't enough light to reveal the other end.

She returned to her room and grabbed her cell phone, turning on the flashlight function. With the help of the light, she traversed the tight passageway, constantly looking behind her, unable to shake the fear of being followed.

She breathed a sigh of relief when she reached the end until she discovered she was in Petro's bedroom. Petro had a secret passage that led to just one of the guest rooms. No doubt he placed anyone he wanted to spy on in that room.

She hadn't been in this room since the day of her wedding. Petro had taken her and Hanna on a tour of their new home, and he'd been particularly pleased to show them the bedroom the three of them would share.

Even now, bile rose to her throat, just as it had that day, when she'd fought back images of Petro touching her, kissing her...raping her. She couldn't even begin to imagine what her life would have been like if she hadn't managed to escape. If Lazar hadn't helped her.

What if Lazar was the mastermind?

Shoving the unwanted thoughts away, she fought to focus on her reasons for being here. Though the room was perfectly tidy, she couldn't be certain none of the servants would venture in here for some reason or other.

Nyx wasn't sure what she'd expected to find. Most likely nothing. The mastermind had proven to be a worthy adversary, one who had eluded capture time after time. If Petro was the mastermind, it was highly unlikely he'd have a manifesto or serial killer and bomber correspondences just lying around his bedroom.

Petro's walk-in closet was immaculate, every article of clothing hanging according to type, tuxedos on one side, expensive suits on another. Casual attire—blazers, lightweight jackets, sweaters, polo shirts, everything was organized according to style and color. She began with the built-in drawers, opening each in turn, careful not to disturb anything that might reveal the room had been searched. Apart from clothing, there was nothing in the drawers.

She turned back to the closet and started going over the clothes, checking pockets and shifting things aside to look at the wall behind. Shoes lined shelves along the bottom, all in perfect condition. She checked them next, but besides shoe forms in a few of the leather pieces, they were empty.

She stepped back, turning in a slow circle. Nyx suspected she was looking at hundreds of thousands of dollars' worth of clothing and shoes. And while that thought disgusted her, it certainly didn't prove Petro was anything more than the narcissist she'd always known him to be.

Leaving the closet, she went through the main chamber, the bedroom itself, checking under the bed, glancing in decorative boxes, and perusing the books on the bookshelf. She sucked in a breath when she opened the nightstand drawer. She had saved that drawer for last, her gut instinct warning her she might find something she didn't want to see.

She'd been right to avoid it.

Inside was a dog collar, whip, and a muzzle. Nyx, despite her recently lost status as a virgin, was not unaware of the role these items could play in consensual sex—one couldn't study religion without also studying sex, after all.

However, she doubted Petro used these on Hanna as part of consensual role play.

Closing the drawer, she walked to Hanna's "dressing room"—the walk-in closet with the small bed tucked in the corner—and searched it. Hanna's wardrobe was as expensive as Petro's. It was obvious the admiral liked dressing up his beautiful wife.

Hanna's "room" revealed very little about the woman. There were no photos of family or friends, no books, no journals, no personal knickknacks that might reveal a hobby or interest. Nyx felt a cold ball of ice form in her stomach as she realized just how lonely Hanna's life had been. What must it be like to live in this palatial place but have only this small space to call her own? The dressing room, which was large by the standards of any normal bedroom, let alone a closet, seemed to be shrinking, closing in. Had Hanna felt that, the sense of being trapped and alone?

But the other woman seemed to embrace her life with Petro, seemed to love the man, though Nyx couldn't decide if those emotions were genuine or manufactured by a world-class actress.

When her search yielded nothing, Nyx returned to the main bedchamber, which was, in reality, Petro's space, her gaze drawn to the door that led to what would have been her dressing room.

Nyx stood rooted, staring at it for several minutes, fighting back the irrational fear that told her if she walked into that room, she would be trapped there, forced into the life she'd run away from all those years ago.

"He isn't here," she whispered to herself.

With those words playing in her head, she steeled herself to make the journey across the room to open the door.

It was meticulously kept, with clean white bedding on the small mattress, the wood of the built-in drawers and cabinets glossy, and even a vase of fresh-cut flowers on the vanity, as if Petro had actually believed she would come home at any moment. On the nightstand was a photograph of her with

Petro and Hanna, taken right after their binding ceremony. Nyx couldn't recognize herself, couldn't find herself in the terrified face of the eighteen-year-old girl looking back at her. Walking to the nightstand, she picked up the framed photograph and threw it against the wall, the glass shattering. It would be evidence that she'd been here, but Nyx didn't care. The soulless man had placed the picture there for her to find, another reminder of whom she belonged to.

Her fears vanished, replaced by white-hot rage. It was time to finish the job.

She started opening drawers and unzipping the garment bags that hung from the racks. Hanna had told her that she occasionally bought dresses for her, and the proof of that was in the garment bags—beautiful, elegant gowns, most of them in shades of gold and silver. In the drawers, she found matching shoes, more than a few sets of lingerie, but for the most part, everything was empty. Or at least it felt empty, given its size, the dozen or so garment bags taking up a mere fraction of the hanging space.

She was about to leave when she decided to check under the bed. At first glance there was nothing there—but after letting her eyes adjust, she saw it.

Tucked in the back corner was a scuffed duffel bag that looked out of place.

Nyx reached for the oversized bag, pulling it out and placing it on the bed. It was heavier than she'd expected.

She unzipped it, curious about the contents.

Nyx frowned as she pulled out what appeared to be gun parts or accessories.

She and her fellow librarians had studied sniper equipment and tactics in an effort to understand how the American, Griffin Rutherford, had been able to do so much damage. There was a scope, a wind meter, binoculars, ammunition, a folded-up mat and a square sandbag, which accounted for the duffel's weight.

Nyx searched the closet again, but there was no gun.

Her heart started to pound. This was a gun kit, with everything but the gun. Was the missing gun the one that had been used last night?

Petro had been shot through his office window, but she couldn't recall Grigoris saying anything about the specifics of the weapon used. If he'd been shot from outside, did that mean it had to have been a long-range weapon? She looked at the pieces, sure that these went with a rifle, rather than a handgun.

She returned to the bed and sat down next to everything she'd found. She needed to pack it up and carry the duffel to Grigoris' room. Perhaps he could glean additional information from what she'd discovered.

She picked up the sandbag, but it slipped slightly, as she'd misjudged the weight of it. The sound of paper crinkled under her fingers. Examining the bag more closely, she realized there was a zippered pocket in the side. Unzipping it, she pulled out several large sheets of paper, folded and tucked inside.

She recognized the black silhouette of a man on targets that were standard at every shooting range in the world. These used targets had clearly been kept, though given the placement of the bullet holes, Nyx wasn't sure why. On the center of the body, there were numbered circles—seven, eight, nine—all leading to X marks the spot in the middle.

None of the holes on these sheets had hit any rings of the target. Instead, they all pierced the right shoulder of the figure.

Nyx inhaled sharply.

Petro had been shot in the right shoulder.

Grigoris said Petro's injury wasn't self-inflicted, but that didn't mean he hadn't orchestrated it. Hadn't planned the shooting, and made sure the person with the gun was skilled enough to hit a non-vital but still serious spot. His right shoulder, rather than left, which would be too close to the heart, held no major organs, and if his lung was damaged, it was one of a pair.

She looked at the top target sheet again. Studying it, she caught sight of something small penciled in on the lower-right corner.

A date. Written in an elegant feminine hand.

And written in Polish.

Hanna's first language was Polish.

She considered Hanna's room, the dual sense of loneliness and confinement.

Nyx knew what lengths she herself had gone to in order to escape her fate.

But how far would Hanna go to escape hers?

Suddenly, Nyx wasn't so sure this was about the mastermind at all.

CHAPTER THIRTEEN

Grigoris was rudely awakened when something heavy dropped onto his stomach, forcing the air from his lungs.

He lunged up, moving through the pain, shoving whatever was pinning him off to the side as he whipped his knife from the sheath. He stopped the blade mere centimeters from Nyx's throat.

She ignored the blade. "Hanna is the shooter."

Grigoris collapsed back on the bed, panting in horror. "I almost stabbed you."

"You wouldn't have stabbed me. Hanna shot Petro."

"I could have stabbed you." Grigoris lifted his head. "I came at you with a knife. Are you all right?" After what she'd been through, having a knife that close to her body had to trigger some bad memories.

Nyx looked down at him in irritation. "I don't have time for unnecessary emotional reactions. Hanna is the shooter, and potentially the mastermind."

"Unnecessary..." Grigoris sheathed his knife and then threw his arm over his face. His heart was still racing.

"Hmm, no, she might be too young to be the mastermind. Then again, discounting someone based on youth might be a folly." Nyx lifted his arm, peering down at him. "It appears you aren't fully awake. Would it help if I slapped you?"

"Don't slap me."

"Then get up and pay attention."

Grigoris sat up, a sense of déjà vu taking him by surprise. It took only a moment to realize that this conversation reminded him of when he'd first met Nyx. The thought made him smile. It was nice to see her returning to her former self.

Nyx stared at him. "Are you sure slapping you wouldn't assist in waking you up?"

Grigoris slid one arm around her waist and jerked her onto the bed. She landed on his lap with a surprised squeak. He kissed her long and deep, and when he was done, she was the one who seemed not quite awake. With a smirk, he slid out from under her, quickly pulling on some clothes before turning back.

She was fully dressed, and the heavy thing she'd dropped on him turned out to be a battered black duffel bag. His amusement turned to outrage.

"You went out without me? Nyx, that was dangerous."

"Hmmm?" She touched her lips with her fingertips.

The caveman part of him was happy he could distract her so thoroughly. The knight part of him wanted to shake some sense into her.

"Nyx, focus," he commanded.

She blinked, then looked at him. Her eyes narrowed. "You did that on purpose."

"Payback, for making me almost stab you."

"You wouldn't have stabbed me."

Her faith in him was...alarming. "You shouldn't have left the room without telling me."

"You are not my keeper."

"No, I'm your bodyguard, and I can't guard your body unless it stays with me."

"You needed sleep."

This was going nowhere. "Why do you think Hanna is the shooter? Where did you go?"

"I went to Petro's room. The master suite."

"*Skatá*, Nyx!"

"Stop cursing and look in the bag."

Grigoris jerked the duffel to the edge of the bed and ripped open the zipper, his irritation at her fueled by his fear that something could have happened to her, making his movements short and choppy. He looked into the bag and froze. "This was in Hanna's room?"

"Actually, it was in my room." Her lips twisted as she said the words.

"Your bedroom in the master suite?"

"Petro would not allow his wives their own bedrooms," she said with a sneer in her voice. "But the master suite has two large dressing rooms, huge closets with small beds in them. I'm assuming that sleeping in those beds, rather than in the massive bed in the main room, is intended as some sort of punishment."

Grigoris wanted to haul her into his arms, to promise her, even if he had no right to make that promise, he would keep her safe. That she would never have to see Petro again.

If Petro is the mastermind, I can kill him.

If I say he's the mastermind, kill him, and then it turns out he isn't, Petro would still be dead. Then I could blame the real mastermind for orchestrating my mistake.

Those disconcerting thoughts were both abhorrent and tempting.

"These are pieces for a long-range rifle. It would fire .223 rounds."

"Is that what shot Petro?"

"According to Ivan. I need to call and get an update."

"Lazar or Hans might have spoken to Petro, or at least to Hanna."

"True." Grigoris ran a hand through his hair.

Nyx reached into the bag and pulled out folded target papers. She carefully unfolded them, laying them on the bed then watching him with an air of expectation.

He flipped through them, blood starting to hum with adrenaline. Each target showed a cluster of shots in the right shoulder, almost exactly where Petro had been hit. Nyx pointed to the handwriting in the corner.

"This is Polish. Hanna's first language, though by the time I knew her, she predominantly spoke Hungarian."

"Hanna is the shooter," Grigoris cursed. "And she left with the admiral. He might be in danger."

"He *is* in danger. I think she may also be the mastermind."

Grigoris wanted to agree. He wanted it to be that simple. But it wasn't. Nothing about this was simple. "Or, she doesn't love him and saw an opportunity to kill him, to free herself, and hope the blame would fall on the mastermind."

Nyx looked down at her hands. "It's not a bad plan."

Grigoris searched through the bag a second time, then glanced at Nyx. "You said you found this in your room?"

"Yes."

"*Skatá.*"

"What?" Nyx asked.

"She might be planning to frame you for the shooting. You show up after years of avoiding Petro and he's shot."

Nyx's eyes went round with shock. "But I wouldn't write a date in Polish."

"Do you speak Polish?"

"Some."

"Nyx..."

Nyx bounced to her feet and started to pace. "If she's the shooter, she could have written the date in a language we both know, but people might assume would be hers. Then she placed the gun accessories in my room to make it seem like I was planning to frame *her*, instead of her framing me."

Nyx stilled, frowning. "But then why wouldn't she put the gun pieces in her own closet? If I were framing her, wouldn't it make more sense for me to plant evidence there?"

"Yes, and no. It could be Hanna isn't involved at all," Grigoris said. "There's a saying—when you hear hoofbeats, a horse is more likely than a zebra."

"She hates me," Nyx said quietly. "She said before they left that she'd see me burn."

"Damn it," Grigoris cursed. "That points more to her trying to frame you for shooting Petro rather than to her being the mastermind. And I keep coming back to timing..."

"But if she's such a good shot, why didn't she kill Petro? If she hates him, why not shoot him in the head?" Nyx remembered what he'd said and parroted his words back.

Grigoris opened his mouth, closed it. "We have too many possibilities and not enough answers."

"Unless," Nyx said slowly. "Unless Petro planned it with Hanna. He had Hanna shoot him in a nonlethal spot, made her practice first. That way he was removed from suspicion."

"Hanna wouldn't have had time to circle around..." Grigoris stopped, frowning. "Unless she came in directly through the shattered window. A straight shot, a quick sprint, and she hides in the room, waits for the first responder to run out looking for help, then she goes to Petro, pretending she just slipped in. It's tricky but possible."

"Don't forget about the bomb in the helicopter. He would have been on that helicopter when the bomb went off if we hadn't gone searching for it."

"And he could have planned for that," she insisted but then frowned. "Bomb-making seems to be a more unique skill than proficiency with firearms."

"Agreed, and dogs went over the whole property. If Hanna, or Petro, was hiding explosive materials, the dogs would have found them."

"Then Petro had one of his pet bomb-makers plant the bomb. Maybe the bomb was on the helicopter the whole time."

"That's convoluted and complicated planning," Grigoris said gently.

"Which is what the mastermind has been doing."

"I know you want it to be him," Grigoris said. In truth, he wanted it to be Petro too. "But it would be too easy to twist the evidence to fit the theory. Right now, my major concern is that you are being set up."

Nyx's composed confidence had fractured, and she stepped closer to him. "What do we do next?"

Grigoris wrapped an arm around her and kissed the top of her head. "We get more information. It's time to wake some people up and start asking questions."

"What do you want me to do?"

Grigoris looked down at her. "You stay with me. I don't trust anyone right now. We remain together."

Nyx nodded, her cheek rubbing his. "Are we starting with Nikolett? I don't want it to be her."

"No," Grigoris said. "We're going to talk to Lazar. You have good instincts, and the fact that you were worried about what he said tells me we need to talk to him again."

"What do we do with the duffel?" she asked.

Grigoris repacked the bag, zipping it shut. "Show me that secret passage."

"AH, feck ye for a game of soldiers."

"You know there is no game, Colum?" Josephine asked, twiddling one of the knotted strings on her peasant blouse. She was bored, and had been ever since Eric had assigned her the task of working with her brother in the archive in Dublin. Meanwhile, all the other librarians were out in the field, investigating suspects, searching for clues.

Darn Eric and his overprotectiveness. While the fleet admiral would never admit it, she was certain he'd given her this task because he was trying to keep her out of harm's way. Given the fact Karl and Nyx had been put in very dangerous and nearly deadly situations while doing their parts to track down the mastermind in Bucharest, she could understand that, but it didn't please her to be stuffed in some...well... stuffy archive.

"There's no actual game," he grumped, looking up from the paper he was examining. He had on a jeweler's headset and one of his eyes looked huge, thanks to the magnification.

Josephine rolled her eyes. She loved her brother dearly, but he was confusing as hell. "What are you looking at?"

"Letters from members to past fleet admirals. I'm looking for any that show dissatisfaction with the way the organization is run."

"Ooooo. Anything juicy? Gossip?"

"I can't read the fecking handwriting."

"Lemme look," she said, trying to shove her brother out of the way. He was immovable, unwilling to give up his seat. "Come on," she pleaded. "You never let me see anything."

"I'm the archivist."

"Yeah, and that and two pounds will get you a box of Barry's."

"Get on with ya," he grumped again, peering at the faded cursive handwriting on a very old-looking piece of paper.

"Eric sent me here to help you. You aren't letting me help, you gobshite." She'd come straight to the archive after Eric had held his Viking traitors meeting. She'd helped him come up with the name, and even now it still made her giggle, though there was nothing funny about what they were trying to do. She wished Eric had given her a more exciting assignment. Sending her to work with her brother in the archives was the equivalent to watching paint dry. And all they had to show for their efforts was...nothing. So far, only a few people had come looking for information, and the likelihood that some old letter would hold the key to the current problem was slim.

"I don't know why he sent you here, except to feck with me. Everything I have is thirty years old and older. I don't have emails, and if this daft fucker is alive now, and was stupid enough to have emailed Kacper something about how he hated him, I wouldn't have a record of that."

Josephine sighed. "Give me the letter. Let me do something. I'm going out of my mind here, boyo."

Colum sighed and reached into a case, pulling out a second letter encased in two thin, rigid pieces of plastic. "Here. Read this."

Josephine scanned the paper, silently agreeing with her

brother. The handwriting was nearly illegible. But it was better than looking at the top of Colum's head, listening to him grumble and curse all day. She turned to a clean sheet of paper in her notebook and picked up a pencil, ready to transcribe the entire thing. If she could.

Was that first letter an A or an H?

Several hours later, Josephine sat up, stretching her back even as she frowned. So far what the letters had told her was that most objections from the membership had to do with the Masters' Admiralty's involvement, or lack thereof, in various political issues of the day. So far, the one thing they *hadn't* run up against was any sort of political motivation.

"Fancy going to get a pint at the pub with me? I need to give my eyes a rest," she said when it got too hard to focus on the page.

Colum didn't even look up from the paper, shaking his head.

"Maybe I'll just take a walk then. We've been sitting here for hours. Wanna come with me? Even vampires need fresh air every now and again."

Colum waved her away. "Just bring me some."

"Bring you some fresh air?"

"Food, drink, whatever." Colum jotted some notes on a pad of paper, then selected another letter from the case beside him.

Josephine sighed. She'd eaten alone every night since she'd started working with her brother at the archive. Not that she should have been surprised by that. Colum didn't do people, in general, and as far as she knew, she was the only one—with the exception of Eric—who occasionally got eye contact and two minutes of real conversation.

She smiled down at the top of his head, feeling affection for the oaf. Then she bent over and placed a kiss on his brow.

Colum swatted her away like she was a bothersome gnat. "Get on with ye. You know I hate that shite."

Josephine laughed, and in true annoying little sister style, she kissed him again on the cheek. "I love you too, Colum, ye gobshite."

"*Imigh uaim*," he muttered.

Josephine laughed at his usual, un-endearing way of saying go away instead of goodbye. "You're going to miss me when I'm gone," she singsonged...her usual reply.

She left him alone in the archive, debating whether or not to have the chipper or Chinese takeaway.

CHAPTER FOURTEEN

I t was late afternoon by the time Grigoris was able to speak to Lazar. His attendant Patty had given the vice admiral something to help him sleep, and Grigoris hadn't been willing to go so far as to slap the sick old man awake.

By then, he'd spoken with most of the other guests, and let anyone who wasn't a member of the Masters' Admiralty go. His afternoon round of interrogations had included Nikolett, who had questioned him as much as he'd questioned her.

Fedir's questioning of the staff had been slightly more productive. Petro's estate had a live-in staff of four people, plus the full-time residents, Petro, Hanna, and, surprisingly, Lazar himself. The four staff members included an estate manager, cook, chauffeur who was also a pilot, and Patty, who also served as assistant to the estate manager. Those four individuals had rooms in what Grigoris was now referring to as the servants' wing of the house. In it were six small bedrooms, a restaurant-style kitchen—separate from the smaller kitchen Petro and Hanna had for their personal use—

and industrial laundry facilities as well as the estate manager's office.

The servants' wing was only accessible from the rest of the mansion via a single door in a back hall. Besides that, there were four entrances that opened directly onto the grounds, but the servants' wing was on the opposite side of the massive building from Petro's office.

Two full-time maids came in on a daily basis but didn't live on-site. There were also gardeners and vintners and a roster of regular service people—exterminators, plumbers, electricians—who all used one of the servant entrances, usually going to the estate manager's office to check in.

That was a whole lot of people who knew how to enter and exit the estate without tripping a door alarm. Grigoris had developed an eye twitch when he found out that, though the entrances to the servants' wing were connected to the house's security system, the doors usually weren't alarmed, given both the odd hours most of the staff kept—the chef usually arrived before dawn to make bread for the day—and how often they went in and out. The security system alerted the guards when a door was opened or closed and told them which door had been opened.

Apparently, the annoyance of having the system constantly chiming was of greater concern than the utter lack of security. It was bad enough that there weren't any cameras on or in the house itself, but to have four unmonitored doors was beyond ludicrous. Petro didn't seem like a stupid man. An evil, misogynistic asshole? Yes. Stupid? No.

That meant it was hubris that was responsible for the glaring breach in security. It also meant that Hans and Lazar hadn't had the balls to stand up to Petro and demand that he maintain better security.

As the chorbaji, he was the leader of the janissaries and

technically reported to Eleni, the vice admiral of the Ottoman territory. If Hande's residence had such shit security, he would have said something. Eleni would have said something.

And that brought up another good point—Petro was using the knights for personal security. While there wasn't a problem with that, and most admirals had a knight or two stationed in whatever city they called home, the knights weren't meant to be personal security. They were the law and order of the territory, and that usually meant traveling to wherever they were needed, dealing with whoever had broken the rules, protecting members who were in danger.

Once again, Grigoris was questioning himself. Maybe he was just looking for reasons to hate Petro. But it wasn't just hate, he feared the man too. Not for himself but for Nyx. Every time he considered how differently Nyx's life would have been if she hadn't managed to escape, it made his blood run cold.

Grigoris' working theory of the crime was that the shooter had, rather than run away from the house, run around the building and slipped in via an entrance in the servants' wing, then back into the main house by the back hall.

Two additional chefs had been brought in to help prepare last night's meal, and they'd been the last people to leave through the main gates, several hours after the few guests who hadn't stayed had departed. Every bedroom in the house was occupied, and a relief guard had been sleeping in one of the two unoccupied servant bedrooms. That brought the total number of people in the house to over twenty.

Very few people had verifiable alibis, which wasn't unexpected. They'd all been asleep alone.

The estate manager had mentioned seeing Hanna in the servants' wing not long before the shooting, but said she'd come to ask that someone take care of the dress she'd worn to dinner, which had a stain on it. Since Hanna had left with Petro—after he'd told her not to—he had no way to ask her where she'd been and possibly catch her in a lie.

Lazar's attendant Patty appeared in Petro's office, which Grigoris had taken over as his command center. With the broken window and bloodstained carpet, no one else had been eager to spend any time in the room, which meant he and Nyx had privacy. It also meant he'd been able to search through Petro's desk and books. He'd found a few documents relating to the Masters' Admiralty membership and business, but most of what was in there was related to Petro's various businesses and real estate holdings. Some of them were owned by the territory, which appeared to have a functioning corporation as a front for the secret society, but most were Petro's personal assets.

If Grigoris was reading this right—or more accurately, reading Nyx's translations right—the man was a billionaire, with most of that wealth amassed in the last ten years. Before that, it seemed he was relying on the admiral stipend paid by the Masters' Admiralty to cover his personal expenses, and this estate had been on loan from one of the wealthier members of the territory, a Ukrainian mining tycoon who owned real estate all over Eastern Europe. The Ukrainian man had died eight years ago, killed in what had been ruled a political hit. He'd left this house to Petro personally, as well as a few other properties, including land in Romania outside Bucharest, large parcels in Bulgaria, and Moldova.

Grigoris had to consult a map to be sure, but some of the properties Petro owned were firmly in the Ottoman territory. There was no law that prevented members from working or owning land in territories other than their own, but as a knight of Ottoman, he didn't like that the admiral of Hungary owned property in his territory, and he hadn't known about it. Common courtesy would demand that Petro tell Hande about any real estate interests that crossed the not entirely precise border between Ottoman and Hungary, which cut through Ukraine, Moldova, Romania—and in particular, divided the capital city of Bucharest—Bulgaria, and the easternmost edge of Greece.

"Janissary?" Patty asked hesitantly.

Grigoris rose, glancing at Nyx, who had taken a seat in one of two armchairs and was flipping through a file and making notes in English, as her written English was far better than her written Greek.

Nyx carefully tucked the pad of paper into the folder before closing it, then rose and came to Grigoris' side. Patty looked relieved and turned to address Nyx in Hungarian. Nyx nodded, before translating. "Lazar is awake and able to talk to us now."

"Good. We'll go to him."

The attendant led them through the house to a first-floor bedroom suite. It was an odd mix of elegant furnishings and medical equipment.

Nyx turned to Patty, and they exchanged a few words. Lazar was hunched and looked small and weak.

What did it mean that Petro had a vice admiral whose health most likely didn't allow him to perform his duties? There was no other admiral in the Masters' Admiralty who would allow their second-in-command to continue in their position if they were this infirm.

Nyx dismissed the attendant, then leaned into him as they walked across the room, whispering, "Lazar has an autoimmune disorder. It's caused severe rheumatoid arthritis."

"Lupus?" he asked.

She frowned. "It's never lupus."

"You said disorder, not disease," Grigoris said.

Nyx raised a brow but stayed focused on Lazar. "His doctors think the condition may have been caused by drugs. There is drug-induced lupus, but apparently this isn't quite that. Patty tried to get him to go to a clinic in Switzerland that is doing research, but he won't leave the territory."

"Drug induced," Grigoris breathed.

Nyx looked at him. "You're thinking about the former fleet admiral, Kacper."

"Yes."

"Don't whisper, it's rude," Lazar said in English. They'd been speaking Greek. His voice sounded stronger than it had yesterday.

"I'm sorry, Lazar." Nyx went to his side, taking his hand and dropping into the chair beside him. "We didn't want to disturb you."

"Then you wouldn't be in my room." The words were sharp, but Lazar was smiling at Nyx.

She smiled, and it wasn't the half smile she'd been doing lately but a grin. The scar deformed the expression, and he could tell the moment she remembered, the moment she adjusted her mouth so as not to draw any more attention to the damage.

Lazar patted her hand, then gave it a squeeze. "How are you doing, Nyx?"

"I'm...I'm happy."

Nyx didn't look at him, but the words made him warm inside. While he was frustrated as hell and exhausted from traveling all over Europe in search of a madman, Grigoris realized he was happy as well.

"That is all I wanted for you. I'm glad you found it."

"Lazar, it's so good to talk to you. Yesterday, you seemed..."

"Insane? Old? Drugged?"

"Yes, all of those."

Lazar wheezed, clearly appreciating her honesty. "The medicine, the treatments, they affect me differently."

"Differently how?"

"I'm taking some trial drugs." Now Lazar looked away from Nyx, out the window. "I didn't take today's dose because this latest drug fogs my mind."

Nyx and Grigoris shared a look. "Your helper said you didn't want to go to Switzerland and participate in the trials."

"Checking up on me?" Lazar asked.

Nyx's expression was haunted. "I should have."

Lazar weakly waved that away. "No need, no need."

"Yesterday you said...you said that Petro didn't do anything you didn't deserve."

His expression shuttered and he leaned back in his chair. Grigoris winced. He should have taken over questioning. Nyx was too close to the situation. "I disobeyed my admiral."

"You mean when you helped me get away from him." Nyx's voice was vehement. "You saved me. You didn't deserve to be punished."

"You needed to be free. The man Petro used to be, when he was my friend...he would have seen that. But Petro changed when he became the admiral."

"Lazar, did Petro make you sick? Did he give you something to make you sick? Is that how he punished you for helping me?"

Lazar stared out the window and said nothing for a long time.

Grigoris knew how to wait. Nyx did not, but he was able to silence her with a look.

"No," Lazar said finally. "No. Petro is my friend. He is a good admiral. When I got sick, he took me into his home. He's made sure I have access to the best care."

Grigoris and Nyx exchanged another look. Nyx scooted to the edge of her chair, squeezing Lazar's hand. She switched to Hungarian and began speaking to Lazar in low tones. Grigoris backed away to give them some privacy.

Lazar himself had admitted the experimental medication he was on affected his mental state, but Grigoris couldn't help but feel that his last statement had been rehearsed, something said by rote. Maybe something Petro, or one of the people in this household, had forced him to say whenever he was questioned.

There was no denying that Lazar's illness was too similar to Kacper's for the similarity to be ignored.

Grigoris walked back. "Lazar, may I ask how long you've been sick?"

The vice admiral looked surprised, and answered, "Eight years."

Grigoris nodded in thanks and retreated. Nyx looked at him curiously, her pale eyes bright with intelligence. He could almost see her following his train of thought. She nodded and turned her attention back to Lazar.

Grigoris retreated and opened up an encrypted messaging app on his phone. He sent a message to Antonio, asking if he would be available later to set up a video conference call.

He couldn't help but roll his shoulders, trying to ignore the itchy sensation between his shoulder blades. With each moment that passed, he was more and more sure that the mastermind, or someone very close to the mastermind, was right here.

This time, he wasn't going to let them get away.

COLUM LOOKED up from another letter, stretching until he felt his vertebrae return to their normal positions. Eric had ordered him to be available to answer questions, which meant he had even more reason than usual to faff about, looking at old documents. He picked up his phone and considered sending something to Eric about how he'd changed his mind and wasn't going to answer any fecking questions. As the archivist, he was the one person in the Masters' Admiralty who could tell the fleet admiral to feck off. He wouldn't do it, not only because Eric didn't deserve any more stress right now but because he wanted to be useful.

Eric's inner circle, a motley collection of newly married trinities, were faced with a nearly impossible task. In the days since the fleet admiral had sent them out on their assignments, Colum had been doing nothing but work. Which was slightly different because normally his days were work, run, watch hurling, then work. He'd eliminated watching hurling and settled for running around Merrion Square rather than going to Phoenix Park. Every request for information had been answered immediately—though there were precious few—and in his downtime, he went through old records, in case there was something there that might help.

As long as he had Josephine to actually talk to the people, he was able to focus on finding, assessing, and cataloging information. Josephine answered the phone and handled all those social niceties he didn't understand, then, if she thought he'd better hear the information request himself, she passed him the phone. Of course, she only did that after blithely warning the caller that he didn't like people and could be a bit brusque. He'd glare at her, she'd smile, and then they'd get down to business.

Josephine, who could talk for Ireland, had been covering for him, lying for him, for years.

Colum secretly loved people—as long as he could read about them, rather than actually interact with them. His crippling social anxiety, born of a youth spent with nary a clue how to interact with people, had taught him that the best way to avoid awkward and humiliating interactions was to avoid people altogether. Much easier to bury his nose in a book and learn about people, and the world, that way.

It was a secret he and Josephine had kept even from Eric. Colum had been the one to break into Eric's house all those years ago. He hadn't just been after the books they'd glimpsed through the windows. Colum had been curious about the huge blond man but wouldn't dare talk to him. No, in Colum's mind, breaking into his house and snooping around, then stealing a few books, was a safer solution than a simple conversation.

Josephine had been the one to quickly think of a lie, saying that Colum was being "a bit of a shite." Colum had embraced that lie, hiding his awkwardness behind a gruffness and curse words he wouldn't have dared use in front of his mum. Now he had a reputation for being an ass, and it kept people away, stopped him from having to explain things he was too embarrassed to say aloud.

And it had all started that day when Eric had caught him. Josephine's quick thinking had worked, Eric hadn't ratted on them, and had instead let them treat his house like a lending library. He owed Eric for all the support he'd given them. Without the Scandinavian man, college wouldn't have been realistic, despite the fact that Irish citizens didn't have to pay for university. Eric's help had covered books and living expenses, all those things that weren't tuition and would have made a college degree financially out of reach.

Rising from his chair, he turned off the ring-light magnifying glass. It took a moment for his eyes to adjust, but once they did, he walked out of the light-tight preservation room. He locked the door with a fingerprint scanner and stretched again as he looked around the front office.

The archive occupied all five floors of a narrow building on Merrion Square. It would have once been a fashionable residence, but the gray stone attached buildings, which towered over the sunken green park-like space that was Merrion Square, were now occupied by architecture firms and high-profile organizations like the offices of the Royal College of Anesthesiologists. The plaque on the black front door of the archive said merely Admiralty Archive. Next door was the Irish Architectural Archive, and between the two of them, they'd retrofitted a chunk of the building with state-of-the-art fire suppression systems to guard their precious paper records.

The front office was on the main floor, which was actually half a flight of stairs up from street level. Occasionally they had a maritime enthusiast who came knocking on the door, thinking they had maritime records. The plaque on the door also declared they were by appointment only, but the front office had a fairly standard-looking desk, filing cabinets, and a calendar on the wall. If the curious peeked in, he wanted them to find his archive bland and boring. Then they'd go away and leave him, and his precious books and papers, alone.

Looking at the window, he realized more time had passed than he'd realized. It was dusk, and thanks to a brief afternoon shower, the pavement sparkled, while Merrion Square itself seemed to glow green in the last rays of golden light of day.

It was long past lunchtime, and his stomach rumbled.

Josephine hadn't brought him back anything. He had to pause and think—had she popped her head in, and he'd just ignored her with the ease of long practice?

He jogged up the stairs to a small kitchenette just off the lone conference room one floor up. Because the remodeling of the building was public record, the archivist before him had chosen to make sure the building plan gave no one reason to doubt that it was anything other than a business and had therefore included a little breakroom, complete with kitchen. He liked having access to the kitchen because his flat on the very bottom floor—half a story below street level—could only be accessed from the footpath. This way, if he wanted a cup of tea, he didn't have to go outside, nip down to his own kitchen, and then run back up.

"Josephine?" he called out, then added, just to irk her, "Sorcha?" Josephine wasn't a traditional Irish name, and his grandmother had objected to it. She'd started calling Josephine "Jenny" before finally abandoning any pretense and using her traditionally Irish middle name of Sorcha. Josephine hadn't liked either Jenny or Sorcha. She'd always insisted they use her full first name. The one time he'd tried "Jo," she'd chased him around the farm with Vise-Grips.

He checked the counters and fridge for food in case his sister had brought something back and left it for him, but he discovered nothing that hadn't been there this morning.

"Sorcha?" he hollered again, closing the refrigerator door. He rarely called her by her middle name—it was a private thing, one used in times of seriousness or sadness, as using it always reminded them of Mamo.

Odd that he suddenly had the urge to use it.

He turned on the kettle and pulled his phone from his pocket to text her. His sister was brilliant but an utter scatterbrain. She'd probably gotten distracted or found someone interesting to talk to, and forgotten all about bringing him food.

Colum rubbed the back of his neck, frowning at the vague sense of disquiet that made his skin prickle.

Her phone rang once, then she answered.

He waited for her to speak, but there was no sound. He held the phone away from his ear and checked the signal strength. The call should be clear.

"Hello? Josephine?"

No answer.

"Josephine? *Sorcha, an bhfuil tú ceart go leor?*"

He thought he heard her breathing, and then the sound of air moving, like she was in a car with the windows down.

"I can't hear you, Josephine."

There was a burst of sound, something he almost thought was a splash, and then the call went dead. He redialed, but it went straight to voice mail.

What the hell had just happened?

The sense of disquiet was now pronounced. Eating at him. Had someone stolen her phone? Or was it just in her pocket, and she didn't even know she'd answered it? Colum paced back and forth, dialing her over and over again.

With a curse, he realized he had the login to track her phone. He wasn't thinking straight. He ran for his computer and logged into her account.

The last location the phone had recorded was near the Royal Canal, north of the river Liffey. Why would she have been north of the river?

He pinged the phone, having it sound an alert, then waited, hoping for his phone to ring as she dug the madly beeping device out of her purse or pocket and called him to ask what he was doing.

Nothing happened.

He paced, pausing every minute or so to either ping her phone or call it again.

Hoping turned to praying.

After fifteen minutes of nothing, his fingers were shaking so badly that he could barely scroll through his contacts to find the number he needed.

"Colum," Eric answered.

Colum opened his mouth but no sound came out. He closed his eyes, swallowed, and started to stammer out "She-she-she—"

"Are you drunk? I know you're Irish but—"

"Feck off!" Colum blurted out. He took a breath, in control of himself once more. "Josephine's missing."

There was silence, then Eric's words came out, low and scarily soft. "What do you mean missing?"

THE ESTATE MANAGER served a formal dinner that night. Grigoris got the sense that she didn't know what to do with this houseful of people who didn't want to be there, so she defaulted to plying people with food and drink.

The meal wasn't as elaborate as it had been the previous night, and the wineglasses were filled more often. Grigoris had one glass, which he nursed, while counting everyone else's consumption. Nikolett was slowly sipping her second glass of merlot.

Beside him, Nyx, along with several others, had a glass of Zwack before the meal started, but now she was having sparkling water, though she'd asked for it in a short glass, and he suspected she was hoping others might think it was an alcoholic beverage.

Lazar hadn't come to dinner, but Hans was there, and he

was starting to say things that made more than a few eyebrows raise.

"When I'm admiral, the first thing we'll do is install cameras in the house. For security."

"When you're admiral?" Nikolett asked.

"Do you think it would be you?" Hans guffawed.

Nikolett raised a single eyebrow.

"Is Petro dead?" Nyx asked bluntly.

A few people sucked in food or alcohol instead of air and started to cough.

Nikolett snickered.

Hans sneered at Nyx. "You'd like that, wouldn't you?"

"For you to confess to the attack? It would simplify things. And confirm my belief in your intelligence."

Hans' face flushed, and Nikolett howled with laughter. Grigoris shifted forward in his chair, ready to protect Nyx if Hans came for her.

"I didn't attack the admiral." Hans leveled a finger at Nyx, the florid color still riding his cheeks. "But with him wounded, someone will have to take control of the territory, and Lazar is a whipped dog. I will have to do it." Hans smiled wide. "And the first thing I'll do is make sure any disobedient little girls obey their marriage vows."

Nyx's expression didn't change. She was like a beautiful statue worked in gold and ivory, her pale eyes unnerving. In another time, another place, her beauty would have been too different, too strange.

Nikolett inhaled, carefully set down her wineglass, turned on Hans, and let loose. She'd switched to Hungarian—they'd been speaking English—but Grigoris didn't really need to understand what she said to know she was laying into the security minister. The expressions on the faces of the other people at the table told the story.

He was so engrossed in the drama that he almost didn't feel his phone vibrate in his pocket.

He fished it out, intending to silence it completely, when he saw who was calling.

Nyx shifted her attention to him when he rose, one brow lifted in question. He turned the screen so only she could see it. He knew the moment she read the display "Eric Ericsson" when her eyes widened before narrowing. He tipped his head toward Nikolett, who was still going, and Nyx turned her attention back to them. He trusted her to listen and hear not only what was said but what was left unsaid. After dinner, they'd pick it apart.

He didn't intend to spend another night at the estate. Once everyone else was in bed, he and Nyx were going to drive to the hospital where Petro and Hanna were.

It was time to question them.

He slipped into the hall and answered the phone, prepared to tell Eric both what he'd learned and what his plans were.

"Fleet Admiral, I have—"

"Get back to Dublin. I need you here."

"What?" Grigoris hadn't expected that.

"Leave Nyx. She's safer there. Get to Dublin." Eric's sentences were short, his words guttural.

"I won't leave Nyx," he said immediately. "What do you mean she's safer here?"

Eric inhaled and exhaled with audible slowness, almost as if he were mindfully controlling his breathing. It was a technique people used to stay calm.

What had happened that Eric needed to stay calm?

"Come to Dublin." That was an order, and Grigoris stiffened, but the fleet admiral's next words stopped him. "We need you here."

The call ended.

Grigoris returned to the dining room, already checking airline websites on his phone. There was a direct flight from Budapest to Dublin, leaving in two hours. If they hurried—and took a helicopter—they could make it.

CHAPTER FIFTEEN

The fleet admiral stared down at the basket, his mind perfectly blank, like an unmarked sheet of white paper. Soon enough, red would bleed through, red like the blood he was looking at, and once that happened, once the anger took control, he wouldn't be able to stay calm. Wouldn't be able to think clearly.

For now, he would hold on to the blank feeling, let it insulate him from the rage that was coming. The rage and the grief.

"They've landed, Fleet Admiral," Lancelot said quietly. The knight from England had flown in from London earlier to help with the search. The search for Josephine. It was the same reason Eric had called Grigoris, who was smart, deadly and, despite his size, able to both blend in and put people at ease.

Things had changed—everything had changed—since that phone call to Grigoris.

"They?" Eric asked softly.

"Nyx is with him."

"Don't let her in."

"I won't, Fleet Admiral." Lancelot paused. "Do you want me to wait here so you don't have to?"

"I'm staying."

Something in Eric's voice caused Lancelot to rear back. The rage was starting to seep through. Eric fought it back, his fingers curling into fists then relaxing rhythmically.

"I'll stay," Eric said, but more softly. He took a knee, far enough back to not contaminate, but close enough to provide protection. Protection that was no longer needed. Eric bowed his head and breathed deeply.

The air smelled like blood.

Grigoris wrapped his arm loosely around Nyx's back as they hurried across the cobblestones toward the Old Library at Trinity College. Nyx had been quiet on the flight back to Dublin, though he wasn't sure if her silence was due to exhaustion or stress or, most likely, both.

While the investigation they'd been conducting had led to more questions than answers, Grigoris couldn't shake the feeling that what they were seeking was in Hungary. Regardless, he was happy for an excuse to get Nyx, if even temporarily, away from Petro's seat of power.

He'd been able to get a bit more information out of Eric via text while he and Nyx raced to make their flight. Someone was missing. He hadn't heard *who* was missing, but the update text that had been waiting for him when they turned their phones back on after landing directed them to come to Trinity, and they'd taken a taxi directly from the airport.

They were almost to the door to the Old Library when a large man stepped out of the shadows in front of them, blocking their entrance.

"Violaris," Lancelot said. "Dr. Kata."

"Hello, Lancelot," Nyx replied. "The fleet admiral has summoned us back."

Lancelot's face could have been chiseled from stone. "He summoned Grigoris back," he said, gently.

Grigoris squared his shoulders. "Nyx goes where I go. I've been charged with keeping her safe and that's what I intend to do."

Lancelot gave him a quizzical look that made it clear he didn't think that had been his assignment...or not entirely. Eric had told him to accompany Nyx as backup. Serving as Nyx's full-time bodyguard was a task of his own making. "The fleet admiral is inside. He's waiting for you, Grigoris. Dr. Kata, I'm going to have to ask you to wait outside with me."

Lancelot stressed the *with me* part. Grigoris assumed that was meant to reassure him. "I would prefer—"

"This is nonnegotiable. Dr. Kata cannot go inside."

There was something in Lancelot's tone and eyes that told Grigoris whatever was inside was bad. He was operating on the assumption that the library was the search headquarters. If the search hadn't been going well, if there was bad news...

If that was the case, he was grateful to the knight and Eric for shielding her from it.

"I understand," he said to Lancelot, before turning to Nyx. "You'll stay with Lancelot?"

"I want to go with you," she insisted.

He gave her a forced smile. "I know, but I need to figure out exactly what's going on, then I'll bring you in." He cupped her cheek, ignoring Lancelot's raised eyebrows at his affectionate touch. He switched to Greek, hoping the knight didn't know his native tongue. "*Meínete edó gia ména, agápi mou.*"

Stay here for me, my love.

Nyx nodded just once. "Be careful."

It seemed like an odd thing for her to say when he was walking into a meeting—or more likely a council of war—and given her expression, she'd realized the moment after she spoke that it wasn't quite right, yet it felt appropriate.

Grigoris pushed that thought away and slid through the door.

He tried to protect the people he was in charge of. He tried, and yet he always failed. He'd failed Dahlia and Trina, his wives. He'd failed some of the missions he'd taken on in the dark years after he'd lost his trinity, and before a young brother and sister in rural Ireland started to bring him out of the darkness into the light.

He'd been successful some of the time too, but no one counted the successes. Only the failures mattered. Because when he failed, people died.

Eric stared around the beautiful Long Room of the library. Thousands of people walked through here every day, tourists who came to view the Book of Kells, kept in a special light-tight room half a floor below them, then to walk through the Long Room, a place that made even those who weren't bibliophiles yearn to run their fingers along the spines of the books, to pluck one from the shelf and see what mysteries and knowledge were hidden in the pages.

No one would be walking through here for a while. They'd have to close the Long Room, the whole Old Library.

He looked at the wicker basket that had been placed on top of one of the glass display cabinets centered in the aisle. Thin trails of blood ran from the base of the basket down the angled glass, obscuring the illuminated manuscripts on display inside the case.

She would have hated that. Would have worried that the case wasn't liquid-tight. That the books might be damaged.

Eric rose, and when he straightened to his full height, he was able to see what was in the basket. Bile rose in his throat, though he'd seen far worse in his life. Still, mutilation on the battlefield wasn't as horrific as this deliberate desecration of the victim and mocking placement of the basket with its grisly contents.

He stared down into the basket, at the decapitated head inside, and wondered what the killer had done with her body.

Grigoris wasn't sure what to expect when he entered the Long Room. Part of him was prepared for a crowd, a large team of security officers and Spartan Guards. Or maybe they had a suspect and wanted Grigoris' help questioning that person, though if that were the case, Lancelot—or more precisely, the man he had been, Charlie—was a far better option.

Whatever it was that had prompted Eric to pull him away was serious enough that he expected a gathering that was dangerous, grim, or something in between. What he didn't expect was to find Eric alone, staring into space, unaware of his arrival.

"Fleet Admiral?" Grigoris said, trying to capture Eric's attention.

Eric turned at the sound of his voice. Grigoris sucked in a harsh breath at the fleet admiral's expression. Fury. Despair.

"What is it? What's happened?" Grigoris asked, though instinct told him whatever it was, it was very, very bad.

Eric glanced at a basket that was situated on top of a display case in the middle of the room, then back at Grigoris.

"It's Josephine."

Grigoris fought to swallow around the lump that had suddenly clogged his throat. He knew Josephine O'Connor through Nyx. They were both librarians, but more than that, Josephine had become a friend to Nyx, and Grigoris was certain his lovely lady didn't have many people she trusted enough to let get that close to her.

"Is she the one who's missing?" Grigoris forced himself to ask.

Eric's teeth were clenched when he said, "No. She's dead."

Grigoris shook his head, as if willing those words away. This would devastate Nyx. "Are you certain?"

Eric glanced at the basket once more. He didn't look back at Grigoris as he said, "I am."

"The mastermind?" Grigoris asked.

The cool, white calm he'd been holding on to disappeared, burned away in a flash by rage. Eric whirled, picked up a chair, and hurled it down the length of the Long Room. It sailed through the air, crashing to the floor and splintering into dozens of pieces. It wasn't enough. He wanted to rip someone apart. He wanted blood to coat his hands, enough blood that it would wash away the feelings of helplessness.

"He killed her," Eric whispered. If he didn't whisper, he'd scream the words in rage. "He killed her, mutilated her, and then left her here for me to find."

Grigoris' gaze flashed to the basket, his eyes widening,

before a professional mask slid over his expression. "Tell me what happened."

"He killed her. Him or one of his pets." Eric's throat was starting to hurt from the effort it took not to howl, to wail, to curse the heavens above. "I will bathe in his blood." The last sentence might have been in Danish, rather than English, but Eric's control was slipping.

Grigoris took a step and looked into the basket.

Eric knew what he saw.

Josephine's head. Just her head. The ends of her dark red hair matted with blood, her eyes open and staring, her face slack, like a rubber mask.

Grigoris looked at him. "You found the—remains. What time was that?"

Eric's throat worked, but he couldn't speak.

"Fleet Admiral. We need to work fast. What time did you find this? Who was the last person to see her alive? Did you come to this location specifically to look for her? If yes, why? Have the Irish police been contacted?"

The words hammered at him, but the rage was choking. He picked up a second chair, but Grigoris snapped it out of his hand.

Eric turned on the Greek, and in his rage, lunged.

Nyx started past Lancelot when she heard the crash.

"No." He put his arm out to block her. "You can't go in there."

"Why not?"

Lancelot's face was unreadable.

Nyx stared him down—then punched him in the throat the way Grigoris had showed her and darted around him when he stumbled back, choking.

She raced into the library and up the stairs to the Long Room.

"Nyx."

She turned at the sound of her name, surprised to see James limping toward her, too fast for his injured knee, stopping her in the small antechamber before the entrance to the Long Room.

"James. Lancelot wouldn't let me in. What's happening? What's going on?"

James pulled up short. "That's what I'm here to find out. I was in Dublin doing research when Arthur called and said Eric had asked him to send over a couple knights to help with a search, and then he called again saying something had happened at Trinity. He and Sophia are on their way."

"Search for what? Or is it for whom? And what happened?" Nyx repeated.

James glanced at Lancelot, who'd followed Nyx in. "That's what I'd like to know."

"How the fook did you get in?" Lancelot wheezed.

"Our normal secret entrance," James said.

"Fookin' 'ell, la," Lancelot cursed.

The doors to the Long Room were partially open, and she could see bits of wood that might have once been a chair. That explained the crash. She could also hear Grigoris' voice, though he was too far away for her to make out the words.

"You two can't be here," Lancelot said, grabbing Nyx's and James' arms.

A roar of rage seemed to shake the building. The three of them turned to look at the doors.

"The fleet admiral," Lancelot said in horrified awe.

"Grigoris is in there." Nyx's heart started to pound as she lunged for the door.

She yanked it open in time to see Eric attack. Grigoris backpedaled and slid to the side, evading Eric's hold.

Heedless of her own safety, Nyx took off at a run. All she could think about was protecting Grigoris, as ridiculous as the idea was.

Eric spun, his face a mask of rage, his focus on Grigoris, though she got the sense that the fleet admiral didn't really see him. She ran as fast as she could, but the room was long and narrow—it was, after all, the Long Room—and she wasn't going to get there in time to stop Eric from hurting Grigoris.

Nyx had met James after his rugby career, after the terrible accident that had destroyed his knee and forced him off the All Blacks and into life as a numismatist. But she saw the rugby player now.

He powered past her, arms and legs pumping, despite his bad leg. Grigoris saw James coming and hopped back. Eric followed him, lunging, which put him right in James' path. James lowered his head, brought one shoulder forward, and took the fleet admiral down in a brutal tackle that would have broken through the fiercest scrum.

Lancelot materialized beside them. Quietly and quickly, he flipped Eric over, cuffing his hands together behind his back. Eric lay still, either unable to breathe or finally calm, though she couldn't tell which.

She skidded to a halt beside Grigoris, panting. As she turned to look at him, she caught sight of something wildly out of place. A wicker basket was set on top of one of the manuscript display cases, and it was leaking. Nyx frowned and reached for it. Whatever it was, it shouldn't be there. It might damage the manuscripts inside.

"Nyx, no!"

Grigoris grabbed her wrists before she could touch the basket, but not before she got a look at what was inside.

Her brain and heart stopped, her blood turned to ice, her mind insisted she wasn't really seeing what was in front of her.

In the next second, everything sped up, her mind processing, accepting, that Josephine's decapitated head was in a basket.

She opened her mouth and screamed.

CHAPTER SIXTEEN

Nyx stood under the shower in the hotel room. They were back at the Westin, near Trinity. When Grigoris booked it from his phone just before they'd left Budapest, Nyx realized she'd begun to think of this as "their hotel," which was a foolish game to play, even if it was just in her head.

She was struggling to remember how she'd gotten here. One minute she'd been looking into a basket...

Nyx's teeth began to chatter. She was so fucking cold.

She reached for the spigot, turning up the hot water, and closed her eyes.

Josephine.

Her eyes snapped open. Every time she closed them, she saw...

"No," she murmured. "No. No. No."

Somehow that word worked for her. Each time she started to fall apart, she simply repeated the word over and over, pushing the pain deeper until she could retain control.

Grigoris had stayed with her as long as he dared. She

knew him well enough to know he hadn't wanted to leave her here alone, but he'd been pulled in two different directions. He'd been called here to help find a missing person, she remembered him telling her at some point, but now it was a murder investigation. They needed him, but her lover had wanted to remain with her, to comfort her, protect her.

Nyx sank down in the shower, sitting on the floor, pulling her knees to her chest tightly as the scalding-hot water poured over her like fiery rain. Despite the steam rising around her, the heat wasn't penetrating her skin. She fixated on that fact, pondered it, let it erase everything else in her mind.

She'd done the same earlier when Grigoris had been here. She'd swallowed down every ounce of agony until she'd found the strength to tell him she was fine. That she was going to lie down and he should return to the investigation. To the fleet admiral.

Eric.

Eric wasn't pushing his pain away. His was erupting into a white-hot violence that would take down everyone in his path. Better that Grigoris was with him, helping him.

She would be fine.

She was fine.

Nyx shivered again as that face—Josephine's once lovely, now-dead face—flashed before her eyes.

"No. No. No. No."

Sucking in a deep breath, she forced herself to stand and turn off the water. Then she stepped out of the shower and dried off before returning to the bedroom. Grigoris' suitcase was next to hers. He'd reserved only this one room for them. To share.

She tried to let her imagination conjure up visions of

another night of passion, spent lying in his arms in this bed. But there was no longing, no desire.

The only emotion she could summon was gratitude. She couldn't sleep in that bed alone. Not after...

Nyx sucked in a deep breath and the pain went with it, buried even deeper. Hopefully, she'd manage to get it deep enough it could never escape.

Lifting her suitcase to the bed, she rummaged through it, trying to decide what to wear. It was too early for a nightgown. Besides, she couldn't bear the thought of climbing into that bed alone. So instead, she opted for a comfortable pair of jeans and a lightweight sweater.

She'd heard voices outside when Grigoris left, and a quick peek through the peephole told her that her lover had commissioned Lancelot to remain outside as a guardian to watch over her.

Now, she heard voices again. Both male, but from the British accents, she could tell in an instant Grigoris wasn't one of them.

She jumped when there was a knock at the door. Peering through the peephole, she saw James, looking just as somber and, well, wrecked as he'd appeared in the library.

Nyx opened the door.

"We're all here," he said, as if that explained something to her.

If she'd been in her right mind, it would have, but instead she heard herself asking, "We?"

"The rest of the librarians."

Nyx glanced at Lancelot, recognizing the anxiety in his expression. He'd been charged with guarding her, but it was easy to see he was torn. His new husband, Hugo, was a librarian and in danger as well.

"We're meeting at a pub near here. We've got a snug so it'll be somewhat private," James explained.

The librarians had never met anywhere besides the Long Room, and they'd never all convened somewhere so...social.

Nyx merely nodded. "That would be lovely," she said, as if she were accepting an invitation to dinner.

James waited as she grabbed her purse, then stepped aside. Lancelot shot James a nervous look.

James returned it with a scowl and, "What?"

Lancelot muttered, "It's your head if anything happens to her. The Cypriot was very explicit in his instructions that she stay inside this room and safe."

James glanced at Nyx. "You want to go back to your room?"

Nyx shook her head. Now that she was out and with people, she didn't feel quite as cold. In the room, she'd feared frostbite and loss of limbs. Now it was only a shivery, *why didn't I pack my parka*, kind of cold. "No. I want to see the others." Once she said it, she realized it was true.

This team of intellectuals had only been formed in the past year, drawn together by James and his belief that the mastermind wouldn't be defeated merely by might and procedural investigative tactics, but by academics who could study the esoteric clues and decipher them. Though they'd only met in person a dozen times or so, Nyx had formed a connection to these people. She'd found in them kindred spirits and even...friends.

The moment the word flashed through her brain, she saw Josephine's face again. The lively Irish woman had annoyed Nyx greatly at the beginning. Josephine, with her bouncing knee and effusive energy, was her polar opposite and not the type of woman Nyx would ever have called a girlfriend.

Josephine had proven her first impression wrong and

bounced her way right into Nyx's heart. Now, a piercing pain stabbed that same heart.

"No," she whispered.

James pulled up short. "Sorry?"

She shook her head. "Nothing."

The three of them stepped out onto the street together, the large men flanking her, shielding her. She'd become used to the same protection from Grigoris, however, now, rather than feeling safe, she shared the same high level of anxiety that seemed to eat at her bodyguards as their eyes shifted from side to side, analyzing every person they passed, trying to determine if they were a threat or not.

"Who is going to save me from the fleet admiral when Grigoris guts you like a fish for inviting her out?" Lancelot asked when they'd traversed half a block.

"Grigoris does not dictate where I go. I am not a fool or a child," Nyx said.

James looked chagrined, but Lancelot shrugged. "Not going to stop him from going mental when he finds out you left the room."

"Hugo is waiting in that pub. Are you seriously trying to tell me you wouldn't rather be where we're going?" James tossed back.

Lancelot didn't reply at first, he didn't need to. It was clear he was deeply concerned about his new spouse. None of them knew what Josephine's death meant.

Had she stumbled upon the mastermind's identity?

Or had the mastermind discovered theirs? Was it now open season on the librarians?

"I don't think it's smart for all of you to be in the same place at the same time," Lancelot retorted. "If Eric knew about this, he'd lose his fookin' mind."

"I fear he already has," James said somberly.

Nyx gave him a sideways glance and saw the fear and anguish on his face. Strangely, she took comfort in knowing she wasn't alone in her pain.

"We're stronger together," Nyx said after they'd walked three more blocks.

James paused for a moment, then he nodded. "That's what I think. We need to be together now."

Nyx latched onto his words as if they might heal her. "We will start with the coins. I know you've been over them, but if we start at the beginning, if there's something we've missed. I'm certain if we—"

She stopped talking when James gave her a look that appeared sympathetic. Nyx couldn't decipher what it meant.

"We're here," he said gently, like he was speaking to a confused child.

She followed him into the pub toward a back corner snug. She and James were the last to arrive. Lancelot gave Hugo the same disapproving glare he'd given James, but his spouse countered it with a ghost of a smile.

"I'll be right out here," Lancelot said, ever the knight, ready to stand guard at the door.

James put a hand on the man's shoulder. "Thank you, Lancelot."

The tension that had been brewing between them ever since they left her hotel seemed to dissipate. "Make it quick, la?" Lancelot asked.

James merely said, "I'll do my best, mate."

Nyx stepped into the snug, glancing first at the small area. The private room—if she could call it that—held only a long table surrounded by six comfortable leather chairs. The walls didn't extend all the way to the ceiling, stopping a couple feet shy of that. So while they were in a semi-private spot, there was no way to ensure someone in the main pub area couldn't eavesdrop if they were so inclined.

Unable to avoid it, she let her eyes roam around the table, exchanging glances with the others seated there. All the librarians were in attendance.

Everyone...except Josephine.

Cecilia gave her a slight, watery smile, the puffiness of her eyes proof that she'd been crying. Nyx tried to return the smile, but the damaged muscles in her face tightened, so she merely nodded her head.

Hugo was seated next to Cecilia, his somber expression something she'd never seen on the political science professor's face before. Typically, he was affable, thoughtful, at ease. Tonight, his shoulders were tense, almost hunched, and there were deep grooves beside his pursed lips.

Karl was at the end of the table. He pulled a handkerchief from his back pocket, swiping his nose with it. He was pale, and she thought she detected a slight tremble in his hands. Like her, Karl had suffered greatly at the hands of the mastermind and Ciril. He'd spent days strapped naked to a chair, held completely motionless, without food or water. Karl confessed to her in the hospital after her own attack that he'd been dying by inches, and he preferred a much quicker path.

Nyx had considered that at the time and decided, given the pain she was in, that he'd raised a good point.

She wondered if Josephine had suffered.

The second the thought popped into her mind, she shut it down again with her silent mantra.

No. No, no, no.

James pulled out a chair for her, then claimed the one next to it. In the past, the librarians met at Trinity College, and Josephine was always there. Every conversation she'd had with these people had pertained to the investigation, to disseminating the information in order to catch an evil killer. They didn't socialize, and they'd never been out in public together.

Despite that, Nyx realized she felt close to them. All of them. They were the first group of people who'd included her and made her feel not only welcome but needed, appreciated.

James rubbed the back of his neck, but he didn't speak. Nor did Cecilia. It appeared no one knew what to say.

Nyx cleared her throat, wishing the huge lump that had taken residence there since she'd seen that basket—

No. No, no, no.

The others glanced her way, and she realized her actions led them to expect her to speak.

"I..." She cleared her throat again. "I believe that if we reexamine what information we've been presented with, starting with the artifact items left in the cave murders in Rome—"

James placed his hand over hers. It was a gentle touch, but it caught her by surprise. "Nyx," he said kindly. "That's not why we're here."

"Why else would we be here?" She frowned, confused. Weren't they here to used their combined intellectual expertise to ferret out any hidden meanings, to figure out anything, any clue that Grigoris and the others working the investigation might have missed?

"To be together," James responded, as if his answer should be obvious.

Glancing around at the others at the table, Nyx saw Hugo nodding in agreement, as Cecilia sent her another of those sympathetic smiles.

"I wanted to be with all of you because I knew it would bring me comfort," Cecilia said.

Before Nyx could respond to that, the door of the snug opened and a waitress stepped into the space with a tray of drinks.

The waitress placed pints of beer in front of all of them as Hugo said, "I took the liberty of ordering us a round of Guinness."

The waitress asked if they needed anything else. James shook his head and thanked her, none of them speaking until she was gone, the door closed behind her.

"I figured maybe this was what Josephine would have ordered at a pub," Hugo said, his voice thick and hoarse.

"This or something pink with an umbrella in it," Cecilia said with a slight smile.

"I've never had Guinness," Nyx confessed, feeling off-kilter.

"I think you'll like it," James said, lifting his pint glass. "This is for our redheaded academic, Josephine. I'm going to miss her bouncing knees under the table."

Karl grinned sadly, lifting his pint and adding to the toast. "I'm going to miss the way she hogged the whiteboard."

Hugo was next. "And the way she always made me play secretary."

Cecilia laughed briefly. "And all her secret texts to Eric." Cecilia finger-quoted Eric's name, as all of them had always been curious about Josephine's close relationship with the fleet admiral, and the way she'd been the only one comfortable enough to call him by his first name during those early meetings.

With each shared memory, Nyx found it harder and harder to push the pain down. In fact, it was rapidly rising to the surface.

The other four looked to her. It was clear they expected her to add to the toast, but Nyx's throat was completely clogged. The only word that escaped was a whispered, "No."

James lowered his pint and grasped her hand again, giving it a friendly squeeze she assumed was meant to be comforting.

All it did was push more of the pain up. She opened her mouth, intent on telling him she was fine, but the words were swallowed up in the sound of a sob.

"No," she said again, louder this time. She fought to regain control, to force the agony back down, but it wouldn't go away. The sheer anguish was overflowing; her body couldn't hold all of it in.

She needed to get out of here, but she made no move to rise. Her hands were shaking and she wasn't completely sure her legs would hold her.

"Please," she said again, staring at the pint of Guinness in front of her. "I can't..."

Cecilia moved closer to her, wrapping an arm around her shoulders. Nyx's focus suddenly homed in on James' hand still holding hers, the warm weight of Cecilia's arm around her.

She couldn't stem the tears, but it didn't matter. She felt safe here, with her...friends.

James had told her they were stronger together. She'd interpreted those words wrong, believing he meant their combined knowledge, their ability to analyze data.

Now, she understood. The strength he'd mentioned had nothing to do with their intellect. They were holding her up, supporting her emotionally and spiritually.

Nyx let the tears slide down her cheeks, let the pain escape. Cecilia tightened her grip around her, and from the other woman's stuttered breathing, she could tell she was crying too.

The five of them sat in silence for several minutes, until Nyx's tears subsided. Lifting her gaze, she let it travel around the table, and she felt the same pain she was suffering reflected in their faces.

Strange how there was comfort in that.

She'd spent a lifetime alone, but now, now she had friends. Friends who challenged her intellectually, but more than that...friends who would share her joy and her pain.

The cold numbness that had set in since seeing Josephine lifted slightly. She still had more tears to shed, but knowing she was surrounded, was encapsulated in this cocoon of love, made that somehow bearable.

She lifted her pint of Guinness. "I will miss her sweet smile and her kind heart."

The others lifted their glasses, tapping them together and taking a sip. The sweet, malty beer was creamy and thick and it warmed her as it slid down her throat.

They remained in the snug for another hour, and two more rounds of Guinness, much to Lancelot's dismay. Especially when Grigoris appeared at the door. He looked furious until his gaze landed on hers. Then he took in the others at the table and his shoulders relaxed.

"Ready to go back to the hotel, Nyx?" he asked in such a way she thought he'd willingly stand guard outside with Lancelot if she needed more time with her friends.

She nodded, and as they stood to leave, she accepted Cecilia's hug and Karl's promise to call tomorrow to check on her. She smiled when Hugo reached for her hand, giving it a quick squeeze, and she nodded in agreement when James promised her they'd catch the mastermind and make him pay for what he'd done.

Grigoris placed a strong arm around her shoulders,

tucking her close to him as they stepped back out onto the street.

"Are you angry at me for leaving the hotel?"

He shook his head. "No."

"How did you know I was here?"

"Lancelot sent me an encrypted text fifteen minutes ago when he realized there was a chance I'd get back to the hotel before you."

"I needed to see them. To be with them. After losing..." She swallowed heavily and Grigoris saved her from having to speak Josephine's name aloud.

"I know. I'm glad you weren't alone tonight."

With his kind words, a fresh round of tears started to fall. Grigoris picked up the pace, neither of them speaking again until they reached their hotel suite.

Locking the door, he turned to face her, his arms outstretched.

And she took the invitation, stepping into his embrace, crying out more of the endless pain.

Grigoris held her through it all, then carried her to the bed and undressed her as she lay there, too weak and exhausted to take off her own clothing.

He tucked her under the blanket, stripped off his own outfit, then joined her beneath the soft duvet. Pulling her into his arms, he held her as she cried herself to sleep.

CHAPTER SEVENTEEN

Nyx opened her eyes, blinking a few times to focus them. When she did, she smiled, not bothering to shield the expression and ignoring the way the muscles pulled.

Grigoris lay next to her on his back. While she slept on her side, curled up into a ball, he resembled a starfish, his arms thrown above his head, outstretched, one leg pressed against hers, the other hanging over the side of the bed.

She thought he looked younger in repose, peaceful, at ease. Nyx knew one tiny sound of distress from her would change that state. That he would bolt upright ready to protect her life with his own.

Nyx propped herself up on her elbow, studying his features, his thick lashes and the dark stubble on his face. His hair was mussed up in such a way she longed to run her fingers through it.

Ever since she was a young girl, she'd eschewed thoughts of what it would feel like to wake up next to a man she was in love with. She'd allowed herself to dream of that for a brief period of time just before she turned eighteen, when she actually thought she could convince Petro to set their betrothal aside. But since then, she'd shut those desires down, never letting them see the light of day.

Grigoris had awakened them, and she feared the time when he would be placed in his trinity by Hande. She didn't let herself picture what her life would be like if she was forced to return to Lake Balaton and her marriage to Petro. Both eventualities were too painful to consider.

Grigoris' eyes opened slowly, finding hers instantly. He smiled, the beloved expression warming her from the tips of her toes to the top of her head.

It took less than ten seconds for him to recall yesterday's events, and his happiness faded, replaced with concern.

"Are you all right, Nyx?"

She nodded, her heart clenching when she thought of Josephine. "I'm struggling to convince myself it really happened," she confessed.

"That's normal. You lost a dear friend. It's going to take time for that to sink in."

"I don't want it to sink in."

Grigoris sat up and she did the same. He cupped her cheek affectionately. "That's normal too."

"I'm perfectly aware of the five stages of grief, *motănel*. What I find myself struggling with is the evil behind this act. What would drive a person to kill such an innocent, sweet soul? What did Josephine discover, what did she see or discover that might precipitate such violence?"

Grigoris sighed. "Based on our retracing her steps, and the fact that she was assisting the Archivist, rather than participating in an active investigation, there is a chance," he paused, and she could see it gave him no joy to say, "she found nothing. Saw nothing. It is possible the mastermind killed, or more likely *had* her killed, as a warning or message to us, to Eric personally. Or maybe she died simply because she was accessible."

Nyx hadn't considered such a thing. She needed there to be some meaning, some purpose to Josephine's death. The idea that it was a senseless act of cruelty felt like a worse crime than the decapitation. Josephine was brilliant, kind, important. To think someone could destroy all of that on a whim or as a way of hurting others made it so much worse.

"I can't..." Nyx swallowed hard. "Can we not..."

Grigoris kissed her brow. "Put it away for now, *ángelos*. We have a long day ahead of us. Eric is expecting me at the library in an hour to continue the investigation while Arthur works on damage control."

"I want to come with you."

"Nyx. I wish you could—"

She held her hand up. "But I can't."

He paused, and it was clear he was surprised that she wasn't putting up a fight.

"I can't go back there," she said. The library at Trinity College, the Long Room, had long been one of "her places." All libraries were. The books brought her comfort in a world where she didn't always fit in.

She wasn't certain she could ever step foot in the Long Room again.

"Lancelot will be just outside. He may be a knight, but he used to be a security officer. He'll fight fair if he can. If he can't...I know he'll do whatever is necessary to keep you safe."

Nyx nodded. She knew Grigoris would never leave her unprotected, and he wouldn't entrust her care to just anyone. The fact he trusted Lancelot spoke volumes about the English knight.

"What happens next in the investigation?"

Grigoris didn't respond immediately, and she realized there was more than one ongoing investigation. "We won't stay in Dublin. It's possible you and the other librarians are targets. But there's something else. I want to speak to Eric on your behalf, Nyx. I want to plead your case, find a way to get you out of your marriage."

"I've explained why that's not prud—"

Grigoris clasped her face in his hands, pulling her toward him. He kissed her roughly, passionately.

Her lips parted, welcoming his tongue, drinking in his taste. She would never get enough of him.

When he released her, they were both breathless. "I can't bear the thought of losing you," he confessed.

"I feel the same." Nyx considered Josephine, realized she'd never properly told the other woman how much her friendship had meant to her. Their world had gone mad. None of them could be certain there would be a tomorrow. "You have come to mean everything to me."

Grigoris rested his forehead against hers, the two of them closing their eyes, relishing this quiet moment when they could push the rest of the world away, could pretend it was just her and him and that their time was infinite.

Grigoris pulled away first. "I have to leave."

She smiled. "I know."

"I don't want to."

Her smile didn't waver. "I know."

NYX'S EYES were closed though she wasn't asleep. She'd thought perhaps rest would still her thoughts, help her find a way to relax, but she couldn't make the transition from wakefulness to sleep. She hadn't managed more than a few hours' sleep since they'd left Dublin two days earlier. That was due in part to the fact that, in the interest of safety, she and the other librarians had been sent into hiding after taking convoluted journeys all across Europe in the hope of ensuring Josephine's killer, and the mastermind, wouldn't be able to track them.

Instead, she was in that cognizant state of dozing, and her thoughts were whirling, touching on too many things.

"Time for our council of war," Eric said softly.

Nyx sat up. She'd been lying on the bottom bed of one of the eight metal bunks that lined the walls of the large underground room. Grigoris' thigh had been serving as her pillow, his hand occasionally stroking her hair. It had felt odd at first, showing any kind of public affection with Grigoris, but her need for his touch overrode her habitual secrecy. When they'd been in Lake Balaton, hiding her feelings for Grigoris had been absolutely necessary. Hiding her marriage to Petro had been a point of pride, and a way to hide the shame she felt whenever she thought about her "betrothal."

The people who'd taken shelter in the bunker with them all knew that she was, technically, married to Petro, but no one had said anything about her obvious relationship with Grigoris. Even Eric—who, as Fleet Admiral, probably should have said something—hadn't passed comment.

She stood and rolled her shoulders. Grigoris also rose, placing his left hand on the small of her back. He held his knife, unsheathed, in his right hand. The sheath, which was normally hidden by his sleeve, was visible, since he was wearing jeans and a tight white undershirt.

A large table in the center of the underground room had enough seats for ten people. One by one they took a chair, sitting down on cold, uncomfortable metal with various levels of grimaces marking their features.

Eric was at the head of the table. He'd been quiet and eerily calm since they'd left Dublin.

Antonio ushered Leila and Karl to chairs but didn't take one himself. Leila and Karl were having a hard time staying in the bunker. When Ciril had kidnapped them, he'd kept them in a concrete basement room, and their current situation clearly brought back bad memories. Karl's face was tight, and he kept adjusting his glasses, touching them almost protectively. Leila kept hold of a very large gun with the hand not holding Karl's.

Antonio looked over at his father, as if considering helping him, but then abandoned the thought and backed up, leaning against the wall where he could see the steel door that was the only entrance into the bunker, while also watching over his spouses. Antonio, as the acting admiral, wasn't staying in the bunker. He was the only one who was allowed to come and go.

His sister, Sophia, glanced at him, then took the handles of their father's wheelchair. She helped Giovanni to the table, placing him in the spot opposite Eric.

"It is high time we treated this as war," Giovanni said. The admiral of Rome looked formidable, despite the fact that he was in a wheelchair. His hair was short, and there was a visible lack of growth where there was a scar, thanks to the head injury he'd suffered when the *Villa Degli Dei* was bombed. Still, his bearing was nearly regal, and his dark eyebrows and salt-and-pepper hair were striking.

After helping her father, Sophia took a seat beside James. "Father, many brilliant people have been working diligently. Your statement might be interpreted as a reprimand or dismissal of that work."

There was a reason they called Sophia Starabba the *principessa*, even after her marriage to James and Arthur, and move to London. She was regal, and managed to convey both censure and disappointment while keeping the words crisp.

Nyx had spoken briefly with James and knew that Arthur had resorted to ordering his spouses to leave. Too many of the mastermind's attacks had taken place in the territory of England. When Giovanni had been injured, Sophia hadn't been able to return to Rome due to security concerns. She and James had decided to take some time away from the stress of the situation and were followed by a killer. If not for the man who was now known as Lancelot, they might have been the victims of yet another of the master-mind's pets.

The fact that they'd been targeted once, so close to home, had prompted Eric to send them to the territory of Rome, where Antonio could protect them.

"Antonio, sit down," Eric said softly.

Nyx and Grigoris exchanged a silent look of worry. The fleet admiral was...distressingly calm.

Antonio pushed off of the wall and took a seat across from his trinity, on Nyx's other side. She relaxed a little, glad that he was no longer standing against the wall and therefore at her back.

Once Antonio was in place there were nine people at the table.

Nyx glanced at the empty chair and then away.

Of the original six librarians, three of them were in this room—herself, James and Karl. Cecilia and Hugo were holed up in a second secret, secure location with their trinities, and Josephine was dead.

Nyx wavered between moments where she could put her friend's death out of her mind enough that it was as if it hadn't happened, as if Josephine hadn't been brutally murdered. Then reality would crash in on her again and the now-familiar sharp pain that pierced her heart returned with a vengeance.

"Who's the mastermind?"

Eric's blunt question hung in the air. Several people exchanged glances, but no one spoke.

Nyx cleared her throat. "Petro."

Grigoris winced, but it was a micro expression. She wouldn't have noticed it if she hadn't studied his wonderful face so extensively.

Eric stared at her. "If you are using this situation to get rid of a husband you don't like..."

Grigoris sat forward, his mouth open to protest, but Nyx put a hand on his arm. He paused and looked at her, then sat back. One of the things she loved about him was that while he protected her, and God knew she'd needed to feel safe, he also trusted her.

"I assure you that if I were able to set aside my moral objection to premeditated murder, I would be far more subtle about it."

Eric grunted. "Good. Then why is it Petro?"

"Hungary's vice admiral is suffering from an autoimmune disease, which may be drug induced. His health and symptoms seem similar to how James described Kacper."

Eric rubbed his jaw, three days' worth of stubble right on the borderline of becoming a full-fledged beard. "Lazar is poisoned and Petro is shot...that points to the leadership of Hungary being a target, not that Petro is the mastermind."

"Another admiral was shot?" Antonio asked.

"And there was a bomb," Nyx added.

Antonio and Giovanni stiffened.

Grigoris jumped in then, quickly describing everything that had happened in Lake Balaton.

"Hanna was the shooter," Nyx said. "Petro asked Hanna to shoot him."

"You caught her?" Eric asked.

"We found her gun accessories," Nyx explained. "Her weapon would have used the same caliber of bullet as that which shot Petro. We also found evidence that she practiced." Nyx touched her shoulder. "A deliberately nonfatal shot that would appear like it was a near miss."

Grigoris cut in, explaining the setup of the estate, and how it would have been impossible for a shooter to have line of sight to the office from beyond the walls. It had to have been someone who was there. He also detailed the paper targets and gun information.

"But any links directly to Ciril? The Rutherfords?" Karl asked.

"We didn't have time to finish our investigation," Grigoris said. With an apologetic glance at Nyx, he said, "I'm not entirely sure that someone at the house didn't just use the situation to get rid of Petro."

Eric put his head in his hands and started to curse in Danish.

They talked for another half an hour, analyzing everything Nyx and Grigoris had learned. The group came to the same general conclusions they had—that Hans and Nikolett both had solid motives to want Petro dead.

Then again, so did Nyx.

However, it was unlikely that either of them was the mastermind. Hans was discounted because he wasn't bright enough, more brawn than brains. Nikolett was smart enough, more than, but the timing was wrong. Nikolett was too young to have perpetrated the earlier crimes.

That led them back to Petro.

"Hanna," Leila asked. "Could she be the mastermind?"

Nyx shook her head. "No. We don't think so. She's too young."

That started another round of conversation.

"Does Hanna hate Petro?" James asked.

"She should," Grigoris said vehemently. "He's a pedophile."

Eric's head snapped up. "What?"

"He picked out Nyx and Hanna when they were kids. Picked them out to be his wives, set up betrothals when they were fourteen and fifteen, then married them the moment they turned eighteen."

Everyone looked appalled.

Nyx slid her hand over Grigoris' thigh under the table and squeezed. "That's true, but I don't know if she hates him." Nyx swallowed hard. "I think she might love him. That he trained her to love him. To obey him."

"If he waited until they were legal adults, we're tabling his pedophilia." Eric looked at them. "We can't focus all our time on Hungary without a more direct connection than the vice admiral's sickness."

"I have a question." Giovanni steepled his fingers. "Why?"

"Why what?" James asked his father-in-law.

But Nyx understood. "Two reasons—first, in order to throw suspicion off himself. Second—to get away from Grigoris."

"From me?" Grigoris looked at her. "You're suggesting those are reasons why Petro would have arranged the shooting."

"Yes. And the fact that he went to the trouble of doing it is further evidence he's the mastermind."

"I'm not convinced," Eric said. "Convince me. Petro is a good admiral."

Nyx demurred. "Petro is brilliant."

"So are you," Leila said.

Nyx cast the woman a glance and smiled. Leila's gaze slipped to the scar, her cheeks draining of color. Nyx thought she must be remembering the day they'd been attacked. Leila had been the one to pull the trigger, killing Ciril.

"Thank you, but Petro's brilliance is a form of arrogance. The opposite of Dunning-Kruger. He is brilliant and he knows it."

"That doesn't explain why he would start recruiting serial killers and resurrecting both the Domino and the Bellator Dei," Sophia pointed out.

Nyx had had a lot of time to think about this. From the moment James had called the librarians together, they'd been working the problem of the mastermind from an intellectual angle. Spending time with Petro again, especially the night he'd appeared in her room, had clarified things to the point she was now confident enough to articulate her theory.

"I am a religious scholar, and in my opinion, when examined as a whole, the mastermind's actions have no defining moral motive. It also doesn't appear that the mastermind is a philosophical hedonist. I believe it is more about what he feels he is owed."

"I thought he was trying to punish the Masters' Admiralty?" Leila asked.

"Punishment would be better achieved through other means. The mastermind isn't always logical, but he *is* clever." Nyx looked around. "Petro feels he is owed things. He feels he is owed his choice of young women for wives because they are his due. Their opinions and wants don't matter. The arranged trinity marriage merely provided a framework to give him what he wanted."

Giovanni stiffened, and Sophia and Antonio very carefully didn't look at their father.

"I believe that Petro feels he was owed the position as fleet admiral. That is why he seduced, by proxy, Manon. It's why he eventually killed the former fleet admiral."

"But he wasn't selected," Leila pointed out.

Nyx turned to Giovanni. "No, he wasn't, but we have the unique opportunity to talk to someone who was at the conclave. *Both* conclaves."

"It is not lost on me that most of the reasons you gave for naming Petro as a suspect also apply to me," Giovanni said smoothly.

"I did consider you. We all did."

Antonio slumped a little in his chair and Sophia looked at the ugly concrete ceiling.

"However," Nyx went on, "your love for your children is well-known, and I don't believe you would have put them in danger."

Giovanni smiled. "Excellent deductions."

"You're still on my suspect list," Nyx informed him.

Giovanni's smile turned into a grimace.

"The events and discussion that happened in the second conclave may uncover a reason why Petro's actions switched from orchestrating circumstances, thereby ensuring he received what he was 'owed,' to creating chaos and fear." Nyx glanced at Eric. "I believe his end game is to damage the society, kill you, take the fleet admiral position, and then use the weakened society to do something like consolidate all the territories, or rewrite our rules to further suit himself and what he is 'owed'."

That statement hung over the room. More than one person looked grim.

"That makes a horrible kind of sense," Karl said.

"It does," Antonio said, agreeing with his husband.

Eric tapped his fist on the table. "It's not enough."

"Petro is a capable leader," Giovanni said, and for a moment it sounded like he was going to defend him, but then Giovanni slumped, and for some reason, that drew Nyx's eye to the wheelchair. It made the man seem more fragile than he had a moment ago. "But he hasn't been the same since the accident. Very well, let us begin with the second conclave, since the first one, the attack, has, I'm sure, already been discussed. At the second conclave—"

"What accident?" Eric's voice rumbled like distant thunder.

Everyone stopped speaking and turned to the fleet admiral. He was gripping the edge of the table, and she thought she heard the metal creak in protest.

Giovanni considered the man they called the Viking. A man who seemed to be very close to his breaking point.

She did not want to be trapped in an underground bunker with a berserker.

"About seventeen years ago, Petro was injured in an accident. He wasn't expected to live, due to the trauma to his brain, but he was medevacked to one of the best surgeons in the world—a member of the Masters' Admiralty, of course—and she was able to save him."

"Where did this happen?" Eric asked in that too-soft voice.

James looked back and forth between them, then at Sophia.

"Spain," Sophia breathed. "Was he taken to Spain?"

Giovanni stared at his daughter. "How did you know?"

Eric looked at James. "Get Arthur on the phone. Now."

James reached for the receiver of the secured line Antonio had set up for them shortly after their arrival.

Nyx held her breath as they all watched him dial the number before pushing the speaker button.

"Arthur," the admiral of England said, answering on the second ring.

Eric didn't bother with niceties. "What have you learned about Mateo's parents?"

It spoke to Arthur's relationship with Eric that he didn't hesitate to answer, didn't question the urgency in the fleet admiral's voice.

"I spoke with a neurosurgeon, Gabriela Lopez, in Spain, whose older brother did his residency with Mateo's mother. She was the easiest to approach because she and her family are also members of the Masters' Admiralty."

"Why didn't you talk to the brother?" Eric asked.

"He was killed in a car accident a couple of years after Dr. Bernard's murder."

"What did Dr. Lopez say?" Antonio asked.

"Dr. Lopez simply said her brother had been devastated by the murder of her mentor, said Dr. Bernard's death was a huge loss in the field of neurological surgery."

"Did she say if her brother suspected anyone?" Eric asked impatiently.

"I asked if she or her brother had known of anyone who might want to hurt Dr. Bernard. You have to understand, Gabriela was ten years younger than her brother, close in age to Mateo. She said her brother insisted that Dr. Bernard was loved by everyone, and that he'd struggled with her death for many months afterwards. Especially when it was discovered her records had been destroyed. I get the impression the brother had been trying to connect some dots at the time of his unfortunate accident."

"Most likely another fucking murder we can chalk up to the mastermind." Eric slapped his hand on the table.

"Dammit. We were asking the wrong question. What's the woman's number?"

Arthur paused, and Nyx thought she heard the sound of the admiral flipping through some papers. After a minute, he rattled off the number. "Eric. What is this ab—"

Eric disconnected the call without answering Arthur's question. "Dial the doctor," he instructed James.

James did so, then sat back down, leaving the interrogation to the fleet admiral, obviously put out over Eric's treatment of his spouse.

Sophia rested her hand on her husband's but said nothing.

The Spanish doctor answered. "*Buenos dias.*"

"Dr. Lopez. This is Eric Ericsson."

"The fleet admiral?" Dr. Lopez asked, alarmed.

"Your brother did his residency with Dr. Bernard."

"Uh, yes, yes, he did." She sounded slightly bewildered but was doing an admirable job of trying not to let confusion seep into her words. "I spoke with the admiral of England about this."

"We have new information. Dr. Bernard treated a patient shortly before her death. If we describe the injuries, do you think you can tell us how they might change a person?"

"I can try," Dr. Lopez responded, "but without the medical records..."

"This person's records would have been the first to go missing," Eric said with that eerie calm. He looked at Giovanni, who had been silent since mentioning the injury.

The older Italian man cleared his throat. "As I recall, a piece of rebar pierced his head, right in the front, during a terrorist bombing."

"His frontal lobe, well..." Dr. Lopez hesitated.

"Well, what?" Eric asked.

"If it was a frontal lobe injury, it may have damaged his ability to feel empathy. In short, he might have ended up a psychopath. Or it may have made him very docile. Depending on the specifics of the injury, it might have in essence been a lobotomy. Is this person still alive? I could interview them, or even better, do a CAT scan. With that, I'd know more."

Eric shot James a look that the other man interpreted easily.

One word in the doctor's statement kept jumping out at Nyx. Psychopath.

James quickly thanked Dr. Lopez and disconnected the call.

Eric turned to Grigoris. "Where is Petro right now?"

"Back in Lake Balaton. Ivan has been keeping me apprised. He was released from the hospital yesterday."

"Pack your shit. We're leaving." And with that, the Viking strode to the bunker door, slammed the bolt open so hard the sound reverberated painfully, then mounted the steps two at a time.

Grigoris grabbed her hand, and Nyx raced up with him.

CHAPTER EIGHTEEN

"Still no answer from Ivan." Grigoris ended the call, then grabbed the handle on the door as Eric took the corner too fast.

Nyx was smiling and appeared to be enjoying the death-defying ride to Petro's compound. Eric was driving, and while he appeared supremely calm, he was driving like a madman. Milo, a security officer from Rome, was in the front passenger seat. He was, unhelpfully in Grigoris' opinion, egging on Eric by providing advice like "you can accelerate more as you come out of the turn."

They'd taken an eight-seater private jet from the smaller of the two airports in Milan—which was where the bunker had been—and flown directly to the tiny Hévíz–Balaton Airport on the western tip of Lake Balaton. There was no way that someone in the Hungary territory leadership didn't have regular monitoring set up for arrivals to these airports, given how close they were to Petro's estate. It was one of the reasons that Eric was driving so fast.

Grigoris had explained to the fleet admiral that the

element of surprise wasn't really an option, but Eric had simply ignored him, while Milo had checked the safety on the several guns he had strapped to his body. Clearly Milo was listening, and understanding what Grigoris was trying to say—there was no chance they were going to surprise anyone at the estate, so if Petro was in fact a psychopath, and the mastermind, they might be walking into a deadly trap.

"Nyx, try the house again," Eric commanded.

Nyx grabbed a new burner phone out of the messenger-style bag she had flung across her chest. Antonio had loaded them up with phones, all of them programed with Hungarian numbers, before they left the bunker.

They took a turn too fast, and Nyx slid sideways and crashed into him. Grigoris wrapped his arm around her waist, anchoring her in place. She tapped out the number for the estate manager's office and raised the phone to her ear. She raised her voice several octaves and added a perky tone that was very un-Nyx-like. She spoke a language Grigoris didn't know. The conversation lasted several minutes before she hung up.

"The manager just said Petro was unavailable and wouldn't give an ETA. I told her I was calling because the Romanian Society for the Arts and Bucharest National Opera wanted to honor him as a patron. He loves the opera. That should have enticed him to the phone."

"I can call," Milo said. "Or perhaps my admiral—"

"Don't want to tip our hand," Eric said.

Grigoris gritted his teeth, annoyed that Eric wasn't listening. With the fleet admiral here, Grigoris was no longer in charge of the operation. If it had been up to him, he would have planned an infiltration, rather than a blitz. He also would have left Nyx safely in the bunker in Italy. When Eric had declared his intention to go and confront Petro, Grigoris had assumed Nyx would be staying behind.

That assumption had been short-lived when Eric asked Grigoris how many Eastern European languages he spoke fluently. Nyx was here as both their interpreter and the person with the best working knowledge of Petro and the main players in the territory, despite the fact that she'd spent her adult life avoiding both.

They came around the corner to discover the gates of the estate were standing open.

"Turn back," Grigoris said immediately. "Fleet Admiral, this could be a trap. Give me a few days, and I'll go in as one of the daytime workers. They won't even know I'm there."

"I'm not waiting days to rip the head off the man who killed Josephine."

Milo cleared his throat. "Fleet Admiral, based on what my own admiral told me before we left, it seems unlikely that Petro Sirko, who was in surgery at the time of the Irishwoman's disappearance, killed her."

"No. He had someone else do it. And I'll kill that sick fuck too." Eric's hands, which despite his insanely aggressive driving, had been light on the wheel, now tightened. "It is time to raise Nidhogg into the light and separate the worm's head from its body." Eric's accent was thicker than it had been a moment ago.

Grigoris looked down at Nyx questioningly. As they barreled through the open gates in the vast wall surrounding the estate, she laid her hand over his, where it rested on her waist.

"Nidhogg is an evil creature from Norse mythology," she said quietly in Greek. "Not a worm. A wyrm, a dragon, that bites and chews the roots of the world tree."

"The mastermind isn't a dragon," Grigoris replied quietly. "He's a hydra. Cut off the head and two more grow."

"Then we must cauterize as we cut."

"Or we ignore mythology and do something besides a frontal assault."

"Enough," Eric barked in English. "Let go of her and be ready to go in."

Grigoris released Nyx. "I want you to stay with us. Leaving you in the car would be too dangerous." Grigoris slid his knives from their sheaths, glad when Nyx moved out of his way, though he regretted losing her touch. "Coming with us is also too dangerous."

"I am not afraid to die," she said quietly. "I am afraid of the pain of death but not afraid to die."

"You have made your peace?" Milo asked.

"I'm a religious scholar," Nyx said, as if that were an answer.

Milo twisted to look at her and raised a brow.

"I'm agnostic," Nyx explained. "Anyone who studies religion is sure of humanity's great capacity for both good and evil."

Grigoris shot her a sharp glance. He hadn't known that about her. He switched his attention back to the windshield. The estate was in sight, and Eric wasn't slowing down.

"If there is a higher power, it's a cruel and petty god," Eric said.

"Perhaps it would be easier to simply believe that in the end, Petro's fate will match his actions," Nyx suggested.

"That works." Eric braked hard, turning as he did, so they rocked to a stop with the passenger side, where Milo and Grigoris were, only inches from the lowest step of the grand entryway.

Before the car had fully stopped, Grigoris and Milo were

out. Milo went up the center of the steps, a two-handed hold on his gun, his eyes scanning side to side. Grigoris ran to the side, leaping over some shrubbery to peek in a window. It was the front parlor, where they'd made the guests wait while looking for the bomb, and it was empty.

Grigoris took several running steps and jumped up onto the wide stone railing of the stairs, then leapt down behind Milo, who'd stopped in front of the door.

He tapped the other man on the shoulder, and Milo adjusted his grip on the gun, then reached for the ornate door handle.

He didn't even have to depress the latch. The moment he touched the door, it swung inward.

Grigoris checked for Nyx, who was coming up the steps with Eric. He was big enough that he served as an effective human shield. Grigoris nodded at her, then winked before following Milo into the house.

Milo swept the foyer, then paused, glancing at Grigoris and jerking his head. Grigoris slid in front, taking point. They weren't totally silent, but they were moving quietly. They swept the main rooms on the first floor. There was no one there. Nyx whispered something to Eric and pointed. He nodded and she dashed away, toward the back hall.

Grigoris straightened, ready to protest, but the look Eric shot him would have frozen boiling water. Grigoris subsided. He had no desire to get in a fight with the fleet admiral right now and, more importantly, he trusted Nyx.

He also thought he knew where she was going—through the back door and into the servants' wing, to the estate manager's office. Perhaps she could get some information out of the servants who lived on-site. If not where Petro was, then how long he'd been gone and who else was here.

Grigoris hurried to finish the last section of the main

floor, which was a small suite of rooms, including a small kitchen and informal living space, which were Petro and Hanna's private space inside the larger residence. When they'd done the sweep looking for the bombs, Ivan had explained that most of the estate was used for territory business, but Hanna liked to make the occasional meal all on her own, rather than having the chef cook.

The fact that no harcosok had met them at the door made it unlikely that Petro was here, but Grigoris wouldn't make assumptions, and he suspected the fleet admiral wouldn't be happy until they'd opened every closet and cupboard.

Then he might raze the place to the ground.

Grigoris paused as he pushed open the door into the small foyer of the private living area, which was like a single apartment within the larger building. There were two open arches off the apartment foyer leading to the kitchen and combination dining/living room. A single door to his left led to a large storage closet. There was also a half bath but no bedroom.

Directly above them was Petro's master suite. Thinking of the narrow bed tucked into the closet, the bed that had been intended for Nyx when she wasn't forced into the massive bed with Petro, made Grigoris' stomach lurch.

He shoved that feeling aside. Now wasn't the time for emotion.

Milo stepped up beside him, Eric, a giant blond shadow, at their back.

"How do we know that he hasn't left and rigged the house to explode?" Milo asked conversationally.

"We don't," Grigoris replied softly.

"Ah. *Non avere peli sulla lingua.*"

Grigoris didn't know enough Italian to translate, so he just assumed Milo figured they were all fucked. He slid into the living room, which was empty and tidy, but not as formal as the rest of the house. Same for the kitchen. They checked the storage closet, and Milo opened a few of the cedar boxes, finding carefully packed linens. There were also plastic tubs holding holiday decorations, skiing equipment, and other odds and ends.

There was something so mundane about the presence of carefully packed German glass ornaments that it gave Grigoris pause.

"Petro is gone. And he has been since yesterday," Nyx said from the apartment's small foyer.

They exited the closet. Grigoris was the last one out, and he frowned as he closed the door.

"Where did he go?" Eric asked.

"The estate manager wasn't sure. Petro came back after he was released from the hospital, but then he and Hanna left again. She assumed it was for one of his other properties. He has homes in most of the major metropolitan centers of Eastern Europe."

"I'll get her to tell me." Eric's calm words were more terrifying than an out-and-out threat would have been.

"I doubt she knows. I told her I'd had a change of heart, that I wanted to be Petro's wife in truth." Nyx's face was impassive. "She looked happy, relieved, and said the next time he called, she would tell him. "

"Why was the gate open and the door unlocked?" Milo asked.

"She didn't say." Nyx frowned, as if disappointed in herself. "I'll go back and ask."

"Wait," Grigoris said. "Who else is here?"

"The estate manager and Patty."

"Patty?" Milo asked.

Nyx explained. "Lazar, the vice admiral, is here, so his

246 MARI CARR & LILA DUBOIS

attendant is too. The others, and the day staff, have been given time off. They'll be back soon."

"Who went with Petro?" Milo asked.

"Fedir and Ivan, though Ivan went with them immediately, and Fedir stayed here last night. He left only several hours ago." Nyx frowned. "The fact that the staff will be returning is most likely why the gate is open, though it doesn't explain the unlocked front door."

"Lazar," Grigoris said. "Let's talk to him." He once more took point, leading them out of the private apartment and up the stairs. Rather than checking each room, he went right to Lazar's quarters.

Grigoris paused at the door. "Fleet Admiral, you might want to stay out of sight. Let me talk to him."

"It's too late to hide the fact that I'm here."

"I'll go in first." Nyx slid out from behind the fleet admiral, walked up to Grigoris, and then past him, opening the door, while Grigoris was still sliding his knives into the concealed sheaths so he wouldn't alarm Patty.

Nyx stepped into the room—and froze, her body tightening, her fingers white around the door handle.

He knew Nyx. Knew how she moved, knew what the smallest shift of her weight meant, the way a smile that barely touched her lips would be present in her eyes.

But right now what her body was communicating was horror.

Every instinct he possessed went on high alert.

One knife still in hand, Grigoris rushed through the door, grabbing Nyx and thrusting her behind his back. Only then did he look around.

Grigoris had seen his share of blood and pain and sadness, but that didn't dull his reaction to what lay before him.

What he saw here was horrifying. Having seen Josephine's decapitated head, he had a new threshold for the word horror, but horror was appropriate in this instance. The mutilated corpse that had once been Patty let out a moan, and Grigoris' terror doubled.

"They're still alive," Nyx whispered.

"Milo," Grigoris shouted. "Help me get her down."

Milo, who, along with Eric, had stayed out of sight, dashed into the room, moving fast in response to Grigoris' tone, then slid to a stop, his eyes sweeping across the room.

Patty hung upside down from the ceiling, her fingertips a foot from the floor. She was suspended from meat hooks that had been pierced through her ankles, between the bone and the Achilles' tendon. Blood ran in thick trails from her ankles to her knees, then disappeared into the legs of her loose pants, which had fallen in gathers at her thighs.

Her face was black and blue, as if she'd been beaten before she was strung up, and blood had leaked from a laceration on her forehead to make a small puddle on the floor.

Grigoris grabbed her around the waist and lifted, hoping to take her body weight off her ankles. Milo grabbed a chair and leapt onto it, starting to work at the bolts that held the meat hooks into the ceiling. Up close, he could smell the stink of her sweat and other, more base smells. She'd pissed herself, probably losing control either from the pain or from fear.

He turned his head, and it was then he saw Lazar.

The vice admiral lay on the bed beyond Patty's dangling body. Blood coated his face but was concentrated in rivulets that ran from his nostrils and the corners of his eyes.

"Lazar," Nyx breathed. She started to run to him but stopped when Patty mumbled something.

"What's she saying?" Grigoris asked.

Nyx backpedaled and dropped to her knees. She started

to reach out for Patty, maybe to comfort the woman, but stopped short of touching her. There wasn't a millimeter of her face that wasn't bruised.

Nyx spoke softly, gently, but the words didn't seem to be calming Patty. She was rapidly becoming hysterical and kept repeating a single word over and over.

"*Vikinh. Tse vikinh. Vin ziyshov z rozumu. Vikinh.*"

Nyx looked up at him, her eyes wide, then she glanced at the door. "Fleet Admiral, run! You need to get away from here!"

Grigoris' blood ran cold. "Nyx, what is she saying?"

"Got it. Brace yourself." Milo was calm and cool, clearly a good man to have in a crisis.

"Shit," Eric said softly from the doorway. "Shit!"

"That is the opposite of running away," Nyx pointed out.

Grigoris concentrated on lowering Patty to lie on her back. She took great gasping breaths, her eyes, which were nearly swollen shut, closing.

"Do you hear that?" Milo asked.

"Hear what?" Eric demanded.

Nyx watched Patty carefully, and didn't react to what they were saying.

Milo carefully pulled up Patty's shirt, which had been tucked into her pants.

The silver head of a knitting needle and ten centimeters of the shaft protruded from the left side of her chest. It had been hidden by her shirt.

"Don't touch it," Grigoris said quickly.

"I can hear air whistling." Milo bent closer. "Her lung...I can hear air escaping."

Nyx looked at the bed, then jumped up and rushed over. "Lazar."

"No, you must go," the man wheezed in English. "Greek. You love her. Take her and go."

"Who did this? Was it Petro?" Eric asked.

"Fleet Admiral, you should not—" Lazar coughed, blood spurting from his mouth. "Go!"

Grigoris left Milo doing what he could for Patty and rose. "What's going on, Nyx? Why does Eric have to leave?"

Nyx's face was ashen, almost as pale as her hair. "Patty is speaking Czech. She says the Viking did this to her." She glanced at Eric. "You're being framed. And you're about to be caught at the scene of the crime."

For one sharp, terrifying moment, Eric's calm facade cracked. He spun around, picked up a side table that was solid wood and had to weigh a hundred pounds, and threw it at the wall. It was a quality piece, and it didn't shatter on impact, instead leaving an impressive dent in the wall.

"And now your fingerprints are on that," Nyx observed.

"Nyx, I am so...so sorry." Lazar's words were barely audible.

She whirled back to him, carefully taking his hand. "Don't be. You saved me."

"I didn't. You were—" Lazar's breathing sounded crackly. He coughed then started again. "You were never really free. It came at a cost."

"He hurt you. I know. I'm so sorry, Lazar. If I'd known, I wouldn't have run."

"No. He knew. He always knew where..." Lazar coughed again, his eyes sliding shut. "Go," he whispered at last. "He knew you were coming. He wants you to be found. The harcosok will kill—"

"She's dead. I think when we took her down it shifted this thing. *Dannazione!*" Milo cursed. "I'm starting CPR."

Grigoris looked at Lazar, then at Patty, and finally to Eric.

"Stop," Nyx ordered. "We're leaving. Now."

"We have to render aid," Milo said stubbornly.

"The fleet admiral is about to be framed for murder and we are too far from a hospital. Neither of them will survive." It was a cold, brutal truth, and someone who might not know Nyx well wouldn't see what it cost her to say the words.

Grigoris briefly felt an odd sort of pride in her strength. Then he considered everything she'd suffered in order to become that way and the pride shifted to pain.

"Go," Lazar breathed again.

Eric grabbed Milo by the collar and hauled him to his feet. Grigoris raced to the table Eric had thrown and used the tail of his shirt to swipe at the leg before running out into the hall to join the others.

"This way," Nyx demanded. She took them away from the main stairs and to the bedroom she'd stayed in. Grigoris realized what her plan was the moment before she opened the secret panel. In silence, they raced down the passage, emerging into the master suite.

Without hesitating, she opened a door to reveal a spiral staircase. Grigoris cursed himself for not realizing earlier that Hanna, who he assumed was the one who'd decorated and maintained the private apartment, would also want a way to access it from the bedroom in privacy. The stairs weren't exactly concealed, the way the secret passage had been, but they weren't obvious. The harcosok would have known about them and probably searched them when they did the bomb sweep.

Before he could take the lead, Nyx started down the stairs, Eric behind her. Grigoris took up the rear, using a clean section of his shirt to close the door, so he wouldn't leave a smear of Patty's blood on the handle.

When he emerged into the apartment kitchen, through a

floor-to-ceiling cabinet door, Nyx and Eric were already at the main door, listening. Milo was doing another sweep of the living room.

He realized how foolish he'd been to think he knew this place, even after he'd been part of the bomb sweep team. Petro was the mastermind, he was sure of that now, and he was also sure that Lazar's words were true. This whole thing had been orchestrated so the Hungarian knights would discover Eric standing over the body of Patty and Lazar. The knights would detain all of them, even Eric.

If Eric was in his right mind, that wouldn't be a problem. The issue was, Eric wasn't all there. Grigoris and Milo exchanged an uneasy glance, both of them looking at Eric. He was an unknown factor in an explosive situation.

The safest course of action would be to make sure Eric wasn't here when the knights found the bodies.

Nyx had hypothesized that Petro wanted to depose Eric and destabilize the Masters' Admiralty. Painting the fleet admiral as a murderer, then killing or discrediting those who supported Eric, was a very effective way to do it.

"I don't hear anyone," Nyx whispered. "But our car is at the front. We will have to go out that way."

Grigoris opened the closet door and stared in. Something had bothered him when he'd checked in here earlier. Petro had at least one secret passage, plus a well-hidden staircase in his home. Why not more?

Grigoris walked over to a stack of boxes that wasn't quite flush against the wall and slid them out of the way. It took less than a minute before he found the correct place to apply pressure to make the hidden door pop open.

"Nyx, Eric, Milo," he called out softly.

The others were with him in an instant. Together, they peered into a large square room painted matte black. It looked like a security control room, mixed with an office. A bank of monitors to the left showed live footage of every inch of the estate. There were cameras. Cameras even the security staff didn't know about. To his right was a narrow counter with neatly filed, clear poly envelopes in stacks. Above those, on a black dry erase board, were lists of information. It was all written in Hungarian, but it looked like names with contact information, locations, and notes written in white.

Several of them had large red X's.

"What does it say?" Eric asked.

Nyx's fingers found Grigoris', grasping tight. She pointed to one X'd out entry. "That one says 'use term my friend. Hedonistic lust. Requires logistics support. Targets Leila Virtanen, Karl Klimek.'"

Grigoris closed his eyes. "Ciril. That's Ciril. I read the report. Ciril always referred to his 'friend'."

"The date in red, just under the X..." Nyx had to pause and gather herself. "The date is the day he was killed. The day Leila shot him."

"The day he hurt you," Grigoris said softly.

She nodded once.

They hadn't gone inside, were all standing at the door, as if some silent accord had kept them from entering a place steeped in evil.

Eric started to enter, but Grigoris stopped him, his mind thinking past the rage, horror, and relief at this confirmation that Petro was the mastermind.

"He might have it booby-trapped," Grigoris said. "We need to proceed with extreme caution."

"Do we have time?" Milo asked.

"If the woman is dead, there's no one left to try to frame me," Eric pointed out.

"We shouldn't assume that either," Nyx said. "Petro

would have redundancies in place. We didn't search Lazar's room."

"I'm the fleet admiral."

"And the knights will detain and question you. They'd have to. That's their job."

"Not happening. I'm not waiting around here while they pull their heads out of their asses."

"Fleet Admiral."

"I'll fuck them up if I have to."

"And doing that would make it look like you were the murderer. And the knights would detain you then."

"They could try."

"I'd fight you, and kill you if I had to if I thought you'd gone mad and murdered someone from my territory, tried to kill my admiral," Milo said.

Eric just looked at him.

Grigoris was distracted by the desk that was on the wall directly opposite the door. There were two computer monitors, one of which was on. The display showed a large map, with a blinking green dot over what he was sure was their current location. Lake Balaton was a distinctive shape, and though the map didn't have names on it, he was sure of that much.

There was a smaller window in the bottom right corner of the monitor that showed a map of Europe. A pale green line led from Italy to Hungary.

The exact path their plane had taken.

"Nyx," Grigoris asked urgently. "What does it say, see the title bar above the map on that monitor? What does it say?"

She peered, then jerked back, as if she'd been struck by something.

"Nyx?"

"It says...it says *soție neascultătoare*."

Eric and Milo were watching her warily. The silence grew heavy with grim anticipation.

"Nyx," Grigoris said gently. "What language, and what does it mean?"

"It's Romanian...my first language." Her hands were trembling. She seemed to realize it and pressed one against her stomach where a knife had violated her, the other over her cheek.

"What does it mean?" Milo asked, his tone as gentle as Grigoris' had been.

"It means disobedient wife." She turned wide, luminous eyes to Grigoris. "The smaller window says 'past twenty-four hours.'"

Grigoris closed his eyes, needing a minute to hide the rage. Suddenly he understood Eric's need to tear something—anything, anyone—apart.

"He's tracking me. He knows where I am. How? *How?*" Nyx's voice grew panicked.

"Are you wearing anything he gave you?" Milo ask.

"Never," she said vehemently. "Never. But he must have, when I was here, somehow he..."

Grigoris looked back at the board, eyes scanning the addresses peppered among the other text. Then he looked more carefully at the desk. If he went in, he'd be able to see everything, but he was more sure than ever that they couldn't enter that room.

Eric took out his cell phone and started snapping pictures.

Apparently the fleet admiral was the only one who was thinking clearly. Grigoris did the same, focusing on a piece of paper tacked to the wall next to the monitor. He stepped back, out of Eric's way, then zoomed in on the list.

His stomach sank.

The header on the page was "*Soție Neascultătoare*," but the rest of the text was in Hungarian. He could make out enough words to know that this was a list of addresses related to Nyx.

And a list that included his home on Cyprus. A place she'd been before they came here, which meant Petro had been tracking her, somehow, before they'd showed up here last week.

He turned his phone so she could see the screen.

She started to read, her expression morphing from fear-laced anger to something more. Something far worse.

Dread.

"That's the address of my first flat in England. And the coffee shop I studied at in Germany. This is...this is every place I've been. Any place that was important." She looked up, and the expression in her eyes pleaded with him to make this false, to scrub away the evidence he now held. "He's been tracking me since I left. That's what Lazar meant. I was never free. I was always his. I..." Her gaze drifted back to the list. "No," she whispered. "No."

Milo and Eric had both turned to them, listening silently as Nyx's perception of life fell apart. "*Háromság főiskolai könyvtár*. Trinity College Library." She stumbled back a step. "I... I..."

Nyx ran.

CHAPTER NINETEEN

"Nyx!" Grigoris caught her halfway through the foyer of the private quarters. "Wait."

Nyx was lightheaded and struggling to get air to her lungs. It was her fault...her fault...

Karl.

Josephine.

She'd given away their identities, their locations, allowed the mastermind...

No, she wouldn't give him the benefit of that name anymore.

Petro. He'd used her to hurt countless innocent people, her friends.

"Nyx, please. Stop!"

He wrapped his hand around her upper arm, attempting to halt her escape.

She whirled on him. "No! Let me go. This is my fault. All of this."

"No." Grigoris rarely raised his voice with her, and she'd

only heard this commanding tone of his when he was controlling a bad situation.

Or in the bedroom.

"You aren't to blame for any of this."

"He was always one step ahead because of me.
Because..." Her hands shook as she considered where the
tracker might be. How, and when, had Petro placed it on her?

No, *in* her.

Her stomach roiled and she feared she might be sick.

"Because of me, he took Karl. He killed J-Josephine."

Grigoris scowled. "Nyx. I know you're upset, but if you
think about this logically, you'll see none of that is true. Karl
was taken because he was traveling. His capture was based
on convenience."

"That's what we thought, but now we know Petro knew
about my meetings at Trinity College. He could have discovered who I was meeting with and chosen to torture Karl
because of our association."

"That's not what happened."

"Ciril knew where to find Leila in Bucharest because she
was with me. He knew where we were just hiding in Rome. Oh
my God, James, Sophia...the others...we have to get them out!"

"Nyx, take a breath."

"And Josephine..." Tears slid down her cheeks, her
breathing becoming louder, more labored.

"Dammit." Grigoris slipped his hand in hers, dragging
her into the empty den. He closed the door behind them,
roughly, then took her face in his hands and kissed her hard.

She was shocked for a moment, her brain shutting down
completely, too devastated to find comfort.

He released her briefly.

"You can't kiss me senseless, Grig—"

He kissed her again, with more passion.

Nyx's tears slowed as she lifted her hands to his strong shoulders.

They parted once more.

"I mean it. I can't—" she started, when he went in for a third kiss.

By the time he released her, she found herself with her back pressed against the wall and his hands under her shirt, his fingers stroking the bare skin beneath.

She was silent the next time he pulled away.

"I'm only going to say this once, so I need you to listen and understand," he said gruffly. "Petro is the villain here. No one else. The things he's done to you, to your friends, to other members of the society, will be answered for. But the fault lies with *him*. Josephine and Karl, as well as the rest of the librarians, understood the risks involved in taking part in the investigation. They made their decision to help the same way you did. Once you've had time to process what's happened, I want the logical, intelligent, savvy," he kissed her forehead, then continued, "part of your brain to kick in. Karl was taken because he was traveling. Josephine's death was an obvious attack against Eric. Petro must have discovered their past association and decided to use it against the fleet admiral."

Nyx wished Grigoris' reassurances would sink in. The words made sense, but her emotions were too close to the surface for her to accept them. "But what if—"

"No. No what-ifs. You forget, Nyx. You suffered terribly at the hands of a man who dared to call himself your husband. Ciril attacked you on Petro's command. Don't let him take anything else from you, don't give him the power to beat you down again, to destroy your peace of mind. Don't do it."

Words defeated her, so instead she reached out, wrapping her arms around Grigoris' waist, grateful when he pulled her into a tight embrace. She pressed her face against his shirt, letting the soft cotton comfort her even as it dried her tears.

"*Se agapó*," she whispered in Greek.

I love you.

"*Ki ego se agapo*," he murmured, his lips pressed to the top of her head.

I love you too.

The door next to them slammed open and Eric strode in. The two of them parted slowly as Eric took in their embrace, then he jerked his head toward the front entrance. "We're getting out of here. I've called in the Spartan Guard to deal with this fucking mess of a territory. Someone here knows something, but as much as I'd like to stay, we can't risk some overzealous knight—or worse, someone Petro mentally fucked —shooting us."

"Hans, the security minister, and the knights..." Nyx said.

"Are going to be renditioned to the dungeons at Triskelion Castle," Eric said coolly.

"And we're going where?" Grigoris asked.

"We're flying to Cyprus."

"Cyprus?"

"Oh yeah," Eric deadpanned. "Did I forget to tell you? You're about to have houseguests. Me, Nyx, and Milo." He looked at Nyx. "I've had your X-rays from the hospital in Bucharest sent to that doctor in Spain, Gabriela Lopez. Perhaps she can discover exactly where the tracker is. We're getting that fucker out of you as soon as possible."

Nyx nodded, wondering if perhaps Eric would blame her for unwittingly revealing so many aspects of their actions to the mastermind. When he said nothing more, she replied, "I want it out too. More than I can say."

Eric's jaw clenched, though his eyes softened. "He's going to pay for everything he did to you, Nyx. For everything he did, period."

She accepted Grigoris' hand, and the two of them followed Eric to the car.

For a moment, it felt like she was going home.

Then she realized the irony of the situation.

Because the truth she'd never accepted was...*this* place was supposed to be home, and now she was leaving.

CHAPTER TWENTY

Grigoris led her, Eric, and Milo through his home on Cyprus, pointing out the bathroom and bedrooms as they walked past, though all anyone was interested in was Grigoris' home office. According to Grigoris, his office was wired with state-of-the-art dedicated secure connection ports and a private server. He pulled out two laptops, keyed them to Milo's and Eric's fingerprints and made sure the phone in the room was routing through Israel, rendering it all but untraceable.

Fengári began rubbing around Eric's ankles. Nyx started to reach for Grigoris' cat, but Eric beat her to it. She was shocked when the fleet admiral cradled the small creature in his arms, absentmindedly stroking her soft fur as Fengári rolled to her back and purred loudly.

"Get me Gabriela on the speakerphone," Eric said to Grigoris. "I want to know how the hell Petro is tracking Nyx."

Nyx swallowed hard.

"And then I want a plan for how we check to make sure no one else is being tracked."

Grigoris rubbed the back of his neck. "If we'd gone into that room, we could have... But no. It was too great a risk."

"Agreed."

"I shouldn't be with you," Nyx said softly. "I'm the Achilles' heel."

Milo was on one of the computers, his eyes scanning the screen. "My admiral sent a message."

Eric walked over, bracing one hand on the back of Milo's chair. "Talk."

"He safely evacuated everyone from the bunker since Petro knows the location. He's rigged it as a trap, in case our enemy makes an appearance."

"Lethal or containment?"

"Containment."

"Good. Petro will suffer before he dies." Eric's calm words were as alarming as a scream would have been.

Grigoris looked up from dialing to glance at her, his eyes widening in comical alarm. She relaxed a little more, smiling quickly in reply.

Nyx had been in shock when they'd fled the estate, but when they reached the airport her brain engaged, and she'd tried to stay behind.

Grigoris, Eric, and Milo weren't safe as long as she was near them, and any place she went was immediately compromised. When she pointed that out, demurred about going to Cyprus with them, Grigoris had been two steps ahead and already had an answer. He'd assured Eric he had the best security system money could buy, plus some things that weren't commercially available, and most importantly, it was a place Nyx had already been, so going there wouldn't reveal any new information.

Nyx had selfishly felt relieved when Eric stuck to his decision that they would all go to Cyprus together.

This was Grigoris' home turf, the place where she felt the safest.

Grigoris set the phone on speaker, and as it rang, Eric straightened and walked away from Milo.

"*Buenos dias*," Dr. Lopez answered in a friendly, breezy manner.

"It's Eric Ericsson," the fleet admiral said. "Did you get the X-rays?"

Nyx could almost imagine the young doctor standing up straighter when she replied, "Yes, sir. I've been awaiting your call."

"And?" Eric asked impatiently.

"The medical report said that the patient had several surgeries to treat a facial wound and a knife wound to the abdomen. Are those the only surgeries she's ever had?"

Eric glanced at Nyx, who nodded.

"That's correct," the fleet admiral replied.

"That's interesting, because I looked at all the X-rays, and the only thing that seemed out of place was something that looks like a dental implant."

"Implant?" Nyx asked.

Gabriela clearly hadn't expected to hear a female voice. "To whom am I speaking?"

"The patient," Nyx replied. "Those are my X-rays. I've never had a dental implant." Suddenly, she recalled something else. "I had my lower wisdom teeth removed when I was sixteen. They were impacted, so I had to be anesthetized."

"I see," Gabriela said. "You never had an infection in one of your back molars? Maybe cracked or broken the tooth?"

"No."

"I have to caution you, I'm not a dentist, but I checked on this. You *are* missing your third molars—the wisdom teeth—on the bottom, but one of your second molars, tooth 18, is an implant, and the post is perhaps a bit larger than normal. I noticed it because that's an odd tooth to implant."

"Why wouldn't the doctors in Bucharest have seen this?" Grigoris asked.

"I'm sure they noticed, but there was no reason to question it," Gabriela replied. "After all, dental implants are fairly common. It's possible an oral surgeon or dentist would have remarked on the oddness of having that tooth be an implant on someone Nyx's age, but the injuries they were treating didn't include the necessity of dental work."

Nyx closed her eyes and tried to recall if she'd damaged a tooth when she was younger, but she honestly couldn't remember. She was careful with her oral hygiene.

Gabriela's next words made her blood run cold. "I think it's possible the implant could have been put in at the same time the wisdom teeth were extracted. That's the most likely scenario. You wouldn't have thought the mouth pain odd because it would have been blamed on the extraction, and since you were under sedation, you wouldn't have been in a place to count how many teeth were removed."

"You said part of it was bigger than normal?" Eric asked.

"The post. It's a metal rod that's inserted into the jawbone, leaving a small amount sticking out through the gums. The false tooth is attached to the exposed end of the post."

"That's got to be the tracker," Milo said grimly.

Sixteen.

It fit, given the long list of addresses Petro had kept on her whereabouts. Nyx swallowed the bile that clogged her throat. He had been tracking her since she was sixteen years old.

Grigoris must have come to the same conclusion because she heard him curse under his breath.

"Thank you, Gabriela," Eric said, nodding at Milo, who reached over and disconnected the call before the doctor could say goodbye. "We pull the post," Eric announced.

Nyx nodded, ready to open her mouth and do the deed herself. All she needed was a pair of pliers.

"I'll call my dentist," Grigoris said. "Find an oral surgeon. Set it up immediately."

"Sooner than immediately. As long as that thing is in her mouth, we're sitting here with our dicks out." The fleet admiral sat down at Grigoris' computer, the cat curling up on his lap as Eric made himself at home.

Eric tapped rapid-fire on the keyboard, doing God only knew what, as Milo pulled out several guns doing what appeared to be a weapons check. Grigoris reached for his cell phone, getting the name of an oral surgeon, then scheduling an appointment for her.

Nyx watched the three men as if they were all moving in slow motion. Life had been in fast-forward ever since she'd left this house the last time, traveling to Dublin, to Lake Balaton and back again—with a quick detour to Italy—before returning here.

She was still trying to wrap her head around everything that had happened.

"Okay," Grigoris said. "I've made the arrangements. We're going off books and paying cash."

"I have money," she said immediately.

"I don't care about the money." Grigoris slashed his hand through the air.

"When?" Eric asked.

"The oral surgeon can do it now, if you're ready, Nyx."

"She's ready," Eric said, not looking up from the computer.

Grigoris frowned, and she thought he might call Eric to task. Nyx placed her hand on his arm and gave him a genuine smile.

"I'm ready."

GRIGORIS PARKED his car in the driveway, nodding when Milo stepped out on his front veranda. The security officer had obviously been watching the perimeter cameras positioned around his property and seen Grigoris' return.

Grigoris walked around to the passenger side and opened the door for Nyx, grinning as he did so. She was loopy from the anesthesia and painkillers. She'd talked the whole way back from the dentist, waxing poetic about what she considered his very sexy ears. More than that, she'd giggled. A lot.

It was a sound he wasn't sure he'd ever heard from her, but one he'd give pretty much anything to keep hearing.

He reached down to help her out and she drunkenly swayed, struggling to get out of the car. She slipped, falling into his arms.

"*Opa!*" she cried out, giggling once more. Grigoris caught her then, much to her delight, bent over to pick her up in his arms.

Milo gave her a shocked look when Nyx said, "*Ciao bello,*" to the security officer.

Grigoris chuckled. "Good drugs," he murmured, but he couldn't resist adding to the joke. "Although you really are a good-looking man."

Milo shrugged. "I'm Italian; of course I am good-looking." He stepped back and held the door open to allow Grigoris and Nyx inside. Then the security officer did a quick scan of the surrounding area before following them in.

In her new position in his arms, Nyx could now touch his ears, and she giggled as she tugged on them. "I want to bite them," she said, her confession setting off a new round of giggles.

"Later," Grigoris promised quietly as Eric walked out of the office.

Grigoris tried to gently place her on the couch. She wrapped her legs around his waist and started humming what sounded like a sea shanty.

"Oooo," Nyx cooed when she caught sight of Eric. "*There's* a tree I'd like to climb."

Eric's brows rose and his lips twitched. "Later," he said, making it clear he'd heard Grigoris' response to Nyx biting his ears.

Once Grigoris was free of Nyx's clinging grip, he stood and quickly explained, "Painkillers."

"Might steal a couple for after we catch this bastard. Oblivion looks good. Tracker?" Eric asked. Grigoris had become used to Eric's cutting wit, but he'd been different since Josephine's death. Calm, but not in a good way. In a fucking terrifying way.

"I broke it, but brought the pieces so we could have someone analyze them. Given its size, and how long it lasted, the tech used was more than just state-of-the-art."

"Good." Eric jerked his thumb toward the office. "We found some things while you were gone."

Grigoris and Milo followed Eric to the office, while Nyx remained on the couch, apparently fascinated by her hair.

Milo handed Grigoris some printed-out pages. "First of

all, we got our hands on Hanna's dental records. She has the same implant."

So Petro had put trackers on both of his wives. Grigoris didn't think knowing that would make Nyx feel any better. He nodded solemnly. "What else did you discover?" he asked Milo.

"We pulled up flight information, plugging in all the airports within three hundred kilometers of Lake Balaton. We got a hit, though I'm not sure it's an accurate one. It looks like Petro got on a flight bound for the United States yesterday afternoon, but we can't track him because he doesn't appear to have actually entered the country."

"Getting information from the States is tricky," Grigoris said.

"On our own, it is," Eric agreed.

"You have some other way?" Milo asked.

Eric sighed, grimacing. "Unfortunately, I do. We have to call the fucking Americans again," he said as he pulled his cell phone out of his pocket and scrolled through his list of contacts. Then he handed the phone to Milo. "That number. Conference call."

Milo dutifully plugged in the number as Grigoris and Eric stood next to the desk.

The Grand Master answered on the third ring. "Juliette Adams."

"Grand Master," Eric drawled.

"Shit."

Grigoris heard the phone knocking around a bit, then Juliette's voice sounded farther away. She'd put them on speaker.

"Now what?" she asked after a few moments.

"I need information," Eric said. "A favor."

"Another favor," Juliette reminded him. "You already owe me. Are you sure you want to be deeper in debt?"

"My offer of sex as reparation is still on the table."

"Well..." Juliette replied, sounding for a moment like she might consider that deal.

"No," a male voice cut through the line. At the same time another man with a slight Hispanic accent said, "I'm not up for it physically, but I'd love to watch."

Eric chuckled. "Ah, the husbands, Devon and Franco. Anyone else there? What about your bulldog, Seb?"

Grigoris could envision the scowls on the Americans' faces when the bulldog corrected him. "I prefer Sebastian."

"No, you don't," Eric egged him on. "How are you feeling, Franco?"

"Better every day," the Hispanic man replied pleasantly.

"In the interest of expediency and getting this conversation over, what do you need, Eric?" Devon asked.

"Fugitive tracking. Two names." Eric spelled Petro and Hanna's names. "They boarded a flight to Chicago yesterday, but their passports weren't scanned in at arrival."

"What did they do?" Franco sounded merely curious.

"How the hell are you accessing U.S. immigration control data?" Devon growled.

"Given the fact you're calling for our help, we can assume this man is dangerous? Do we need to intervene?" Sebastian asked.

The pleasantry in Eric's voice faded, warning dripping from each of the next words he spoke. "I'm going to deal with Petro Sirko myself. All I need to know is where he is."

"If he's on American soil, you'll be dealing with more than just him. You'll be dealing with us," Devon reminded him.

"None of your members need to be involved. We can handle this ourselves."

Grigoris was surprised by Eric's relatively normal tone. There was nothing in his voice, in his comments, to reveal the bloodlust Grigoris could see in his eyes right now.

"I believe you said that last time," Juliette said shortly. "And my husband was nearly killed."

"In all fairness, the *American* shooter," Eric drew out Alicia's nationality, "was aiming for two of my people."

Juliette's tone was cool. "Who weren't supposed to be where they were."

Apparently Eric wasn't interested in rehashing ancient history, though Grigoris figured two months ago hardly classified as ancient. Hugo and Lancelot had traveled to America to capture the American sniper's wife, Alicia, whom they'd discovered was another of the mastermind's acolytes. At the time, she'd been their best hope of discovering the mastermind's identity. The information she'd given them helped lead them to where they were now. Petro had been smart to escape to America, relying on the contentious relationship between the two societies to offer an extra level of protection.

"Can you get the information or not?" Eric asked.

"Of course I can." She blew out a long breath, as if debating whether or not she wanted to. Then, mercifully, she asked, "Is this the number where you can be reached?"

"It is."

"I'm assuming you need this immediately."

"I do."

"This information isn't free."

"I'll owe you a favor."

"You will, but you will also give me details as to who these people are, and why they're running from you."

"You don't need to know that."

"You presume to know what I do and don't need?" Juliette's question was silky.

The fleet admiral stared at the phone, his face stark. "He likes to blow up stuff and recently killed someone very important to me."

The dark silence that followed that statement had an almost physical weight.

"I'll be in touch," Juliette said softly.

The call disconnected.

FOR SEVERAL HOURS, Grigoris and Milo went through every flight record, attempting to find anything they might have overlooked, as Eric spoke with Antonio and Arthur about everything they'd discovered since leaving the bunker in Italy. Nyx had alternated between dozing on the couch and entertaining herself by singing bawdy pub songs Grigoris could only assume she'd learned while attending Oxford.

It was nearly midnight, and they still hadn't received a call from Juliette.

Milo was the first to cry uncle. "We can't work through the night. We're going to have to be ready to move when the Grand Master calls with the flight information. Once that happens, we will move fast. You need to get some rest now, Fleet Admiral. We'll take shifts."

Grigoris hated to stop, but he couldn't deny the security officer was right. He'd run enough investigations in the past that he knew a lack of sleep dulled the senses. They were up against a deadly, dangerous foe. And they all needed to be one-hundred percent ready if they hoped to defeat him.

Grigoris stood up and stretched. "I need to move Nyx to

272 MARI CARR & LILA DUBOIS

the bedroom." He left the office, walking to the couch to rouse Nyx.

When she opened her eyes, he noticed they were more focused and, sadly, the adorable grin she'd worn all day was gone again, replaced by the same pensiveness and concern he'd grown accustomed to.

She blinked a few times, glancing around the room. "The tracker?"

"Gone."

She lifted her hand to her jaw, feeling the place where the implant had been removed. Because of Nyx's desire to have the tracker removed immediately, there hadn't been time to replace it. That was something she would need to deal with after...

God, just after.

They'd been chasing the mastermind for so long, Grigoris had stopped considering what happened after this nightmare was over. At least in terms of mundane things like dentist appointments and getting his car detailed. Everyday things had fallen away in the face of so much death and suffering.

However, there was one thing he hadn't been able to stop thinking about ever since they'd put a name to the mastermind, ever since Grigoris realized Nyx was going to be free from her sham of a marriage.

Nyx slowly pushed herself up.

"Are you in pain? I can get you another one of the painkillers the dentist prescribed."

She shook her head. "No. I'm fine. I don't like the way those things make me feel."

Grigoris grinned. "Does this mean you don't really find my ears sexy?"

Nyx frowned, confused, though he thought perhaps bits and pieces of her day were starting to come back to her.

Eric stepped into the living room.

"There's our Nyx," Eric said, his tired smile revealing he'd witnessed her silliness.

Nyx grimaced but didn't mention her embarrassing afternoon. "What did I miss?"

"I'll let Grigoris catch you up. A bedtime story. Milo offered to take the first shift watching the security cameras. I'm relieving him in two hours. You're relieving me two hours after that," he said to Grigoris. "If we don't have a call from Juliette by morning, we're going to have to come up with a plan B." Eric bent down and scooped up Fengári. "Come on, sweetheart. You're sleeping with me."

Grigoris and Nyx were quiet until Eric slipped into the guest room and shut the door.

"I think I lost my cat."

Nyx gave him a tired smile. "I'll steal her back for you, *motănel*. Come. You need your rest."

They walked to Grigoris' bedroom together. How many times had Grigoris imagined Nyx in his bed? He'd spent countless sleepless nights with her just across the hall, longing for her until he thought he'd go mad with desire.

Now, she was here, and though he knew it wasn't wise, Grigoris couldn't stop the tiny kernel of hope taking root inside that told him Nyx was free.

Once they'd captured and killed Petro, Grigoris would ask Eric to place him in a trinity with Nyx.

"Juliette?" Nyx said, obviously recalling the fleet admiral's last comment. "The Grand Master of the Trinity Masters?"

Grigoris quickly filled her in on everything they'd discovered while she was sleeping off the anesthesia and enjoying her painkillers, then he recapped the phone call with the Americans.

Nyx looked at Grigoris' bed, then back at him with a shy, sexy look.

Grigoris stepped closer, unbuttoning her blouse, unhooking her bra, then drawing her pants and panties off. Once she was naked, she took over, stripping him out of his clothing as he stood still, relishing every stroke of her fingertips, every soft kiss from her lips to the various parts of his body she bared.

Together, they crawled into his bed. Nyx shifted to her back, her legs parting as Grigoris knelt between them. He ran one finger over her clit. She was already wet, ready for him.

He guided his cock to her entrance and slid inside with one steady, smooth motion.

Being inside her felt as natural as breathing.

Grigoris kissed her gently as he thrust in and out, neither of them in a hurry. Rather than a rough, frantic, passionate lovemaking, they simply melted together, two bodies, two hearts.

It felt like one of the most powerful moments of his life.

"*Se agapó*," he whispered. They'd spoken the words before, but that didn't weaken their impact. If anything, the emotion grew stronger each time he told her how he felt.

"Grigoris." She kissed his shoulder, his neck.

He stroked her breasts, pushing deeper with each return to her body. He allowed himself to dream of the day when the two of them would make a baby together. He wanted a little girl with Nyx's white-blond hair and translucent blue eyes.

"Come with me," he murmured, when he reached the precipice. He could tell from Nyx's accelerated breathing, her soft mewls, that she was close too.

He reached between them and pressed on her clit,

rubbing it the way he knew she loved, her hips rising and falling more rapidly as she tried to draw in even more of him.

"Nyx," he said, when he felt her orgasm begin, her inner muscles clenching tightly on his cock. "God."

Her back arched as she cried out, dragging him over the edge with her. Grigoris worried briefly about how much Eric could hear from his room across the hall. He cast the thought away. The fleet admiral had stolen his cat after all.

He held himself over her as their climaxes faded away and he withdrew. He kissed her once more, then his lips slid along her neck.

It was late and they needed sleep. Grigoris could tell himself those things over and over, but they didn't serve to make him tired. When he was with her, he felt as if he could run a hundred marathons in a row.

Nyx kissed his cheek, and then she nipped his earlobe.

He pulled back for a moment, uncertain if her action had been deliberate.

When her soft laugh escaped, he chuckled.

"Now if only I could find that big blond Viking," she teased.

He gave her a stern look. "Biting my very sexy ear is one thing, but you are not climbing Eric's tree."

Nyx's amusement erupted into a full-fledged laughter that he shared.

"Jealous man," she mused as their laughter subsided.

"With you. Always."

He meant his words as a compliment, but something flashed in Nyx's eyes and a shadow fell over them. Only for a moment before she twisted to her side to fully face him, her hand resting on his hip.

He wanted to ask her what he'd said, but she yawned and

blinked tiredly. Though she'd dozed all day, there were dark circles under her eyes that he hated seeing there.

They still had a thousand miles to walk, a million bridges to cross. There was so much he wanted to say to her, but right now, the only thing that mattered was sleep.

He kissed her good night, closed his eyes, and played out all his hopes for the future in his dreams.

CHAPTER TWENTY-ONE

Nyx was sitting in the office, ice pack held to her jaw to help reduce the swelling from having the tracker removed. The spot where there had once been a tooth felt like a gaping hole, though intellectually she knew it wasn't. After some contortion in the mirror this morning, she'd been able to catch a glimpse of the blank space in her mouth and a single stitch in her gum.

There was something morbidly amusing about the fact that the tracker had been on the left side of her mouth, meaning that she now had a scar on the right side of her face, and the left side had been, pre-ice, swollen to the point that she looked like an animal storing nuts in its cheek pocket.

Since her face hurt too much for her to focus on anything —and she'd be even less focused if she took the prescription the oral surgeon had given her—she was playing receptionist, stationed by the phone in case it rang.

Last night had felt like an escape, a brief moment spent in paradise, considering the chaos raining down on their heads every other minute of the day. With Grigoris, she was able to forget...everything. Then the bright, harsh light of day would crash in again. It took everything she had to get out of bed this morning, which would have made sense if Grigoris had still been there, but the tireless man had only managed a few hours' sleep before rising to keep watch over the house.

The phone rang.

"*Parakaló*," Nyx said, using a formal Greek phone greeting.

"I'd like to speak to Eric." The clipped woman's voice spoke English with an American accent.

"Hello, Ms. Adams. A moment, and he'll be here." Nyx put the call on speaker and rushed out of the office. Eric was standing on the terrace stroking Fengári.

"Fleet Admiral," she called out.

Even as Eric turned, Grigoris appeared at her side. He was careful not to approach her from the back, and as his arm slid around her waist, she relaxed into him.

Milo had appeared in the office, seemingly out of thin air. His hair was slicked back from his head, showing off a widow's peak that made him seem a little wicked.

No one spoke until Eric entered the room. His face was calm, almost placid, his hand gentle on the cat's back, but his eyes... There was rage in his gaze, a rage so vast and deep that it reminded her of the perhaps overused Nietzsche quote, "*Und wenn du lange in einen Abgrund blickst, blickt der Abgrund auch in dich hinein.*"

And if you gaze long into an abyss, the abyss also gazes into you.

Eric paused, then seemed to gather himself. A good-natured smirk transformed his face, but the expression didn't reach his eyes.

"Grand Master. How are you and your posse?"

"Posse?" Devon asked in an irritated voice. "We are her advisors."

"Franco's the brains, Seb is the dumb muscle, and you're the irritated logistics guy," Eric said.

"Thank you," Franco sounded pleased.

"What the fuck?" Sebastian yelped.

There was a noisy sigh from who Nyx assumed was Devon.

Juliette, however, laughed. "Fleet Admiral, your manners are, as always, lacking."

Eric, apparently, had exhausted whatever patience, or perhaps "facade or normalcy" was a more appropriate term, he'd been able to summon. "Where's Petro?"

"I need to clarify a few things before I give you any information."

Eric's hand stilled on the cat, and he must have started to squeeze her because Fengári bit his finger. Eric jerked, looked down at the cat, and his expression softened. "What do you want to clarify?" He resumed petting the cat, who looked haughtily pleased for having put the big man in his place.

"If you commit murder on U.S. soil and are caught, we will not come to your aid."

"Because murder is wrong," Franco said.

Milo's brows rose and Eric looked at the ceiling.

"Um, yes, of course. Because murder is wrong." Juliette cleared her throat. "But more importantly because you have yet to pay us back for the first favor. I'm not sure it would be worth it to me to continue to help you without recompense." Juliette paused. "To put it simply, you're writing checks I'm not sure you can cash."

"Do not underestimate me, Grand Master."

"Don't forget that I am your equal, Fleet Admiral."

There was a pregnant silence. Even the cat looked at Eric warily.

"Of course, Grand Master. I'm..."

"Sorry," Nyx mouthed.

"Sorry," Eric said through gritted teeth.

Juliette hummed. "We tracked people matching Petro and Hanna's descriptions getting off the plane in Chicago, though they used other names."

"We're checking to see why they were able to get through, despite the fact that the names they used at passport control were not listed on any flight manifest," Devon said.

"What names did they use?" Milo asked.

"It doesn't matter because they left Chicago and flew to Honolulu, using another set of aliases. From there, they traveled by boat to Kauai, before finally flying to Guam. As of right now, we think they're on Guam," Sebastian said.

"Guam?" Milo frowned. "Micronesia?"

"Yes. It's a U.S. protectorate, and home to Joint Region Marianas, a combined Air Force and naval base," Devon added.

Franco muttered something about colonialism.

"You understand this took considerable effort," Juliette added. "And whoever these people are to you, they took great pains to make sure you couldn't find them."

"He must be unaware that you and the leader of the Trinity Masters have started to open up lines of communication," Grigoris added.

"And promised some light sexual favors," Franco added.

That broke the tension, and Eric went back to stroking the cat. "Grand Master, we're requesting permission to follow our man into your territory."

"Permission granted, and I'll even help you with accommodations on Guam. Rear Admiral Smith, the commanding officer of the base, is one of my members."

"Thank you, Fleet Admiral." A ghost of a smile touched Eric's face. "Since you're being so accommodating, I'll abandon my plans to keep wooing the Hayden triplets to my team."

"Are you the reason they haven't accepted their memberships yet?" Franco asked.

"Franco, shut up," Sebastian snapped.

"They haven't accepted?" Eric looked intrigued.

"Yet," Juliette said smoothly.

"Oops," Franco muttered.

"Let me know when you've finalized your travel arrangements," Juliette said smoothly. Then added, "And this makes two, Fleet Admiral."

The Americans ended the call and everyone looked at Eric. He was still for a moment, then turned to Grigoris. "We need a strike team."

Grigoris nodded. "The three of us, Dimitri, Lancelot, and Leila. I want a sniper."

"I'm coming," Nyx declared.

"You're staying here," Grigoris said immediately. "I'll get another janissary, or a security officer from Ottoman, to come stay with you. My house is secure."

"No place is perfectly secure," Nyx countered.

Grigoris opened his mouth to protest, but Eric cut him off. "She's coming. She's the only one we've got who knows what's going on and speaks all the same languages as Petro and Hanna."

"I won't risk her," Grigoris said stubbornly.

Eric faced him, that cold, dangerous calm sliding over him again, but before he could reprimand Grigoris, Nyx slid up to him, letting the back of her hand brush against his.

282 MARI CARR & LILA DUBOIS

"I feel safest with you," she whispered.

Grigoris' shoulders slumped, and he turned to press a kiss to her temple. Eric watched them.

"It's going to take us twenty hours to get there," Milo said from behind his computer. "And that's if we leave now."

"Then let's go," Eric commanded. "We'll make the rest of the arrangements in flight."

GRIGORIS HELD Nyx's hand as they followed Milo and Eric from the car they'd rented at the Antonio B. Won Pat International Airport, more commonly known as Guam International Airport, and walked toward the home the Trinity Masters had arranged for them to use while they were on the island.

Devon had emailed Eric directions to the house on Nimitz Hill. The home itself was single-storied and flat-roofed, with a covered area to park cars, but no garage. Delicate palm trees swayed, and long expanses of green lawn connected the homes, which didn't have fences to mark the property lines. During the grueling trip to get here, they'd had plenty of time to research Guam, looking not only for any clues as to why Petro would have gone there but also gathering information on the political situation. Grigoris and Milo had both been concerned there might be a CIA black site on the island, and it would be far too easy for the Trinity Masters to remand them into a nameless prison, never to be seen or heard from again.

Everything Nyx knew about Eric told her that the fleet admiral should have been far more worried about the possibility, but with every kilometer they got closer to Petro, Eric seemed to care less and less about the details, something that was making Grigoris more uneasy by the minute.

A guard at a small gatehouse near the entrance to the neighborhood had checked Eric's passport, then silently given him a ring with two identical keys on it and a map of the neighborhood, with the house they were using circled. The area was, they had learned, classified as on-base housing and meant for sailors and airmen who brought their families with them when they were stationed here. They'd passed two brightly colored and well-maintained playgrounds on the way through the neighborhood.

Nimitz Hill was also where the command of the Joint Region Marianas had its headquarters. There were two military bases on the island, a U.S. naval base and Anderson Air Force Base. Some time ago, they'd been combined into the Joint Region Marianas. The man in charge of all of it was a Rear Admiral Smith, who they knew was a member of the Trinity Masters, though from the information they found online, he was a happily married family man who seemed staid and conservative. He and the wife in the pictures were doing a very good job hiding their third spouse.

The Grand Master seemed determined to keep an eye on the fleet admiral. Nyx recalled Hugo sharing about his experience in the United States when he and Lancelot traveled to South Carolina to track down Alicia. They'd spent a great deal of time playing cat and mouse with the Trinity Masters during their hunt for the dangerous woman. A game that ended when Lancelot captured Alicia, however, not before Juliette's husband was shot.

Hugo had also found his trinity during that trip, returning home with Sylvia Hayden, whom Eric made a member, then bound to him and Lancelot in marriage.

As they reached the front door, it opened and two men

stepped out. Both gentlemen were attractive, tall, and formidable.

"Seb," Eric said, speaking to the clean-cut, dark-haired man who was scowling at them. So much for a welcoming committee.

"Sebastian," the man corrected, looking over the fleet admiral's shoulder at her, Grigoris, and Milo. "Is this your team?"

"Others are still en route," Eric replied.

Sebastian's brows rose slightly, obviously surprised that Eric was bringing so many people to track down one man. "Who is this Petro Sirko?"

Eric ignored the question, turning instead to the other man. "Langston. Given any thought to my offer?"

Langston was the polar opposite of Sebastian. While the Grand Master's advisor was stiff and clearly distrustful, Langston was more relaxed, laid-back. He had close-cropped hair and an easy smile that reminded Nyx of his sister, Sylvia.

"Eric," Sebastian warned. "You told Juliette—"

"I know what I said." Eric's words were soft and low.

Nyx didn't know Sebastian, but she shot the man a warning look. He met her gaze briefly.

Sebastian stepped aside and Eric led the way into the house. Nyx glanced around, surprised to find the home well-furnished and cozy-looking. Traversing through the bright, sunny foyer, they turned left into a large living room, complete with an overstuffed couch and ottoman, a recliner, and two wingback chairs. Everything was tastefully decorated in muted tones of navy and beige.

She and Grigoris sat down, sharing the couch with Langston. Milo claimed one of the chairs. Neither Sebastian nor Eric sat. Eric stood with his back to the wall as Sebastian claimed a spot near the front window.

Eric quickly did the introductions, then said, "You've met everyone. Now leave."

"We're not going anywhere," Sebastian stated.

Eric stiffened, and Nyx braced herself for an explosion. Grigoris must have sensed the same thing because he rose from the couch and put himself between the fleet admiral and Sebastian. "We appreciate your offer of help," he said genially. As always, Nyx was impressed by his smooth, almost gentle tone. No one upon first meeting Grigoris would realize how intelligent, how deadly he was.

Sebastian sized up Grigoris for a moment. "We're not here to help you. We're here to watch you."

"I'm here to help. Sylvia called and asked me to," Langston said, rising from the couch as well.

"Wasn't sure you'd be able to make it," Eric said.

Sebastian narrowed his eyes at Eric. "Our members aren't at your disposal, Fleet Admiral."

Eric crossed his arms, his grin slightly frightening. "According to Franco, he's not a member yet. And *my* members obey me. Sylvia told you what we needed?"

"Yeah. Hold on a second." Langston dashed out of the living room, returning a minute later with a large trunk on wheels. He placed it in the center of the room, unlocked it, and threw open the lid.

"What the hell?" Sebastian muttered as all six of them stood around the trunk and peered inside.

Langston had presented them with a mobile armory as Nyx studied the array of weapons—everything from large knives to handguns, scopes, ammunition.

"You said that was your drone." Sebastian frowned, his hands on his hips.

Langston gave Sebastian a shit-eating grin before turning

to Eric. "Sylvia called and said y'all needed some firepower. This was all I could fit in the trunk."

Milo bent over the trunk, pulling out two of the guns, looking like a kid in a candy shop. Grigoris had mentioned on the plane that one of his first tasks when they landed would be securing the weapons they needed to capture and kill Petro. Luckily Guam was a part of the U.S. and had the same laughable gun safety laws. Eric hadn't mentioned recruiting Langston via Sylvia, so he must not have been sure help would arrive from that front.

He was grateful Langston had taken care of the task of securing weapons for them.

Eric looked pleased for the first time in days. "I like you. You sure you don't want to join the fun team?"

"You're the fun ones?" Langston asked, looking around.

Milo blinked, then smiled and did an awkward thumbs-up, clearly trying to look nonthreatening, fun, and American.

Grigoris regarded Milo with a pained expression. Sebastian looked stupefied. Milo gave up with a shrug, then went back to petting his new guns.

"Jesus." Sebastian walked to the corner of the room and retrieved several large sheets of paper rolled up. He carried them to the coffee table and unfurled them. "Devon asked the rear admiral for maps of the island and suggestions of potential places your man could be holed up."

Eric slapped Sebastian on the back. "So you *are* helping."

Sebastian glanced down at the trunk, and then scowled at Langston again. "Apparently we are."

Grigoris pulled a tablet out of his jacket pocket, then tapped the screen, pulling up a list of addresses. "We've been looking into any connections Petro has to Guam also."

"Maybe this will be easy, and there will be overlap," Milo said hopefully.

"If there is, we'll need to know if I can kill him there or at a secondary location," Eric said.

Langston laughed, but quickly fell silent when no one else joined in. "Oh, he's serious?"

Nyx declined to join the circle of men around the map, not fully comfortable with the idea of leaving her back unprotected. Instead, she took a seat in an armchair tucked against the wall and listened, trusting her mind to sort and store what she heard as they narrowed the list down to a few, with one location that seemed to rise to the top as the most likely location.

An hour after they'd arrived, Lancelot, Dimitri, and Leila arrived, loaded down with bags filled with tactical gear.

Leila and Nyx exchanged hugs, Leila squeezing her tight, before whispering in her ear. "I'm so sorry I didn't realize. I saw you and Petro together that day. I knew something was off, but I didn't...I never..."

"Nothing about this is your fault," Nyx said immediately.

Leila looked at her. "And it's not your fault either. You know that, right?"

Nyx went silently back to her seat.

Langston nearly cried tears of joy when Leila set up a state-of-the-art 3-D printer and began printing out the parts for a computer-aided sniper rifle. She'd been equally impressed by him when he suggested a couple of tweaks to her blueprint, and she scavenged pieces from a few of the weapons in the trunk.

Grigoris took the list of possible hiding places once they'd finished compiling it and left, intent on doing some preliminary recon that would help them narrow down the list as well as prioritize it.

Five hours later, he'd returned with their three best options—two were unoccupied buildings, one of which had been undergoing a remodel to turn it into a boutique hotel for several years, the project apparently stalled out, thanks to funding issues. One of the backers was an investment group based in the southeastern part of Belarus—a strip of that country fell within the territory of Hungary.

The second was a defunct MWR center—Morale, Welfare, and Recreation, according to Sebastian. Not far from where they were now, it had been sold to a private developer after the newly formed Joint Region Marianas built new leisure facilities with state-of-the-art entertainment and recreation. The old center, with its small hostel-like housing, pool, bowling alley, and ballroom, had been vacant for years. It had been bought by an NGO that planned to turn it into a community center to serve Chamorros using funds and grants from the U.S. government. The interesting part was the NGO, though it had a branch in the U.S., had primarily done work in eastern Europe.

The third option Grigoris had identified from the long list was a mortgage and title company that had major financial backing from K&H, one of the largest banks in Hungary. It maintained offices but was located away from other businesses, and there was a large warehouse across the lot from it. If Petro had any connection to it, either the small offices themselves or the warehouse could be where he was staying.

"The unoccupied ones," Eric declared. "Full tactical assault. Which one is our best bet?" He studied the map again.

Grigoris hesitated. "I think we should try covert recon at the title company. That's the safest, least obtrusive."

Eric shook his head. "We're taking him down now." Eric glanced at the window. The sun was starting to set. "Tonight."

Grigoris looked back at her. Nyx could see he was frustrated, but he was hiding it. He turned back to the map and pointed. "The hotel. It has what appears to be a working security system, which makes sense if it's being remodeled— that means tools, materials, items that are worth a lot of money and need to be protected."

"Good. Gun ready, Leila?"

"Almost finished, Fleet Admiral. I had the parts least likely to cause alarm at customs already assembled and in my luggage. Plus, I was able to take shortcuts, thanks to what Langston had."

"Good. Milo, this is a tactical assault. I want you in command, I'll do first entry."

Lancelot started pulling tactical gear out of bags. "How many people are we outfitting?"

Milo looked around, his gaze dark and assessing. "We'll need at least five. Myself, Lancelot, Eric, Grigoris, and Dimitri on breach. Leila, you find high ground."

"I'll only be able to cover two sides." She looked at the map and pointed. "If I can get onto the roof of this building, I'll be able to see the north and east walls."

"Nyx is coming too," Eric said.

Nyx raised an eyebrow but didn't say anything. Grigoris, however, looked like he was going to explode. Before he could say anything, Eric raised a hand. "She's the only one who speaks all the same languages they do."

"Then we put her on the coms," Grigoris said desperately. "She should stay here with Sebastian and Langston."

"I'm coming with you." Sebastian selected a Kevlar vest and helmet.

"Uh, I'm not," Langston said immediately. "I'm more of a Q than a double O."

"Then Nyx can stay with him," Grigoris said.

Nyx cleared her throat and stood. That was enough to get

290 MARI CARR & LILA DUBOIS

Grigoris' attention. Their gazes met. She would not stay here with a man she didn't know. Wouldn't remain hidden away and safe while he went into danger, not when there was a possibility that she could help.

"She comes with us," Eric said softly. "Dimitri, fit her with a vest."

Milo took over then, assigning breach and entry teams, walking everyone through the plan. Nyx would be at the back with Grigoris.

The last thing Milo handed everyone was two cans of Silly String each. Grigoris nodded his approval as he tucked them into pockets in the vest.

"We go in slow," Milo said.

"That's what she said," Lancelot muttered.

"We've been studying the mastermind, but we don't know what he's capable of on his own. We know what his pets do."

"What if there's a bomb?" Grigoris asked.

"We back out," Milo said immediately. "But, given that we think Petro himself is in there, a bomb isn't high on the list of possible booby traps. I'm more worried about incendiary trip wires, alarms. It's why we have this." He tapped a can of Silly String.

Nyx nodded, then reached up to hold the heavy helmet in place. It was a tad too large. Grigoris reached out and undid the chin strap, then started making adjustments to the inner padding while she spoke. "We should be prepared for the possibility that he isn't alone. He may have come here because he has other pets here—bombers, serial killers, and Hanna who appears to be a sniper."

"If there's a bomb, can I have it?" Langston asked.

Everyone turned to look at him.

"He's strange. I like him," Milo declared.

"We don't give him time to attack. We slide in, kill him, and leave," Dimitri said softly. Like Milo, he was a security officer, which meant when he went out to execute someone, it wasn't like when Grigoris had to deliver justice. It was the kind of killing where they never found the body.

"We need him alive to question," Grigoris pointed out.

Dimitri and Lancelot exchanged a glance but then nodded.

Eric crossed his arms, his muscles bulging, his expression ferocious. "This ends today."

CHAPTER TWENTY-TWO

A tarp-backed chain-link fence surrounded the hotel. Grigoris dropped to one knee, took the tin snips out of his pocket and cut a vertical line through the wires, holding aside the chain link so the team could slide through. As Nyx slid in, Grigoris squeezed her shoulder, reassuring himself as much as her.

"Still quiet," Leila said, her gently accented voice clear through the headphones built into the helmets. She was on the roof of a building not far away, with a clear line of sight to two sides of the building. For safety, they were breaching the fence on the short side, where they weren't visible from the street but where Leila could see and protect them.

Eric barely fit through the opening, his tactical gear giving him the proportions of a comic book character. Once everyone else was through, Grigoris slid in and turned, using a few short lengths of wire to close up the fence. He'd have preferred leaving it open for a quick getaway, but in a place filled with military personnel, they didn't want to risk someone noticing the damaged fence.

Once that was done, they tucked the tarp back into place. It hid their movements from street view, but Leila would still be able to see them, at least until they went inside the building.

Milo raised a hand, motioned right, then left. Silently, they split into two teams. Eric, Grigoris, Nyx, and Sebastian were going to breach via the front door, while Milo, Dimitri, and Lancelot went in the back. Milo's strategic assessment had been that the front door was more likely to be potentially booby-trapped, while there was a better chance of success of getting into the building through the back door.

Grigoris and Nyx were going to the front door because Grigoris didn't want Nyx in the building, didn't want her creeping through the dark hallways of an old hotel with the man who'd destroyed her life potentially lurking behind every corner. He would much rather keep her with him and attempt to go in the front door, where they would no doubt be stymied by some sort of defensive measures. Then he could take Nyx back to the vehicle and wait until the rest of them had captured Petro and Hanna.

"Team one, go," Milo said quietly.

Nyx did as they'd practiced, standing behind Eric as the fleet admiral used a short crowbar to force the door open. Eric was large enough to be a full-body shield. Perhaps Grigoris should feel bad for thinking of the fleet admiral as nothing more than a walking, talking barrier between Nyx and danger, but Eric was the one who'd insisted on bringing her *into* danger, so Grigoris didn't feel the slightest bit of remorse. Besides, he was beginning to believe the fleet admiral was bulletproof.

Eric finished popping the door, then stood to the side, Nyx moving with him. He pushed the door open with one hand. Grigoris and Sebastian flattened themselves to the wall on the other side of the set of wooden double doors.

"Team two breaching," Milo said.

They waited, listening for the sounds of team two needing help.

"We're in. Going up." Milo's voice was cool and calm, proving that this wasn't the first, or even fiftieth, time he'd done something like this.

"Team one going in," Eric said, then motioned for Grigoris to go first.

Gun at the ready, Grigoris whipped around the open door, pausing, gun trained on the darkened foyer and reception area. They'd been able to pull both the original hotel plans, and the construction permits with the new plan for what it would look like after the remodel. The problem being, they weren't sure what the actual state of the building was. Luckily, floors one and two—the hotel rooms—and the reception area of the ground floor were the same.

Grigoris pulled a can of Silly String from a pouch on his vest and sprayed it over the area just beyond the doors. The stuff was light enough to lay on, rather than trigger, any trip wires. The bright pink sticky ribbons fell to the floor.

"Clearing second floor," Milo said.

"Foyer clear," Grigoris responded. Sebastian, Eric, and Nyx joined him.

Nyx, dwarfed by the tactical gear, took up position just inside the door, her body angled so she could see outside and, more importantly, Leila could see her.

"Eyes on Nyx," Leila said.

Grigoris looked at her and winked. Nyx gave him a little half smile.

Eric tapped him on the shoulder, and Grigoris refocused on the task at hand. Moving in tandem, he, Eric, and Sebastian swept through the foyer, then behind the reception desk. Eric shoved open the swinging door behind the desk, and Grigoris ducked in, gun sweeping the small office.

"Clear," he murmured.

Next, they cleared the bathrooms and a storage area under the staircase. Eric tapped his shoulder and pointed to the elevator shaft. Grigoris and Sebastian took up positions on either side of the doors as Eric swung his gun onto his back, then forced the elevator doors open.

The hotel was dark, but moonlight filtered in the windows, providing enough illumination to work by. Compared to that, the elevator shaft was pitch-black.

Grigoris took a knee, then flipped on a pen light attached to the top of his gun. He swept the base of the shaft, seeing nothing, then leaned in, looking up, to check where the elevator car was.

He looked up just in time for the beam of his flashlight to catch a slender hand tossing something into the elevator shaft.

"Pull back!" Grigoris snapped, scrambling back himself. "Female on the second floor at the elevator—"

The flash bang went off, sound and light incapacitating Grigoris. He gritted his teeth and waited for the ringing to stop. He'd closed his eyes before the flash, but when he tried to look around, he still saw spots, the blast of light bright enough to temporarily blind him even through closed eyes.

"Flash bang," Eric shouted. "She's on your floor, Milo."

"We see her," Dimitri said. "We're going—"

Another burst of sound, but this time it was coming through the com link. Petro and Hanna had thrown a second flash bang.

Eric snarled and started up the stairs, taking them three at a time.

"Fleet Admiral!" Grigoris called.

"We've fallen back into one of the rooms." Milo's voice was strained.

"Do they have anyone with them?" Grigoris asked.

"Visual confirmation of Hanna only," Milo added.

"Where's Petro?" Eric snarled.

"We're exiting the room. Headed west down the hall to target's last-known position." Milo's voice had lost some of the strain. "Ericsson, hold your position in case they retreat down the stairs."

There was a sound like a growl, and then Eric said, "I want them alive. So I can kill him, slowly."

Grigoris looked back over his shoulder, exchanging a glance with Nyx from across the dark foyer.

For a moment there was tense silence, and then a pop, followed by shouts. Grigoris tensed.

"Elevator shaft!" Sebastian shouted.

Grigoris whipped around in time to see something silvery fall through the darkness. A second later there was a pop, and then a gagging, stinging smell filled the foyer. Grigoris' eyes burned, and the inside of his nose felt like it was on fire.

"Pepper spray." Milo coughed out the words. "Coming down."

"It's here too," Grigoris choked. He raced across the foyer, elbow over his mouth, and grabbed Nyx, hauling her outside where the air was clear.

"Gun." Leila's voice was clear and calm.

Grigoris' body reacted before his brain—distracted by the burn of the pepper spray—had fully processed, and he stopped abruptly.

The concrete of the circular driveway at the front of the hotel chipped and exploded a meter in front of Grigoris' toes. He backpedaled, shoving Nyx behind him.

"Where is he?" Eric demanded.

Grigoris turned and shoved Nyx back toward the open front door.

"First floor, fourth window from the corner," Leila said coolly. "Female. No sign of anyone else. You can't use the front exit, unless I lay down cover fire, but that will attract attention."

"Hold your fire." Milo's voice was hoarse.

Grigoris and Nyx were back in the foyer. Sebastian had been thinking fast and shoved the elevator doors closed, which protected them to some extent.

"For fook sake, why didn't we bring masks?" Lancelot wheezed.

Eric, and then the three members of team two, stumbled down the steps into the foyer. Milo used hand signals to guide them all out of the foyer and into the construction zone in the restaurant kitchen.

Nyx ran to a small handwashing sink and grabbed paper towels from an old dispenser that hadn't been removed yet. The water was off to the building, but when Nyx handed him the stack of paper towels, Grigoris grabbed a small silver pouch of water from the supplies tucked into the cargo pocket of his pants and ripped it open with his teeth, dousing the towels, and then passing them around.

Everyone wiped their faces, and the air in the kitchen was clear enough that after a few deep breaths and a lot of coughing, they were able to speak normally.

"Leila, do you still have a visual?" Milo asked.

"No."

"We exit the building and flush them out with tactical crowd disbursement," Milo said. "They know we're here and going after them in close quarters is an unnecessary risk."

"If she's still one floor above us, let's get under her and shoot up through the ceiling," Lancelot suggested.

"And give away our position so they can shoot down on us?" Grigoris asked.

"If we kill them, they won't be able to," Lancelot snarked.

"The fleet admiral wants them alive," Dimitri reminded him.

"Are we sure Petro is here?" Nyx asked. Everyone looked at her, and she raised a brow. "Have we seen anyone besides Hanna? And are you sure it *is* Hanna?"

"I saw her well enough to say it was Hanna," Milo said. "But I haven't seen anyone else."

"We can't stay here," Eric growled. "We have to move. You think you can flush them, her, out, Milo?"

"Yes."

"Then we go out the back and come at this a different way."

"No," Leila said immediately. "There are windows that face the back of the hotel, she can walk into a room on that side and take you out, and I won't be able to protect you."

"We go out the front and run for it?" Nyx asked.

"Leila, did you see what kind of gun?" Milo asked.

"Long-range rifle. I wouldn't bet your lives on the vests and helmets being able to stop one of her bullets."

Nyx looked around. "We're trapped?"

"No," Milo said. "We need a distraction. Keep her focused on one person while the others get out."

"We're not sacrificing someone," Eric said immediately, then his cool demeanor cracked and he grabbed a large metal cabinet, picked it up, and began methodically smashing it against the cracked tile floor.

They watched him in silence. When the cabinet was warped, Eric dropped it, his shoulders sagging.

"Feel better?" Lancelot asked.

Grigoris pinched the bridge of his nose. "Well, the noise will have alerted her as to where we are."

"How did one fucking woman with a gun manage to fucking back us into a corner?" Eric growled.

"Don't underestimate one woman with a gun," Leila said.

Milo's eyes narrowed. "Leila, you think you can shoot her before she shoots me?"

"I thought I wasn't supposed to shoot her?"

"Can you shoot to wound?" Eric asked.

"I can try, but I can't promise."

Milo adjusted his grip on his gun. "Here's the plan."

Nyx was strangely calm. Despite the fact that she was effectively trapped in this hotel with a gun-wielding mad woman, who also happened to technically be her wife, which should have panicked her.

She kept one hand curled loosely around Grigoris' belt. Eric's outburst in the kitchen had made going with Grigoris the far more preferable option. She and Grigoris were on the top floor, hunkered down in a stairwell landing. Eric and Dimitri were on the first floor, Sebastian and Lancelot on the ground floor. Eric and Dimitri were closest to Hanna's last-known location, but it was Milo who was in the most danger. He was about to run out the front door, lure Hanna into the window, and then Leila was going to incapacitate her.

"Going in three, two, one," Milo whispered through the coms.

Nyx waited, tense, eyes closed so she could focus on what she was hearing.

"I see you," Leila said. "Stay close to the building. I need her in the window."

"Understood," Milo said.

"I have movement." Leila's voice was tense. "She's on the second floor, center window."

Nyx's eyes popped open, and Grigoris cursed softly. While they'd been in the kitchen, Hanna had moved, going up a floor, meaning she and Grigoris were now the closest ones to her.

"Stay here," Grigoris breathed, pressing her gently against the wall by the stairwell door. He eased the door open, wedging it in place with a short knife he pulled from his ankle, the handle thick enough to serve as a doorstop.

There was the crack of a gunshot, and Grigoris and Nyx both froze.

"You're too far out," Leila said. "Get closer to the building, make her come into the window to get the angle."

Faintly, Nyx heard a curse, but it wasn't coming through her headset. Hanna was close enough that her snarled words were audible. Fear pooled in Nyx's stomach, but she yanked the helmet off so she wouldn't be distracted. Grigoris gestured frantically for her to put it back on, but Nyx pointed to her ear, gesturing that she was listening.

Grigoris cupped a hand over his mouth, murmuring into the communications link while she inched closer to the open door, straining to hear.

"*Basszon agyon a kenkoves istennyila!*" Hanna snarled.

Grigoris looked at her, and Nyx mouthed the words, "Fuck you," though a literal translation was, "Get fucked to death by lightning with sulphuric stones."

There was the sound of metal clinking, then breaking glass.

Nyx took a deep breath, and then crawled out of the stairwell and into the doorway to the hall, hoping she'd be able to hear better.

"You said there was a plan," Hanna muttered in Hungarian. She sounded tired. Defeated. "You said it would end. But it will never be enough!"

Was she actually talking to someone? They hadn't seen Petro or anyone else.

There was another crack of gunfire, and Hanna cursed again, calling Milo several names and wishing that a wheelbarrow of small monkeys would fuck him. Hungarian curses really highlighted the lack of creativity in other languages.

Grigoris crept up next to her and placed a hand on her shoulder.

There was a noise of triumph, another crack of gunfire. Hanna had fired again. Had she gotten Milo?

As those questions whipped through Nyx's head, there was another, distant crack of sound.

Hanna cried out.

Grigoris was up and moving, Eric—who'd crept up the stairs—pounding after him, Nyx scrambling to her feet to follow.

Grigoris was already through the door and had Hanna's gun in hand by the time Nyx raced in. Eric was on his knees, pressing his hands to the wound in Hanna's abdomen.

He'd pulled her shirt up to get a look at the wound. The bullet had partially destroyed two of the tattoos on her stomach. Her entire abdomen, from waist to breasts, was covered in intricate designs.

"Hanna," Nyx murmured in Hungarian. "Where is he?"

"I won't tell you."

"He has to be stopped."

"He cannot be stopped." She grimaced, clearly in pain. "You cannot stop the sun from shining."

"Hanna, he was injured, a brain injury. That's why he's like this. We can stop him, maybe help him."

Hanna's brows knitted for a moment, but then her face smoothed out. "Even if I wanted to, it's too late."

"It's not too late. Whatever you did, it was because of him."

"She's going to bleed out," Milo said as he dropped down beside them. "It looks like the bullet hit the abdominal aorta."

Lancelot yanked a small first aid kit from one of his pockets and pulled out a gauze pad. The instant Eric lifted his hands, blood gushed from the hole in Hanna.

"Not too late for me. Too late for *them*." Her hands raised, fluttering down to rest on her stomach. Nyx wasn't sure if she was trying to push away Eric's hands, where he was desperately trying to keep her blood in her body, or help him stem the flow of her lifeblood.

"Nyx, where is Petro?" Grigoris asked in English.

"She didn't say."

"Find out," Eric snarled.

"Hanna," Nyx asked once more in Hungarian. "Hanna, where is he?"

Hanna's eyes slid closed.

"No pulse. She has no blood pressure. If we race her to a hospital..." Grigoris had his hand on her wrist.

Eric sat back, bloody hands on his knees. "No."

Nyx lay a hand on Hanna's head and offered up a prayer in several languages, and to different deities. "Let her be at peace."

They were silent for a moment, then Eric looked around. "Burn this place to the ground."

"They'd find the bones in the rubble," Sebastian said quietly. "I'll take care of the body."

"See?" Eric said. "You *are* here to help."

GRIGORIS CLOSED the door to their bedroom, leaning against it wearily. Nyx was already dressed in her nightgown, sitting up in bed, waiting for him. He'd insisted she head to the bed without him as Eric demanded that he, Milo, Lancelot, and Dimitri go over every detail of the raid, dissecting it and trying to decide how they could prevent making the same mistakes again. Even with all of their tactical knowledge, Grigoris wasn't sure they could out-plan Petro.

Especially since now Petro knew they were there. Once again, they'd lost the element of surprise.

Since Josephine's death, Eric had been distant, flashing between fits of white-hot rage and a cold calm. Both were equally terrifying. Every now and then, there were times when Grigoris thought the fleet admiral was pulling himself together—he'd crack a joke or make a sarcastic comment—but it was becoming very clear that those times were shams, a show. The rest of the time, the Viking, who was like an irritated bear on a good day, appeared to have become a large, dangerous snake, coiled up still and seemingly calm but ready to explode at any moment.

The berserker was lingering just below the surface and Grigoris no longer worried *if* that crazy killer would emerge. Now his concern was when. Because there was no doubt Eric wouldn't be able to hold it together much longer.

"You didn't have to wait up," he said, when Nyx gave him a tired smile. She didn't try to shield the scar any longer with him. He was touched by her trust, her ease with him. He was sad she couldn't manage those same things in the presence of others, but he knew her scars were not merely skin-deep. It would take time for her to overcome her inability to have anyone standing behind her. In truth, that may be something she never conquered.

"I wanted to see you," she said as he pulled off his shirt. "And I had a lot on my mind."

"I'm sure you did. Are you upset about Hanna?"

Nyx shook her head. "I didn't really know her. I've felt a great deal of guilt over the years, feeling as if I'd left her behind to take the brunt of Petro's abuse. There is still an element of that guilt."

"She was complicit in some of his schemes."

"Because that is her nature, or because he brainwashed her when she was still young?"

"He didn't brainwash you."

"No, I got away, but at what cost?"

"Nyx, you can't blame—"

"You mean I shouldn't. I shouldn't blame myself. You are a proponent of moral responsibility. I am responsible for my actions, and only my actions."

"Er, I'm not a proponent of—"

"But that raises the age-old dilemma because moral responsibility hinges on freewill, but do we truly have freewill, when so much of who we are is causally determined?"

Sometimes Grigoris forgot just how intelligent she was. Before this turned into a philosophical lecture—not that he didn't love listening to her talk about these kinds of things— he put his hand over hers. "Whether Petro brainwashed her or she was a true follower, in the end, she was with him because she chose to be. She would have killed all of us today if she'd gotten the chance. Maybe if we'd been able to take her alive, she could have gone to a prison with a mental health facility, but that's not what happened."

"No. She is dead, and that is a kind of finality that cannot be unspooled."

They sat in silence for a moment.

"Your trinity is gone, Nyx." Grigoris realized this probably wasn't the best time to bring up this conversation, but he was tired of pushing it off because their lives were insane. He wanted—no, he needed—to know that something positive, something good was going to come out of all this.

"Grigoris," she said. There was hesitance, a sadness in her tone that should have warned him to stop, but he didn't.

"No, please. Hear me out. Hanna is dead, and I'm pretty sure Petro won't live long after Eric gets answers out of him. You'll be free." He squeezed her fingers. "We'll ask the fleet admiral to place us in a trinity together. I realize it's not common to match people from different territories, but Eric's last several trinities have all gone against the norm. Given everything we've done to capture the mas—"

"I can't ask Eric to do that."

Grigoris sighed and stood. "I know this isn't a good time. With Petro on the run, with so much still uncertain, hanging in the balance, but we're going to find him. And Eric is going to kill him."

"I understand that, and I pray he does. What Petro has done, the atrocities, the torture, he deserves to die a thousand painful deaths. But..." Nyx's fingers tugged at the sheets anxiously and were the cotton paper, she would have shredded it. "I can't ask Eric because I don't want to be placed in another trinity. The thought of it terrifies me."

Grigoris had been in the process of taking off his pants, but he stopped. "What?"

"I told you before I came to your bed. This," she pointed to him then to herself, "what's between us could only be temporary."

"Because you were married," Grigoris said, wondering if stress was causing Nyx to be confused. "You aren't anymore. Hell, you never were. Not really." He ran his hand through his hair, wishing now he had waited to bring up this discussion. They were both running on empty.

He shrugged off his pants and climbed into bed next to her. "We can talk about this tomorrow."

She shook her head. "No. I think it's best if I say this now." She shifted to face him, her hair haloed by moonlight. "I love you, Grigoris. I feel things for you I never thought I would feel, never thought possible."

"Then I don't understand what we're talking about here. We know we're good together. More than that, we were made for each other, Nyx. I'm sure you'll give me a million academic, religious reasons why soul mates isn't a real concept, but there's not a doubt in my mind that you are mine. I feel it all the way to my bones."

"Actually, you're wrong. Many religions do embrace that concept. In the Hindu culture, it's called *lehnu*, the link you share with another who helps you lead a life that serves a higher purpose. It's similar in Judaism. But I prefer the Buddhist idea that we are all reborn an infinite number of times, and relationships carry over from one lifetime to the next."

He was always fascinated by her intelligence, drawn to it.

"In fact," she continued, "I've often felt as if my soul knew you the first moment I saw you scowling at me outside the airport in Bucharest."

Grigoris smiled at the memory. "I'd given specific orders for Antonio to stay away. Not only did he ignore that directive, he showed up with a posse that included this gorgeous, haughty, brilliant religious scholar who challenged every single word I said."

He saw the sheen of tears in her eyes, but her expression told him she wasn't touched, wasn't moved by the memory. For some reason, it hurt her.

"You've come to know me very well, Grigoris. Better than anyone in my life. You know what the attack in Bucharest did to me, but more than that, you know, understand, why I've lived my life the way I have. Hiding." She swallowed heavily before adding, "Looking over my shoulder, trying to outrun a monster. You're the only person I've ever trusted enough to get close to...to give my heart to. You're the only man I let touch me."

Grigoris reached for her hands. "Nyx, everything you're saying only proves—"

"Our society requires arranged trinity marriages. Even if we were to ask the fleet admiral to allow us to marry, there would have to be a third. We don't live as couples.

"It would mean letting a stranger into my life. Letting a stranger touch me, not just physically—though I find the idea abhorrent—but emotionally."

She was breathing fast and his heart was breaking.

"I don't have it inside me to trust someone else. I'm not even good at being around people I consider friends. You're the only one." She looked up, and there were tears in her eyes. "And you were my choice. Our third wouldn't be."

"We could find someone—"

"And marry them, knowing I'd resent them? Be scared of them? Cold to them? I am not unaware of how I can seem."

"I don't want to hurt you, Nyx. I want to be with you."

"And I want to be with you. And that's why I'm here. In your bed, and I'll stay with you, for as long as I can."

"And that can be forever if we—"

"I've been in a trinity. I've fulfilled that part of my membership to the Masters' Admiralty. Please don't ask me to do that again."

He considered her words, trying to find a way around her concerns, some way he could alleviate them and convince her they could make it work. He couldn't think of anything. "Then we won't ask Eric. Won't get married. We'll simply remain together."

"And what happens when your admiral places you in your trinity marriage?"

Grigoris rubbed his jaw wearily. He was two days overdue for a shave. It was a strange thing to think of when it felt as if his heart had just shattered into a million tiny pieces. Then he realized that didn't have to be the case. "Fine. Hande can put me in a trinity. I'll fulfill my duty as well. But I won't give you up. We can still be together, can still be lovers—"

He stopped talking when she shook her head, and the first tear slid down her cheek. "We can't be together after you're married. You're an honorable man, Grigoris. It isn't in you to not do the right thing."

"For you, Nyx, you might be surprised how dishonorable I can be. I'd do anything for you."

"I wouldn't allow it."

Grigoris swallowed heavily, his throat clogged as the weight of what she was saying sank in. He'd started his conversation because he wanted this part over, wanted Petro killed, wanted to go back to Cyprus to a future with her. Now, he suddenly needed time to stop. Right here, right now, in the midst of this hellscape. "I can't lose you."

"You have me. For now. That has to be enough. Because there can't be more. Perhaps if I were braver, I could...but I am a coward."

"You are not. You have every right to be terrified of an arranged trinity marriage, though I'd be there, I'd be with you, we could—"

"—could close ourselves off to this third person? They would enter the marriage expecting a trinity and instead find a couple who resented them. Is our love worth the damage that would do to someone else? The guilt you would feel, the shame that would eat at me?"

Grigoris didn't have a response to that.

She cupped his cheek and gave him a soft kiss. Then she lay down in bed. And turned away from him. She trusted him enough to have him at her back.

She was crying. He could tell from the slight quiver in her shoulders. And though his heart was broken, he couldn't allow her to suffer alone.

He shifted closer, spooning her from behind. "I love you, Nyx. If this is all we can have..." Grigoris couldn't make himself say the rest.

Nyx placed her hands over his at her waist, nestled her back against his chest, and though they were both exhausted, they lay there, motionless, without speaking, for hours as sleep eluded them.

NYX'S EYES were scratchy the next morning, thanks to a sleepless night. She knew Grigoris hadn't really slept either, something that concerned her, given Eric's determination to find Petro as soon as possible. The fleet admiral acted very much like a man possessed and it was becoming more and more frightening.

Grigoris needed to be alert, focused, ready for anything. However, after their talk, she feared she'd destroyed all chance he had of achieving any of that. She would have been wiser to keep her feelings to herself until all of this was over, but she'd been aware of Grigoris' hopes for a future together and to let him believe it possible felt crueler than speaking the truth.

After the failed first raid and Hanna's death, the element of surprise was now gone. Petro would know they were on Guam and he would be ready for them. Eric had come to their bedroom just after dawn to rouse them, though Grigoris had already been up and dressed. Neither of them had managed to grab more than a few minutes of restless dozing.

Nyx sat on the wingback chair in the corner of the living room, quietly listening to their plans. Despite their early start, they had spent most of the day planning, and didn't start getting ready to leave until late afternoon. Today, they were attacking on two fronts at the same time. Grigoris had argued against that idea, but the fleet admiral refused to listen. Confidence among everyone in the group was low. Petro had proven himself to be a worthy adversary and in this instance, dividing and conquering didn't feel like the wiser option.

Grigoris planned to infiltrate the mortgage and title company, while Eric was leading the tactical team to the now-defunct MRW center as soon as the sun started to set. Leila would be with Eric's group and would once again take up point as sniper, choosing the roof of an adjacent building as her vantage point. Lancelot, Milo, Sebastian, Dimitri, and Eric would all be on the ground.

Her name and Langston's weren't mentioned at all.

"What about me?" Nyx asked.

Eric glanced at Grigoris briefly before turning his attention to her. "You're staying here with Langston. Sebastian arranged for a soldier to come as a guard. He'll be inside with you, since the rear admiral doesn't want us to attract undue attention."

Nyx started to shake her head, but the fleet admiral didn't give her the opportunity.

"That's the plan," Eric said, the finality in his tone warning her that arguing would be pointless. "I wanted you there in case we could overhear Petro and Hanna talking, but without her, there's no point. You'll help question him when I bring him back." Eric turned to the others. "Suit up and grab your weapons. We're leaving here in ten."

Nyx shifted, rising. Her heart was in her throat and her hands were trembling. She hated how she and Grigoris had left things last night, hated that their previous evening had been so strained and sad. But most of all, she hated that he was leaving without her.

Ordinarily it was her own safety she feared for, but this morning, she was terrified something bad would happen to him.

She wanted to find something to say to fix the way they'd left things, but she couldn't. Couldn't take back what she'd said because her feelings hadn't changed.

Part of her feared he'd leave without saying goodbye at all, but she knew him. Knew he'd never do such a thing.

Grigoris put on a thin Kevlar vest, pulling a dress shirt over top of it then donning a necktie. While he looked like a prosperous businessman on the surface, underneath the clothing, he was dressed to kill. He had a knife strapped to his ankle, another to his arm. He strapped on a shoulder holster, the gun tucked beneath the suit jacket.

Once he was ready, he picked up a second jacket, though it looked too small, too feminine for him. He looked at it for a moment, then glanced up at her, his brows furrowed as if he was debating with himself over something.

He released a long breath, then walked over to her. "Langston is staying here with you," he said.

Though the American didn't give off any threatening vibes, she still couldn't shake the fear of remaining here alone with him and a second strange man.

"We'll practice not getting shot," Langston said.

Unlike her, Langston didn't seem to mind missing the action. Despite his desire to remain behind the front line, he seemed to be quite knowledgeable about weapons and tactical assault.

"Stay clear of the windows, keep the curtains drawn," Grigoris ordered.

"I will," she promised.

He held up the women's jacket. "Nyx. We've lost our element of surprise."

"I know that."

"I wouldn't leave you here if I didn't truly believe this was a safe place for you. It's just...with Petro, anything could happen. And I want to be sure we're ready for it."

"A reasonable precaution." She wasn't sure what he was trying to say, but it was obvious he was nervous.

"There's a tracker sewn into the seam of this jacket. I know how much it upset you when you learned Petro had put one on you. I don't want to—"

"Give it to me." Nyx held out her hand. "Petro's reasons for putting that tracker on me was so that he could possess me, watch me. It was a violation and something done to an animal. You're protecting me, Grigoris. Of course I'll wear it." She slid her arms into the jacket.

"Don't take it off."

"I won't." She longed to embrace him, to kiss him, to tell him she loved him, but after last night, she didn't feel as though she had the right. She'd hurt him enough.

"Let's go," Eric said, filling the frame of the doorway, looking for all the world like a thunderous god. He appeared calm at first, but if she looked closely, it was easy to see the calm wasn't real. She halfway expected him to start shooting thunderbolts from his raging eyes.

"Nyx," Grigoris said, turning to her. He didn't reach out

to her, didn't say anything more than her name...almost desperately.

He'd called her his soul mate, and he'd been right. She could see his feelings, even though he said nothing.

Reaching out, she squeezed his hand and simply said, "I know."

A sad smile broke the heaviness in his face for just a moment, then it was gone.

He gave her a quick wink, the gesture never failing to reassure her, even if only briefly.

Then he turned and followed the others out.

CHAPTER TWENTY-THREE

Grigoris straightened his tie before grabbing the empty briefcase he was using as part of his disguise from the passenger seat of the rental car. Actually, the briefcase wasn't completely empty. He'd placed a second gun inside. After yesterday's fiasco, he wasn't taking any chances.

While he wasn't expecting to run into any problems at the mortgage company, he'd also learned to never underestimate Petro. The man collected pets the way some people collected coins.

His plan was to pose as an auditor sent from the home office. He'd spent the better part of two hours the previous night researching the mortgage company. He'd memorized the names of the CEO and the board of directors and familiarized himself with their services. His game plan was to speak English with a slight Hungarian accent in order to pull off his role as an auditor from the K&H Bank backing the company—as far as he could tell from the staff list on the website, no one on staff was Hungarian.

He walked into the small office, casually looking around.

There was a waiting room with four cushioned brown chairs and a coffee table laden with old magazines and mortgage brochures. There was one door to the left labeled conference room and four other doors leading to the private offices of the employees who occupied them.

He'd purposely waited until an hour before closing to arriving, certain that would assure several of the employees were already gone for the day. The fewer people he had to fool with his act, the better his chances of pulling it off.

The receptionist smiled as he approached her desk. According to the placard in front of her computer, her name was Isa. "*Hafa adai,*" she said.

Grigoris nodded briefly at her casual greeting. She was young, which left him a couple of options as far as which character he should play. He toyed with the idea of flirting with her, but discounted it when she shyly tucked a strand of hair behind her ear. Intimidation, he decided, would work better and quicker with this woman. "Hello, Isa. I'm here to meet with Tano Apatong."

The receptionist's smile faded. "I'm sorry, but Mr. Apatong isn't in the office today."

Grigoris knew that. He'd discovered Apatong, the office manager, was off the island, away on business this week. Grigoris shook his head in obvious disgust. "This isn't going to look good on my report."

"Did you have an appointment?" she asked timidly.

"I contacted Mr. Apatong two weeks ago to warn him of my arrival. I'm an auditor from the home office of K&H Bank."

"Auditor?" Isa said, glancing around somewhat hopelessly. Given her alarm, Grigoris suspected his luck was even better than he'd hoped. It appeared everyone was gone for the day.

"I'm afraid I wasn't made aware of this audit." She reached for her phone. "If you'll give me just one moment, I'll contact Ms. Hocog. She's running the office while Mr. Apatong is away. She only stepped out of the office for a few minutes."

It was an obvious lie. He'd bet his home on Cyprus the employees all kicked off early with the boss out of town. When the cat's away...

Grigoris held up his hand imperiously. "That's not necessary. I don't need to speak to anyone. I merely need access to the mortgage and titles records. You know where those are, I presume?"

Isa was clearly new to her position, and if Grigoris had to guess, she wasn't a day over twenty-two. She hesitated.

"Isa. I spent the entire day yesterday traveling here, and I have a return flight booked for tomorrow. I got a very late start today, thanks to lost luggage and an issue with the rental car. I don't have time for this. Show me the records so I can do my job, or I promise you, the fact that your boss isn't here and you're hesitating to show me what I need will reflect poorly on my report. My audit often determines which offices remain open and which ones," he paused for dramatic effect, "are closed. I assume you like your position here?"

Isa rose nervously. "Oh, I'm not hesitating. Honestly. It's just..." Her words faded when he crossed his arms and huffed out an impatient sigh.

She turned to one of the private offices. "If you'll just follow me, I'll show you the records."

Grigoris grinned when she turned her back to lead him inside. He'd just cleared the first hurdle.

NYX SAT BESIDE LANGSTON. The guard Sebastian had arranged to stay with them was standing in parade rest near the door. His silent presence wasn't threatening, but it didn't make her feel comfortable either. Between the two of them, she preferred Langston, so she joined him on the couch.

"You are Sylvia's brother, correct?"

"Do you know my sis?"

"I met her briefly and only once." Nyx didn't know how much the young man knew about what was going on in the Masters' Admiralty. From what she gathered, he'd been offered membership to both societies—a rare, though not unheard of offer—and so far had joined neither.

She wouldn't tell him that Sylvia's husband Hugo was, like her, a librarian, and therefore possibly being targeted by a serial killer who had already beheaded one of them.

"So how many languages do you speak?" Langston asked.

"Fluently? Conversationally? Written and oral, or just oral?"

"I'm going to guess a lot."

"I speak many," Nyx agreed. "It's why I should be with them, in case they encounter Petro."

"But after yesterday, they decided to leave you with me. Us non-dangerous types have to stick together."

Nyx looked at the weapon pieces he'd laid out on a large square of felt. "I very much doubt you are non-dangerous."

"Aw heck, ma'am. That's sweet of you to say."

Nyx glanced at the clock on the cell phone beside the weapon pieces. They'd been gone just over an hour, and the sky was painted magenta, orange, and gold by the sunset. "It would help if we knew how long this was supposed to take," she murmured.

"We should distract ourselves. Want to learn to assemble a gun?"

"Yes, I think I would enjoy that."

The soldier standing in the corner looked alarmed, but only cleared his throat and shifted a bit.

Langston snickered. "How much do you know about how a gun works?"

"Very little."

"So what you're doing is creating a small explosion and directing the force of that explosion with the barrel. Here we have—"

There was a knock on the door.

FROM A TACTICAL STANDPOINT, this was probably going to be a game of cat and mouse. Eric waited as the rest of the team fanned out, trying to cover the many exits and entrances to the sprawling building. They were focused on the larger building, which included a ballroom, restaurant, a few classrooms and, most importantly, sleeping quarters.

They hadn't been able to get accurate, current blueprints to the building, but Milo had sketched out a floor plan using photos of events and activities that had taken place in the center before it closed. Based on that, he'd assigned tactical entry paths. Eric was going in with Sebastian.

He should have cared that he had a stranger at his back. He should have cared that he and Sebastian had been given the least-interesting entry point—the front doors. He didn't care about any of that.

It was hard to care about anything. The rage burning in him was so hot that it singed away anything else he might feel.

And that rage was getting harder and harder to control.

Sebastian was standing out in the open, wearing a

construction jumpsuit to hide the Kevlar and a hard hat instead of tactical helmet. Hopefully that would prevent anyone from reporting them, since the former MWR site was on the apex of a low hill, with nothing but a few scattered palm trees to obstruct the view from the road on the inland side of the hill. It was one of the reasons they'd had to wait until dusk to enter. From where he stood, if he wanted to, he could turn and look out over the water, a seemingly endless expanse of blue ocean and brilliantly colored sky.

He didn't because he didn't give a shit. All he wanted was to find someone he could make pay for what had happened to Josephine.

They hadn't found her body. All they had was her head.

"Entry team one, go," Milo said in his ear.

Sebastian stepped up to the door, positioned the bolt cutters, and snapped the chain. Eric slid out of the shadows and through the now-open door. Unlike Sebastian, he was in full black tactical gear, gun raised. He paused by the door, waiting for Sebastian to join him, and once he felt a tap on his shoulder, he moved forward. They were in what had once been a reception area. He paused after sweeping the room.

He could abandon the plan and scream a challenge. Declare that he was there and demand that Petro come out and face him. That would be much more satisfying than playing a game of cat and mouse.

Sebastian, now wearing a black helmet and holding a gun, tapped him on the shoulder. Eric didn't move because for a moment he couldn't, the struggle between his control and the need for blood, to let the rage inside him burn away everything, was so real that it caused his muscles to tense, his heart rate to quicken.

"Ericsson?" Sebastian whispered.

"Problem, team one?" Milo's accented voice was sharp.

"No," Eric said. The word came out like a growl. He shoved down the rage, and as he did, he could feel the core of it, a feeling much more destructive than hot anger. Grief. And guilt.

Josephine was dead, and that regret was too great for him to deal with, so it turned to anger, an anger that would consume him if he let it. After his wives had died, he'd let guilt take over. He'd lost himself to the berserker for years, taking on missions so dangerous they'd been death sentences, but he'd always made it out. He'd gone from noble young fool to soulless mercenary.

Josephine, Colum, and the time he spent in Ireland pulled him back, helped him find a new version of himself. He would never be that noble young knight again, but sarcastic badass was better than out-of-control rage-monster.

Eric swung open the internal door that should open to a hall. Milo's plans had been right, and there was a long, dark hallway beyond. Sebastian cracked a couple of glow sticks and slid them along the floor so they illuminated the hallway.

"Reception clear," Eric whispered. "Team one moving into the hall."

His control back in place, Eric pulled out a can of Silly String, and sprayed it in the hall, checking for any trip wires. There weren't any, so a second later, he and Sebastian moved in.

THE SOLDIER STIFFENED and looked at Nyx and Langston. "Are you expecting anyone?"

"No," Nyx said.

"Please move to the back of the house, out of sight." The soldier peeked out the front window as Nyx and Langston retreated through the living room. Langston, gallant man that he was, stood in front of her. Nyx kept her back pressed to the wall.

"Can I help you?" the soldier called through the door.

"Delivery."

"Come back later," the soldier said.

"I need you to sign." The voice was, at first, bland and American—but Nyx knew accents, and she knew this voice all too well.

"No!" she shouted, racing around Langston.

There was a crack, and the soldier was blown back, his body limp on the floor. The door smacked against the wall, before bouncing against the guard's legs.

Petro stepped into the house, through the door he'd blown open, carefully lowering the small box he held in one hand to the floor. The other hand held a gun with a silencer.

Langston grabbed Nyx, started to pull her back.

"Don't go anywhere, wife," Petro said in Romanian. "This box contains a bomb. If you come with me, I will wait to detonate it, and that will give your friend time to escape." Petro's gaze slid to Langston, and he switched to English. "Let go of my property."

"What?"

"He means me," Nyx said quietly. "There's a bomb in that box."

"Well, fuck."

"I'm going to leave with him. He says he'll give you time to get out. Can you drag the soldier?"

"Wait, wait, you can't go with him. He won't detonate the bomb, not with himself inside the blast radius. Call his bluff."

Petro shifted the gun and shot the guard again. The young man had been breathing heavily but had remained silent as he lay on the ground. Now he cried out in agony after Petro shot him in the knee.

Nyx stepped in front of Langston, shielding him with her body as she spoke to Petro. "I'll come with you. You have to give them time to get out."

"I will if you're a good girl," Petro said with a smile.

Bile rose in her throat. "I will be."

"No!" Langston said. "Don't go with him. I can—"

"You have to get him out." Nyx looked over her shoulder at Langston, not caring that he was at her back when the real threat was standing several meters away by the door. "Don't trust him. Move fast."

"Come to me, my wife," Petro said, once more speaking Romanian.

Nyx walked across the room and into Petro's arms.

———

"VERY WELL. I have all that I need." Grigoris dismissed Isa once she'd shown him the company's files.

Once again, she seemed hesitant to leave him alone, but when he raised one imperious eyebrow at her, she scampered back to her desk quickly enough, closing the door behind her.

Grigoris waited for the sound of her footsteps to retreat, then plugged an external hard drive into the computer, downloading the contents, before he took his gun out of the holster and quickly slid out of the private office. It took him less than five minutes to search the rest of the building, carefully staying out of Isa's line of site. Petro wasn't here, and it didn't look like he had been. That had always been a remote possibility.

He returned to the office, checked the progress of the drive, and then started his search of the physical office.

Grigoris quickly rifled through the desk drawers, finding the standard office fare, pens, pencils, several calculators, a stapler. There was a stack of photographs of what appeared to be Mr. Apatong and his family. Grigoris flipped through a few of them, pictures of the middle-aged man with an attractive woman and two young kids laughing in the ocean. He tossed them back onto the desk.

Rising, he walked to the filing cabinets, opening each one, scanning the tabs in search of something that might give them an idea of where Petro might be hiding.

Every file folder tab was written in English, none of the names or services found there standing out. The computer download would give him a list of properties the company had done titles for, and later he'd cross-reference them with their original list, assuming Eric didn't find Petro at the MWR. Grigoris quickly worked his way through every drawer, his sense of futility growing when he reached nearly the back of the bottom drawer.

There was a tab written in Hungarian that stood out immediately.

Apostolok.

Apostles.

Grigoris pulled the file out and discovered only three pages, a ledger of sorts with code names, also written in Hungarian, followed by what appeared to be a payment schedule. He laid the three pages out on the desk, snapping pictures of each with his phone. His Hungarian was rusty. Nyx would have a better idea of what was written here. There was no time to try to decipher it now.

He quickly put the papers back in the file and tucked it in the drawer where he'd found it. Grigoris scanned the rest of the office then, running his hands along the picture frames on the wall and feeling around the furniture for hidden compartments.

He recalled the secret entrance Petro had used to enter Nyx's guest room at his home. Grigoris was leaving no stone unturned.

He was just about to leave when one of the scattered photos on the desk caught his eye. It was of a man's bare tattooed chest. There was no face, no distinguishing marks except for the tattoo, which looked like some sort of religious symbol placed over the left pec, just above the heart.

Grigoris tucked the photograph into the pocket of his jacket just as his cell phone rang.

"WE HAVE MOVEMENT." Dimitri's voice came over the coms.

Eric froze, Sebastian at his back. They were in the second of four classrooms. There were tables and chairs stacked against a wall, and part of the drop ceiling had been removed near the front, exposing the structural girders and wiring in the ceiling.

"Where?" Eric demanded.

"Hold your position," Milo commanded.

"Where?" Eric snarled.

There was a pregnant silence, then Milo—brave man that he was—said, "Fleet Admiral, team two is in the hostel area, however, I need you to finish your sweep."

Milo was right. It was dangerous to go off plan.

Eric didn't care.

"Have there been any booby traps so far?" Eric asked.

"No, Fleet Admiral, which probably means it isn't—"

He was no longer listening. The rage made his ears buzz. Eric stormed from the classroom and wound his way toward where the sleeping quarters were. He didn't check for trip wires or traps. He didn't wait for his partner. He slammed open doors, his vision haloed by rage.

"Team two, I'm coming to you." Milo's voice had a tinge of worry.

"We're breaching now," Dimitri said.

"Where do you want me?" Leila asked.

"Southwest corner," Milo replied.

The conversations were just background noise.

"It's not our target," Dimitri said as Eric reached the door he was looking for. He slammed it open, wood cracking. The interior of the large room beyond was lit by the acid-green light of glowsticks. Dimitri and Lancelot stood with a third figure, who was looking up at them, in their full black tactical attire, in terror.

Not Petro. This man wasn't Petro. It was a young Asian man in disheveled clothes. There was a backpack on the ground near the closest bunk bed.

"Who are you?" Eric demanded. He didn't stop once he entered the room but kept right on walking. Only Lancelot's hold on his shirt stopped the terrified young man from scrambling backwards.

"I'm sorry, I'm sorry! I'll go, I'll go!"

"How do you know Petro?"

"I don't know anybody." The young man shook his head, the large gold cross he wore on a chain swinging out from under his shirt collar, which had been yanked to the side, thanks to Lancelot's hold.

Dimitri opened and then upended the young man's bag. No gun, no bomb-making supplies. Clothes, toiletries, a passport, and a bit of cash.

Eric reached for the young man, but Lancelot hauled him back out of Eric's grasp.

Eric turned cold eyes on the English knight. "What are you doing?"

"This target is a bust."

Milo slid into the room, Sebastian right behind him.

Eric considered Lancelot. He was a big man, but it wouldn't be hard to incapacitate him. It might even be fun.

Eric's phone vibrated in his pocket. He ignored it, but it vibrated again. Only when it rang the second time did he remember that this was a new phone, a burner that they had purchased when they'd arrived, and it was only to be used in emergencies.

He ripped it out of his pocket, pausing in confusion for only a moment when he saw it was a conference call. He answered, and Grigoris' voice filled the line. "Langston?"

"He took her," the American man panted. "Nyx! He took her and there's a bomb and I thought you both should... Shit! This is tricky. Gotta go."

The line went dead.

Eric turned to the door and ran, the rest of them right behind him. No one noticed the young man adjusting his rumpled shirt, pulling the collar back in place, hiding the top of a tattoo he had on his chest, right over his heart.

CHAPTER TWENTY-FOUR

Nyx walked quietly to the white van parked at the curb. It, like Petro's shirt, bore the logo of a shipping company. "Did you kill someone to get this vehicle?"

"You think so poorly of me?" Petro asked as he gallantly helped her into the back of the van. There were no seats, but instead, shelves with boxes and white plastic tubs full of envelopes.

"You're a psychopath," Nyx informed him. "It's not your fault, your brain was—"

Petro backhanded her across the face, splitting her lip. She winced, but straightened, facing him as if she weren't terrified. Petro didn't look angry, he looked calm. He wiped the back of his hand, which was speckled with her blood, on the uniform shirt.

He climbed in after her, and Nyx couldn't stop herself from scooting frantically away. He chuckled but slid between the front seats, dropping down behind the wheel.

"The bomb," she said. "You said you wouldn't set it off until we were gone. Where is the trigger?"

"Oh, it's on a timer. It will go off in one minute." Petro seemed supremely unconcerned as he started the car and pulled away from the curb.

Had that been enough time for Langston to get the soldier out? Maybe, but they wouldn't be far enough away to escape the blast. "They need more time."

"What they need isn't my concern."

Nyx licked blood from her lip, then, mustering her courage, rose and slid into the passenger seat. She'd feel much better if she went to the back of the van. If there hadn't been a mesh screen behind the driver's seat, dividing it from the storage compartment, she might have tried to find something to strangle him.

And if she failed, what would he do to her?

"I'm asking you to please give them more time," she said softly. "Can you disarm it remotely?"

"What a good wife you could be," he murmured. "But even if I wanted to, which I do not, the bomb is on a timer."

Nyx stared straight ahead as Petro waved at the man in the gatehouse as he drove out of the neighborhood. She waited, braced for the sound of the explosion.

None came.

She closed her eyes in relief. It had been at least a minute, probably two, no bomb.

Her relief that Langston and the soldier were safe was short-lived because *she* was most definitely not safe.

Petro's gaze was dark with anger as he pulled over into a small shopping center. He parked the truck around back, by the dumpsters, then climbed out. Nyx held her breath, watched him circle around the hood to the passenger side. When he was at her door, she moved, dashing to the driver's seat and out the driver's door. With the car between them, she had the advantage of youth and adrenaline on her side. She raced for the corner of the building.

She would have made it, would have outrun him, the panic of knowing he was behind her, lending her speed. The taser darts sank into her back and 50,000 volts of electricity dropped her to the ground. She couldn't breathe, couldn't move. Pain lit up every nerve ending in her body.

Petro crouched beside her. He wiped his fingerprints from the stun gun and then tossed it away. Casually, he grabbed her chin, turning her face to look at the scar, then tsking. She couldn't move, could barely breathe as he lifted her shirt, rolling her onto her back to look at the scar on her abdomen.

"All this can be fixed," he said consolingly. "Though I suppose I could keep you damaged. *Kintsugi.*"

Nyx didn't have the breath to scream when he grabbed her by the hair and dragged her across the alley to a second car he had concealed behind a dumpster. He yanked, and she felt a clump of hair, or maybe scalp, rip. She reached up, trembling fingers grabbing his wrist. Disgust ran through her at the skin-to-skin contact.

Grigoris will find you. Grigoris will come for you. You have the tracker.

Unless the taser had just short-circuited it.

Three minutes after Langston disconnected the call, Grigoris' phone rang again. He was running toward the rental car. God only knew what Isa thought about the so-called auditor's hasty exit. Not that he cared.

Petro had Nyx.

"What?" he said, answering his burner phone. It could only be one person.

330 MARI CARR & LILA DUBOIS

"Come get me."

Just what he thought. Eric was on the phone and making demands. Grigoris, in a saner frame of mind, would have responded differently. Instead, he said, "Fuck off."

"Come get me *now*," Eric said.

"You left her alone. Virtually unprotected. I knew—"

"Is she wearing the tracker?" Eric asked, cutting him off.

It was the first thing Grigoris had checked before running for the car.

"She is."

"We can follow them, find him."

Grigoris gritted his teeth, his anger flashing hot. "Did you leave her there as bait?"

There was a pregnant pause, and Grigoris could swear he felt the heat emanating from Eric through the phone. "I won't lose another woman to this man. Come. Get. Me."

Grigoris was on the road, following the blinking red dot on his GPS that told him where Nyx was. She and Petro were heading north. Detouring to pick up Eric would take him in the opposite direction, would cause him to lose precious minutes.

"Stop thinking," Eric said, his voice deadly calm. "Follow orders. We both want the same thing, Grigoris. We want this man to die the worst death possible. I can make that happen."

"No." There was nothing that would convince him to turn his car and drive away from that red dot, from Nyx.

"I'm going to catch you, Violaris. And when I do—"

The call went dead. Grigoris looked at the phone, uncertain if Eric had disconnected it on purpose or accident after issuing half a threat.

For days, he'd feared what would happen when Eric's calm cracked. Feared the release of the berserker. Now Grigoris needed him. Wanted him.

However, Eric was going to have to catch him first.

He took a hard left onto the main road and pressed on the accelerator. There were no interstates on Guam and the posted speed limit was thirty-five. Grigoris was switching lanes, passing cars, at sixty. He'd only made it twenty miles when he spotted a car coming up behind him...fast. Given how quickly the car was catching up to him, it was safe to say the other driver had to be doing ninety, changing lanes smoothly to pass other vehicles on the road. When the car pulled up even to him, Grigoris looked over in time to see Eric pointing to the side of the road.

Grigoris hesitated, unwilling to stop, but he also wouldn't put it past the fleet admiral to run him off the road if provoked. He slowed down, pulling into a gas station parking lot, and Eric followed.

Eric leapt out of the other car, hopping into the passenger seat. "Go!" he barked once he was inside.

Grigoris merged back onto the road. "Where did you get that car?"

"Stole it."

"How did you find me?"

"Milo pulled up Nyx's tracker signal. Figured I'd catch you or meet you there."

"What about the others?"

"They took our vehicle back to the house to deal with the bomb." Eric picked up the GPS, calling out directions. "Drive faster," he demanded.

Grigoris lowered his foot on the accelerator, praying they got to her in time.

NYX CLOSED HER EYES, tried to locate the courage and

strength she'd found through those months in Cyprus with Grigoris. She was loved by a good man, a brave man who thought she was beautiful and brilliant and strong.

Those thoughts calmed her enough that she was able to fight through the pain, the residual tremors from the taser.

"Well done. Resilient," Petro said when she opened her eyes.

Ignoring him, she looked around. He'd tossed her into the front seat of a small sports car. He'd strapped a thick vest around her chest. Her heart stopped as she looked at it, sure she'd see it was packed with explosives. It wasn't, at least not that she could see. Curiously, Petro was also wearing a vest.

Luckily, he'd placed it on her over the top of the jacket. She didn't have time to worry about that anymore, so she focused on what else he'd done.

There were handcuffs on her wrists, but instead of a single set holding her wrists together, there were two sets. The second cuff on her right side was secured to the door handle, while the one on her left hand was secured to his belt, her palm resting on his thigh.

She jerked away the instant she realized she was touching him, and he laughed. Though he dressed elegantly and expensively, he was a heavy, muscled man, with the physique of a back-room brawler. She wouldn't be able to use the handcuff to yank his weight around enough to stop him from driving.

But there were other options. Slowly, she lay her hand back on his thigh.

"Well done, but you should know, if you try to harm me, all it will do is increase my creativity."

That threat was far more terrifying than if he'd simply said she'd made him angry, and that made her rethink her initial plan, which was to grab his dick and attempt to rip it off.

"What are your plans?" she asked instead. "Whatever they may have been, the fleet admiral, and many of the other admirals, know you're the mastermind."

"The mastermind? A good name. I enjoy that." He chuckled. "And I did have plans. I was going to be fleet admiral, maybe change things, but if that doesn't happen, it's no great loss."

"You wouldn't abandon your plan so easily?" she asked.

"That's one plan of many. I enjoy...anarchy." He chuckled again. "I enjoy watching people try to make sense of it all. Surely you understand that."

She did. Religion was, after all, humanity's attempts to make sense of the world. "You see yourself as chaos? Entropy?"

"I see myself as free."

"Free of what? Or from what?"

"Morality."

"That is because you have brain damage," Nyx said coolly. "You are not enlightened or superior." Petro took his right hand off the wheel while she was speaking. "You're no longer fully human because you lack the capacity for the kind of empathy-driven decisions which define—"

He reached behind her seat, grabbed a tire iron, and then brought it down with a crack on her left arm.

Nyx's word cut off as the horrible sound of bone breaking reached her ears a moment before the pain registered. The strength behind that swing proved Hanna's target practice had paid off. Petro had full use of his arm, despite being shot there just a few days earlier.

She understood now why he'd stretched her left arm across the space between the seats. Not to make her uncomfortable by forcing her to touch him, but so that her arm was exposed and available for his abuse.

She screamed in agony, waiting for the sharp pain to dull to a throb, but it didn't. Her stomach heaved, and she felt the vomit rise in her throat.

If she threw up on herself, he might make her take off her clothes. Take off the jacket.

She forced herself to swallow, to live in the pain because there was nowhere else to go. She thought of the view from the pool at Grigoris' house. Thought of Fengári curled on her lap, and the way Grigoris' eyes sparkled when he winked at her.

When she was able to open her eyes, they were on a winding road heading up a cliff. It was full dark now, and the stars were beautifully bright.

"It's not broken, only cracked," he told her confidently. "And heavily bruised."

"Why did you do that?" she asked coolly, as if her interest was only academic.

"It's important you understand you are not smarter than I am and that you are helpless. Though you are, of course, intelligent, as well as beautiful. I was quite pleased to discover that sharp mind of yours as you grew older and tried to find ways to outwit me."

"You think brute force indicates intelligence? It is, in fact, the opposite."

She braced for him to lash out again, but he merely smiled. "By itself, yes, but brute force applied methodically, and to elicit specific reactions, is an artisan's tool. Given your intelligence, it's one of the reasons I chose to use it with you. With Hanna, psychological influences were more effective."

Hanna.

Nyx's guilt redoubled. No matter what Grigoris had said,

Hanna had been a victim, brainwashed and trained to obey Petro, her mind warped by his treatment of her.

"I should have come back for her," Nyx whispered, unable to keep the words inside.

"She wouldn't have gone with you. I am, was, her husband. She knew her place."

"Her place was as your equal. Not your prize. Not your servant."

"You could, perhaps, have been my equal." Petro slowed and turned into a small driveway. There was a gate across it, and a sign that said "Two Lovers Point" as well as a "closed" sign.

Petro undid his belt, freeing the loop of the cuff around her broken arm. Her arm dropped uselessly, but there was no fresh stab of pain, only an increased throbbing.

He lifted bolt cutters from behind the seat, and Nyx flinched. He grinned as he turned off the car and climbed out.

Nyx looked around frantically, then, taking a deep breath, grabbed the shifter with her left hand, her arm screaming in pain, and threw the car into neutral.

GRIGORIS CONCENTRATED on the road as Eric spoke on the phone.

"Put it on speaker," Grigoris said.

Eric hit the button. "Did the bomb go off?"

"No, sir," Milo responded. "Langston defused it."

"Where are the Americans?" Eric asked.

"We left Sebastian at the house with Langston. The car is still loaded with all the tactical equipment and fire power, Fleet Admiral, but we need your coordinates to follow."

Grigoris responded, "We're heading north on Route 1, along the coast."

"Very good," Milo said. "Dimitri, Lancelot, Leila, and I are en route now."

"Drop a pin and share our location with them," Grigoris said. Eric did so, though his movements were stiff, choppy, as if his hands were primed and ready to destroy anything he touched. Given the fleet admiral's tight grip on the phone, he was afraid Eric would crush it.

"Got it," Milo said over the phone. "We're thirty minutes behind you."

"Too late," Eric said.

"Fleet Admiral," Milo said. "I think you and Grigoris should wait until—"

Eric disconnected the call. "We're not waiting."

Grigoris nodded. For the first time since embarking on this mission on Guam, he and the fleet admiral were in complete agreement.

NYX LOOKED OVER HER SHOULDER, out the back window. The adrenaline pumping through her body made each fraction of a second stretch, and some disconnected part of her mind marveled at how subjective the idea of time was.

The car rolled backwards a meter, and Nyx was ready to grab the wheel. She wouldn't be able to do much to control the car, but she hoped she could keep it from going over the cliff. She'd get away and that would give Grigoris time to get to her.

The car jerked to a halt.

Nyx whirled to face forward, almost expecting to see Petro grabbing the front bumper, like a supervillain in a movie. He was standing at the gate, the snapped chain in one hand, the bolt cutters in the other. The headlights illuminated his face, and he was smiling.

The parking brake. The parking brake was on. She looked frantically at the console, trying to find a button or lever. It was no use, it was a foot pedal brake. She lunged herself across the seat, trying to reach the pedal, a sob ripping at her throat.

The passenger door opened, yanking her right arm so hard it felt like it had been pulled from the socket.

She shrieked in rage and fear as Petro hauled her from the car, using the bolt cutters to snap the right cuff chain rather than bothering to unlock one of the bracelets.

Petro reached for her hair, but she dodged back, slapping his hand away with her right arm, cradling her left against her stomach.

Petro's smile dropped, and he swung the bolt cutters underhand, cracking the heavy head against her shin. Fresh pain shot through her, and she let out a sob, too consumed by pain to fight him when he grabbed her by the right arm and hauled her through the gate into a small parking lot. Above and to their left was a white pergola-like structure perched on the crest of the cliff. Around the bottom of it, built into and then extending out from the cliff face, was a circular walkway.

"Let me tell you a story. How much do you know about Guam?"

She sucked in air, limping behind him as he dragged her by the upper arm. She knew Grigoris was coming for her, the jacket a comforting weight around her upper body.

But at the rate Petro was hurting her, there might not be enough of her left to put the pieces together.

"It's rude not to answer, wife."

338 MARI CARR & LILA DUBOIS

"Not...not much," she gasped.

"You're lying to me, but I understand physical pain can inhibit mental processes. When I considered bringing you home, I had planned to use some sort of permanent remote-controlled stimuli to keep you in line."

"You could never have kept me under your control," she gasped.

"You still think this? I know you took out your tracker." Petro paused in the process of hauling her toward the steps up to the circular viewing platform. He forced her mouth open, peering inside to the space where her tooth had been. "I'll fix that too."

Nyx jerked her head out of his grip. "You never controlled me. You merely knew where I was."

Petro's gaze darkened. He grabbed her neck, jerking her face close to his. "Make no mistake. I allowed you to be free because if I'd had to control you, I wouldn't have been able to focus on my other plans."

Nyx's breath stopped, and not because of his grip on her throat. If she'd been with him, stayed with him, thereby challenging him, forcing him to focus on breaking her, controlling her, he wouldn't have had time to cultivate his pets. He wouldn't have recruited the Domino's apprentices, Ciril, or the bombers.

"I let you enjoy your illusion of freedom because I didn't have the time to devote to you. It was a mistake because it allowed you to be damaged." He looked at her cheek again. "Though I did enjoy Ciril. Simple man, but creative."

How many people had died so she could be free? A freedom that had, as he pointed out, only been an illusion.

"I see you start to understand. Do you know that when Hanna cried, I told her it wouldn't have been that way if you'd been there? And once she was mine, I had to find more challenging pursuits."

Horror overwhelmed her. As he dragged her up the last few steps, she was barely aware of what was happening. "Now for that story. This is called Two Lovers Point." Petro gestured out at the view, and then yanked her to the glass-paneled railing. He grabbed the back of her head and forced her to bend over so her upper body dangled in nothingness, and she stared down at the jagged rocks below. She could see a small speed boat anchored not far from the rocks, and the crashing surf foamed and frothed beautifully.

"The place is named for the beloved daughter of an esteemed Spaniard and his beautiful wife. She ran away with her true love, a poor, young Chamorro warrior, rather than the powerful Spanish captain her father had chosen for her."

Doomed lovers, like her and Grigoris.

In that moment, consumed by pain and guilt, she started to lean forward, to let more of her body weight tip over the railing. Her freedom, which had been a sham, was what had given Petro the time and space to become the monster he was.

That's a false equivalency. Correlation does not equate causation.

Nyx took a deep breath, centered herself, and then firmly planted both feet on the deck. Petro was still forcing her head forward, but she relaxed so that as he pressed down, her neck bent, chin touching her chest, but her shoulders didn't move. Every part of her hurt, from her back where the taser darts had pieced her to her broken arm and battered shin. She had, thanks to the pain, become highly emotional, and those emotions had pushed her to say and do things she logically knew were nonsensical.

She took some calming breaths while he continued to

blather on about the two mythical lovers, then she prepared to fight back with her best weapon.

"The woman in the story chose to follow her heart, her true path rather than succumb to false gods—wealth, power, prestige. She was the true hero of that story. Something you could never understand." She let go of the emotion and focused on this as if it were an academic discussion, using her intellect to put distance between the terrifying reality of her situation and her conscious mind. "Arguably the reason you became a mass murderer," she said, interrupting him as he laughed at her assessment of the story, "is the brain damage, though there are plenty of people with similar injuries who didn't become psychopaths, which leads me to believe it is either a natural or learned moral failing of yours that was exacerbated by the injury."

Petro yanked her up. "Trying to make yourself feel better, wife? If you'd been obedient, if you'd been—"

"You would never have let me stay, because short of imprisoning me or lobotomizing me, you would not have been able to hide your activities from me. That is why you didn't try to force me to return. You were afraid of what I would discover."

His lips quirked in a smile. "If that's true, if you'd been a good wife, a good partner in our trinity, you could have stopped me."

"No, had I gotten close, you would have killed me. In which case, I would not have been alive now and able to help track you."

"You're trying to make yourself feel better." He made a tsking sound.

"Tell me, what is it like to understand the concept of guilt but not feel it?"

He grinned. "Freeing."

She kept talking. Kept him focused on her. Prayed he wouldn't hear the car coming, the car whose lights she'd seen slicing through the darkness as it wound up the cliff road.

"I researched psychopaths, once I realized what you were."

"My little academic." He reached for her, and Nyx didn't try to pull away. He didn't have the bolt cutters any longer, but she was already so physically impaired, she didn't want to risk anything, even another slap. His fingers caressed the undamaged side of her face, and though she held still, she couldn't stop the shiver of revulsion that shook her.

"I think," she said, forcing the words out as his fingers slid across her lips. "That you want to blame the doctor who did your surgery, me, Hanna, for what you are. What you've become."

"Blame implies guilt. Which, as you pointed out, I don't feel."

"No, blame needs anger. And you're angry." Nyx opened her eyes. "You're angry, resentful, and maybe afraid, consciously afraid, since based on my reading, your ability to perceive and process dangerous situations—unconscious fear —is compromised. *You* are compromised."

"The doctor *was* to blame. She did a bad job. I woke up different. Angry, so angry." Petro scoffed but he didn't seem so sure of himself. "I killed her, and then I did things to her body and her husband's. Unthinkable things that were suddenly natural."

"And you recruited others, your pets—"

"Pets? I quite like that."

"—but I still don't know why. What did you hope to gain? To be fleet admiral? If you wanted it, why didn't you orchestrate your own nomination at the conclave?"

"I could have, but I wanted to see what would happen. If

Giovanni had been made fleet admiral, I would have intervened, but Ericsson was an unforeseen piece, a new player."

"You haven't answered."

"You want to know why?" He merely smiled. "You, of anyone, should know the answer to that."

She was looking into the abyss, and it was most definitely looking back. "You're afraid," she stammered, needing to keep him distracted. The sound of the car engine had stopped. Grigoris was here. *Please gods, let Grigoris be here.*

"And what do I fear? Your lover?" His hand slid over her jaw to her neck. He wrapped his fingers around her throat. "The fleet admiral? You?"

He leaned in to kiss her.

All she had to do was let him, and maybe that would distract him enough that Grigoris would arrive, have the element of surprise that had eluded him until now.

She couldn't do it. She couldn't.

As his lips pressed to hers, Nyx used her good hand to shove him back. He must have been expecting it because he grabbed her left wrist and yanked.

She felt bone screech on bone and her vision flashed white. A scream of agony pierced the air, and she was so lost in the pain she didn't even register the noise was coming from her.

GRIGORIS AND ERIC had been running toward the cliff's edge, but when they heard Nyx scream, the run became an all-out sprint. Both of them had pulled their guns, turned off the safeties. The moment Petro came into view, Grigoris was killing the bastard.

"He's mine," Eric said through gritted teeth, his breathing

heavy with the exertion it took racing full-speed ahead up a steep hill.

Grigoris shook his head.

"Mine," Eric repeated.

When Grigoris reached the overlook, he saw two silhouettes against the gray ocean sky. The sun was nearly gone, leaving only smears of amber and crimson. Two Lovers Point was illuminated in low-watt floodlights built into the path. He lost sight of Eric, but he didn't care. He wasn't going for stealth.

This was a full-frontal attack.

He watched as Petro twisted Nyx's arm, and her scream of pain and fear rent through the quiet night once more.

CHAPTER TWENTY-FIVE

"Let go of her, Petro!" Grigoris' shout cut through the sound of her second scream.

Nyx opened her eyes, blinking away tears, and realized the nightmare had gotten both better and worse. Better because Grigoris stood on the platform, a meter from her, gun in hand. He looked tall and safe and calm. Her panic abated, only to redouble when she realized Petro was behind her, holding her back to his front, the exact way Ciril had.

Petro's hand was around her throat, and as she reached up to try to pull it away, fresh pain from her left arm made her sway. Petro tightened his hold on her throat and she coughed, scrambling with her right hand to loosen his hold.

"Nyx, *o ángelós mou*, stay calm," Grigoris soothed.

"That's my wife you're addressing," Petro said, the smug amusement back in his voice. She'd gotten to him before, when she questioned him, but he was back to tormenting and torturing her, and now with an audience.

"There's no way out of this, Petro. Let Nyx go and you'll live."

"Do you know the story of this place?" he asked Grigoris.

"I think he's going to throw us both over," Nyx said, her voice reedy. "I think he intends to commit suicide."

"I wouldn't let it end that easily," Petro murmured in her ear, at the same time Grigoris said, "I'll shoot him first," in a wonderfully calm voice.

Petro reached a hand into his pocket, and the next thing she felt was the muzzle of a small gun pressed against her temple. "I'd prefer she experience the fear of falling, but I'm willing to compromise and put a bullet in her temple."

Every time he spoke, she could feel his chest moving, his breath fanning her hair. She tried to pull away, needing space so the panic would abate. She couldn't think, couldn't breathe. There was something hovering on the edge of her mind, something she needed to figure out, but the pain and fear were making it hard to think.

"Yes, wife, you stay with me," Petro murmured in Romanian. "And don't think you'll escape me in death." The gun shifted away from her head, and when he pulled the trigger, the sound was like a physical blow, despite the small size of the weapon. She felt a breeze on her legs, and then the gun was back on her temple.

"There we are," Petro said in English. "Now we don't have to worry about you heroically grabbing her as I take us over."

Petro used his hold on her neck to turn her head. He'd shot one of the clear panels that made up the waist-high wall of the lookout platform. Where there had once been a solid barrier, there was now the cragged edges of safety glass and a meter-wide gap. One step to their right, and all he'd have to do was lean back, and they'd both go over.

Petro's cheek rubbed against her ear. He seemed calm, happy.

"Is kidnapping me all that you need?" Nyx asked. "You're done with all the other games and plans?"

"Oh no, wife. There are plenty more games," he replied in Romanian. "Pieces in play that will continue on even without me. Though I'm not out of the game yet. The Masters' Admiralty will never be the same."

"Why hurt the society you're a member of? Why destroy something that has given you what you want?" She spoke in English, hoping he would do the same. After she and Petro were dead, any clue that might help Grigoris hunt down the rest of Petro's pets would be a help.

"It might be the same answer as to the question of why I do this at all. But maybe the answer is because the Masters' Admiralty is the only worthy adversary."

"Nyx, what's he saying?" Grigoris asked.

Petro tightened his hand, preventing her from speaking.

Grigoris shifted his gaze to her. She was going to die, but that wasn't so bad, as long as it meant Petro died too. She tried to smile, but she knew she was crying.

Grigoris rolled his shoulders as if working a kink out of them, then reached up and touched his right cheek. Had she touched him there when they made love? She was sure she had. It was his goodbye, it was...

Nyx blinked slowly.

The corner of Grigoris' lips twitched, as if this were all a game. Petro was holding her around the neck, not the waist, and her left forearm and hand were useless, but she could still do it.

Grigoris wasn't touching his cheek as some secret goodbye. He was reminding her of when she'd managed to take him down.

Step one, elbow to the face.

Petro's left hand was around her neck now, his right holding the gun to her head.

Nyx took a breath, then winked at Grigoris. She bent forward, and then let the weight of her head and neck rest in Petro's hand. The unexpectedness of it meant his grip loosened, and she was able to drop her shoulders a precious few inches, gaining her the space she needed.

She jabbed her right elbow up and back, striking not his face, but the wrist that held the gun. It clacked as it fell, and Petro snarled.

She was already moving again, jabbing with her left elbow, though the blow missed. It hurt too much to move that arm, so she didn't try again with that side. She jabbed back with her right again, catching him in the stomach. As Petro bent, she danced away, grabbed his left arm with her right and pulled forward as she kicked his legs out from under him.

Petro snarled as he hit the ground, the momentum of his fall causing him to slide...

...right through the broken section of glass wall, and over the edge.

ERIC TOOK TWO STEPS, emerging from behind the column that supported the small pergola above where Nyx, Petro, and Grigoris were. He leapt over the metal-reinforced railing on the upper viewing platform just as Petro slid over the edge.

A grisly death smashing on the rocks a hundred meters below was too good for him.

Petro grabbed on to the edge of the concrete platform as he went over, but it wouldn't have been enough to stop him from plummeting to his death if Eric hadn't landed in a crouch and grabbed Petro's wrist. He braced his shoulder on the still-whole barricade to his right.

"Who killed Josephine?" Eric demanded.

Petro, dangling over the edge, held up by nothing but Eric's hands, laughed. "Pull me up, and I'll tell you about them. Or let me go, and have your revenge."

Out of the corner of his eye, Eric saw Grigoris hustling Nyx back away from Petro, his gun trained on the empty space where Petro's head would emerge when Eric pulled him up.

And Eric would pull him up, but not for the reasons Grigoris thought.

Vaguely, in the dim light, he saw the others emerge. Milo. Lancelot. Leila. Dimitri. Langston.

Eric tightened his grip on Petro's wrist, even as he let go of his self-control. Rage, fueled by grief and guilt, consumed him.

He stood straight up, drawing Petro up by one hand. A display of strength that had even the psychopath looking alarmed.

What did it say about him that he scared a mass murderer, an amoral killer?

Maybe nothing. After all, he was a killer too.

Petro opened his mouth to say something, but Eric didn't care. His free hand shot out, wrapping around Petro's neck. He squeezed, hard.

"Fleet Admiral, we need to question him."

"No," Eric snarled, all pretense of calm gone. "He won't tell us anything. He'll fuck with us—and I'm done."

He could snap his neck, but that was a quick death. Petro didn't deserve that. The other man's nails raked Eric's arms, but he ignored it, barely feeling the pathetic attack. He shoved Petro against the railing, pinning him there by driving a knee into his gut and keeping it there, leaning his own body weight into that knee so Petro couldn't move.

"I think...I think this wasn't a suicide." The hoarse feminine voice belonged to Nyx. "This vest..."

"This is a parachute," another voice was saying.

"I saw a boat. He was planning to get away."

"We took Hanna from him, so he needed to have me, for the sake of both his id and his ego."

"So if he was planning to escape...why did he wait here for us?" someone else asked.

"Ohh, look. Another bomb!" an American voice exclaimed.

"Run!"

"No, I can disarm it. But we would have been very dead if it went off."

None of that mattered to Eric. Not anymore.

He had always liked physics. When he'd been a knight, when he'd had a sword, he'd loved to study the physics of swordplay, how the length of the blade added speed and force.

Here he had no blade, and a clean beheading was too good for Petro.

He'd killed Josephine.

Not personally, but he'd ordered the hit. This putrid creature was the reason Josephine was dead, Colum was grieving. He was the reason good men and women had died, the reason Leila and Karl still went to therapy. Why Nyx was scarred, always looking over her shoulder.

Eric grabbed Petro's right shoulder with his left hand, locking his elbow. With his right hand, he reached around behind Petro's head, then waited for Petro to open his mouth to say something—Eric was no longer listening. The berserker didn't care what the enemy had to say.

350 MARI CARR & LILA DUBOIS

Eric hooked the fingers of his right hand in the right side of Petro's mouth, grabbing onto his lower jaw. Petro bit down, hard enough to make Eric grin. The grip was awkward because Eric's wrist was behind Petro's head.

But it was all about the physics. Blood-soaked, wonderful physics.

Eric pulled, forcing Petro to turn his head to the right. Then he just kept pulling. Petro's jawbone broke, but it still worked as a handle to slowly force the man's head around. Not jerking, as that might break the neck, and that would be quick.

Petro was going to suffer.

Someone screamed, someone else was shouting, but Eric just kept pulling, forcing Petro's head to turn, his knee and left arm holding the man's body still. The skin and tendons of the neck strained, and Petro was keening in pain, the sound fainter now that his esophagus was so twisted he could barely breathe. Eric was aware there was blood in one eye from a blow the other man had landed, but it didn't matter.

He'd once calculated it would take nine thousand, four hundred and eight Newtons of force to separate a head from a body. Hanging, even when the body was dropped several feet, was enough to break the neck if the recipient was lucky, but not to physically separate the head. A three-foot sword or ax could do it.

There were people who would say it wasn't possible for a man to rip another man's head from his body. And it might not have been, if Eric hadn't known to pin the body, hold it still so all the force he was exerting had nowhere to go but the neck. And besides, Eric wasn't a man any longer. He was a creature of pain and rage. An enraged bear in human flesh.

He pulled, muscles straining, and there was a pop. Petro's

head was now, quite literally, on backwards. The neck had finally broken, but Petro might still be alive.

Eric hoped he was.

Another soft tug, and Petro's head kept turning. The flesh of his neck, stretched beyond the point of its own elasticity, started to separate, rending with a sound not unlike fabric ripping. A jagged red line appeared, stretching from the point under one ear then down almost to the opposite shoulder. Petro's jaw was now over his left shoulder, two hundred and seventy degrees around from where it had started, the rest of his head several degrees behind that.

Eric adjusted his grip, wrapping his big hand over the man's face. The jaw dangled loose and useless.

Eric gave a final yank, now sure that Petro was dead, and jerked the head back to face front. The aorta separated from its anchor point in the brain and blood splashed Eric's face.

There was another spurt. The heart was giving its last few beats.

Eric reached in and yanked on the few remaining tendons that held the head to the body. Rather than severing them, he yanked down, unseating them from their mooring in the head. Petro's tongue separated and slithered out through the hole that had once been his windpipe when Eric yanked that free.

Eric stepped back, still holding Petro's face in one hand, the way some people held soccer balls or basketballs. The body fell to the ground, blood pouring from the jagged stump.

The fleet admiral turned, blood-soaked and holding a severed head, to look at Nyx, Grigoris, all of them. He let them look, let them see what he was.

Eric turned to the night-dark ocean, raised his arm up and back, and screamed in primal challenge. Let the gods know what he'd done. Let them judge him...and fear him.

Snarling, he released the coiled tension in his body and tossed Petro's head off the cliff. There was a distant tapping noise when it hit the rocks below, before being swallowed into the crashing surf.

Eric waited, waited for the guilt to ease, for the grief to abate, but they were still there. All he knew was the fire of that pain-fueled rage.

"Search the body, then throw it over," he growled.

When he walked toward them, they scrambled out of his way. They feared him. They should. In the end, everyone feared him.

Being scared meant they wouldn't get close to him. And being scared was better than being dead.

CHAPTER TWENTY-SIX

Nyx glanced at the large table that had been set up in a corner of the pub. It was piled with food, though most of it had gone untouched. She'd tucked herself against a wall near the front of the pub, where she could see everyone without fear of anyone approaching from behind her. The PTSD she'd suffered ever since Ciril's attack had been exacerbated since Petro had kidnapped her and dragged her to Two Lovers Point.

She wore a sling over her shoulder, cradling her fractured arm. It hadn't been a clean break; there had been loose bone fragments, and she'd needed surgery before she'd been able to leave Guam. Luckily, with the Trinity Masters' help, she'd been treated at the naval hospital with no questions asked.

They were here to mourn Josephine.

Apart from that one brief night in this same pub with just the librarians in attendance, no one had had the opportunity to grieve, to say goodbye. James had convinced the owner of the pub to close the establishment down for the evening, so they had the entire place to themselves.

Cecilia had organized the wake, insisting that now, with Petro dead, it was time to properly memorialize Josephine, and Colum had reluctantly agreed. Not because he didn't want to honor his sister, but because it meant socializing, something the man simply couldn't seem to manage.

Nyx felt as if she understood Colum better than the others. She, like him, was more comfortable living inside her own head. Interaction with others had always been something she struggled with, and it appeared it was even more difficult for Colum. And grief was a very private thing, something hard to share or let be seen.

Even now, Josephine's brother sat alone in one of the corner booths, looking around the room, his expression shadowed, subdued. Cecilia had tried to interact with him, but small talk was beyond Colum's capabilities, so she'd moved on after a few awkward moments. Nyx had been slightly amused by Colum's obvious relief when he was alone once more.

It was a quaint little pub, and while she couldn't force herself to eat anything, the delicious smells emanating from the shepherd's pie and Irish stew were comforting, and they evoked one of Nyx's earliest memories. She'd only been five or six, and she had been sitting at the kitchen table, watching her grandmother cook. As her beloved *bunică* had made *lángos* and *gulyás*, the warmth in the kitchen, the mouthwatering aromas, made her feel safe and loved. At home.

Nyx couldn't help but think Josephine would have loved every minute of this. Unlike her brother, she was perfectly at ease with people, actually enjoying the times when the librarians were all together, though those meetings had been steeped in uncertainty, frustration, and fear as they searched for a brutal killer.

Petro was dead.

Those three words managed to slip into her psyche every so often, repeating themselves, fighting to penetrate the part of her brain that couldn't quite believe he was truly gone. After so many years of running, she wasn't sure how to simply...stand still.

The room was filled with people who knew Josephine, who mourned her, a group that included the only people Nyx had ever called friends. The majority of the people in attendance were the librarians and their spouses. Milo was also in attendance, as well as several of the Spartan Guard, who were genuinely shaken by her death, which proved that Josephine's friendship with Eric had involved lots of visits to the Isle of Man.

Bringing everyone together like this had been a good idea.

Nyx looked around, spotting James, Cecilia, Karl, and Hugo. She considered how much all of their lives had changed since being called upon to serve as librarians. The others had found their spouses. She'd found Grigoris. And Josephine...

Nyx wouldn't finish that thought as her gaze drifted to another table, where Cecilia had set up a display of photographs of Josephine that Colum had shared with her. They showed Josephine as a baby, a young girl, and there was one of her in her university graduation robes. There was a photo of her and Colum with a couple who appeared to be their parents, and there was a large picture in the center of the table of her and a younger Eric, sitting together on a wooden fence, talking in the midst of a field of sheep.

The fleet admiral looked at peace in the photo as he smiled at Josephine, whose hands were raised, her mouth open. Anyone who knew her could tell Josephine had been animatedly chatting, as was her habit, and Eric...well, there was no mistaking the obvious fondness in his expression as he listened to her.

Eric.

His was the most obvious absence at the wake. Given the way Colum's gaze kept shifting toward the door, it was apparent Josephine's brother was surprised Eric hadn't come.

But Colum hadn't been there. Hadn't been on Guam. Hadn't seen the berserker rip Petro's head from his shoulders and toss it into the ocean.

Eric had disappeared after that, not returning to the house they'd all been sharing on the base, but instead, chartering a private plane that took him back to the Isle of Man alone. One of the Spartan Guards here tonight said Eric hadn't left his quarters in the week since his return. Not once.

Sophia touched James' arm, and her husband stood, clearing his throat as he raised his glass. "To Josephine. In a field full of roses, she was a wildflower. Wonderful, unique, special in her own beautiful way."

Everyone else lifted their glasses. Nyx's eyes welled with tears at James' sweet toast, recalling Josephine's mass of curly red hair, the glasses she could never keep pushed up on her nose, and her constant bouncing, whether sitting or standing.

Grigoris, who had been talking to Lancelot, came to stand next to her after the toast. "How are you doing?"

Nyx swallowed back her tears, determined she wouldn't fall apart. Later, in the privacy of her own bed, she would shed these tears for her beloved friend. For now, she was determined to remember Josephine in a way the Irishwoman would have wanted—with laughter and fondness, surrounded by friends. "I miss her."

Grigoris wrapped his arm around her waist, tugging her against him as he placed a soft kiss against the top of her head. "I know," he murmured into her hair. "I'm sorry."

Grigoris hadn't left her side since Guam, the two of them returning to Cyprus for a few days before traveling here for the wake. Neither of them had mentioned the future. Instead, they clung together, treating each second as if it was the most precious thing they had, falling asleep in each other's arms, making love, kissing, touching.

Nyx wouldn't—couldn't—think about the moment when her time with him would end, so she didn't.

The other librarians took a turn sharing funny stories about Josephine. Colum remained in his booth in the corner, though he was watching them, listening. Twice, Nyx even caught the ghost of a smile on the man's face as Karl spoke.

The smiles and laughter came more easily as the hour grew late and the conversations, which in the past had all revolved around solving the mystery, were now about mundane things. Sylvia, Hugo's American wife, wondered how anyone could stand to live in such a chilly place as Ireland, when South Carolina was sitting right there, warm and inviting on the other side of the ocean. Arthur and Sophia chatted with Antonio about small concerns within each of their territories. Leila and Dimitri were in a heated, though friendly debate with Milo about which model of sniper rifle was the best in windy situations.

Grigoris had convinced her to eat, and she'd been delighted by the savory lamb in the stew. It tasted even better than it smelled. She drank two pints of Guinness, much to Grigoris' amusement, who claimed he wouldn't have pegged her for a beer drinker.

No one mentioned the horrors of the last year or the mastermind. Nyx knew that omission was on purpose. None of them was willing to give Petro one more moment of attention. Their final act of vengeance was to do the one thing the psychopath would hate the most—forget him, erase him from the narrative completely.

They'd all been about to leave when the door of the pub flew open and Eric strode in. His hair was disheveled, as if he'd just stepped out of a windstorm, and he clearly hadn't shaved since leaving Guam. His pants and shirt were wrinkled—Nyx suspected he'd slept in them—and there was still thunder in his eyes, easier to see now that the mask of calm was gone.

Though he'd killed their enemy, brutally, Eric hadn't found the same peace the others had. It was the first thing Nyx had noticed tonight. It was as if everyone had started to breathe again, live again. Hope again.

The same did not hold true for Eric.

All conversation died and the room went silent as the fleet admiral glanced around, his gaze landing on each face before shifting to the table displaying the pictures of Josephine.

He crossed the room to the photographs, his eyes softening. If Nyx hadn't been standing close to the table, she would have missed it.

Eric reached out and ran his finger along one of the photos, touching Josephine's cheek as she smiled widely in her doctoral robes, holding up her diploma proudly. Then he picked up the picture of the two of them together. His fingers tightened on the frame, the only sign of his sadness. "You shall fly to Valhalla with the sun on your face, my brave warrior," he whispered.

His gaze lingered there briefly, then he glanced over at Colum. The two men stared at each other, neither of them speaking a word. It was clear they shared the same terrible grief, though while tears fell down Colum's cheeks, Eric was stoic, his face chiseled in stone.

When Eric looked away, the fleet admiral was back...sort of.

There was no denying the berserker still lingered. Especially when he said, "You are all to report to the Isle of Man tomorrow. This isn't over yet."

GRIGORIS TOOK Nyx's uninjured hand as they walked the path that led to *Cashtal Ny Tree Cassyn,* which was located on the northern tip of the island, far from Castle Rushen—a medieval castle and major tourist draw—and the cities of Douglas and Port Erin.

The fortified manor house looked as formidable and imposing as it always did, given its location near the cliffside. The arched Gothic windows, steeply angled roofs, and intricate carved capstones made it feel like a castle, or even a cathedral. It was weather-beaten from nearly six hundred years of wind and waves.

He and Nyx had traveled here by ferry, departing from Dublin and docking in Douglas. Several others had chosen the same means of transportation, and they'd passed the time crossing the Irish Sea talking with Lancelot, Sylvia, and Hugo.

They were met by a Spartan Guard at the front door, who instructed them to report to the Great Hall.

The occasion felt far more formal than he'd expected, and Grigoris wished he was wearing his sword, which knights commonly did at formal events. Lancelot also seemed uncomfortable without a weapon.

"There's an armory somewhere in here," Lancelot muttered. "If not here, then in the Spartan Guard quarters."

"Do you know who else is going to be here?" Grigoris asked quietly.

"No, and I don't know what the fookin' hell this is about."

He felt Nyx's hand tremble slightly and he squeezed it gently, hoping to reassure her. When they entered the Great Hall, Grigoris saw many familiar faces, which wasn't unexpected, since he knew everyone who'd been at Josephine's wake would be there. Nyx's fellow librarians were already inside, along with the admiral of England and both the official and acting admirals from Rome, and the thirds in their trinities. Antonio had his hands on the back of a wheelchair, in which sat his father, Giovanni. Grigoris feared for the older man's obvious ill health, worried this trip would weaken him even more.

Milo stood not far behind Antonio, and Grigoris wondered if he was there as protection for his admiral and admiral's spouses, or because he'd been part of the team to take Petro down, and at Josephine's wake. He recognized the new Head of the Spartan Guard, who stood not far from Colum, and...

"Is that Nikolett?" Nyx asked.

They'd both spotted the Hungarian politician at the same time Nikolett saw them. She gave them a wary smile and nodded as she approached them.

"Janissary, Dr. Kata," Nikolett said. "It's nice to see you again. I was concerned about both of you after some of the reports I'd heard from Guam."

Nyx raised a brow. "Reports?"

"Don't worry, Dr. Kata. Most of what happened on that island is secret, except to say the leadership is aware that Petro is dead."

"You aren't the leadership," Grigoris said plainly.

Nikolett grinned. "I don't deal well with a lack of information. I like more details. Hungary's leadership is in tatters. The admiral and the vice admiral are both dead, the security minister, as well as half the knights and all of the security officers and finance ministers, were arrested by the Spartan Guard."

"Hans Molnar was inept," Nyx replied.

"Or in Petro's back pocket," Nikolett said. "He worked closely, day in and day out, with Petro. For him to say he wasn't aware that his boss was the mastermind makes him look incredibly stupid."

"But to say he was aware..." Grigoris started.

"Makes him a criminal," Nikolett finished. "Either way, he is in the custody of the Spartan Guard and I'm guessing being questioned. No matter what the outcome, Hans is out and Hungary is in a state of crisis."

"Is that why you're here?" Nyx asked.

"I'm here because I was summoned by the fleet admiral." Nikolett looked around the Great Hall. "Given what I've heard about Eric Ericsson, I'm very interested in meeting him."

"The two of you have never met?" Grigoris asked.

Nikolett shook her head.

Nyx tilted her head, studying the other woman. "I'm very interested in *him* meeting *you*."

Grigoris tried to hide his grin, agreeing with Nyx. Nikolett was a strong-minded woman who didn't kowtow to others. In many ways, she felt like Eric's equal when it came to not suffering fools and speaking forthrightly. He sobered quickly, however, recalling Eric's current state of mind. Perhaps Nikolett and Eric meeting under these circumstances wasn't such a good idea.

Nikolett's voice lowered as she looked over their shoulders. "Well, this party is getting more compelling. It would appear all the key players are making an appearance."

Grigoris followed Nikolett's gaze to the entrance of the Great Hall.

He blew out a soft breath when his admiral, Hande, arrived with several of his knights. His admiral had given him permission to work the mastermind case months ago—not that she'd had much choice, given that Eric had requested he personally head the investigation. At the time, he'd been honored by the request. Now, after everything he'd seen, returning to his duties as leader of the knights of Ottoman would be difficult. In a lot of ways, he felt more like a security officer now, one of those trained to do whatever it took to bring the bad guys to heel.

He hadn't returned to his normal duties in the week since defeating Petro. Seeing Hande made him realize it was time for him to return to work, though doing so meant leaving Nyx, something Grigoris didn't want to consider. He was still stealing every moment he could, though it was becoming clear their days were numbered.

"I should speak to my admiral." Grigoris squeezed Nyx's hand, then went to greet Hande, and then the other knights.

"You've accomplished your task for the fleet admiral?" Hande asked once they'd exchanged pleasantries.

"I believe so, Admiral, though the fleet admiral hasn't yet given me leave to return to my normal duties."

The truth was, he hadn't asked. Based on her expression, Hande knew he'd been home to Cyprus but hadn't checked in.

Shortly after her arrival, the rest of the admirals began filing in. It was nearly unprecedented for all the admirals to be called together to meet like this. Normally it only happened for conclave, to appoint a new fleet admiral.

The muscles between Grigoris' shoulders tightened as he realized that whatever Eric was doing here, it was going to be big. Around the room, he saw other people shift uneasily.

Cezary Lis and Santiago De Leon, from Bohemia and Castile, respectively, walked in together. Hugo walked over to greet the French admiral, Victoire Dubois, when she entered. The last two admirals to arrive, Dolph Eburhardt from Germany and Alma Ivarsson from Kalmar, both traveled with knights from their territories.

Eight admirals, when there should have been nine.

Five librarians, when there should have been six.

The Great Hall could hold hundreds, yet because everyone spoke in hushed voices, it seem as if no one was there at all. A pall rested over the room, everyone uneasy.

The summons from Eric had plagued Grigoris all night.

This isn't over yet.

He had a feeling this was about more than just identifying and capturing Petro's remaining pets, a task that would be much easier, thanks to the Spartan Guard managing to disarm the booby traps on the hidden room in Petro's estate and gather all the files and information in there. He wasn't sure who was working on untangling all that information, but he hadn't been asked to take the lead, and part of him was glad.

He wouldn't have called all the admirals here if it was just about finishing up the investigations.

He didn't have long to ponder that concern when Eric appeared on the interior balcony that looked out over the Great Hall.

Unlike last night, he was clean-shaven, his black pants and shirt pressed but tight over the muscles of his arms and shoulders. He towered over them, looking down on them like a god. Those standing under the balcony took several steps back so they could see him better.

Eric remained silent for a moment as his eyes traveled the length of the room as if he was taking roll in his head.

Satisfied everyone was in attendance, he lifted his hands. If the gesture was meant to silence them, it was unnecessary. No one had spoken a word since he'd entered the room.

Eric looked all business, but Grigoris had come to know the man over the past few months. He'd seen the subtle changes that had taken place in their fleet admiral as they continued to search for the mastermind.

However, those changes paled in comparison to the man he'd become since Josephine's death.

The sight of Eric literally ripping a man's head off, of him soaking in blood, digging his fingers into the neck to loosen tendons and rip flesh, would be featured in his nightmares for years to come.

"Everyone in the room knows that our enemy is dead. Petro Sirko was responsible for organizing and enabling the Domino's apprentices, the serial killer Ciril, and the bombs in Bucharest and Rome."

"Why did he do it?" Nikolett called out.

Eric focused on her, some of his stony facade melting in apparent surprise. "This isn't a Q&A."

"Nyx, what is the Hungarian word for 'abort'?" Grigoris asked Nyx out of the corner of his mouth.

"I know the answer to that," Nyx said to Eric, her voice loud enough to carry. Everyone turned to look at her and Nikolett.

"You abort too," Grigoris whispered.

"This is my fucking meeting," Eric muttered, leaning on the railing so he could hear better.

"You know why he did it?" Nikolett asked Nyx.

"I asked him. Before Eric beheaded him."

"You didn't tell me this," Grigoris murmured, looking at Nyx.

Nyx smiled sadly at him, then turned to the front, addressing Eric. "I asked Petro why, and he said I knew the answer."

"The brain damage," Eric replied.

"No," Nyx said, her voice cool and strong. "There is only one real answer to the question of why." She looked around the room, then back to the fleet admiral. "Why not?"

"He did all this...because he could?" Nikolett asked.

"Yes. Because he could. Because whether from injury or natural malformation of the brain, he felt no empathy."

"He wasn't always like that," Giovanni said sadly. "Petro was once a good man."

Nyx didn't say anything in reply to that.

"Are you done?" Eric asked sarcastically. "Can I have my meeting back?"

"I have several more questions," Nikolett called out.

"You have got to be fucking—okay, change of plan. I'm starting with you." He leveled his finger at Nikolett.

She smiled and crossed her arms. "Yes?"

"The territory of Hungary is a fucking mess."

Nikolett stiffened slightly. Though she'd just said the exact same thing, it appeared she could talk bad about her family, but no one else could.

"Your admiral and vice admiral are dead, and your security minister is as dumb as a box of rocks. I questioned him personally. Right now, all that's left in Hungary are three knights who were stationed away from Petro's headquarters. They're the only ones I'm sure aren't either too fucking stupid to live, or in on it."

Grigoris winced. Just losing an admiral was enough to

rock a territory, cause instability that could shake the foundation of not just that territory but world governments.

"Nikolett Varda," Eric called out.

Nikolett stepped forward confidently. "Yes, Fleet Admiral."

Eric studied her, quiet for a moment. "I am naming you the new admiral of Hungary."

Nikolett's eyebrows rose incrementally, though she remained silent.

"You have nothing to say?" Eric asked.

"I'm trying to decide if this is an honor or a punishment."

Eric's lips twitched, and for one hot minute, Grigoris thought the fleet admiral might smile. He didn't. "Don't run," Eric commanded. He disappeared from the balcony.

Antonio fake coughed and said, "Punishment."

Eric appeared in the Great Hall a moment later, walking straight toward Nikolett. "Kneel," he commanded.

Nikolett knelt before the fleet admiral, though she held her head high, her eyes locked with Eric's. "Nikolett Varda. You are, by directive of the fleet admiral..."

At this, there was a low murmur of confusion and disapproval by the other admirals in attendance. According to tradition, the conclave of admirals selected another territory's successor, not the fleet admiral alone.

Eric ignored them. "You are appointed admiral of Hungary." He offered his hand. Nikolett placed hers in his, and he pulled her to her feet. As she rose, Nikolett kept hold of Eric's hand, her face lifted as he looked down at her. Though the moment might have lasted mere seconds, it felt like longer as the new admiral of Hungary and the fleet admiral stared at one another. Grigoris had expected sparks between them but not *these* sparks. Sparks that felt more like sexual tension than those resulting from a contentious relationship.

Eric dropped her hand, cleared his throat. "Your vice admiral will be—"

"Someone I choose," Nikolett said confidently.

Eric's eye twitched. "Your territory is in shambles."

"No, we are in a transition period. Language matters, please don't use that term again."

"You need—"

"I can handle it."

Eric and Nikolett stared at each other. Eric opened his mouth, closed it, opened it again, then turned away. Anyone the fleet admiral couldn't see smiled. Those in his line of sight wisely kept their expressions neutral.

Eric rolled his shoulders, then looked around the room again. "James Rathmann, Cecilia St. John, Karl Klimek, Hugo Marchand, and Nyx Kata, please step forward."

Nyx reluctantly let go of Grigoris' hand, stepping forward with her fellow librarians.

"Thank you for everything you did as the librarians, to help with the investigation."

Each of them nodded in response.

Eric's expression hardened. "As of now, the librarians are disbanded."

Nyx's body jerked as if she'd been shocked. James cleared his throat. "Fleet Admiral, we think that—"

"I'll make it really fucking simple. The five of you are never to be alone in a room together again. No member of the Masters' Admiralty is to step foot in the Old Library at Trinity. Am I understood?"

The words hung angry and dark in the air. It was an insane order, nonsensical even. And yet it made complete sense. Eric was trying to protect them.

There was a gentle clearing of a throat, and Grigoris turned to see that Colum, who was leaning against the back wall, had made the noise.

"What?" Eric asked the Irishman.

"Dublin is neutral territory. You can't give orders for Dublin."

"Really? Because I just did."

Colum looked deeply uncomfortable, maybe even panicked, but he didn't back down. "As the Archivist, I reject the order and issue a standing invitation to all librarians to the archive. They are welcome. Singly or as a group. Always."

Eric snarled, then pointed his finger at the former librarians. "You aren't librarians. I don't want to hear about the five of you meeting anywhere, do you hear me?"

There were unhappy nods. Grigoris was surprised someone didn't argue, but maybe they were all too aware of where the order was coming from—a place of grief, and grief didn't always make sense.

Eric took a step back, as if trying to retreat not from them but from his feelings. He turned and walked out of the Great Hall, and everyone looked around, questioning if the meeting was over.

Eric reappeared on the balcony, and it was clear that he'd deliberately gone there to put space between them. It was odd and out of character. Eric was a hands-on leader.

He looked over the group once more, and to Grigoris' surprise, Eric looked directly at him. "Grigoris Violaris. Kneel."

Grigoris hesitated for just a moment, uncertain about what was coming next. The entire meeting had been one surprise after another.

Eric looked to Nyx. "Nyx Kata. Stand beside him and kneel as well," he instructed.

Nyx glanced toward him questioningly as she walked over to him, but Grigoris didn't know what was going on either.

"Fleet Admiral," Grigoris called out, adopting Eric's formal title, not wanting to inadvertently prompt the beast from its lair. "If I have displeased—"

"Kneel," Eric repeated.

He and Nyx looked at each other, and then, his lovely woman dropped gracefully to her knees, careful of her still-bruised leg. Grigoris knelt next to her.

Eric leaned forward. "I hereby bind you, Grigoris Violaris, Janissary of Ottoman, and Nyx Kata of Hungary, in marriage."

The words fell over the crowd, and it took Grigoris a moment to process what had been said.

Hande cleared her throat. "Fleet Admiral, you haven't—" She was silenced instantly after a malevolent look from Eric.

The fleet admiral continued with the ceremony. "Your union will serve to better and protect the people of our proud and ancient society. It is your duty to love, protect, and keep your spouse. I will hear your pledge to not only keep and protect one another but to strive to better our world."

Grigoris was speechless, too many facts, too many truths, pushing in on him. Nyx didn't want to marry. Though her argument against it was because she didn't want to be placed in a trinity. Which brought to mind Grigoris' primary concern.

Who was their third?

"Eric," Grigoris said, using the fleet admiral's first name, hoping perhaps that informality would somehow drag the man back to reality. Their reality.

"Say. Your. Vows." Eric's words were clipped, short. He

expected them to obey. But how could Grigoris do that, knowing that Nyx—

"I pledge on my honor and," Nyx swallowed heavily, tears in her eyes, "as your spouse—"

"Nyx," Grigoris interrupted. "You don't have to—"

She reached up and cupped his cheek with the hand of her uninjured arm, finishing the vow, her smile full and genuine. "To love, protect, and keep you all of your days. *Motănel, agápi mou.*"

My dear. My love.

She had taken the vow, bound her life with his. He'd asked her once if she could trust him to take care of her and protect her in a trinity. She hadn't been ready then, but apparently she was now.

Grigoris took her good hand in his, squeezing it tight as he repeated the words. "I pledge on my honor as janissary, and as your spouse, to love, protect, and keep you all of your days, *o ángelós mou.*"

They moved toward each other and kissed. It lingered, a soft merging of lips and hearts, the clasped hands pressed together between them.

"You may rise," Eric said.

"Eric," Sophia said gently. Grigoris admired the *principessa*'s courage. "Who is their third?"

Eric didn't look at her. Instead, his gaze remained steadfast on Nyx. "Josephine," he said at last. "Their third was Josephine."

EPILOGUE

"Vice Admiral, I have your—"

"Do not call me that."

Grigoris grinned at her, then very deliberately repeated the words, "Vice Admiral, I have your report on the financial status of the territory."

"Husband, your failure to accept my proposal that we run away together is most distressing."

"No more running, remember?" He set the paper on her desk and kissed her head.

Nyx's cast thunked against the desk as she swiveled in her chair. She'd gotten the previous one wet having newlywed sex in the tub with Grigoris. This time she'd gotten pink and purple stripes. Josephine would have liked it.

"I don't want to be vice admiral," she whispered as he hitched one hip onto her desk.

Grigoris' eyes softened. "I know."

After marrying them, and the heartbreaking declaration that Josephine would have been their third, Eric had made one more announcement, then walked out of the Great Hall.

He'd given Sophia Starabba the power to confirm marriages, a duty normally carried out by the fleet admiral. When she'd asked him why, he'd just smiled almost sadly before leaving without another word.

No one had seen or heard from him since. The Spartan Guard had started a manhunt, until one of them had found a letter pinned to the door of their hotel room in Hanover by a knife. The letter had stated that he didn't need a babysitter and to go home.

The Spartan Guard hadn't stopped looking for Eric, but they were, apparently, much more subtle about it now.

That day in the Great Hall, when she'd still been reeling from her marriage, and Eric's sudden departure, Nikolett had appeared at her side. She'd congratulated her, asked her how she was feeling, then appointed her vice admiral.

Nyx had refused. Nikolett had laughed and told her she would see her at the headquarters in Hungary in two weeks' time—which her new admiral had declared was enough time for her honeymoon.

Nyx had pointed out that her husband was the chorbaji of the Janissaries in Ottoman, and that she would be moving to Cyprus. Nikolett merely smiled and ignored her refusal once more, repeating that she would see her in Hungary in two weeks.

At that point, Hande had come over and demanded to know what was going on. There had been a spirited debate between the two female admirals. Nikolett had given Hande the half of Bucharest that was in Hungary, in exchange for Grigoris.

Grigoris had looked slightly offended and very shocked. Sophia, who'd walked over at the sight of a potential girl fight, had patted him on the shoulder and told him he was like a medieval princess being married off in exchange for power and real estate.

Nyx had laughed so hard she'd almost cried. Nikolett had studied her, then nodded, proclaiming the two of them were going to work very well together.

The laughter had stopped when she remembered that she had to be the vice admiral.

And now the honeymoon was over, and she was vice admiral of Hungary.

"I'm a religious scholar, not a lawyer or financial sector professional," Nyx told Grigoris. It was hardly the first time she'd said this. Given that the vice admirals oversaw the knights, who served as the law and order for the territory, and the finance ministers, it was far more common to have a vice admiral who had themselves been a knight or had some level of financial acumen.

"No, but you're brilliant."

"I'm sorry you had to give up being a janissary."

"Please stop apologizing. My previous job, and apparently the capital of Romania, are a small price to pay to be with you."

For now, Grigoris was helping her vet and train new knights, along with help from Mateo and Dimitri. Before marrying Cecilia and Mateo, Dimitri had been a security officer in Hungary. He and his trinity had been living at the bed-and-breakfast they owned in the Lake District, but with Hungary in such a state of chaos, Dimitri had agreed to take on the role of acting security minister.

Prior to his marriage, Mateo had been captain of the Spartan Guard, a position he'd had to give up upon marrying Cecilia and Dimitri. Mateo, who hoped to be a doctor one day, like his parents, had taken a leave of absence from medical school to come to Hungary with his spouses. Unfortunately, he couldn't transfer to a medical school here, as he didn't speak Hungarian.

Cecilia had fared better because she had a job she could do from anywhere. Which was fortunate because while Nyx had no financial acumen, Cecilia did. She was, in secret, teaching Nyx the basics of accounting and how to read budgets, quarterly reports, and other common financial documents.

Luckily, it turned out money wasn't one of Hungary's problems. Petro had amassed a fortune both personally and for the territory. Nikolett had asked Nyx to figure out if any of that money had been obtained illegally so they could return it.

It was on Nyx's list. Her very long list. Her list used to consist of making sure to peer review articles for various academic journals, not checking for blood money.

"There's something we have to talk about," Grigoris said. "I told Nikolett it would be better if I talked to you about it."

Nyx looked up at her new husband. Outside the window behind him, she could see the skyline of Budapest.

"What is it?"

"They officially found Petro's body. Well, his head. It was ruled an accidental drowning."

"And Hanna?"

"I don't know. Do you want me to look into it?"

"No, I will. It's my job."

"A job I'm happy to help you with."

They hadn't talked about it yet, but Nyx hoped that once he was fully fluent in Hungarian, and conversational in at least one other language spoken in the territory, Grigoris would apply to be one of the harcosok. "Thank you," she replied.

"There's more." Grigoris' face was serious. "You were Petro's heir."

"What?" Shock made her shoulders tight.

"In his will, all his money, property...it all came to you."

"That can't be right. Hanna was his legal wife."

"She wasn't. He never legally married her, and she's not listed in his will."

"Why would he..." There was no point in asking that question.

"I'll deal with it," Grigoris assured her. "You don't have to do anything."

"Does it include the property in Lake Balaton?"

"Yes, why?"

Nyx stood and walked out of her office, across the hall, to Nikolett's office. They'd decided to set up their new headquarters in a modest three-story building, with a nice café around the corner.

"Admiral," Nyx said. "Would you like to go with me to blow up a building?"

"What building and why?" Nikolett didn't look up from her computer screen.

"Petro's estate in Lake Balaton. Apparently it's mine. And I would like to blow it up."

Nikolett tapped the last few keys, then turned and grinned. "Let me get my coat."

AND FOR THOSE of you who are curious about what's coming next in this series, we can tell you in two words - THE TRIPLETS! We are returning to the Trinity Masters world to tell the stories of Langston, Oscar and Walt, but don't worry! We also have big plans for future Masters'

Admiralty books, including Colum, Eric, Nikolett, featuring the librarians and other beloved characters as well.

IN THE MEANTIME, Lila and Mari both have new releases in their other series coming out in January 2020. Fancy some kidnapping/BDSM role play? Or maybe a red hot menage? Then read on...

FROM LILA DUBOIS.
    K is for...
    Is it really a kidnapping if you know it's coming?

OLIVER SANZ IS INTRIGUED by the opportunity his BDSM club's new checklist game presents. Assigned to the letter K, he gets to kidnap the lovely submissive Kumiko. One weekend together with a list of items and a new sub—a touch of novelty, which for an experienced Dom can be hard to come by—and then they'll part ways.

KUMIKO ALCOTT DOESN'T KNOW who her Dom is, but she knows she's been assigned "K", and kidnapping. Too bad she doesn't need, or want, fantasy role play. What she needs is a serious Dom to help her get out of her head. There have been far too many changes in her once carefully planned life. A new partner, and a new game, might be one adjustment too many.

THE FIRST TIME they touch they realize there's a problem

—what's between them is explosive, making their scenes too intense, and the kidnapping seem all too real.

Preorder now.

AND FROM MARI CARR.

Wild Side

How can "no strings attached" feel so confining?

LAYLA MOVED to Baltimore in search of a fresh start. After too many years in a lackluster relationship, she's ready to embrace her wild side. Casual is her new middle name and the last thing she wants or needs is a serious relationship.

FINN AND HIS BEST FRIEND, Miguel are ALL IN on showing Layla a good time. After all, neither one of them is looking for love either. Or so they think.

UNTIL FINN FALLS for Layla and Miguel falls for Finn and Layla falls for...both men. Then it's a wild side freefall as the three lovers try to make one plus one plus one equal the perfect match.

Preorder now.

AFTERWORD

We, the authors of this book, apologize for any mistaken translations. Due to potential compatibility issues with different e-readers and software, we elected to use the English alphabet for all. For example, Greek words are presented in their English translation, rather than in the Greek alphabet. And because we are barely fluent in English, we relied heavily on Google translate and travel blogs.

ABOUT THE AUTHORS

Virginia native Mari Carr is a *New York Times* and *USA TODAY* bestseller of contemporary sexy romance novels. With over one million copies of her books sold, Mari was the winner of the Romance Writers of America's Passionate Plume for her novella, *Erotic Research*.

Join her newsletter so you don't miss new releases and for exclusive subscriber-only content. Find Mari on the web on Facebook | Twitter | BookBub | Email: mari@mari-carr.com.

Lila Dubois is a top selling author of contemporary erotic romance. Having spent extensive time in France, Egypt, Turkey, England and Ireland Lila speaks five languages, none of them (including English) fluently. She now lives in Los Angeles with a cute Irishman.

You can visit Lila's website at www.liladubois.net. She loves to hear from fans! Send an email to author@liladubois.net or join her newsletter.

Made in the USA
Monee, IL
22 September 2021